Janie Crouch has loved to read romance her whole life. She cut her teeth on Mills & Boon Romance novels as a preteen, then moved on to a passion for romantic suspense as an adult. Janie lives with her husband and four children overseas. Janie enjoys traveling, long-distance running, movie-watching, knitting and adventure/obstacle racing. You can find out more about her at www.janiecrouch.com.

To my grandparents: Mittie and Quinton King, as you celebrate your 70th(!!!) wedding anniversary this very month. All the romantic stories I'll ever write will never compare to the true love you've lived in a lifetime together. You've taught me that marriage is 80% adoration and 20% exasperation, but no matter what, it is always filled with respect. Thank you for being a living example of what love is to your children, your grandchildren and your great-grandchildren.

Your legacy is many things, but most important, it is love.

SPECIAL FORCES SAVIOR

BY
JANIE CROUCH

First Published in Great Britain 2016
By Mills & Boon, an imprint of HarperCollins*Publishers*
1 London Bridge Street, London, SE1 9GF

© 2016 Janie Crouch

ISBN: 978-0-263-91892-2

46-0116

Our policy is to use papers that are natural, renewable and recyclable products and made from wood grown in sustainable forests. The logging and manufacturing processes conform to the legal environmental regulations of the country of origin.

Printed and bound in Spain
by CPI, Barcelona

Chapter One

Pinned down behind his car with someone shooting at him from across the street was not how Omega Sector agent Derek Waterman had planned to spend his afternoon. He wasn't exactly sure how he had planned to spend his afternoon, but this was definitely not it.

Derek slid closer to the ground as a bullet whizzed past his head and shattered the concrete behind him.

Whoa. Too close.

The saving grace in this situation was at least the entire block was empty of any innocent bystanders. No upstanding citizen had much reason to be in this section of West Philly. The less upstanding citizens had exited when Derek and his team had shown up, obviously law enforcement, and the shooting had started.

"Uh, what exactly was the intel you got on this place again, Derek?" Jon Hatton asked from where he was also pinned down a few feet away. Although highly trained in weapons and combat as all Omega Sector's Critical Response agents were, Jon was primarily a behavior analyst in the Crisis Management Unit.

"What's the matter? You having problems remembering how to use your weapon, Jon? Too much analyzing, not enough action in your life?" Liam Goetz, the other team member, smacked his gum and grinned. As a member of

Omega's Hostage Rescue team, no one ever asked Liam if he remembered how to use a weapon. Liam had pretty much been born with one in his hand.

"I'm just asking to see if there is any sort of plan here besides hide behind the car until the bad guys run out of ammo," Jon responded. "Which, at the rate they're shooting, should be sometime next week."

True, the number of shots being fired at them seemed to be dwindling. The people in the building obviously weren't trying to kill Derek and his team, just keep them pinned. But damned if this entire situation wasn't starting to piss Derek off.

The empty apartment building across the street gave the enemy the tactical advantage. That advantage wasn't something Derek, as the lead tactical team specialist of Omega's SWAT generally gave up.

But the intel they'd received on this location had required an immediate response. Time for tactical analysis hadn't been available. Thus, the taking cover behind their SUV as the bullets flew by their heads.

Derek had moved in on this location so quickly because it had been the first substantial lead pertaining to a terrorist attack on Chicago two weeks earlier. A bombing that had killed or injured over five hundred people.

None of the leads Omega had followed up on until now—and there had been hundreds of them—had provided any useful intel. Each location had been totally cold.

Another bullet flew by. This location definitely wasn't cold.

"All right, to hell with this." Derek looked over at Liam. "Jon and I will lay down cover-fire. You head around to the back of the building."

Liam was grinning like an idiot. He loved this sort of thing, danger be damned. "Now you're talking."

Derek nodded. "Remember, we need them alive, if at all possible."

"Hey, it's me!" Liam actually winked at them. "I wouldn't hurt a fly."

Derek rolled his eyes and heard Jon groan under his breath as Liam made his way down the line of abandoned cars parked on the street. Still using their SUV for as much cover as possible, Derek and Jon began firing their weapons toward the abandoned building, hoping to draw any return-fire back at them and away from Liam.

But there were no shots at all coming at them from the house.

Derek looked over at Jon. "Again."

Using the hood to brace his arm, Derek fired three shots at the house while Jon did the same from the rear of the vehicle. Still no return-fire. Out of the corner of his eye he saw Liam make it across the street at the side of the building. No shots were fired at him, either.

The bad guys weren't in the building anymore; they must be on the run. Whoever had been shooting at them just a few moments ago was Omega's best lead in Chicago's terrorist attack. They were the *only* lead. And now they were about to get away.

"Move in, but be careful," Derek said to Jon as they made their way forward, weapons still raised.

Derek was reaching for the knob of the door, Jon covering him from a cross angle when they heard a rapid burst of gunfire from the back of the building where Liam had been heading.

Both men backed out of the doorway and sprinted around the building without a word. Each of them knew that getting inside was secondary to helping Liam if he was under fire. As they rounded the building, Derek was relieved to see Liam unharmed, chasing a suspect farther down the road behind the apartment building. Derek and Jon continued running to catch up with them. Helping capture a known suspect was better than sticking around for what may or may not be in the house.

"Stay with them," Derek told Jon, then made a sharp turn. He would run down a parallel side street and try to cut off the runner. He forced more speed out of his legs.

As he made a sharp turn around the next group of buildings, Derek saw the perp slowing down with Liam only a few yards behind him, Jon just beyond that.

It was obvious Liam was going to catch the guy at any moment, and the perp knew it, too. He fired his weapon at the Omega agents behind his back in some haphazard fashion without even stopping his run, but the bullets didn't come anywhere near either of them.

Derek turned again and began running toward them.

"Stop!" he called out to the man, and saw distress wash over his face. The man stopped running altogether, sliding to an awkward stop.

"You're under arrest," Derek continued between breaths. "Place the gun on the ground and put your hands on your head."

The man turned around, frantically looking for another way out, but didn't put his gun down. All the Omega agents gripped their weapons tighter. Nobody wanted to shoot this suspect, he was too important. But they would if necessary. Especially if he turned his weapon on them rather than where it currently lay in his hand pointing at the ground.

"Put your weapon down," Derek repeated. He nodded toward the ground with his forehead, as the man turned back in his direction. "Do you understand? All we want to do is ask you some questions."

That wasn't entirely true, but Derek just wanted to get the man's gun out of his hand.

The man nodded and Derek eased his finger off the trigger just the slightest bit. But then, almost as if it was in slow motion, and before any of them could react, the guy brought his gun up to his own temple and fired. He crumpled to the ground, dead instantly.

Derek's curse was vile. Jon rushed up to the man and crouched down to take his pulse at the wrist, but Derek knew it was too late.

Their best lead—their *only* lead—had just blown his brains out rather than be taken into custody.

He looked over at Jon and Liam. "We need to call this in. Omega and local PD."

Liam already had his phone out. "On it."

"Okay, stay with the body until they get here." Derek turned back toward the house. "Jon, let's go see if there's anything in the house. Maybe we'll get lucky."

They hadn't gone more than a few steps before they smelled it. Smoke, coming from the building the potential terrorist had just vacated.

If possible, Derek's curse was even more vile. A burned house would destroy all possible evidence. The poor dead guy had probably just been a decoy to lure the Omega team away so whoever was left could start the fire.

Jon and Derek sprinted back to the house. Smoke was pouring out of the windows. If they were going to be able to salvage anything useful, they'd have to do it in a hurry. As safely as possible, Derek opened the back door, throwing a latex glove onto one hand to grab anything that might be useful for the investigation. Then he took off his jacket to use as a filter over his mouth.

Inside, everything was in flames. Whoever had been here had used some sort of accelerating agent, probably gasoline, to make the place burn more quickly. Bending low under the smoke, he and Jon made their way farther inside.

They'd been in the house less than a minute, squinting their way through the smoke and heat, when Jon pulled on Derek's shoulder, gesturing back toward the door. Jon was right. This was too dangerous. They needed answers about the terrorist attack, but it wasn't worth either of them losing their lives.

Derek saw a few pieces of some sort of computer hardware sitting broken on the floor. He crawled to them, wincing as his hand was burned picking up the more substantial pieces and placing them inside his jacket pocket. Jon was pulling on him again and Derek could feel the hairs singeing on his arms from the heat. It was time to go.

As they rushed to get out, Derek saw something just under the layer of smoke lying near the edge of the kitchen table. It looked like some sort of communication device, or maybe some sort of drive, about half the size of a cell phone. Derek pushed Jon toward the door, then dropped to his hands and knees to crawl to it. The smoke was now too heavy to remain upright. Derek smelled the putrid stench of burning flesh just before he felt pain on his shoulders and back. He was too close to the heat and it was burning his skin. He grabbed the device and wrapped it in his jacket, then began crawling for the door.

Or at least he hoped he was crawling in the direction of the door. He could no longer see in the smoke. Breathing was becoming damn near impossible. Derek kept crawling forward.

Hands reached from in front of him, grabbed him under the armpits and dragged him out of the building and into blessed clean and cool air.

"You are one stubborn son of a bitch," Jon murmured to him as he dragged Derek down the three steps onto the ground.

"I'm okay," Derek wheezed out, crawling a few more

steps before sprawling on the ground. The pain in his back and shoulders was uncomfortable, but not excruciating. His lungs, though, felt seared. Both men lay, watching the building burn for long minutes, Derek's lungs finally feeling a bit of ease as he continued to breathe clean air. Eventually he could hear the sirens signaling the firefighters' arrival.

"I hope you got something in there," Jon told him, obviously hearing the sirens, too. "Because the only thing that destroys evidence quicker than fire—"

"Is extinguishing it," Derek finished for him. Water, foam, the firemen themselves. All were hell on evidence. "Yep."

"I think I might have gotten something important." Still lying in the mostly dead grass of a lawn that hadn't seen proper care for decades, Derek explained about the communication device. "We need to get it back to the lab so Molly can try to recover information from it."

Jon snickered. "Uh, o-o-okay, D-Derek." The stuttering was completely for show.

Sitting up, Derek rolled his eyes. "Shut up, Jon. She's not that bad." Derek knew he shouldn't try to defend Molly Humphries, the forensic lab director. Yeah, the pretty pathologist tended to get a little tongue-tied around Derek. But the more he tried to defend her to his colleagues when they mentioned it—which was as often as damn possible—the worse everyone teased.

Jon smiled. "Hey, you know I like sweet Molly as much as anyone. But I have to admit that watching her go from the most intelligent scientist I know to a blushing, stammering schoolgirl around you is one of my favorite pastimes."

"Shut up, Jon," Derek repeated. "Just focus on the case."

Jon was wise enough not to say anything else about Molly Humphries.

Both Jon and Derek were seen by paramedics as they waited for the firefighters to finish their job. Derek was decreed as suffering from first-degree burns on his shoulders and smoke inhalation, but didn't require further medical attention. As he and Jon watched the firefighters work diligently, neither held out much hope of finding any further evidence. They would still check.

Liam joined them once local law enforcement came to pick up the body of the guy who had shot himself. Liam had taken the dead man's prints and his weapon, as well as a sample of the man's DNA. The body would be delivered to the Omega morgue later. All the items Liam had collected would go straight back to the lab.

A dead suspect, a burnt building and a few broken pieces of possible evidence. All in all a pretty terrible day. Definitely not any closer to solving the terrorist attack on Chicago. And Derek knew they were going to get chewed out again for it. Govermental-type bigwigs all the way up the food chain were demanding answers for the bombing. Derek was scheduled to provide an update to a committee via teleconference in just a few hours.

Derek wasn't looking forward to that. Especially not now, with nothing to show.

Derek's only hope now was that Molly, with all her magic in her lab, could salvage something out of this mess. Molly had saved Derek before. He prayed she could do it again.

Chapter Two

Molly Humphries caught a look at her shoes as she carried an armful of case files across the lab to her desk. How she hated her sensible shoes. They were flat, unimaginative and…well, just *sensible*. Plain and brown.

That her shoes were a symbolic reflection of her personal life was not lost on Molly.

She had no idea why the shoes were offending her so much on this particular day, when she'd been wearing them every day for over six months. They'd faithfully seen her through long weeks at the lab where she'd sometimes put in sixty or seventy hours a week. Her shoes got the job done, gave her no cause for complaints and never drew attention to themselves for the wrong reasons.

Oh man, the metaphors just kept coming, didn't they?

She should be thankful for her shoes now, for their comfort and sensibleness, since she'd already been on her feet for ten hours, and the day wasn't close to over. Molly loved her job as director of Omega Critical Response Division's main forensic lab here in Colorado Springs. Her work was challenging and fulfilling. Molly excelled at it, both as one of the leading pathologists in the country and as supervisor of the dozen people who worked daily in the lab.

Molly stopped and added another case file to the pile she was carrying. Not that they couldn't use twice as many technicians working here. That's how much material was constantly brought in for them to process. The forensic lab handled just about everything having to do with evidence: toxicology, trace reports, forensic biology, pathology, prints, DNA and even human remains for all the Critical Response Division cases. Therefore the lab was in a constant state of backup. Hiring more technicians was on Molly's to-do list, but the qualifications and security clearance required to work at Omega made the candidate pool slim.

So for right now Molly planned to continue working twelve- to fourteen-hour days to help keep the lab producing results at the speed they were needed. Like today. She'd arrived at seven o'clock this morning and was still here even though it was nearly eight in the evening. She definitely needed to cut her sensible shoes a break.

The other lab technicians had left a couple of hours ago, but being here by herself wasn't unusual or even unpleasant. Molly didn't expect her lab technicians to put in the same crazy hours she did. Often some of them were willing to stay late or come early if Molly asked, but she tried not to impose unless it was an emergency. These people had family. Molly didn't, so it was easier for her to stay. Nobody was going to miss her at home.

Molly got along well with all the people who worked in her lab. She treated them with the respect they deserved and, in turn, they worked hard. The key was direct, clear, respectful communication. Molly prided herself that she was not only good at the science part of her job, she was good at the communication aspect with her colleagues, as well.

Derek Waterman walked through the swinging double doors of the inner lab.

Well, maybe not *all* her colleagues.

Molly turned away quickly and placed the files on her desk. She put them right smack in the middle so she wouldn't accidentally knock them over. Molly had been known to do stupid things like that while in the presence of Derek.

Jon Hatton and Liam Goetz were with Derek and none of them looked too happy. Molly could smell smoke on them from across the lab, coming from *them*. Derek had been in a fire.

"Are you okay? Is everyone okay?" Molly rushed across the room, her long French-braided brown hair swinging over the shoulder of the white lab coat she always wore. These were three of the most intelligent and able-bodied men she'd ever known, but as active Omega agents they put their lives on the line daily.

"We're fine, sweet Molly," Jon said to her as she stopped a few feet away from them. "Unless you count your boy Derek here almost being trapped in a burning building as not okay."

Molly felt the air rush out of her lungs. She looked over at Derek for just a moment, needing to take in with her own eyes that he wasn't, indeed, seriously injured. His dark brown, almost-black hair had the tousled, disheveled look it always did, the five-o'clock shadow a permanent fixture on his chiseled face. He was leaning against one of the research tables, his long legs extended in front of him. She couldn't see any signs of pain based on his body language or facial expressions. Just a slight stiffness in how he held his back.

Molly knew Derek well enough to know that meant he'd been hurt.

"Did you burn your sh-shoulders?" she asked him, the words barely coming out in a whisper. Molly pressed her lips together and looked down at her shoes. She heard Liam snicker quietly before Jon nudged him.

"Yes, but I'm okay. Very minor first-degree burns on my shoulders and back," Derek responded. "No real harm."

Molly just nodded, relieved the burns weren't serious, although she could tell he had also suffered, at least to some small degree, from smoke inhalation. Derek's sexy voice was even deeper and more gravelly than usual, and although she hated the cause, Molly couldn't help but shiver slightly at the rougher sound of it.

Of course, then she felt like a fool, as she always did when Derek was around, for the way she was acting. Molly turned to a desk behind her and pretended to sort through files. She didn't blame Jon and Liam for snickering. Her behavior every time Derek entered the room was snicker-worthy.

"We've got some evidence from a lead we followed dealing with the Chicago bombing," Liam said as he began unpacking various evidence bags and laying them out on the table.

Molly walked back around to the table so she was on the far side, careful not to look at Derek in any way, not even out of the corner of her eye. It seemed as if they had about a dozen items that needed processing.

"We need a complete work up on all of it," Jon told her. "DNA, fingerprints, any possible trace evidence. Everything."

Molly picked up one of the bags containing some sort of piece of computer hardware inside. "Was this evidence from the burning building?"

"Not all of it," Derek answered her, causing Molly to study the contents of the bag more carefully so she wouldn't have to look at him. "Some of it is from what was left of a suspect before he killed himself. But the rest is from the burnt building."

"Is the body coming in here, too? Will I need to process that?" She looked at Liam and Jon as she said it.

Liam shook his head. "Yes, but not until later. Local coroner will be bringing it by. We brought prints and DNA so you could get started."

"You know, the stuff from the fire will take longer. It will have to be manually run through the system, based on layers of damage. Probably have to use a clean room." Molly put the bag back on the table. "Put it all over on the in-processing shelf. I'll try to get somebody started on it in the morning, but it might be in the afternoon."

Both Liam and Jon started talking at her immediately, voices raised, speaking all over each other. Derek, she noticed, didn't say anything. Molly held up a hand and eventually the two men stopped talking at the same time.

"Molly, this is a priority," Liam said. "It has to do with the Chicago bombing."

"I understand, Liam, but—"

"The largest terrorist attack on American soil in over five years," Jon continued. "We need the results on all of it right away."

Molly glanced quickly at Derek. He was just standing there, arms crossed over his large chest. She looked away again, not knowing what she would do if he interjected into the argument. Molly understood the men's frustration, she really did.

She looked over at the pile of files and packages of evidence on her desk. The problem was, every case was this important to *someone*. Those packages might provide clues to missing children, or someone's murder, or the identity of a serial rapist.

Everybody needed everything right away and that just wasn't possible.

"You guys," Molly looked at Jon and Liam, and even risked a glance at Derek. "I—I'm sorry. We're backed up in here."

"Molly." Liam wouldn't let it go. "We need all this now. It's vital."

Molly threw her arm out toward the files on her desk. "All those cases are vital to someone, too, Liam. And they've been waiting longer than you."

Both Jon and Liam began their arguments again, but Molly tuned them out. She hated being in this position; hated having to tell them to wait. She knew the men weren't making demands arbitrarily—what they needed was important. Brows furrowed, she looked down at the items on the table again, began trying to sort through them a little bit. Maybe if she stayed here all night she could get at least a couple of the pieces processed after she finished the cases sitting on her desk.

But which evidence pieces should she process first if she could only get to one or two tonight? In the midst of categorizing the evidence bags in her mind, and placing them in different groups on the table, Molly didn't realize Liam and Jon had stopped pleading their case.

Or that Derek had come to stand right behind her as she sorted through the evidence bags. He reached over and took the bag out of her hand and laid it on the table, and picked up two others near it.

Startled, Molly spun around, then immediately regretted it as she found herself trapped between the evidence table and Derek's hard body. Oh, dear lord. Was she supposed to be able to come up with actual words right now? Something coherent?

Derek took a small step backward, just enough so he could hold one of the evidence bags up between them.

"This one is most important," he said softly, holding up a small bag with what looked like part of a phone or communication device. "Although I know it's partially melted and will be difficult. The other is just the prints from the dead guy to run for ID. Should be simple. Both as soon as you can manage, Molly. But I know your other work here is also important."

Molly just nodded.

Derek hooked a finger into the hip pocket of her lab coat. He took the two small evidence bags and dropped them in. But instead of letting her go as she expected, he placed both hands on her waist.

Molly pretty much forgot how to breathe.

"Thank you," Derek said, his gravelly voice playing havoc with her insides. "I know this means more work for you, and I'm sorry."

"It—it's okay."

"Did you eat dinner?"

"Um, today?"

Derek shook his head and sighed. "I want you to eat something, all right?" His hands tightened the slightest bit on her waist. "You're too tiny as it is."

"Wh-what?" Since when was Derek aware of her eating habits?

"And not the vending machine. A real, proper meal. Promise me you'll go down to the cafeteria tonight and eat something if you're working here a long time."

Molly nodded.

"And not tomorrow morning. Tonight, okay? In the next couple of hours," Derek asked again. "Promise?"

"I promise." Molly forced the words to come out with no stammer.

Derek smiled, and for a second looked as if he was going to say something else, but then Liam and Jon began talking to each other as they repacked the other evidence to be placed on the in-processing shelf. Whatever Derek had been about to say in that moment was gone.

He dropped his hands from Molly's waist and took a step back. "Thanks for processing that communication device tonight. I'm hoping it may be a key piece in the Chicago case."

Without another word, Derek turned and walked out the lab doors. Jon and Liam said their goodbyes as they left, too. Molly finally began breathing normally again.

But as the doors closed, she heard it, although they obviously didn't mean for her to: quiet laughter and the words *Mousy Molly*.

Molly stayed where she was against the evidence table as if glued there. It wasn't Derek who called her mousy, it was never Derek. But it was everyone else. Molly didn't think Jon and Liam meant any harm by the expression, but it was true. Molly *was* mousy in all its elements: nervous, shy, lacking in presence or charisma. Heck even her coloring was mousy: brown eyes, brown hair.

Okay, yeah, it hurt a little bit. Molly didn't want to be mousy. And really most of the time she wasn't that bad. It was just when she was around Derek that she became unbearable to herself.

Molly brought her hands down to her waist where Derek's had been. Derek had actually touched her. That didn't happen very often. Although they saw each other a few times a week, Derek was very careful not to touch her in even the most casual way.

He really hadn't touched her at all since the time he showed up at her condo three years ago—*drunk*—and they'd had sex.

Molly still grimaced when she thought about it. He'd been inebriated, he'd needed a friend. She should've just made a pallet for him on her couch and let him sleep it off.

Instead of taking him to her bed and having the most wonderful night of her life.

Except Derek had been gone when she woke up the next morning. And he had never brought it up again, so she assumed he didn't remember much about that night at all. But Molly did. She also remembered their embrace in the lab about a year ago… The only other time he'd touched her.

Molly sighed and pushed herself off the table. There was no way she was going to start thinking about this again. She had entirely too much work to do. She would put in a call to David, the newest young tech, and see if he was willing to make some extra money by coming back in and helping her with this processing.

There was a lot of important work to do and she planned to get it done. She might be Mousy Molly like the guys said, but there was one thing she knew how to do well: her job.

Chapter Three

Derek cringed when he heard Jon and Liam's Mousy Molly comments as they followed him out the lab doors. How he hated that nickname. He knew the guys didn't really mean any harm by it, neither Jon nor Liam would ever purposely be unkind to someone like Molly, but Derek still hated it.

"I think you probably could've pushed to get more of our evidence processed tonight," Jon said with a little snicker as they walked down the hallway. "I don't know why Liam and I even tried talking to her. We should've used you from the beginning."

"It's not like that, Jon." Derek kept walking, hoping they'd just drop it. They had a meeting with Omega's Critical Response Division Director Steve Drackett in five minutes, teleconference with state officials not long afterward.

Both men laughed. "Uh, it's *exactly* like that. Of course, it's always like that with Molly when it comes to you," Liam told him.

Jon continued, "Yeah, if you had asked her to process *all* our evidence tonight I bet she would've done it. If she could've managed to get a sentence out."

Liam stopped walking and, with a dramatic sigh, grabbed Jon by the waist and pushed him up against the hallway wall. Liam pulled out a pen and held it in front of Jon's face.

Derek stopped to watch the show that was obviously for him.

"Just this one piece of evidence, Molly." Liam deepened his voice to mimic Derek, wiggling the pen and keeping his other hand on Jon's waist.

Jon's falsetto was even more annoying, especially given he was three inches taller than Liam's six-one. "B-but D-Derek, we're s-so busy."

If anything, Liam's voice got even deeper. "Please, Molly. For me? Because I'm Derek Waterman and I'm the best agent in the world."

"For you D-Derek, anything." Derek watched as his two coworkers embraced, then pulled apart, bowing.

Derek raised an eyebrow and just stared at them. "You morons done?"

He started walking down the hallway again.

"Oh, come on, Derek." Jon caught up to him first. "We like Molly as much as anybody. Hell, everybody likes her, she's so sweet and kind. But she gets so awkward around you, it's pretty entertaining."

"Obviously, she's not your type," Liam continued. "That's cool."

"What do you mean she's not my type?" Derek knew he shouldn't let himself get drawn into this conversation, but couldn't help it.

Of course Liam was right, Molly wasn't his type. Molly was sweet, kind, tender, gentle.

Everything Derek knew he should stay away from. Everything he knew he would destroy if he allowed himself near.

"I just mean you're not interested or attracted or whatever. It's obvious by the way I've never even seen you touch her before today." Liam shrugged. "You don't take advantage of her feelings, which is admirable."

Yeah, Derek tried not to touch Molly, because every time he did it went further than he wanted. Like a few minutes ago. He'd touched her waist, and all he could think about was sitting her up on that table and kissing her until neither of them even remembered what the word *evidence* meant.

"Yeah, I wish someone would get that tongue-tied around me," Jon said. "At least you got her to process the important evidence."

"Molly works hard, you guys. She's probably going to be here all night, doing what we asked *plus* all her other stuff. None of us will be working all night. So stow the comments."

That shut them up. Good. Derek needed to drag his focus away from Molly Humphries and back onto this case since they were walking into the director's office.

"Quite a mess today, gentlemen," Steve Drackett, division director, said as he opened his office door and met them in the hallway. "Walk with me on the way to the teleconference room."

"Yeah, it was a mess," Derek told him.

"What happened?" Steve's tone wasn't angry or condescending.

Derek explained what happened this afternoon, about the suspect killing himself and the house being burned to the ground. Since no harm had come to any bystanders, it was a little easier to report.

"So today was both good and bad," Steve said.

"Mostly bad," Jon muttered.

They made it to the conference room door. Derek opened it and they all moved inside. Steve had been giving daily briefings to a group of DC state officials—a committee of congressmen, senators, members of the Department of Defense and Department of Justice—each day since the Chicago bombing. Since Omega Sector's Critical Response Division was a multiagency task force made up of the best people each agency had to offer, faster, better and more detailed results were generally expected. And they were expected from people very high up in the governmental food chain.

So not having those expected results, hell, not having any results at all when they reported every day was getting a little old for everyone.

"We've got just over seven minutes until the call," the technician working the room told them. In seven minutes they would be staring down five different government officials on different screens.

"The only good thing to report about today is that it was at least an actual *live* lead," Derek told Steve. "We've personally followed up dozens since the Chicago attack which have led to nothing. This at least led to something."

Steve nodded. "Yeah, an important something. Critical enough that your suspect would *kill himself* rather than be taken into custody. That's pretty extreme. Do we know who the guy was?"

"Lab is running prints. We'll know in the morning. Local PD should be bringing the body, too."

"Yes, I got a report that the body was on its way, should be here within the hour," Steve told them.

"Hopefully this guy's ID should provide some sort of clue," Liam said, settling himself in a corner that would be out of the way of the cameras. Smart man. "But not as much as having him alive for questioning. Sorry, boss, if I'd had any inclination that he would off himself, I would've tackled him. I thought he might shoot at us, but not himself."

Steve shrugged. "You did the best you could with the info you had. Don't beat yourself up."

One thing Derek liked about having Drackett as his boss was that Steve hadn't been out of the field so long that he'd forgotten that sometimes things just went to hell for no particular reason. Steve was probably only ten years older than Derek's thirty-three years.

"Was anything recovered from the house before the fire completely burned it down?" Steve asked.

"We got out a few potential pieces of evidence. One looked particularly promising. Some sort of communication device. Looks like it could hold pictures or other data, if it can be retrieved," Derek told him, as Steve took notes. "Molly is rush-processing that for us herself tonight."

Jon and Liam made eye contact with each other at that, but Derek ignored them.

"Molly's got to get more people hired in the lab so she's not at Omega twenty hours a day." Steve scribbled something else on his notepad. Derek hoped it was a reminder to talk to Molly so she could get some of the lab workload off her shoulders. She looked tired.

Pretty, as always, but tired.

"What I find most interesting," Derek said, reining in his thoughts, "is that whatever was there, they burnt the building *to the ground* to get rid of it, definitely using an accelerant. The fire was almost as drastic as the guy killing himself."

"Which means you were really close to something," Steve finished for him. "All right, let's present this to the committee."

"One minute until the call, sir," the technician told him.

Steve nodded and looked at Derek. "You ready?"

"Oh, yeah," he answered, rolling his eyes. "Getting chewed out by government officials who really have no idea how to do police work is the favorite part of my day."

"First caller is connecting now," the technician announced. Derek and Steve sat down behind the computer that would show all the people on the call, and also make Derek and Steve visible to them.

And great, it was Congressman Donald Hougland. Always the first person on the video call and the last person off. And always the most vocal about Omega Sector's lack of results with the bombing.

"Gentlemen," Congressman Hougland said. "Hope we have good news today. Or at least not no news at all, as usual."

Derek reminded himself not to roll his eyes because that could be seen by the other man.

"Congressman Hougland." Steve was a much better diplomat so Derek let him talk. "We're just waiting for the others, and we'll provide an update. We've had a breakthrough. I believe you'll be pleased."

"I doubt it," the older man said. "For an organization that's supposed to be stellar, I've yet to see evidence of that. Of course, I've yet to see evidence of anything." He laughed at his own joke.

Thankfully, the other committee members chose that moment to connect to the conference call so Derek could force himself to swallow his tart retort for Congressman Hougland.

Derek had been raised on a ranch in Wyoming by his reluctant, confirmed-bachelor uncle when Derek's parents had died when he was twelve. So cursing had been a prevalent part of his upbringing.

But telling a US congressman to kiss his ass was probably not going to help any part of this conference call or overall situation. He could see Steve looking over at him cautiously as if preparing to kick him under the table if he opened his mouth. Derek glanced at him and nodded to let him know he wasn't going to do anything stupid.

The head of the committee, and much more amiable, Senator Edmundson, opened the conference. "Director Drackett, Agent Waterman, thank you for speaking with us today. We know your time is valuable."

"Senator," Steve responded respectfully. "Ladies and gentlemen."

"Let's cut to the chase, Robert," Congressman Hougland said, practically cutting off Steve's greeting to the committee. "Drackett mentioned they have some news. I'd be thrilled to hear that." Sarcasm dripped from his words.

Annoyance floated over Senator Edmundson's face before he reschooled it into its polite mask.

"All right, then. Director Drackett, please."

"Agent Waterman and his colleagues received a tip earlier today while returning from Chicago. They changed route midflight and headed to Philadelphia. Upon their arrival at the location, they were met with gunfire."

The men and women were listening attentively from their screens. It made for a nice change from the past two weeks when they'd had nothing of any interest to report.

"One man gave chase, and unfortunately killed himself rather than be taken into custody," Steve continued. "The suspects also burned the location to the ground while the team was chasing the running suspect."

"So basically, Agent Waterman, you had a more exciting day, but still have nothing to show for it," Congressman Hougland jumped in. "Is that correct?"

Derek counted to three before answering. He'd once been thrown from a spooked horse and had to walk the four miles home on a broken ankle. He'd survived that.

He could survive this.

"Actually, Congressman, we were able to retrieve a few pieces of evidence from the house before it was totally destroyed. One piece in particular, a communication device of some kind, looks particularly interesting. Although it was damaged by the fire, we're hopeful the data on it can be retrieved."

Most of the committee were nodding, at least accepting that this was progress. Not Hougland.

"Hopeful," he scoffed. "Not exactly confidence-inspiring."

"All right, Don, let's stay positive," Senator Edmundson said.

"The only thing I'm becoming positive about is that Omega Sector might not be living up to its reputation any longer," Hougland spat back.

Derek's lips thinned. As much as he disliked the congressman, the man wasn't totally incorrect. He and the team had been pretty inept on this Chicago case. They hadn't caught a single break until today.

"We should also have identification of the dead man soon," Drackett told the committee. "That will also point us in a direction."

"The body is there now, at your facility in Colorado?" Senator Edmundson asked.

Steve nodded. "Yes, our lab is or very soon will be, running the prints. We'll also have any other helpful evidence from the body."

"And the communication device? When will you know if that will provide anything useful?" Hougland asked.

"By tomorrow morning," Derek replied. He hoped that would be true. "The lab is working on it tonight."

That seemed to placate everyone. Since there weren't any other questions from the committee and Hougland had evidently gotten tired of poking holes at their case, Steve said good-night to everyone, promising to keep them posted. After the last of the committee had disconnected from the screens, Derek ran a weary hand over his face.

Jon and Liam stood up from their chairs in the corner.

"I am so glad I'm not you guys," Jon said. "That was brutal."

Derek couldn't agree more. He just wanted to get home, change out of his smoky clothes and shower. The burns on his back and shoulders were still bothering him a little. Everyone said their good-nights, agreeing to meet back first thing in the morning.

Derek partly wanted to go check on Molly, but decided it was better to just let her work on her own since his presence tended to discombobulate her so much. But he hated that she had more work on her plate—probably a whole night's worth—because of him. Derek promised himself that when this case was over, he would make sure that Steve forced Molly to hire some more people for the lab.

He needed a good night's sleep. Once they had this evidence in hand, it would hopefully lead them somewhere, and they'd all need to be able to hit the ground running. Derek was still thinking about the evidence through his meal, shower and even as he was falling asleep. Why would someone kill himself rather than be arrested? What was on that device that was worth burning a building to the ground? Molly's results would point them in the direction they needed to go. He drifted off to sleep with it on his mind.

The phone ringing at 2:42 a.m. jerked him out of his sleep. This was not the first call he'd gotten from Omega in the middle of the night. Derek looked at the caller ID: Steve Drackett.

"Steve, what's up?" Derek tried to wipe the sleep from his voice the best he could.

"Derek, I need you to get back to HQ right away. There's been an explosion at the building. I'm on my way in now, but you're closer."

Derek was instantly awake. "Like what, a fire?"

"No. I don't have many details yet, but I know it was an explosion. In the forensic lab."

Derek could actually feel his heart stop beating. "Forensic lab?" he parroted.

"Yes. And I know there's at least one confirmed death."

Chapter Four

Derek's general idea of "help from above" was a sniper on the roof, but he prayed like he had never prayed before as he broke multiple traffic laws driving back to Omega Headquarters in downtown Colorado Springs.

It was nearly three in the morning. The forensic lab had just exploded. One person was dead.

No matter how much he tried to twist it, there was no way to think that it wasn't Molly. Who else would even be there at almost three o'clock in the morning?

Acid ate at his gut when Derek thought of the fact that she wouldn't have been there at all if he hadn't asked her to stay. To do something specifically for him.

But he categorically refused to assume the worst until there was no other choice. Until he was presented with proof positive that it was Molly who was dead.

He hit the gas harder and rounded a corner, nearly blinded by all the emergency vehicle lights parked at Omega. A uniformed officer stopped him from pulling into the parking lot, but let Derek through when he flashed his badge and ID.

Which saved Derek from having to pull his gun on the man. Because there was no way in hell he wasn't getting into that parking lot.

Chaos reigned as Derek parked his car far enough away

not to hinder any emergency vehicles and jogged over to a small group of personnel who seemed to be directing the efforts.

Behind them he could see the building burning, the concentration of flames largest in the southwest corner. Smoke billowed from right where the forensic lab was located—what was left of it.

"I'm Omega agent Derek Waterman, standing in for Director Drackett until he gets here in a few minutes." Derek pulled out his ID, but the men barely glanced at it.

"Captain Jim Brandal, with Station 433," the man closest to Derek, holding a hand radio, said, nodding at him. "You've had some sort of explosion in the southwest corner of the building."

"That's the forensic lab." Derek kept the panic out of his voice.

Captain Brandal looked over at the man standing next to him and both of their faces turned more grim. "That's what we figured. Any hazardous materials there?"

Derek shrugged. He was sure there were, but he didn't know what. "Almost definitely. You have one confirmed dead?" His throat tightened as he said the words.

"Yes," Captain Brandal agreed, and then started to say more before stopping to respond to a report from the radio in his hand.

Derek shifted in frustration. Who was dead? Where? Had the ID of the victim been established?

But looking at the smoke from the forensic lab, so much more than from the house fire today that had been minutes from taking his own life, Derek realized no one could've survived in there.

Derek steeled himself, forced himself to cut off emotions altogether. It was one of the things he'd become an expert at over the years.

The fire department captain turned back to Derek after his radio conversation. "Sorry. Yes, one confirmed dead. But the good news is that the fire doors in the building instantly shut after the explosion. So there should be very limited causalities outside of the immediate blast site."

Some part of Derek knew that was good, but the biggest part of him didn't care if everyone else in the building survived if Molly had died. He managed to nod at Captain Brandal.

Brandal continued, "Based on what the firefighters closest to the blaze reported, it looks like there was an explosion in the lab, which is why we asked about hazardous materials."

"I'm sure there were flammable items in the lab, but the safety record there is exemplary. Never been any problems reported whatsoever," Derek told the man.

He had a hard time imagining meticulous Molly being anything but completely safe in her lab. But she was overworked and overtired. Anyone could make a mistake under those conditions.

The Captain shrugged. "It only takes one time."

Derek felt guilt threaten to overtake him as the man's words echoed his thoughts. But he ruthlessly tamped it down. There'd be time for guilt later. Right now he had to know the answer to the question burning a hole in his gut.

"Has the body been identified yet?" he asked through gritted teeth. Then an ugly thought hit him. "Can it even be identified here on scene?"

Maybe there wasn't enough left of the body to be identified visually. The thought made him sick to his stomach.

"Hang on." Captain Brandal spoke into the radio again and waited for a response. "The body is over by the paramedics. I'm sorry for your loss, but truly, with an explosion of this size, it's nothing short of a miracle that only one life was lost."

Nothing felt further from the truth to Derek. He wiped a hand over his face. "Thanks," he murmured.

"Paramedics said you should probably be able to ID the guy visually. If not, we can use other means."

Derek's head jerked up. "*Guy*? Paramedics are sure the victim is a man?"

Brandal spoke into his radio once again, then turned back to Derek. "Yep. Young black male. Midtwenties."

Definitely not Molly. Derek felt relief flood through him.

But where was she?

THE EXPLOSION ROCKED the whole building. Molly had been staring at the vending machine in the break room outside the lab, feeling guilty because she had promised Derek she would eat hours ago in the cafeteria, when she found herself thrown back against the wall and crumpling to the ground.

For long, panicked moments she couldn't hear, couldn't see. She struggled to get her bearings, feeling around along the floor. The emergency generator lights kicked on, casting a ghoulish gray light around the break room. But at least she could see.

The vending machine lay broken on the floor, the chairs and table knocked over and scattered across the room. The coffeemaker was hanging precariously off the side of a shelf, held by just its cord plugged into the wall. Dust floated around everywhere, like snowflakes in slow motion, moving in all directions.

Molly began moving toward the hallway, trying to shake off the ringing in her ears. What had happened?

Not an earthquake. It was too loud. Definitely some sort of explosion.

She needed to get back to the lab, but once she rounded the corner from the break room she realized the lab was on fire. In all the chaos it took her longer than it normally would've to realize that the explosion had come *from* the lab.

Oh, no. David had been working in there.

Molly rushed forward, but after only a few feet ran into the clear fire wall. It had automatically lowered, as it was meant to do, to keep damage from spreading. Looking into the area where the lab had once stood, she knew there was no way the young tech had made it out of there alive.

And if the explosion had happened five minutes earlier, Molly would've been in there with David.

She knew if this door was closed, others around the building would be, too. All she could do was wait for the firefighters to do their job. She sat back on the floor and tried to figure out what had happened. Her ears were still ringing and the room still seemed to spin slightly.

Had something in the lab caused the fire? There were always hazardous materials around, but everyone who worked there—including David—was trained in lab safety. She couldn't think of anything they'd been working on that could've caused something this damaging, but right now it was too hard to even get her thoughts straight.

And, oh gosh, David was probably dead.

Molly just closed her eyes and leaned her head back against the wall. Eventually rescue workers came through and led her out. They wrapped her in a blanket and she was now sitting in the back of an ambulance. Still dazed.

She had been questioned multiple times. What did she think had caused the explosion? What hazardous elements had been in active use in the lab? Had there been anyone else working besides herself and David?

She answered each time as best she could about the causes, but just like when she had been sitting inside, she couldn't figure out what would have triggered an explosion of that magnitude.

And no, no one else had been there besides her and David. The young man's death had already been confirmed.

She didn't know what to do, who to call. It was even more chaotic and loud out here than it had been inside near the explosion. The rescue workers were all moving at a brisk pace, yelling to one another, coordinating the best they could to do their job.

Molly liked order and quiet, not the cacophony of havoc currently swirling around her. She resisted the urge to put her hands over her ears and close her eyes.

And then she saw him.

Derek was walking directly toward her, determination in his eyes. He radiated a definite purpose in his walk, because no one got in his way; instead, they stepped around him. He didn't stop until he was right in front of her.

She wanted to jump into his arms, to beg him to take her from here. But this was Derek Waterman. Jumping into his arms wasn't an option.

She was shocked when he put his large hands on either side of her head and tilted her head back so she was looking into his blue eyes, and found them searching her face intently.

"Are you okay?" His voice was deep, gravelly. "Injured?"

"No, I'm fine. But David Thompson, the new lab assistant, is dead, Derek." Molly could feel herself begin to cry.

To her shock, Derek pulled her to his chest and wrapped his arms around her.

"I know. I identified the body a few minutes ago."

She leaned into Derek's strength. He'd never put his arms around her in public before, but Molly didn't question it. She needed his strength right now.

"I heard they'd found a body in the lab and I thought it was you, Molls. How did you get out?"

"I wasn't in there when the explosion happened. I'd gone out to get something to eat." She leaned back from his chest so she could look at him. "Like you told me to do."

"I told you to do it hours ago." He pulled her back against his chest. "Thank God you suck at following directions."

Everything going on around her, all the noise and chaos, all the danger, didn't seem quite so overwhelming against Derek's chest. "Actually, I'm quite good at following directions," she murmured. "I just lost track of time."

She heard him chuckle before confirming with the paramedic that she hadn't sustained any injuries needing further medical treatment.

"Oh, thank God!" Molly found herself ripped out of Derek's arms and hugged against the even larger chest of Jon Hatton. "You cannot believe how glad I am to see you, Molly."

Molly liked Jon just fine. And heaven knew he was attractive enough—six-four of solid gorgeousness—but right now she just wanted to jump out of the man's embrace and back into Derek's. But the moment had passed. Derek had turned to talk to Director Drackett and wasn't even looking her way anymore.

As if it had never happened.

As usual.

"Are you okay, honey?" Jon released her from his hug,

but kept one arm around her. "When we heard someone from the lab was dead…"

"David Thompson. The new tech." Sadness filled her again. Nobody that young should die.

"I'm sorry, kiddo." Jon squeezed her before letting her go. "But I'm glad it wasn't you."

As she stood watching the firefighters put the last of the flames out, Molly knew how lucky she'd been. And although she was heartbroken over David, she was glad it hadn't been her, too.

Chapter Five

Derek was listening to what Steve Drackett was saying while trying to force himself not to punch Jon in the face. Seriously, the man had been his colleague and one of his closest friends for over five years, but when he had snatched Molly out of his arms and into his own...

Derek reminded himself that Jon had no romantic intentions toward Molly. And even if he did, Molly was free to date whomever she wanted. Derek had no claim on her.

But damned if he wasn't totally relieved when Molly stepped away from Jon. Derek pretended not to pay any attention to them whatsoever as he spoke with his boss. But he knew exactly where Molly was.

Of course, he always knew where Molly was if she was anywhere in his vicinity. It was as if he had an internal radar set solely for her. Not that he could do anything but keep a watchful eye on her. Anything else wasn't acceptable.

"Based on the preliminary report, the fire department feels like it was definitely something from the lab that detonated. Not caught on fire. Actually blew up," Derek told Steve. "One confirmed death. Protection walls came down, so it looks like other damage and causalities are pretty minimal."

The director nodded, then turned to Molly. "You okay?"

"Not physically hurt. But sick about David's death." Molly's voice was strained. Derek had to resist the urge to wrap an arm around her again.

The one good thing about the trauma of the explosion was that it seemed to have made Molly forget to be nervous around him. At least she wasn't stammering.

"Can you give us a report? Do you know what happened?" Steve asked her.

"We were working." Molly shrugged one delicate shoulder. "Nothing out of the ordinary. Our caseload had heightened, so I called David and asked him to come back in. But we weren't working with anything hazardous or explosive."

Molly ran a hand over her face, exhausted. "I'm sorry." Her voice was shaky. "I'm trying to figure out what it could've been. But I don't think it was anything we were working on. I—" She rubbed a hand over her face again.

"Molly, it's okay," Jon said to her, coming to stand close to her again. "We'll get it all worked out. I'm sure it wasn't your fault."

Molly just shook her head, her hand still covering her face.

Jon looked at Derek and Steve, then tilted his head in Molly's direction. He wanted to take her home. She obviously needed to go and really couldn't help anything here.

But over Derek's dead body was Jon taking Molly anywhere. Derek would take her home.

Derek walked over to Molly and touched her gently on the arm. The arm that had been covering her face dropped to her side. Her eyes seemed glassy, dazed.

"Hey." He bent at the knees so they could be eye to eye. He tucked an errant strand of her long brown hair back behind her ear. "I'm going to take you home, okay? We'll figure out what happened tomorrow."

She nodded, swaying slightly toward him. Derek wrapped

an arm around her shoulders. He looked back at the guys, ignoring both of their slightly shocked expressions at how he was treating Molly.

Maybe he'd made too much of a show out of never touching her over the past couple years.

"I'm going to put her in the car and will be right back. She needs to sit down before she falls down." Both men nodded, their gazes flickering to Molly, where she was tucked under his arm. "I'll take her home in a minute."

Steve stepped up to Molly. "Get some rest, okay? We'll work out what happened later. But I have no question that you will be totally exonerated of all blame."

Molly nodded, but didn't say a word. Derek walked her over to his car and opened the passenger door, thankful for the balmy May night that wasn't too hot or cold. But Molly was shivering slightly, so he grabbed a blazer he had thrown in the backseat and put it around her. He knew her reaction was from shock more than cold, but she wouldn't know the difference.

Once he had her settled in the car, he squatted down so he could look in her eyes again. Hers were still pretty unfocused.

"Hey." He wrapped the jacket more securely around her, then grabbed it by the lapels to bring her in a little closer. "I'm just going to finish my conversation with Steve and Jon and then I'll take you home, okay? Five minutes."

She nodded.

Derek kissed her forehead, then closed the door, jogging back toward Jon and Steve who were walking toward his car. Both of them were still looking at him with odd expressions.

"What?" he barked when they didn't say anything.

"Nothing." Jon shook his head. "Just wondering how I

can call myself a behavioral analyst and miss certain facts that are right before my eyes."

"What are you talking about?"

Jon shook his head again. "Absolutely nothing. Is Molly okay?"

Derek glanced back at his car. "Exhausted. A little shaky. Not unexpected, given the circumstances."

"I believe her when she says that they didn't have any flammable materials out in the lab at the explosion site. Molly's record is impeccable when it comes to safety. Hell, when it comes to anything," Steve stated.

"But she's been working long hours. Was tired. Could've made a mistake she wouldn't normally have." Derek's grim expression matched the other men's.

The director nodded. "And if that's the case, we'll deal with it. I share in that responsibility."

Jon turned and looked back at the building. "But if human error or some other accident wasn't the cause of the explosion, then we have to think about what is."

"What are you thinking? That it was some sort of attack against Omega?" Derek asked.

"Maybe not so much attack as sabotage," Jon responded.

Each man processed that for a minute.

"It seems a little extreme, I know," Jon continued.

"Until you take into consideration someone killing himself rather than being questioned, and perps burning that house to the ground today to keep evidence out of our hands," Derek finished for him.

"Exactly."

Derek grimaced. "Whatever we took into evidence must have been pretty important to blow up the whole damn lab for it."

Steve had been quiet up until now. "And if this is all

connected, then we also have to think about who knew we had that specific evidence here." He shook his head.

"Nobody really knew, but us," Derek said. "Unless you think we have some sort of mole?"

There had been moles in other divisions of Omega Sector in the past. But the Critical Response Division was not a clandestine section of Omega. They worked out in the open, not generally undercover or in the shadows. And although they didn't talk publicly about investigations, Derek had no idea why a terrorist would keep a mole inside the Critical Response Division. Information was pretty open there.

"Not necessarily, at least not within our division," Steve responded. "But perhaps amongst the people we've been reporting to every day."

"The government committee?" Derek asked.

"Actually, I was thinking about that very fact last night, after Congressman Hougland was giving you a hard time," Jon said. Derek wasn't surprised to hear his friend doing what he did best as a behavioral analyst: piecing everything together.

"What did you come up with?" Steve asked.

"Like we've already talked about—obviously there was critical information at the location yesterday, based on the lengths the suspects were willing to go to try and keep us from getting it."

Both Derek and Steve nodded.

"This lead was also unique because we weren't here at Omega when you got the info, Derek. We were in the air following up on something else and switched our focus to the new lead."

They'd been on one of the small Omega jets traveling back to Colorado from a lead in Chicago.

"Yeah, that's true. We moved quicker on this lead than we have some of the others," Derek agreed.

"We also didn't follow exact protocol since we were already out. We hadn't called in our exact location, just decided to go to Philly, and then the building, immediately, since the option was available."

Derek was beginning to see the pattern Jon was suggesting. "Unlike every other lead we've investigated for the last two weeks. Where we've followed protocol pretty much to the letter. And all have led to nothing."

Steve grimaced. "You're thinking sabotage." It wasn't a question.

Jon shrugged. "It's hard to believe that every single lead we've followed has been completely dead. Although I guess that's possible."

"No, I agree with Jon," Derek told Steve. "Sometimes it felt like the people we were after were one step ahead of us. Almost ready for us."

They'd had the normal factions attempt to take credit for the bombing, both international and domestic groups. All had been investigated and all had come to naught. Then all other aspects of the investigation—the bomb site, witnesses, the type of explosions—had also led nowhere.

Maybe everything had led nowhere because someone was deliberately running interference on the perpetrators' behalf.

There were very few people who could have done that effectively. A dirty agent inside the Critical Response Division could, but having one there was unlikely.

And since Derek and this investigation had been under such close scrutiny by high-ranking government officials, any one of them could be responsible, too. Which was uglier, but made more sense in a lot of ways.

"Gentlemen," Steve said. "It looks like there's every

possibility that we've got some high-ranking US official who is tied in with the Chicago terrorist attack."

Jon pointed at the now-destroyed lab. "And we're looking at the third extreme example of what that person, or people, might be willing to do to keep us from making any progress on the case."

"Whoever it is has also put us back at square one in terms of evidence." Derek could feel his teeth grinding, knowing they'd been so close to a real breakthrough only to lose it. "Nothing in the lab survived that explosion. It was definitely important, but now it's gone."

All three men looked at the smoke still rising from the building. The fire was out, but the smoke would linger for a while.

"Well, they may have successfully destroyed whatever evidence we'd gotten yesterday, but they also tipped their hand a little too far," Jon said. "They've given us an edge they don't know we have by revealing they have inside knowledge. We should use that to our advantage."

The director nodded at both men. "I agree. I'm going to start keeping much more careful track of what information is going to which offices. The committee we report to every day hasn't been the only ones requesting information. I'll see what I can narrow down. And I damn sure won't be sharing actual pertinent info about the case any longer."

Steve turned away from the lab. "Go home, get some rest," he continued. "Tomorrow you guys head back out to the house in West Philly, see if anything there can be salvaged. Track down where the lead came from and see if you can get any further info."

Derek nodded. He needed to get Molly home, let her rest. But then he'd be coming right back, or at least working out of his house. Sleep could wait for him. He glanced over at Jon and knew the other man felt the same way.

"I'll let you know when the building is open," Steve said. "This fire is meant not only to destroy evidence, but to misdirect us. Give us a lot of other stuff to be worrying about. We're not going to let that happen."

"Damn right we're not," Jon said.

Some of the firefighters were beginning to pack up their equipment.

"I've got to go sign off on all this," Drackett said, shaking his head. "I'll see you later."

He began walking toward the fire trucks, but then turned back. "And boys, watch your backs. If this goes as high up as I'm afraid it might, we all have targets on us."

Derek nodded. He could feel it, too.

He got back into the car and looked over at Molly. She was sitting in the exact position as when he had left, staring straight out the windshield.

"You doing okay?"

"Yeah." She finally nodded. "I'm just trying to go over in my mind if anything we had out in the lab could've caused this."

He wasn't sure if he should tell her that it might have been a deliberate attack. "Molly, we're looking into a lot of possibilities for what happened. But believe me, no one is assuming you're at fault. You run a pretty tight ship in that lab."

She seemed to relax just a little bit. "Everyone's safety is always my first priority."

"I know that. Everyone knows that."

She seemed tiny inside his blazer, huddled in the seat as he drove out of the Omega parking lot and toward her house.

"You know where I live, right?" she said in a small voice.

Did he know where she lived? Was she kidding? He was guilty of driving by her condo sometimes even when it was almost the opposite direction of the way he needed to go.

And every single time he wanted to stop and knock on her door like that one night three years ago.

Knowing she wouldn't slam the door in his face, wouldn't tell him to go to hell, was the only thing that kept him from doing so. She was too gentle, too kind, too soft to send him away.

And he wasn't so much of a bastard that he was willing to drag her down into the dark world he lived in. He didn't want her touched by the ugliness of the sordid things he'd seen and done.

But damned if that wasn't the hardest thing he'd ever done.

"Yeah, I know where you live."

He could almost see the flush move up her cheeks.

"I just mean… The one time you were there you were… not your normal self. A-and I just wondered."

"Hey." He reached over and grabbed her hand. "You've gone the entire evening without being nervous around me."

"That's because I was upset."

"Then stay upset, at me if you need to. No need to go back to nervous."

She shrugged. He knew he made her nervous, made her uncomfortable.

Just like he knew the way she looked at him when she thought he couldn't see. And he cherished it even as he tried to keep himself distant from it.

Her condo wasn't far from Omega Headquarters and soon he pulled up and into her parking space. She was already opening her door when he came around to help her.

"I'm okay," she said, and although her voice was soft,

it wasn't shaky. "Thanks for the ride. My purse was in the lab with my keys in it. Let me get the spare."

He watched as she hunted around her bushes, and saw her pull it out from where she had used electrical tape to attach it to the main branch. Much better than just slipping it under a front doormat.

"Found it!" The small victory had evidently thrilled her.

"May I?" He took the key when she offered it and opened the door for her. "Do you have another set inside?"

"Yes. This is just for true emergencies."

"Okay, I'll put it back out for you." He slipped it into his pocket.

She stood there in the doorway swamped in his jacket, plaster in her hair, smelling like smoke, smiling her slightly awkward smile that always seemed to be uniquely for him.

She was the most beautiful thing he'd ever seen.

All the lecturing he'd given himself on the drive here about not dragging her down into his darkness completely vanished.

Molly was alive and he had to taste her.

He slipped one arm around her small waist under his jacket and threaded his other hand through the hair at her scalp underneath her long brown braid. He backed her up against the door frame and brought his lips down to hers.

He heard her soft gasp of surprise and took advantage of it to slip his tongue into her mouth. A knot of need twisted inside him as he drew her closer. He felt her arms wrap around his neck as her tongue dueled with his.

His jacket falling from her shoulders and pooling at their feet brought some sense of reality back to Derek.

This could not happen. As much as he wanted it to.

He dropped both hands to her waist and took a step back. "Molly…"

She blinked up at him, arms still around his neck.

"Molly, this isn't a good idea."

"Why?" She leaned forward again.

Hell if he could remember why in this moment. Her lips were almost to his. If he kissed her again he wasn't sure he would have the strength to stop. "You have plaster in your hair."

"What?"

"Plaster. It's all in your hair."

Her face that had just been so flushed and soft from his kisses became shuttered. Her arms dropped to her sides, before one came up to her head to find the plaster he had mentioned. Why the hell had he said that? He didn't care about anything being in her hair. He'd just meant that she had been through a trauma and that they shouldn't do anything she might regret.

Or he might regret. Like break her heart.

"Oh. Yeah. I—I probably need a shower pretty badly."

The thought of Molly in the shower had everything in Derek's body tightening, but the slight stutter wasn't lost on him. He hated that he'd made her uncomfortable around him again. And her eyes were wounded.

Damn it. He had to get out of here just to stop the damage he was inflicting.

"I'll pick you up tomorrow at nine, okay?" He glanced down at his watch. "Actually, that's only about four hours from now, so let's make it ten. You'll need to give an official report."

Molly nodded and stepped inside her door. She picked up his jacket and held it out to him, wary, as if she didn't know what to expect.

Derek didn't blame her. He couldn't run more hot and cold if he tried.

He took the blazer from her. "Just get some rest. It's been a crazy day for all of us."

He waited until she closed the door—without a word—then turned and walked back to his car.

Damn it.

Chapter Six

It's been a crazy day for all of us.

Molly turned on the shower water to let it warm up. She slipped her lab coat off as well as her other clothes, all of which smelled like smoke, and just threw them in the bathtub so they wouldn't contaminate her clothes in the hamper.

She glanced briefly in the mirror before stepping into her walk-in shower. Yeah, she did have some plaster in her hair.

But let's face it, Derek could've had giant pieces of cement or paint or a dozen more building substances covering his entire head and Molly would've kept kissing him.

That was the difference between them.

Derek Waterman was out of her league and she needed to remember that. He was glad she was alive and had kissed her. But tomorrow they'd be back to their same old routine: him acting as if nothing had ever happened between them and her acting like a complete nincompoop around him.

As Molly washed the mess from the explosion off her body and out of her hair, she decided it was time to stop the silly way she'd been acting around him all this time. She was a strong, intelligent woman. She needed to act that way.

She completely ignored that she had made that promise to herself multiple times before. This time she was going to do it.

Plus, she had other things to worry about besides Derek Waterman and his kisses. She got out of the shower and dried off, slipping on a pair of yoga pants and a T-shirt, rebraiding her hair.

The explosion in the lab. She rubbed a hand over her face as she walked downstairs to get something to eat. Even if the explosion wasn't her fault, the workload resulting from it would be enormous. Sorting through which evidence was completely destroyed, or whether any of it could be salvaged, would be a daunting task.

Without a doubt many Omega cases would be ruined because of what had happened tonight. Crimes would go unsolved, some criminals unpunished. It was frustrating to consider.

Molly made herself a sandwich, poured herself a glass of milk and forced herself to finish both even though she didn't want to. She was going to need her strength for tomorrow and a full stomach would help her get rest now.

All of the findings for past cases had been backed up on a server in a different building, just in case of a situation like what had happened tonight. But current cases… They would have to be sorted through individually. And almost all findings would now be ineligible in court because they had been contaminated.

Worst of all, a young man—a promising young life— had perished.

Molly got up and put her dishes in the sink and stood there for just a moment, head hanging low. How she hoped they could prove this wasn't her fault. She didn't know how she was going to live with herself otherwise.

For the first time Molly wished she was a drinker. That

she had some sort of hard liquor in the house that she could use to help alleviate all these thoughts in her head just for tonight. Be drunk and just not care.

And maybe, just maybe, she would go show up at Derek's house drunk. And they could have sex again. Turnabout was fair play, after all.

Who was she kidding? Like she'd ever have the guts. She'd be thrilled if she could just talk to him like a normal person tomorrow when he came to pick her up. Which was just a few hours from now. She should get some sleep because she was obviously slap happy, thinking about drinking and having sex with Derek.

She went back into her bathroom to brush her teeth and took another look at herself in the mirror. No plaster in her hair, it was all tidy in its braid. Would Derek mention their kiss when he saw her tomorrow or pretend like it never happened? Again. She was interested to find out.

Crossing into her bedroom, she stopped as she realized the door leading to her small balcony was cracked open. Molly racked her brain. Had she opened it when she first got home? Had it been open when she got into the shower earlier? It was a nice night and now that she wasn't in shock she wasn't feeling so cold. But she still didn't sleep with doors open.

As she crossed to shut it, she saw movement out of the corner of her eye and gasped. *Someone was in the room with her.*

She opened her mouth to scream when the arm of a different, second person came around her head and covered her mouth roughly.

"She saw you. Get the drug. Hurry up," one voice whispered to the other.

Molly began to struggle as hard as she could, throwing her weight back and twisting in the arms that held her. The hand squeezed harder on her face and jerked her head to the side, exposing her neck.

She felt a sharp prick in her neck as the second man injected her with something.

Molly fought to keep her head, to not panic. Whatever they had injected her with would only work faster if she was flailing around. She couldn't fight them both anyway.

She let her body go slack.

"That was fast. Is that how it works?" the second man asked the first.

"How the hell should I know? Let's get her to the car. The plane will be waiting for us." Voice number one.

Plane? Oh God, where were they taking her? Molly struggled to focus over the effect of the drug they'd given her. One man grabbed her feet and the other carried her torso as they took her downstairs, then out the back through her sliding glass door. Molly tried to make her body respond once they got outside. If she was going to try to flee, now would be the best time.

But she couldn't make her body respond as they threw her in the backseat of their car parked right outside her gate. She watched her row of condos get smaller from the window.

She wasn't sure how long the car had been moving, and she definitely had no idea which direction they'd been going when it stopped again. But she could see an airplane hangar and small runway. Not the Denver airport, a much smaller regional one.

Through the fog of her mind Molly figured out that this was her only chance. Once they had her on a plane she'd have no opportunity to escape. The movement would send the drug faster through her bloodstream, but she couldn't wait. And even in the haze she could imagine the terrible things they would do to her.

The men were arguing in the front seat, about something she couldn't begin to understand, obviously not thinking her a threat of any kind. Using all her focus, she opened the door of the car and poured herself through the opening.

She tried to stand upright to run, but the world was spinning too rapidly. In a sort of three-limbed crawl-run she moved as rapidly as she could toward the tree line surrounding the airstrip.

She couldn't hear anything but her own breathing, sobs coming from her chest as she tried to force her body to move faster. Her vision blurred as the drug took greater affect.

For just a moment she was sure she was going to make it. Then a hand grabbed her shoulder, spinning her around and sending her sprawling to the ground. She felt the pin prick again, this time in her arm.

"You're tricky." It was the first man. The one she had seen in her apartment. "But that should do it."

The other man, the angry one, came up next to him. "I'll take care of this the old-fashioned way."

Molly tried to move away from his fist flying at her, but there was nowhere to go and she couldn't get her body to move anyway.

She felt a pain like she'd never known against her jaw, then everything went blessedly black.

DEREK HAD GONE back to Omega Headquarters after dropping Molly off. But Steve had sent both him and Jon home. There was nothing that could be done until all the firefighters were cleared out, and they'd both be more useful after a few hours of sleep.

Molly's house was much closer and Derek was tempted to stop there and catch a few hours of sleep on her couch.

Except he knew there would be no sleeping or couching going on if he did.

So he'd headed back to his own house and spent the couple of remaining hours of the morning trying, not very successfully, to sleep. And trying, again totally unsuccessfully, not to think about that kiss in Molly's doorway.

Or her face when he'd stopped it and told her it was because she had plaster in her hair, for God's sake. This was a shining example of why he shouldn't be with her.

He was too rough and she was too gentle. She would always end up getting hurt around him.

But now he was on his way back to her house to pick Molly up. They both had long, hard days ahead of them.

And so help him, if she still had that sad look of rejection in her eyes when he saw her, Derek didn't know if he'd be able to stop himself from taking her to bed right then and there to prove how much he wanted her. Consequences be damned.

He couldn't stand the thought of her thinking he didn't want her. Because he did. Every moment of every day. But he knew he wasn't good for her. More than not good for her.

Poison for her.

He pulled up at her house and knocked on the door just a couple minutes before ten o'clock. When there was no answer he knocked again.

Nothing.

Had he gotten the time wrong?

Or maybe Molly had finally come to her senses and decided she didn't want to be around him anymore. He couldn't blame her for that. But he still wanted to make sure she was okay. He wished he could call her, but knew her phone had been destroyed in the lab.

He grabbed his phone and called Jon.

"Hey, you on your way in?" Jon answered without preamble. "I'm already here. It's still pretty much chaos."

"Have you seen Molly around or heard from her? I thought I was supposed to pick her up this morning but she's not answering her door."

"No, I haven't seen her, but that doesn't mean she's not here. Let me check with Drackett."

Derek stepped back so he could get a better look at her condo. None of the windows had any drapes open. If she had already left, then she hadn't taken the time to open any blinds first.

"Steve hasn't seen her, either. I don't think she's here, man."

"Okay. I'll see if I can find her." No need to panic yet. "I'll be in soon."

Derek still had her extra key from last night, since he'd been so hell-bent on getting out of there as fast as possible. He knocked harder on the door, but when he received no answer again after a few seconds, he let himself inside.

"Molly? Are you here? I'm coming in." He had been in law enforcement long enough to know not to enter a building unannounced if you weren't on some sort of covert op.

He stopped just inside the doorway to listen for any sounds that would give away Molly's presence: a shower, hair dryer, dishwasher. But there was nothing but silence.

"Molls?" Derek was actually worried now, running through possible scenarios in his head. What if she had been more hurt from the fire than any of them had thought?

He checked her bedroom first, then the bathroom and guest room. Back downstairs he found a dish in the sink, with crumbs from what looked to have been a sandwich. An interesting breakfast choice.

She wasn't here and her bed was made. Which meant

she either hadn't slept in it at all or had already gotten up and was on her way.

Maybe she really was mad at him and had made her way to Omega on her own. Or maybe she just hadn't been able to sleep and decided to go in to HQ where she could do some good.

It wasn't like her to be inconsiderate, but she didn't have a phone to contact him.

There were a lot of reasons why she could be out of pocket. All of them perfectly reasonable. But something about this wasn't sitting right in Derek's gut.

And he knew it wouldn't ease until he found her.

Chapter Seven

Derek didn't waste any time getting back to Omega Headquarters. He hoped Molly would be there, even if she was mad and didn't want to talk to him. At least he would know she was safe.

The scene at Omega was less hectic than the night before. All the rescue vehicles and personnel were gone. Like the fire department captain had said, most of the damage had been contained to the forensic lab. The fire doors had saved the rest of the building.

Derek checked with security first. Everyone had to log in to enter the building. There was no record of Molly's entry. Derek made his way to the main group of offices where his desk was located. The offices were far enough from last night's fire to still be operational. Everywhere he looked, Omega agents were doing their normal jobs. Fighting crime and keeping society safe didn't stop just because of a setback. Even one as large as last night's fire.

"Did you find Molly?" Derek wasn't even to his desk before Jon caught up with him.

"No. You haven't seen her anywhere around here, have you?"

Jon shook his head. "Nope. And I even went outside and looked after you called, just in case. I know Drackett was out at the explosion scene this morning."

Derek sat in his chair. "I checked the security log. No record of her scan card being swiped. I'm a little concerned that maybe she was more injured last night than she let on. Maybe something happened and she called for an ambulance or something."

"Let me call the local hospitals, see if she got brought in."

"Okay." Derek nodded at him. "I'm going to go back to the lab, or what's left of it, to see if she's there. Maybe Steve knows something."

The director was outside, walking around the site of last night's fire. He was talking with multiple people. Derek could only imagine the amount of paperwork headache something like this had to cause. He didn't envy Drackett's position, especially not right now.

When he saw Derek's nod, Steve excused himself from the group of people he was consulting with. "Everything okay inside?"

"Is Molly Humphries out here with you?"

"No. I haven't seen her since you took her home last night."

That was not what Derek had been hoping to hear. "She seems to be MIA. I was supposed to pick her up this morning, but she wasn't at her house. No record of her signing in here."

"It's not like Molly to just not show up."

"Jon is checking hospitals. I'm concerned she may have been more injured than she let on."

The director grimaced. "I hope not. Keep me posted. I've got my hands full out here trying to figure out what happened and how to move forward. As a matter of fact, I could really use Molly's input if she shows up." The older man slapped Derek on the shoulder. "*When* she shows up."

Derek nodded, but wasn't convinced. "I'll send her out here when I see her."

By the time he'd made it back inside and to his desk Jon had a report. "Well, good news, or bad, depending on how you want to look at it. She's not at any of the hospitals. I checked any Jane Does, too, to be thorough."

The itch he'd had at the back of his neck since there'd been no answer at Molly's door was back in full force.

"Something's not right. I just know it." He looked over at Jon. "Am I overreacting?"

"You told Molly you'd pick her up this morning? And she seemed fine when you left?"

Well, no, actually she'd seemed a little upset because—jackass that he was—he'd told her he didn't want to kiss her because she had plaster in her hair.

"She didn't seem injured if that's what you mean."

Jon shook his head. "I've watched her hang on every word you say for the last three years. Watched her eyes follow you all around a room every time you enter it. Feelings which—congratulations to you for being such a good actor and fooling us all—I assumed were one-sided on her part."

Jon was a damned good behavioral analyst, but Derek didn't like to find himself on the other end of Jon's skills. "What's your point, Hatton?"

"Actually, my point is that I agree with you. I don't think you're overreacting. If you told Molly you would be there to pick her up this morning, there is not much that would keep her from being there when that happened if she had a say."

Derek wasn't sure about all that, but he did know Molly was a considerate and kind person. She would've left a note, *something* if she knew she wasn't going to be there for him when she said she would.

Derek wasn't ignoring his gut any longer. Yeah, they

needed to get back out to the house in West Philly, but first Derek was going to make sure Molly was all right. He sat down at his desk.

"What's your plan?" Jon asked.

"I'm going to see what sort of street-camera footage we have on Molly's house. She has a stoplight nearby."

"Give me her address and I'll help look, too."

Accessing camera footage wasn't as easy or as simple as cop shows made it look on TV. Watching it was time-consuming and boring work, often leading to nothing.

But not this time.

If Derek hadn't been watching for it, he wouldn't have seen it since the perps hugged the shadows so well.

"Jon. Look at this."

The traffic light camera provided footage of two men entering the alley behind Molly's condo. Twenty minutes later they left down the same alley, but this time they were carrying someone between them.

The expletives that flew out of Derek's mouth were ugly. Jon's weren't much better.

They watched it again.

"Someone took Molly. Why the hell would someone take Molly?" Jon murmured to no one in particular.

For the second time in twenty-four hours Derek had to completely divorce himself from his feelings. There was no room for panic. There was only room for the task at hand.

Finding the bastards that took Molly and getting her home safely.

Sometimes the toughest part of taking action was when you knew there was no action to take yet. The *why* of someone taking Molly was secondary right now to the *who* and the *where*.

"I'm tasking every available camera in that area to see if we can get an ID or at least a vehicle."

"You take the ones running north and south. I'll start east/west."

Definitely faster this way. Neither of them spoke as they used the computers to find and utilize any cameras near Molly's house. And neither of them gave a damn that they didn't have the necessary prior approval to do so.

If Steve Drackett was pissed at what they were doing, Derek would take the heat. But they were already hours behind Molly's abductors. Derek wasn't going to waste time running outside to get Drackett's written permission.

Every second was precious.

"I've got something. ATM camera." Jon spun in his chair to face Derek. "Same black SUV leaving. Heading west down Monument Street at 5:12 a.m."

Five-twelve? That was barely fifteen minutes after he'd left Molly's house. Derek clenched his fists. As if he hadn't had enough reason to have wished he'd stayed.

Derek concentrated his efforts on the cameras that would pick up the SUV. It was like piecing together a puzzle, figuring out which way the vehicle turned at an intersection, often by process of elimination.

But as the vehicle headed farther out of the city, there were fewer cameras to track it.

"We're going to lose it." Derek's teeth were gritted as he made the statement. "It's heading out of town."

Sure enough, within a few minutes they'd lost the SUV completely. There just weren't enough cameras.

Derek slammed his fist down on his desk.

"Let me see if we can get anything by working with the cameras from different angles or with reflections," Jon told him.

It wasn't as good as getting an actual location where the vehicle had stopped, but it may get them a usable photo of one of the two people who had taken Molly. Better than nothing.

While Jon worked that, Derek went back to footage at Molly's condo. He watched again as the men carried her out, one holding her legs, the other her torso. She seemed to be totally slack, not struggling in any way.

If Derek was working this case objectively, looking at this footage and not knowing it was Molly, he'd say that there was every possibility that the two men were carrying out a dead body.

But Derek refused to even consider that possibility now, even though the stillness of her body frightened him to his core. Damn it, why did it seem as if he was praying for Molly's life to be spared so often over the past twenty-four hours?

"I've got something!" Jon's excitement was palpable. "A clear shot of the driver's face."

Derek rushed over to Jon's computer so he could see. "I don't recognize him at all. You?"

"No, nothing. But let's run him through facial recognition and see if we get a hit."

It was a long shot, but it was the best shot they had. But it also meant more waiting.

"This has to be tied to the lab fire last night," Derek said.

"Yeah, but maybe we were wrong about it having to do with the Chicago bombing case. Maybe it was someone trying to get rid of Molly, and when that didn't work, they took her. There was a lot of evidence in that lab."

Derek had to admit it was possible. "Definitely an angle to consider."

"But it's also a pretty big coincidence after everything that happened in Philly. Unless all the bad guys have gone overboard crazy at once."

"Right now, I'm not ruling anything out. I just want to get Molly back."

"Absolutely." Jon pounded him on the shoulder. "I'm going to look over footage from last night's fire. See if anyone was around."

Derek nodded. "I'm going to look through everything we have from yesterday at the house. If this is all tied together, maybe it could provide us with something."

What it could provide, Derek had no idea. All he knew for certain was that every moment he had nothing was another moment where Molly was in the clutches of some unknown foe.

Using the same method they had earlier, Derek began looking for accessible cameras near yesterday's house in West Philly. The area wasn't nearly as busy, or as wealthy, as the area where Omega HQ and Molly's neighborhood was located, so cameras were more sparse. Most of the ones he could find didn't produce results of any value.

He was about to call it a dead end when an unusual reflection caught his eye in one of the traffic cameras. A black car parked about two blocks from the site. Not an SUV like the one that had taken Molly, but a four-door sedan that looked completely out of place in that neighborhood.

Derek watched as the camera's canted angle showed the perpetrator who had eventually killed himself yesterday walking up to the car. The backseat window rolled down halfway, but Derek couldn't see inside. After a brief conversation, the now-dead man ran away, toward the house where Derek, Jon and Liam would be showing up a few minutes later.

The sedan quickly pulled away and Derek barely caught the most important feature as it sped up the street.

"Jon, get over here and look at this."

"What?"

Derek ran the footage for him and then paused it right at the end, pointing to the license plate of the sedan. A small sticker that made all the difference.

"Secret Service." Jon shook his head as he said it.

"Somebody under Secret Service's protection was meeting with the guy who'd rather kill himself than be taken into custody a few minutes before we got there."

The US Secret Service guarded a lot more than just the president. Their duties included protection of congressmen and senators as well as certain dignitaries. Hundreds of people.

But it was definitely one more link strengthening the theory that someone pretty high in the US Government had some part in the Chicago bombing. They would need to get this info to Drackett as soon as possible.

But it didn't get them any closer to figuring out who took Molly.

As if it could read Derek's thoughts, his computer pinged. Facial recognition had a hit on the picture of the guy from the SUV that had taken her.

Derek printed the findings of the facial recognition program. He and Jon stared at it, both of them trying to figure out the ramifications.

The man they were looking at wasn't important in and of himself. It was who he was a known associate of that drew their attention.

The man worked for Pablo Belisario, a known drug lord from Colombia. Derek tried to wrap his head around that.

What in the hell did a drug lord from Colombia want with Molly?

"Belisario? Is someone in Omega actively investigating him?" Derek asked.

Jon pulled up some info on his computer. "Not that's

listed. I guess someone could be doing undercover work. But what would that have to do with Molly?"

Derek shook his head. "I have no idea." Anything undercover wouldn't be fielded through the Critical Response Division offices. Omega had its own main office in Washington, DC, for undercover ops, and they had their own labs. "I felt sure whoever had taken her was going to be tied into the terrorist attack in some way. But Belisario? He's too chump change for something the size of Chicago."

Belisario wasn't a terrorist. But he was known for his ruthlessness and violence. The thought of Molly in his hands—for whatever unknown reason—was sickening. Something had to be done.

Right damn now.

"We need to run everything we can about Belisario immediately."

Derek and Jon spent the rest of the afternoon tracking down every piece of information they could about Pablo Belisario. Derek found Liam Goetz, knowing the other agent had some background in Vice.

"Belisario is continually on the DEA watch list," Liam told him. "He's become a bigger player over the last year. But I have no idea what he would have to do with Molly."

"Neither do I," Derek told him. "I've run all the cases that were listed in the system that the lab was currently processing. Nothing to do with drugs or Belisario."

"Let me call in a few favors with some old contacts in the DEA. See what the current word is about it."

"Thanks, Liam. I don't know what the hell is going on, but I know we've got to get Molly back."

Liam picked up the phone right then. "As soon as possible. Because Belisario is one mean bastard. I can't stand the thought of sweet Molly in his hands."

Neither could Derek.

Within a few hours—long, agonizing hours for Derek—they had some answers. Belisario was under surveillance by local Colombians the DEA had carefully hired. They reported back daily to the DEA on Belisario's movements. Over the past twenty-four hours there had been no word of Belisario leaving his well-fortified home. But there had been a report of a woman being dragged into the house this afternoon, unable to walk on her own.

A white woman with long brown hair.

Chapter Eight

As soon as he heard the description of the woman, Derek was on his feet. He had no doubt this was Molly. It had to be.

"Listen, man." Liam put a hand on his shoulder. "Evidently women being dragged into Belisario's house is not an uncommon thing. This may not even be Molly."

"A white woman with long brown hair just a few hours after Molly was taken by one of his known associates? It has to be her." It was time to do something. He started walking down the hall.

"Where are you going?" Jon called after him.

Derek didn't even slow down. "Drackett's office. We all know that's Molly."

He didn't wait to see if the other two men were coming with him. He didn't expect them to. Just like Derek wasn't going to the director's office to get his permission. He was going to tell him because he respected Drackett and his boss deserved to know why he would be MIA for the next unknown number of hours or days.

However long it took to get Molly out of the hands of a sadistic drug lord.

Derek knocked once on Drackett's door as he was opening it. The director didn't seem too surprised to see him.

Derek, on the other hand, was a little surprised to find Jon and Liam had followed him into Drackett's office.

"I've already been apprised of the situation," Steve told them without any formal greeting.

Derek should've known Drackett would be aware of what was going on, even with the chaos from last night's fire to deal with. That's why he was the director.

"DEA contacts put a Caucasian woman with long brown hair being forcefully taken into Belisario's estate a couple hours ago," Derek reported.

"Knowing we wouldn't be able to confirm if that was Molly or not—"

"Steve—" Derek didn't need confirmation. He was moving regardless of whether they were 100 percent sure.

Steve held up his hand and started over. "Knowing we wouldn't be able to confirm if the woman was Molly, I immediately tasked a satellite to give us footage of his property as soon as I got word of that."

This was why Steve Drackett was the director of one of the most important law enforcement agencies in the country. The man made decisions and didn't waste time. Derek was tempted to lean over the desk and kiss him.

"Don't get too excited," Drackett told them. "I was still unable to confirm it was her. But I was able to positively confirm that this man was present on the premises this afternoon."

He slid a picture across his desk.

"That's Santiago. He's the one that was at Molly's condo last night. We had positive ID on him."

Drackett nodded. "I know. Which is why I agree that Molly is the woman spotted by the DEA contact being taken into the estate."

Derek had been prepared to move at much less confirmation than this. "I'm going down there."

Drackett stood and looked Derek directly in the eye. "We have zero jurisdiction down there."

"I don't care." Derek knew where Molly was and he was going to get her out. Or die trying.

"No agency of the US Government can send in a team into a situation like this. Not if we don't know for sure who the woman is or why she's there," Jon chimed in.

"I don't care," Derek repeated, nodding at Jon. He knew whatever he was going to do was going to be unofficial. He'd be on his own. Drackett couldn't have any official knowledge of it.

He turned back to Steve. "I just came in here to tell you I was going to need a couple of personal days off. Not sure exactly how long."

Steve looked at him for a long moment. Then finally nodded.

"Oh man, Steve, and I forgot to tell you, I need a few days off, too," Jon said.

Surprised, Derek looked over at Jon. Derek would've never asked this of his friend—it was potentially both career- and life-threatening. But he needed all the help he could get.

Jon nodded at him and shrugged.

"Seriously, you guys? This is so stupid." Liam rolled his eyes and turned and walked toward the office door. "Which is why I just remembered I need time off, too, Drackett. I think I put in the paperwork for it last week, but you probably lost it."

When Derek turned to look at him, Liam grinned and winked. For the first time since he realized Molly was missing the tightness in Derek's chest loosened just the slightest bit. There were no other people Derek would rather have at his back in a situation like this than Liam and Jon.

The director sat back down behind his desk. "Gentlemen, if you don't mind I have a lot to do here with last night's fire fiasco. For the life of me I can't even remember what you came in here to tell me besides to remind me of your time off which was approved over two weeks ago."

"Thanks, Steve." Those two words didn't say nearly enough.

"Listen, you guys do me a favor, okay?" Drackett continued as they turned to leave. "The oversight committee is pretty concerned about security here at the building after last night's episode. Jon, since you're a pilot, I need you to relocate one of the Omega planes before you officially go on vacation, okay? Just go to any of the approved airfields in North or South America. Just so I can keep my superiors happy. And you should probably clear out some of the weapons lockers for the same reason. Security."

"Steve—" Jon started.

Everybody knew that if all this went bad Drackett would have a hard time explaining things. But providing them with an unofficial plane and weapons was probably making the difference between success and failure.

"Why are you guys still here? I don't have time for chatting today. Enjoy your vacation."

Derek looked at Liam and Jon. They planned on it.

DEREK KNOCKED ON *her door. She'd been watching* The Avengers *for the umpteenth time and had honestly thought it was one of her neighbors at the condo. Who else would be knocking at her door at eleven at night on a Friday? When she peeped through and saw it was Derek she'd been so surprised she'd just opened the door in her pajama shorts and oversize Georgia Tech sweatshirt.*

For the first time since she'd known him, which had been for over a year, the gorgeous agent looked indecisive.

"Derek, um, hi. Are you okay?"

He just stood there in her doorway, looking slightly rumpled and all the more sexy because of it.

"Is there an emergency at work?" *she asked him.*

"No. Nothing to do with work."

His deep voice sent heat to places Molly didn't think about very often.

"Oh, okay." *She wasn't sure what to do or say, which wasn't unusual for her. But usually Derek knew what to say. Although evidently not tonight.* "Are you okay?"

"I told myself not to stop by. Then I decided I would because I thought you wouldn't be home."

That didn't make any sense to her. Why would he come by if he thought she wouldn't be home?

"Oh, okay." *And now she sounded like a parrot.* "Um, do you want to come in?"

"I probably shouldn't." *But he took the slightest unsteady step forward.*

And then it hit her. "Oh my gosh, Derek. Are you drunk?"

He cocked his head sideways and smiled, a boyish grin completely at odds with Derek's size and darker features. "I might be just a wee bit tipsy."

Molly's insides completely melted.

Derek Waterman: superagent. Strong, tough and completely cool under pressure was standing right in front of her, a wee bit tipsy.

She'd seen him in the lab multiple times over the past few months and could admit she had a crush on him, but she never dreamed he'd show up at her house. Looking closer at him she could see the tension around his eyes, the slightly haggard look on his face.

Whatever had led to the wee bit tipsy *had been fueled by something much darker and harder. Decisions he'd had to make as an agent. Or violent and terrible things he'd seen. Molly experienced some of that secondhand in the lab, but never up close like Derek did on a daily basis.*

Derek Waterman needed a friend. She didn't know why he'd come to her, but she was more than willing to be a friend to someone in need. Especially someone who had dedicated his life to helping others.

He looked a little surprised when she grabbed his hand and pulled him the rest of the way inside. "You didn't drive, right?"

He looked affronted. "Of course not. The guys and I were at a bar just a few blocks from here." *He rubbed his eyes with his hand.* "It was a bad day today."

The demons in his eyes were evident. "I'm sorry." *She couldn't help herself; she reached up and touched his cheek.* "You can stay here as long as you want."

He closed his eyes and leaned his cheek into her hand, not saying anything.

"Do you want me to make some coffee?" *she said softly.* "I was just watching a movie. We could do that if you want. Or just talk."

Derek opened his eyes and looked at her slowly from head to toe.

Molly wished she was wearing a little bit of makeup. And wasn't in her pajamas. But the look in his eyes said he didn't care. She shivered.

He reached out and touched the hair that had fallen over her shoulders.

"No braid," *he said, taking a step closer.* "No lab coat."

Molly's laugh was rueful. "Yeah, contrary to popular opinion, neither are permanent fixtures on my body."

"This was how I knew you'd look—sweet." He took another step closer, still holding her hair. Molly's breath hitched as he hooked his finger in the loose collar of the sweatshirt under her hair and slid it until it fell completely off one shoulder. He slowly moved her hair to the other side so her neck and shoulder were exposed.

She was very aware that she had nothing on under that sweatshirt. He had to be, too. She knew that she should stop this. That he'd had too much to drink. That he needed a friend.

But watching him transfixed by her bare skin, Molly could no more stop this than she could stop breathing.

But she did stop breathing when she felt his lips against her collarbone, moving with featherlike kisses down the length of her shoulder.

"Derek..." His name came out in a breathy whisper.

"So soft. So gentle. I knew you would be." His voice was right next to her ear, then his lips moved down to her neck and throat.

When Molly's knees threatened to buckle, he wrapped an arm around her waist and backed her up against the hallway wall. His mouth came down in a painless bite right where her shoulder met her neck. Molly moaned, wrapping her arms around his neck and pulling him closer.

"Where's your bedroom?"

She waved her arm in the general direction of the stairway before bringing it back to his neck and pulling his face down to hers, his mouth to her own.

He never stopped kissing her as he slid an arm under her knees and picked her up, not even breathing any harder after carrying her up the stairs. He set her down next to her bed and pulled her sweatshirt over her head and pulled the shorts completely off her body.

Molly was very aware that she was completely naked while he was still fully dressed. She reached for his shirt, but he stopped her, grabbing her wrists gently and holding her arms out to the side.

"No. Let me look at you." He trailed a finger from her cheek, down her throat and over both breasts. "You're so damn beautiful, Molly. So beautiful."

She reached for him again, and this time he didn't stop her, kissing her again after she unbuttoned his shirt and pushed it from his shoulders. He made short work of his pants and they fell into bed together.

Molly tried to take a moment of sanity, to make sure this was what Derek was looking for. That it wasn't just the drinks he'd had that had led them to this moment. She flipped her weight around so that he was lying on his back on the bed and she was kneeling over him.

"Derek, maybe we should wait. Make sure that this is what you really want."

He froze for just a moment, silent, looking up at her. Molly was sure he had come to his senses, that he realized this wasn't what he was looking for, that he was just drunk. Then he reached up and gently touched a strand of her hair from the roots all the way down to the tips where it rested on his chest.

Without saying a word he flipped her back over, grabbing her leg and hooking it over his hip. Molly gasped as she could feel every inch of both their naked bodies against each other.

"Does it feel like you aren't what I really want?"

Molly started to answer, but someone ripped her violently out of the bed and threw her on the floor. She looked around blinking, trying to get her bearings.

This wasn't her condo. She wasn't with Derek, she had been dreaming. Remembering.

Her reality was a room with no window and a filthy cot, and standing over her were the two men who had taken her from her home.

Chapter Nine

The memory of her wonderful night with Derek made waking to this reality that much more terrifying. They laughed as she scampered back until she hit a dirt wall.

Where was she? Who were these men? Why had they taken her? What did they want?

Molly racked her still-fuzzy brain. They'd taken her on a plane somewhere, right? She didn't know for sure, but the plane had been the last mode of transportation she'd seen.

She was still in the yoga pants and T-shirt she'd put on after her shower at home, however many hours ago. Her bra and underwear were still in place, which made her feel better.

Surely they wouldn't have violated her unconscious body and then bothered to completely redress her.

The two men were speaking Spanish with a little English thrown in, and both had dark enough hair and skin to be from Mexico or South America. But narrowing it down to a continent didn't get any of Molly's questions answered.

She definitely had been drugged. Not only did she remember the pinpricks, she could still feel the aftereffects: mushy head, thirsty, tongue feeling swollen. Of course her whole face felt swollen from where Jerk #2 had hit her after she'd run.

"What do you want with me?"

Molly's voice sounded strange, distant, to her own ears, much lower than her normal pitch. A side effect of the drug, no doubt. What had it been? Rohypnol? Ketamine? GHB? Molly had worked dozens of cases in the lab over the years dealing with these common date-rape drugs. She tried to remember specific ramifications of each, but couldn't seem to force her brain to do it.

And then the men were coming toward her and she totally forgot about the drugs. They didn't answer her question about what they wanted with her, just grabbed her under her armpits and dragged her through the door.

Not wanting to get punched again, Molly didn't try to run or yell. Walking without falling over was difficult enough. She'd never be able to escape them, especially with one flanked on either side. Right now she just needed to focus. To gather as many details as possible about what was going on. To try to come up with a plan.

They went down a short hallway before a door opened to the outside. Glancing over her shoulder, Molly realized she'd been held in some sort of servant's quarters or something. They were now crossing under an extended portico to a much larger house. A mansion. She could see men with large guns guarding it.

Despite the fact that the sun was going down, it was still warm. They must have traveled south. Maybe they really were in Mexico or South America. Everyone she had seen so far looked to be Hispanic.

Hysteria swamped her at the thought of being in a completely foreign country, having no idea where or with whom, but she tamped it down. Panic wasn't going to get her anywhere.

And she was afraid panic was going to be her only option in a little while anyway. Might as well save it.

They took her through the back door into the house.

It was beautiful inside, if a touch melodramatic with marble floors and heavy drapery hanging in the windows. Paintings of all different types decorated the walls while vases and sculptures lined the tables in the vast foyer. It was like some weirdly interpreted copy of Tara from *Gone with the Wind*.

The two men brought her into the very formal living room with furniture so fancy it would've made Molly afraid to sit on it even in normal circumstances. She stopped walking and was dragged from the doorway to the middle of the room. A man with black hair combed back and dressed in light linen pants and a dark shirt rose from one of the large leather wingback chairs.

"So you're finally awake, Ms. Humphries. It took much longer than I thought. My name is Pablo Belisario. This is my home."

He spoke in English, but his accent was thick. Although his name sounded vaguely familiar, Molly still didn't know who this man was or what he wanted with her.

He continued, "It seems my men gave you too much of the drug when they first took you. You've been unconscious for over twelve hours." Molly fought not to cringe as he walked around her in a circle. "You're quite petite, the second dose they gave could've been fatal."

He glared at the men holding her. "Fortunately for your sake—and for theirs—it was not."

What was she supposed to say to this? Thank you? She finally decided silence was probably better.

"But your lack of consciousness for so long has caused a delay in answers I need right away." His glare turned from the men to her.

"I'm sorry. I'm not sure what you are talking about. Answers about what?" Maybe it was still the drugs making her fuzzy, but Molly had absolutely no idea what

Belisario was referring to. "I think maybe you have the wrong person."

His sigh was impatient. "No, Ms. Humphries. We very definitely have the right person. I just need to know what you found out in the lab yesterday before it was destroyed. And exactly who you told about it."

Molly shook her head, trying to clear cobwebs. She would be confused even if she didn't have Rohypnol or whatever in her system. Belisario had brought her here to ask her about the lab fire?

"There are—*were*—a lot of items in the lab. Could you tell me, um, what sort of business you're in?"

Belisario's eyes narrowed. "I'm a little disappointed you don't know who I am already."

Molly backtracked. The last thing she wanted to do was injure this man's pride in any way. "Well, I'm a geek, in a lab all the time. I don't get out much." Sadly, that was true. "I probably wouldn't know ninety percent of celebrities if I saw them on the street."

"You've already become acquainted with one of my best sellers. It's what has made you sleep so long. But most of my empire has been built on cocaine."

The true identity of the man suddenly clicked into place. He had told her who he was, but she hadn't made the connection. He was Pablo Belisario, head of one of the largest drug manufacturing and dealing operations in South America. She really only knew about him because of consulting with the DEA a couple years ago.

Molly sucked in a breath as she now understood how much danger she was really in. Belisario's reputation was brutal. Lethal.

"Ah, I see you now have figured out who I am." His smile made Molly's skin crawl. "I must admit that makes me happy."

He stepped closer, more focused on her than he had been just a few minutes before. "You are much prettier than I thought you would be." He touched her cheek.

Molly knew with absolute certainty that the center of this man's attention was a very bad place to be.

"Mr. Belisario, yes, your reputation is very well-known." Molly knew she had to get his attention off her personally, although she didn't know where to direct it. She'd never handled anything in the lab having to do with him. "But I'm sure nothing in the lab had any incriminating evidence about you."

"No, I'm not worried about my operations. I have a partner, who shall remain…unmentioned. He needs to know what you know."

That really didn't narrow it down for Molly. "Mr. Belisario, I was working on dozens of cases in the lab yesterday, and honestly, I don't remember many details about any of them."

He shrugged, giving an exaggerated sigh. "You know, I tried to make that exact point to my partner. I told him to just leave it alone. But he is prone toward the melodramatic."

Almost as if he couldn't stop touching her, he reached over and grasped her chin in his hand, turning her head side to side, as if he was inspecting her. "Yesterday was quite the bad day for him. Seems like evidence linking him to…certain crimes was obtained, despite his attempts to keep that from happening."

Despite herself, Molly pulled her head away and Belisario's eyes narrowed.

"He tried to destroy all evidence at the scene first," Belisario continued. "But evidently a few key pieces were still recovered by your Omega agents. So then he planted a bomb to destroy the entire lab."

Oh, no. All of this was about the evidence that Derek had brought in yesterday. Concerning the Chicago bombing.

He touched her cheek again and Molly forced herself to hold still. "You, my dear, were supposed to have died in the fire, in case you knew anything. But you somehow made it out.

"Once we found out you had survived the explosion, he needed you questioned. And that couldn't take place on US soil, so he asked me to bring you here. He needs to know what you found yesterday in the lab and who you told."

"I don't know anything—"

His backhand nearly knocked her to the floor. If his henchmen hadn't been on either side of her, she would've fallen. Molly tasted blood in her mouth, the pain compounded by the bruise she already had on her face.

"You see, Ms. Humphries, I don't have time for responses like 'I don't know anything.'" He shook his head almost apologetically. "So I'm going to need you to give me specific information about what was in the lab."

He nodded briefly to the henchman on the left. Before Molly even knew what to expect, his fist came piling into her midsection.

Molly doubled over as pain stole her breath in a way she didn't even know was possible. She tried to sob, but no sound or air came out. Almost immediately the other henchman pulled her back upright by her hair.

"Let's be honest with one another." Belisario's tone was almost bored. "You are small, delicate. A scientist. You're not the type who will be able to bounce back quickly from severe questioning. From torture." He grabbed her jaw again and squeezed it painfully. She felt tears stream down her face. "I need specific details, Ms. Humphries."

"I—I…" Molly tried to get her thoughts together, to get

her breathing under control now that her airways seemed to be working. "The agents brought in something from a fire, a building that had burned down earlier in the day."

He released her face. "Yes. Very good. Continue. Which agents brought it in?"

Molly didn't care if they hit her again. She wasn't giving this psychopath Derek's or any other agents' names. She thought fast. "Steve Rogers was the main agent. I can't remember the other guy."

She felt a cruel yank on her hair. "Details, Ms. Humphries."

"He's new, so I'm not sure. I think his name is Bruce something. Banner, maybe." She prayed none of the men were Marvel comic or *The Avenger* fans, since she was basically just listing characters now.

"And?"

"I didn't have a chance to get to any of what they brought in. The lab was backed up. I was planning to work all night. I had stepped out to get a bite to eat, that's why I wasn't in the lab when the explosion happened." That was the truth.

Belisario nodded at the man standing behind her holding her hair. He brought her arm behind her back in a cruel twist that had Molly crying out.

"Just the slightest pressure from Henrico and your arm will break in quite a nasty way. So make sure you answer completely—did you talk to anyone about what was brought in by the agents? Does anyone know anything that could come back to haunt my partner?"

"Not from me, not from our lab. Everything was destroyed. I promise. If there was anything more to tell you I would." Molly could feel her arm being inched up behind her back. Henrico was definitely looking forward to doing damage.

Belisario looked at her for a long moment, then thankfully shook his head at Henrico. He let her go and threw her away from him, anger in his eyes when she glanced at him, rubbing her aching shoulder.

"You see? Not so difficult when you provide the right details," Belisario said. "And I believe you, because I'm sure you can imagine what will happen to you if I discover any part of this is a lie."

Molly shuddered and Belisario laughed.

He ran a finger down her cheek again and Molly blanched before she could help it. This earned her a slap. "I'm supposed to kill you now, that's what my partner wants, in case you talk to anyone. But like I said, he can be a bit overdramatic. There's no need to kill you yet. I'm sure I can find other uses for you."

His finger trailed down her shoulder and Molly looked away.

"Plus, we want to check all those details you gave us. Make sure they were true. And if even one small part isn't, then we'll start this whole questioning process again."

Molly struggled not to vomit right then. It wouldn't take long for whoever Belisario's partner was to figure out that the names she'd given were fake, even if everything else was true.

A phone rang in Belisario's pocket and he moved away from her. "I have business to attend to now. But we'll talk again soon." He turned to his men. "Take her back."

It was dark outside as they returned her to her room.

"I'm sure the boss will let us have our turn with her after he's done," Henrico said to the other guy.

Molly choked back a sob. She was hungry, thirsty, tired and ached all over. The thought of these men touching her was almost more than she could handle. When they opened the door to her room, Henrico reached down and squeezed her buttocks.

Molly elbowed him in the stomach and jerked away, making the other henchman laugh.

Enraged, Henrico threw her down on the floor. He kicked her with one booted foot in the thigh. Molly cried out in pain and scampered backward to try to get out of his reach. He grabbed her by the front of her shirt and brought her torso off the ground.

"And when the boss lets me have you, you will beg me for death." He backhanded her across the face and threw her down.

Although that hit wasn't as hard as the others, it was too much for Molly. She just let the blackness consume her.

Chapter Ten

This was not how Derek liked to go into a situation: totally blind. But he didn't have much choice. He and Liam poured over all of the intel they could get their hands on about Belisario's home—which was more like a compound—as Jon flew them down to Colombia.

Derek liked to have the tactical advantage in all professional situations. He even liked having it in personal ones. But he had to admit there was no real tactical advantage for them here.

"Covert entry is pretty much our only option and our only advantage," he said to Liam. "If we have to go in guns blazing, our chance of success is pretty darn low. We just don't have the manpower needed to take down Belisario in his own nest."

"Quiet, it is." Liam was leaning with his head back against his seat, eyes closed, but Derek knew the other man was aware of everything going on around him. "My kung fu is strong."

Using night as their cover, Derek and Liam would be parachuting out to land closer to Belisario's property. It was risky, but it would get them there much faster. Derek was willing to risk just about anything to get them there faster.

Every additional minute it took them to get there was

a minute Molly was left alone in heaven knew what type of situation.

Jon would have to land the plane almost ten miles from the property in order not to be seen. It was the only place in the dense rain forest with enough clearing for a landing strip. He would have the plane ready for takeoff upon Derek and Liam's return with Molly, backup firearms ready in case they were coming in hot.

Although hostage rescue was Liam's specialty and jumping out of planes into questionable situations was his particular forte, it had been years since Derek had done this sort of thing.

"You'll do fine. It's just like 'Stan, only greener." Derek found Liam looking over at him. They'd both been in Special Forces in Afghanistan for multiple tours. Both knew what it was to take a life, to make the hard call, to do things that left scars on the soul. Even though Derek didn't use that training any more in his day-to-day duties, his time there had made him into the man he was.

As Special Forces, both he and Liam knew how to infiltrate silently and deadly. That's what they'd be doing here. Because if they got caught, there wouldn't be anyone coming to help them. Omega would not be able to acknowledge Derek's mission in any way. The official word would be that they had acted on their own.

"Besides, I know how to speak Spanish, so that gives us an advantage," Liam said.

Derek studied Liam. He'd known the other man for a lot of years and didn't know he spoke Spanish. "You do?"

Liam shrugged. "The important stuff. *Hola hermosa bebé, creo que deberíamos pasar la noche juntos.*"

Derek was pretty sure Liam had just called him pretty and asked him if he wanted to spend the night. Derek rolled his eyes. Knowing Liam, he wouldn't be surprised if that was the only Spanish the other man knew at all.

Of course, Derek also wouldn't be surprised to find out that the man spoke it fluently. You just never knew with Liam.

"Thanks, Liam," Derek said.

"Thanks for calling you pretty?" Liam winked at him.

"For doing this. I know the risks. I know you do, too." Their lives, their careers. Everything. Without Jon and Liam, Derek's chances of getting Molly out alive would be practically zero.

The odds with them weren't terribly higher either, but at least they had a chance.

Liam was serious now, a rare occurrence. "I assumed Molly was irrelevant to you. I think we all did."

Derek stared at the other man for a long minute. "No, she's never been irrelevant to me. The opposite." He hardly had words for what Molly was to him. "She's my light. Pure and lovely and…" Derek shrugged. He wasn't good with words.

"She's everything you're afraid of dragging down into your dark and dirty world. Extinguishing the light." Liam finished for him. "So you've stayed away. Made everyone—including her—think you don't care."

Derek nodded. All of that was exactly right.

"Good thing I didn't ask her out like I considered. I had grand dreams of being the one to help her get over the stupid jerk who didn't seem to appreciate what was right in front of him." And just like that Liam's seriousness was gone. "Would've sucked to have my nose broken when you punched me in the face."

To be honest Derek wasn't sure what he would've done if Molly had gone out with someone else. Especially a friend.

Liam was back to serious. "You'd do the same for me,

if I needed help, Derek. And all of us would do anything for sweet Molly."

"Ten minutes till we're in the drop zone," Jon called back from the cockpit of the small plane.

"Roger that," Derek responded. He turned to Liam. "Any questions about our plan?"

"Rendezvous with each other on the ground. Get into the estate at the weak spot in the wall near the northeast corner. Find our girl and get her out. All undetected."

That was the plan. Now all they had to do was pull it off.

MOLLY DIDN'T PARTICULARLY like autopsies. *She did have a degree in forensic pathology, was a certified medical examiner, so not liking autopsies was probably a little odd. But she had never been able to distance herself from the body on her table, and sympathized about what had happened to them.*

And since she worked at Omega, most autopsies she performed were often pretty gruesome deaths. Most of the time Molly was able to foster out the autopsies to one of the other two pathologists employed by the lab; neither ever seemed to mind.

But sometimes, like now, it had to be Molly. It was late in the evening, everyone else had gone home. The two bodies in the morgue were Omega agents who had been killed in a hostage rescue situation. She knew them. Not as well as she knew some of the other agents, but enough that what she was doing—removing bullets that would later be used in the case against the criminals who did this—was harder. But she wanted to get it done as soon as possible so the bodies could be released to the grieving families.

She felt eyes on her from across the room, and looked up. There was Derek standing silently watching her.

It had been two years since that night he'd shown up

*at her house. The night she thought about all the time.
The night that had haunted her dreams and caused her
to wake up aching for Derek. The night that had changed
everything for her.*

The night the two of them had never once spoken about.

*When she'd awakened the next morning—after multiple
bouts of lovemaking, since every time she'd even slid away
from him, even when he'd been sleeping, he'd pulled her
back to him and tucked her against him—he'd been gone.*

*Molly thought maybe he'd been too drunk to remem-
ber what had happened. But medically she knew that was
highly unlikely. If Derek had been sober enough to...ahem,
perform...that many times, then he hadn't been inebriated
to the point of blocking the night out of his subconscious.*

*Then she had feared even worse: that she'd just been a
one-night stand, a conquest Derek would boast about to
his friends. The thought had made her ill. But there had
been nothing that anyone had ever said or did—no knowing glances or sideways winks—that had insinuated that
Derek had spoken to anyone about it. Since that night,
Derek himself had been polite, respectful.*

Distant.

*He never touched her. Not even casually like he had
before. He was very deliberate in the not touching her,
although Molly didn't think anyone else noticed. It wasn't
as if they'd walked around arm in arm before that night.
But now, nothing.*

*And Molly, pansy that she was, had developed some
sort of stutter anytime he was near. She'd always been a
little awkward around him, but after that night she was
a complete moron. Everyone assumed that she was just a
socially awkward scientist who got tongued-tied around
a super-sexy, mega-hot agent she had a crush on. Which
was true.*

No one suspected her body remembered every single touch and lick and nibble from their night together causing her to go into overdrive every time Derek was around. Which was also true.

Derek did an excellent job of being distant and making sure no one suspected what had happened.

But every once in a while, Molly would catch him watching her with a look in his eyes that melted everything inside her. There was only one word for it.

Heat.

He was quick to blank his face, to school his expression back into its blasted neutrality as soon as he realized she'd seen him. He was so good at it that soon Molly would wonder if she had seen the heat at all.

But now, looking at him across the small morgue attached to the lab, she could see the heat. He didn't do a thing to hide it. She took off her gloves and laid them on the nearby table. He walked over to her without taking his eyes off her face.

And enfolded her in his arms.

She could feel his face buried in her neck, his arms crossing low across her waist and hips. His big body was almost doubled around hers, he had her so close. Molly extracted her arms, trapped between their bodies, so she could wrap them around Derek.

The two dead men had been his colleagues, his friends. As hard as it was for her to have those bodies on the table, it had to be much worse for Derek.

She stroked her hands up and down his back saying nothing. Neither of them said anything. Derek didn't know how to ask for comfort now, for a gentle touch, any more than he'd known how to ask for it when he showed up at her condo two years ago. But that didn't mean he didn't need it.

And Molly would give it, would always give it if it was in her power to do so.

But her leg hurt so badly. And her face.

She moaned. No, pain wasn't part of the memory. There had been no pain in the long minutes where she'd held him before he had gently disengaged himself, kissed her on the forehead, and walked out as silently as he had arrived.

Oh no, she was dreaming again. And was about to wake up to the living nightmare surrounding her. She didn't want that. She wanted to stay here in Derek's arms where she was safe.

"Molly." His finger stroked down her cheek. She felt so secure here. Like nothing could ever hurt her again.

"Molly." The voice was firmer now. She knew she was waking up because everything hurt and Derek hadn't talked to her, he'd been silent.

Well, if she was waking up, she was going to get a kiss in first. She'd always wished she'd kissed him that day in the lab. She drove her hands through his hair and pulled him down to her, not giving him any choice. She kissed him.

And, ah, it felt so good. So real. She so should've kissed him that day. She felt his fingers slip into her hair and pull her closer before moving away. She felt cold without him.

"Molly, sweetheart, I need you to wake up. We've got to get out of here."

She decided not to fight it anymore. She had to wake up and try to find a way out of this. But she wanted to stay in the dream with Derek. "Don't leave me," she whispered to her dream.

"I won't, honey. I promise. But I need you to wake up."

Molly reluctantly opened her eyes to find herself looking in Derek's blue ones, her fingers threaded in his hair.

Chapter Eleven

Molly was alive.

When he'd first seen her lying on the floor at such an awkward angle, Derek had feared he'd been too late. But then she'd moved just the slightest bit and relief crashed through him.

He rushed over to her, cringing as he saw the bruises covering her face, picked her up and laid her on the small cot. She wasn't dead, but that didn't mean she was going to be able to assist them in getting her out of here.

Time was of the essence. The man who had been guarding her door wouldn't be bothering anyone, but all it would take was one person coming to check on Molly and all hell would break loose.

"Molly." He stroked a gentle finger down her damaged cheek. She moved just slightly.

And then she smiled the sweetest smile, cuddling her face down into his hand. Whatever she was dreaming about, it definitely wasn't bad. That reassured him somewhat; better than terror controlling her dreams.

"Molly," he said more firmly. Her smile had faded, but she still hadn't awakened. She could have a head injury or have been drugged.

Then she'd done the damnedest thing: wrapped her hands in his hair and pulled him down to kiss her.

He'd kissed her back before he could even think about it. It was all he'd wanted to do anyway. But sanity soon resumed. No matter how much he wanted to kiss her, this wasn't the time. They had to go.

"Molly, sweetheart, I need you to wake up. We've got to get out of here."

She'd begun to fret and held on to him tighter. "Don't leave me," she whispered.

Derek was so thankful to hear her voice, now she just needed to open her eyes. "I won't, honey. I promise. But I need you to wake up."

And she did.

He watched a plethora of emotions slide over her face: fear, confusion, relief, joy, embarrassment. Her hands dropped out of his hair.

"Derek?"

He smiled at her.

"How did you find me?" she continued.

He framed her face with the gentlest touch he could. "A combination of people committed to finding you and a couple of lucky breaks."

Tears welled in her eyes. "I thought they were going to kill me."

Derek wanted to know why; wanted to know all the details she could tell them about why Belisario had taken her. But not now.

"We've got to go. Every second we spend here is stolen. Liam will cover us as best as he can, but he can't take out all of Belisario's men." Not that his friend wouldn't try if he had to. "Can you walk?"

They'd work on walking first. Hopefully she could run, too. He helped her sit up on the cot, noticing every wince. But she didn't stop or hesitate as he got her up onto her feet.

But she swayed and would've fallen if Derek didn't have

an arm around her. He needed to know exactly what type of injuries they were dealing with. And Molly seemed to have a hard time staying awake. Head trauma?

"Molls, I need you to focus. Can you tell me the worst of your injuries? Do I need to carry you?"

It would make things harder, but Derek was prepared to do it. And despite the kiss that seemed to have rooted from a sweet dream, Derek had to face the very real possibility that Molly had been raped while they'd had her here.

He could see Molly try to gather herself, to concentrate. "My left leg is in a lot of pain—it was kicked—but I don't think it's broken. I was drugged. Rohypnol, I think, or something similar. They gave me too much which is why I keep sleeping."

It was also probably helping to keep the pain under control, or at least make her not focus on it, so the drug wasn't totally a bad thing. But too much still in her system so many hours later was definitely a concern. At least it wasn't a concussion.

And the question he didn't want to ask. "Sweetheart, it's better for me to know now rather than when we're out in the middle of the jungle on the way to the plane—did they…" He couldn't get the word out. "Were you sexually assaulted?"

"No. But it was part of their plan, I know." Her huge brown eyes were laced with terror. "But you got here in time."

Derek closed his eyes. Yes, he was thankful. But they weren't out of the woods yet. Literally or figuratively.

A low whisper came through the headpiece that was attached to his radio. "You got her?"

"Affirmative."

"Can she travel?"

"Affirmative."

Derek heard Liam's short sigh of relief. "Then quit making out or whatever you're doing and get going toward the wall."

"Roger that. Leaving in just a moment."

Very few of Belisario's men were up and around. It was the middle of the night and they had no reason to believe anyone even knew Molly was there, much less expect any sort of rescue attempt.

Their mistake.

Derek knelt down and put a pair of tennis shoes that he'd brought on Molly's feet, since hers were bare. He brought clothes, too, but she was wearing relatively decent clothing, dark yoga pants and a T-shirt, so they weren't needed. Derek wrapped an arm around her and began hustling her toward the door.

"Once we're outside, stay as close as you can to the shadows. This whole place is surrounded by a wall with barbed fencing on top, but there's one place that has an opening we can fit through. We have to cross to the other side of the estate. Liam is covering us and will meet us there."

She nodded and he brought her through the door, deliberately keeping his body between her and the guard who was lying dead outside it. They walked quickly and silently through the dark hallway before Derek cracked the larger outside door, wincing as it made a small sound which seemed to echo in the darkness. Since opening the door slowly seemed to be causing more noise, he jerked it open quickly.

Derek wasted no time pulling Molly through the doorway and outside, shutting the door quickly behind them. It still made a noise, but an open door would be a sure giveaway that something was amiss.

Outside was even more dangerous because there could

be roving guards, or even someone who just came outside to have a cigarette, who could happen upon them and send this entire operation straight to hell. Knowing Liam was out there with his sniper rifle gave them a certain measure of safety. But if he had to use it, things would be going to pot quick, the sound would notify everyone of their presence.

Molly was doing her best to stay with him. To get low when he did, and stick to the shadows. He could tell her leg was hurting her from how she limped. Her shoulders seemed stiff, as if she couldn't get a full range of motion without pain. And one eye was almost swollen shut.

But she didn't complain, not a peep, even when he'd had to throw her to the ground—hard—when a guard had appeared suddenly from behind a nearby building.

They made it to the rendezvous point at the wall, but Liam wasn't there yet. Derek began giving Molly a boost up.

"What about Liam?" she asked.

"He'll be here."

She still looked concerned.

"Baby, hostage rescue is what Liam does. Hell, he thrives on this sort of thing. He'll be here. We've got to make our way through the fence."

Derek was helping Molly through the hole in the fence when from his higher vantage point he saw Liam. But he was running rather than keeping to the shadows. Derek knew that wasn't good, even though no alarm had been raised yet. He urged Molly through faster, and helped her down the other side of the wall.

"What?" she asked him, after seeing his face.

"Liam."

She paled. "Is he hurt?"

"No, but he's running. That's not good."

Out in the thick underbrush of Colombia's rain forest, Derek started moving with Molly. Liam would catch up with them soon enough. They had ten miles to go to get to the plane. Alone, Derek could probably make it in about two hours, given this terrain. But with Molly's condition, it would probably be at least three times that.

They were out of Belisario's estate, but the danger was far from over.

Derek knew Molly needed food and drink, both to give her energy for the journey ahead of them and to continue helping flush the drugs out of her system. He stopped for just a moment as he reached into his small military-grade backpack to pull out water and nutrition bars. He handed both to Molly.

"Here. The bars don't taste the best, but they're packed with nutrition. Try to nibble on one pretty constantly if you can. And water is critical. No doubt you're already dehydrated, which isn't a good way to start a trek through the jungle. That's probably why you still have so many side effects from the drugs. Drink every couple of minutes if you can."

Molly nodded and they started moving; they couldn't stop. Liam would catch up with them. But he was worried about Molly. She didn't seem very steady on her feet.

Lights were coming on at Belisario's estate, and they could hear lots of yelling. Damn it. Now they had no choice but to run, no matter what state Molly was in.

"You okay?" Derek spoke to Liam through the communication unit.

"I'm over the wall," he responded, obviously on the move. "But they definitely know something is up. It might take them a little bit of time to figure out which way we went, but not long."

Derek looked over at Molly and spoke into his mic. "We're going to be slow going. No way around it."

"Plan B?"

Plan B involved Liam, who was moving much faster than Derek and Molly to leave a more obvious trail for Belisario's men to follow in the wrong direction. He would then double back and meet them at the plane.

It wasn't a perfect plan. And it was downright dangerous for Liam. But it was their best option.

"Roger, Plan B. But Liam, be careful."

"*Moi*, not careful?" Liam chuckled, then clicked off.

"We've got to go, baby." She had taken the opportunity to sit while he'd been talking to Liam. Derek hated the way he was going to have to push her, but it was the only way. He trailed a finger down Molly's pale cheek. "Let's go. Right now."

She got up and started following him. "Is Liam okay?"

"He's all right, out of Belisario's estate. He'll meet us at the airplane." No need to tell her the whole plan. She'd just be upset that Liam was at risk. "Getting you out is the priority. He'll be okay."

Glancing over at her, he could tell that Molly didn't like it. But she took a swig of water and kept following. Derek looked down at his GPS, especially formulated for use in the dense terrain. With the shape she was in, he didn't want to add on any more distance than was needed to get directly to the plane.

He grabbed his machete out of the holder strapped to his thigh, but cutting only when absolutely necessary for them to get through. Liam would be leaving a more obvious trail for Belisario's men, but too much hacking would also make his and Molly's route apparent if the men happened on it.

They traveled without speaking. Even though the moon

was full, most of the light didn't make it onto the jungle floor because of the dense trees and bushes. But artificial light would basically be a beacon for their pursuers, so that wasn't an option. The darkness just made everything more difficult. Even so, Derek kept up a pretty grueling pace, determined to put as much distance between them and Belisario's compound as possible. They weren't running full-out, but they were moving much faster than a walk.

Derek heard a soft cry from Molly and turned, but wasn't in time to catch her as she fell all the way to the ground. This was the second time she'd tripped.

"Let's stop," he said, quickly helping her up.

"No." She shook her head. "I'll be okay. I just can't see very well."

With one eye almost swollen closed, he wasn't surprised. But she hadn't stopped, hadn't complained, had kept his grueling pace for the past two miles.

"You're amazing," he told her, meaning every word. He knew trained agents who wouldn't be coping as well as she was.

He could see her roll her one good eye. "Oh, yeah? Did you figure that out before or after I just did a face-plant in the middle of the jungle floor?"

Derek couldn't help his short bark of laughter. He pulled her into his arms and kissed the top of her head. The acerbic wit of hers was going to be his undoing.

"Drink more water." He pulled back and handed her the canteen.

"Won't we run out?"

"No, there's plenty of water sources around here. And this canteen has a triple filter system. It could make a mud puddle safe to drink. So don't drink sparingly."

She nodded and took a huge sip.

"Good." He nodded in approval. "Don't forget to eat, too. You ready to get going?"

"Yep." She smiled, but he noticed her deep breath as if she was trying to steady herself, prepare mentally.

This time he took her hand and hooked it into the back waistband of his pants. "Don't let go. No more face-plants."

"Yeah, well, you'd just better hope I don't try to get fresh with you."

There was nothing he'd like more, but knew that couldn't happen even if there weren't people hunting them. But he smiled at her. At least she wasn't stuttering. "I'll take my chances. You're doing great, honey. About eight more miles to go."

Eight miles was a long way to go for someone traumatized, injured and drugged.

Chapter Twelve

A few hours later all Molly could hear was the sound of her own breathing sawing in and out of her chest. Honestly, she was amazed Belisario's men couldn't hear it and use it to find them. She tried to make herself be more quiet, but found it impossible.

And they weren't even running. Moving fast, but not running. If they were running, Molly was pretty sure she'd have already fallen dead on the jungle floor. Her lungs were burning, the damp, hot air of the rain forest making every breath agonizing.

After an hour of shooting pain, she lost most of the feeling in her hurt leg, thank goodness. Her shoulders and face were quite a different story. Every step she took reminded her of her injuries.

But she didn't want to slow Derek down. Didn't want to stop. Didn't want to do anything that would put them in any more danger.

So she kept moving, despite the pain, despite the fact that she could never seem to drag enough air into her lungs. One step after another. Over and over.

Her hand was in Derek's pants.

She would've giggled at the thought had she any reserve energy in her body whatsoever to do so. Sadly, she didn't.

But that didn't stop her from enjoying the skin of his lower back that she could feel against her fingers.

Derek was here.

She still could hardly believe it. After her talk with Belisario yesterday, Molly had all but given up hope. No one would link her and Belisario, heck she could hardly link herself and Belisario. She would've sworn no one was coming for her.

To be honest, she thought it would be a few days before anyone even noticed she was missing. And by then, well, unthinkable things would've happened to her and she'd probably be dead. That's what she had resigned herself to.

But then she'd woken up from another lovely dream— really, a memory—about Derek. To find not Henrico or another one of Belisario's henchmen standing over her, but Derek himself.

After she figured out she wasn't still dreaming, she'd never been so excited to see anyone in her whole life. Derek was here to get her away from this horror.

Molly didn't think this could be a sanctioned mission by Omega, not here in South America at a private residence. She hoped Derek and the guys weren't going to ruin their careers by getting her out. But regardless, she had to admit she was glad they were here.

The minutes began to blend. One step after another. Over and over. Molly almost felt as if she was floating out of her body.

She was so out of it that she didn't even realize when Derek came to a stop. She plowed right into him, hit his hard back and was about to fall when he reached his arm around behind him and caught her.

He turned and put both hands on her upper arms. She could see concern in his eyes, but didn't even have the energy to pretend that everything was okay. Everything seemed to be hazy.

"Whoa, sweetheart." He helped her sit down on some cleared ground. "Looks like we need a break."

"No, I'm okay."

"Like hell you're okay, Molly. Here, drink." She was thankful he held up the canteen to her lips because she didn't think she could do it.

"I know we need to keep moving." Molly forced the words out after drinking. Derek took out another energy bar and began feeding it to her in tiny pieces. She wondered if she should feel offended that he was treating her like a baby bird. Honestly, she didn't care.

Even sitting up was hard to do now. All she wanted to do was sleep. Derek sat down, leaned against a tree and lifted her into his lap so her back was against his chest.

"Just rest and eat," he murmured against her hair.

He fed her piece after piece, bringing the canteen to her lips every once in a while. It was all Molly could do just to chew the bar and swallow.

"How much farther do we have?" she finally whispered, full volume feeling as if it was too much effort.

"A little over a mile and a half—"

They were both stunned into silence when they heard the chirp of a radio and someone speaking on it in Spanish less than a hundred feet away.

Derek spun them around so they were lying flat on their stomachs and less likely to be seen. Molly tried to understand what the man was saying into the radio, but he was speaking too quickly for her to pick out many of the words.

"Stay here, okay?" Derek whispered into her ear. "I don't think he saw us, but I'm going to circle around the back of him and take him out before he can give any details about where we are."

Molly nodded. She didn't think she could do much more anyway.

THANK GOD FOR Molly's exhaustion. If she hadn't so desperately needed a break—Derek had turned around to find her almost gray with exhaustion—they probably would've run right into Belisario's man.

Derek wasn't sure how he'd found them, if he'd tracked their trail all the way from Belisario's house or if he'd caught it somewhere more recently, but the fact that this area wasn't swarming with bad guys was a good sign. Hopefully he was alone. But Derek knew that all the man needed was proof he was on the right trail and backup would be called immediately.

He couldn't let that happen. Especially when they were this close to the plane. Derek thought about contacting Jon, but it was too risky, the guy might overhear. Plus, even if he sprinted it would take Jon too long to get here to be much help.

The guy kept talking on the radio and although Derek couldn't tell what he was saying, his tone wasn't frantic or excited so that was good. He didn't think they were around here.

Just keep talking, moron. Give me a chance to sneak up on you. Derek didn't want to use his gun, which would be heard for miles. He needed to take this guy out up close and personal. Derek considered going around the opposite side, just in case there was a problem. It would lead the guy away from Molly, but decided speed was more of the essence.

Silently Derek stalked through the jungle. His Special Forces missions in Afghanistan may not have been in the jungle, but they had still required the same patience and focus.

The man never knew what happened, and Derek had not one iota of remorse as he came up behind him, covered his mouth with his hand, and stabbed him quickly where his cranium met his spinal cord at the back of his neck.

The man was painlessly dead before Derek laid him on the ground.

And if this was another black mark on his soul, so be it. This man may have been the one who hurt Molly. Or even if he wasn't, he was in with the group who had. Derek had killed for much less reason.

He heard the unnatural cracking of a tree limb at the same time as he heard the safety being flipped off of a semiautomatic rifle behind him. Derek realized his mistake immediately. He had not checked for a partner.

But there was one. And he had either been smarter or just not as talkative, but Derek had never heard or seen him. And now his weapon was pointed at Derek.

The man spoke to him in harsh Spanish. Derek didn't understand him, but he held both hands up and got up slowly, making no sudden movements as he turned around. He still had a knife in his hand, but that wasn't going to do him any good against the weapon the man had pointed directly at him.

The man nodded at the knife with his chin. "Down," he said.

Derek let the knife fall to the ground. At least the man hadn't already shot him, which meant he didn't have instructions to kill them on sight.

"Woman," the man said. *"Dónde está la mujer?"*

Where is the woman? That much Spanish Derek could understand. "A woman? Dude, I haven't seen any women out here. I wish. Your friend snuck up on me and I got a little carried away with the self-defense, I guess."

The man was obviously trying to pick out whatever words he could understand. Derek had hoped the confusion might buy him more time, at least allow him to lead the man away from Molly, but he was reaching for his radio. Derek listened as the man reported in.

"Matalo. Encuentra a la mujer." The words came from the radio. Derek didn't know what they meant, but by the evil smile that spread across the big man's face, it wasn't good news for Derek.

The man put the radio back in its holder and lifted his weapon. Derek was about to make a dive for it—a total gamble, but better than doing nothing as he got shot— when the man crumpled to the ground.

Molly stood behind him, a large branch in her hand. She had obviously belted the guy over the head with it.

But he wasn't completely unconscious. He turned himself and his gun toward Molly in a rage. Derek didn't hesitate, but dove forward, landing on the man in a flying tackle. The gun flew from his hands and Derek pounded his fist into his face.

The larger man didn't want to go down without a fight. He got in a few punches that had Derek grunting in pain, before Derek was able to get behind him. Derek wrapped his arms around the man's neck and gave a quick twist, breaking it. The man fell dead.

He landed near Molly, who immediately backed up to get away. Derek saw horror in her eyes.

Something in his heart froze. Now she knew Derek was a killer, could kill a man with his bare hands. He supposed she had already known academically that taking lives was sometimes part of his job. But she didn't know the sorts of things he had done when he'd been in the military. The people he'd killed while his skin was touching theirs. Just like the two men he'd killed tonight.

When Molly looked over at him the horror was gone from her eyes, but he knew it would be back. This was why he had always tried to distance himself from her. To keep this blackness away from her light.

"*Matalo* means 'kill him,'" she whispered. "That's one of the few phrases I remember from my high school Spanish."

"What?"

"That's what the voice said on the radio. *Matalo.* Kill him." She was swaying on her feet.

Derek rushed over to her. "Well, he definitely would have if you hadn't clocked him. Thank you. And thank you to your high school Spanish teacher for teaching completely inappropriate phrases."

She started to smile, but then paled even more, if possible. "I'm not feeling so good."

The words were hardly out of her mouth before she turned to the side and was violently ill. Derek tried to brace her at her waist and held a hand at her forehead.

So much for all the food and water he'd tried to get into her. It was on the jungle floor now. Any fortification in her system was gone. They had almost two miles still to go and the second dead guy had called for backup.

They needed to leave now, but Molly wasn't capable of going anywhere.

"I can run," she said.

Derek actually scoffed right in her face. "You can't even stand up straight, much less run."

He took his backpack off and set it against a tree. He would just have to leave it here. "Time for a piggyback ride."

"What?" Despite how she was feeling she still managed to look at him as if he was crazy.

"Carrying you on my back will be much easier than carrying you in my arms. And much more comfortable for you than me carrying you over my shoulder fireman-style."

Evidently the thought of being upside down made her turn a little greener.

"Piggyback."

They didn't have any more time to waste. He swung her up on his back. Her small arms wrapped around his neck.

"Jon," Derek spoke into his mic.

"Damn it, man, I was worried about you. Are you guys okay?"

Derek started to run.

"Yes. We're about a mile and a half out and are probably going to be coming in hot. Someone found our trail and reported back before I could stop him."

"What's you're ETA?" Jon asked.

"I'm carrying Molly, so I'm aiming for twenty minutes. I don't have any guns on me." Talking was harder now as he picked up speed.

"We'll be ready. Liam's already here."

"Roger. Over and out."

Derek focused on running. He still had his machete to cut through brush and whacked away now that he didn't care about whether the trail could be followed.

He felt Molly try to hold her own weight as much as possible with her legs and arms grasping him tightly. But he could feel her muscles start to fail her as they got closer to the plane.

"Hang in there, baby," Derek told her.

As he reached the clearing a half mile from the plane, Derek felt her start to slip from his back, her strength obviously spent. He tossed his machete to the ground, caught her by the arm and swung her around so he was carrying all her weight in his arms.

He heard shots coming from behind them in the jungle.

"Liam." Derek hit the mic on his throat to talk.

"I'm out here and got my sights on you. Just keep running with her."

Having Molly over his shoulder would probably be faster, but Derek wasn't going to take the chance of them shooting at his back and hitting her. She was totally slack in his arms.

Derek heard more gunfire and forced more speed out of his legs. Not only did they have to make it on the plane, it had to take off. The plane wasn't bulletproof.

Five hundred yards.

Four hundred yards.

He heard gunfire coming from in front of him. That was Liam, which meant Belisario's men had broken the tree line.

Three hundred yards.

"I see you, Derek. Keep going." It was Jon in his ears. Derek could barely hear him over the sound of the jet's engines.

Two hundred yards.

"Liam. Let's. Go." Derek had no breath left for full sentences.

A bullet flew wide, over his head. Belisario's men weren't close enough for accuracy yet, but it wouldn't be much longer.

One hundred yards.

Out of the corner of his eye he saw Liam sprint up beside them, then he passed them and made his way up the stairs into the plane. Derek forced one last burst of speed and followed him up the stairs a few seconds later.

He dove for the ground inside the plane, twisting so he wouldn't land on Molly's unconscious form.

"Go!" Liam yelled and the jet began to roll even while Liam was pulling up and securing the door.

There was nothing Derek could do but hold on to Molly and pray that Jon's skills as a pilot could get them out of this. A few moments later he felt the plane leave the ground at a much steeper rate than normal, and make a sharp turn that threw them back against the side of the aircraft.

But then it evened out and they began a more normal ascent to a higher altitude.

Derek heard a loud woot and laugh from the cockpit. Jon called out, "We hope you enjoy your flight on Save Your Ass airline. Now just sit back and relax."

Chapter Thirteen

Once they were safely in the air Derek got Molly up into a seat. Her color was still pale—in the places of her face he could actually see not covered by bruises—but her breathing was pretty even. She'd be waking up soon.

Derek and Liam put headsets on so they could talk to Jon without having to yell.

"Molly okay?" Jon asked.

"She's waking up," Derek told him. "The eight miles was a lot for her in the shape she was in. Although she was a hell of a trouper."

"Looks like someone pounded on her pretty good." Liam winced.

Derek reached over to stroke a stray wisp of hair off her forehead. She moved just the slightest bit at his touch.

"Well, she's alive." Derek looked over at his friend. "And the worst didn't happen, so we'll call this a win."

Liam knew what he meant. "Thank God. I couldn't have stood the thought of that for her."

Derek's jaw tightened just thinking about it.

Molly shifted again and her eyes began to flutter open. Derek positioned himself in the seat next to Liam, across from Molly, so she could have a little space as she awoke.

"Hey, kiddo," Liam said. "Don't be scared by this ghoulish monster sitting next to me. It's just Derek. But he often scares small children."

Derek heard Jon chuckle over the headset.

He watched as Molly became more aware of what was going on. She sat up a little straighter in her seat and looked out the window, then across at them.

"We made it to the plane," she said.

"Yep."

"What is she saying?" Jon was demanding. "Give her some headphones."

Derek got up and grabbed a set, then handed them to her, smiling. "Jon wants to be able to talk to you, too."

She put them on. "Hey, Jon."

"You have no idea how happy I am to hear your voice, Molly."

"Well, you have no idea how happy I am that you guys figured out where I was and came to get me."

"Are you okay?" Jon asked.

"Nothing that won't heal. No broken bones."

"I still want to take you to the hospital when we get back to Colorado," Derek told her. "Whatever drug they pumped you full of, we need to make sure there are no residual effects."

"Yeah, that's probably a good idea." She nodded at him.

They both noticed Liam was looking kind of strangely at Molly.

"What?" she asked.

"Nothing." Liam shook his head, smiling. "That's just the first sentence I've heard you say to Derek without stuttering in years."

Molly looked away for a minute and Derek thought he might have to punch Liam for bringing it back to her attention, but then she regrouped.

"I guess my life being threatened by a real ghoulish

monster like Pablo Belisario taught me there are much bigger and badder things to be nervous about than Derek."

"Atta girl," Jon murmured over the headsets.

"Molly, what did Belisario want with you?" Derek asked her.

"I still don't know, exactly. But it definitely had to do with the explosion at the lab. He wanted confirmation that everything had been destroyed."

"Did you have evidence dealing with Belisario in the lab?"

"No." She sat up straighter. "That's just it. It wasn't about him. It was about someone he called his 'partner' and the evidence you guys brought into the lab yesterday."

This was getting even weirder. "Who is his partner?" Derek asked her.

Molly closed her eyes, obviously concentrating on her memory of the conversation. "He didn't say. He just said someone who couldn't allow me to be found on US soil."

Derek met eyes with Liam. Common criminals wouldn't care about Molly's questioning and/or murder happening on US soil. But a politician sure as hell would.

"That Secret Service vehicle," Liam murmured.

"Exactly." Derek nodded.

"Evidently this partner had a very bad day and needed to absolutely confirm that all evidence had been destroyed in the lab," Molly continued. "I was supposed to have died there. And the partner wanted the names of you guys, too, the ones who brought in the evidence."

"Whoa," Jon said from the headset. "Sounds like someone was going a little overboard in making sure he cleaned up his mess. We'd better watch our six."

"Don't worry." Molly was quick to jump in. "I didn't give them your names. They wanted names, but I told them the agents were Steve Rogers and Bruce Banner."

"Who are they?" Liam asked.

"Superheroes from *The Avengers*," Derek answered. His eyes met Molly's. Did she remember that was the movie that was playing in the background that night he'd shown up at her house? Derek hadn't been able to think of the film since without thinking of Molly.

Molly flushed and looked away, fiddling with the headset. Yes, she remembered.

"That was good thinking," Jon told her. "I'm sure you were under a lot of pressure. We appreciate you trying to look out for us."

"I'm sorry I don't have any more useful information."

Derek wanted to take her hand, but forced himself not to. He needed to keep his distance from her now more than ever. "Don't be sorry. You confirmed some important details we've been working on with Director Drackett."

Her look said she didn't believe him.

"Seriously. Even before the explosion in the lab we were considering that it might be someone high in the US Government—someone who Drackett's been reporting to—who has ties to the Chicago bombing," Derek explained.

"Oh, no."

"It's how they've kept ahead of us on all our leads, knew when we had critical evidence and knew to take you to find out more details," Liam continued. "Belisario wouldn't be able to get that information on his own. It's highly unlikely that he has any clout or inside knowledge when it comes to Omega, without his 'partner' feeding it to him."

Molly nodded. Derek could tell she was exhausted again. "Why don't you rest? We have to stop in Miami to refuel, but then we'll be going straight to Colorado."

She wanted to argue, but couldn't find the strength. Her eyes were closed within moments.

"She still has too much of that damn drug in her system,"

Derek muttered. He slid a pillow under her head where it rested against the plane.

"Not to mention the trauma of all those miles getting out of the jungle," Liam said. "She's a lot tougher than you would think, just by looking at her. I know I'll never call her mousy again."

Derek heard Jon's quiet, "Amen to that."

Derek remembered the horror that filled her eyes when that man had fallen dead at her feet. The man Derek had killed with his own two hands right in front of her.

He looked at her sleeping form. "She's strong, definitely."

But Liam was wrong, Molly wasn't tough. Nor was she hard or cold. She didn't belong in their world. She needed to be back at a lab where she could be safe. Protected from people like Belisario.

Hell, protected from people like Derek.

"Doctors will get her situated, Derek. She's made it through the worst part," Jon said.

Derek hoped so. He tucked another strand away from her sleeping face, but quickly moved his hand back when she turned toward him.

He hoped she'd made it through the worst part. But somehow he knew she probably hadn't. And that the worst part for her, was him.

Six hours later, after a brief stop in Miami for refueling, which Molly slept through, they landed in Colorado. Even though she was feeling better, Derek wanted to get her straight to a hospital. Jon and Liam would take care of the plane and report back to Steve Drackett at Omega HQ.

Everyone agreed that they all needed to watch their backs. Outside of the four of them, and Drackett, no one was trustworthy.

Molly was now hooked up to an IV and had been seen by two different doctors. Derek hadn't left her side the entire time. He'd told the doctors as much as he could without giving away any important details of the case. The cover story was that she'd been carjacked.

"Overall, I'd say you're very lucky. Neither your nose nor your jaw is broken. I imagine the swelling will go down in the next twenty-four hours and there shouldn't be any lasting effects from the blows to your face," Dr. Martin, a kind woman in her midfifties had told Molly.

She flipped through some charts. "The drug in your system is Ketamine. That's a medication mainly used when someone is having surgery, for starting and maintaining anesthesia, although it is used recreationally, also."

"Will she have any lasting effects from that?" Derek asked.

"No." Dr. Martin put the chart down and turned to Molly. "But honestly, given the amount still in your system after nearly thirty-six hours and your size and weight, you're very fortunate that you didn't go into cardiac arrest."

"Well, I've been pretty out of it since they gave it to me. Hard to stay awake," Molly told her.

"I'm sure. It's almost out of your system now, and the IV will help flush out the rest."

"How long will she need to stay here?" Derek asked.

"I'd like to keep her overnight, just for observation."

"Do I have to?" Molly sounded like a child, even to herself. But she didn't want to stay in the hospital.

Of course, Belisario's men had taken her from her home, so going back there wasn't safe. Molly didn't know where she would go after the hospital. Maybe to a hotel.

"Just for one night." The doctor had shaken hands with both Molly and Derek, then left.

Derek sat down on the chair across from her bed. "Don't

worry, I or someone I trust will be here with you the entire time."

"I don't think I said thank-you for coming to get me. Belisario..." She paused then restarted. "I would've been in real trouble if you hadn't shown up when you did."

Molly shuddered. She didn't even want to think about what would've been happening to her right now if she was still back in Colombia. "I thought it might be days before anyone even realized I was gone."

"I started looking for you as soon as I realized you weren't at your condo when I came to pick you up yesterday morning."

"Well, I wasn't counting on that."

Derek's eyes narrowed just the slightest bit and he tilted his head to the side as if the thought of not picking her up had never even occurred to him. "Why? I told you I would come get you."

Molly shrugged. "It's just, we kissed the night before. Then you left pretty abruptly."

"And because we kissed you thought I wouldn't pick you up the next morning like I said I would."

He was offended, she could tell.

Molly struggled with what to say. She wasn't trying to insult him. But he had a pattern when it came to the two of them and their interactions.

"I'm not trying to say you wouldn't keep your word, Derek." Molly tried to look him in the eye, but it was hard. She looked at the top of his forehead instead, at his thick dark hair. "It's just that after...something happens between the two of us physically, you tend to withdraw. Completely. You don't really talk to me, definitely don't touch me. You just withdraw. For months, even years."

She cleared her throat. "You're still friendly, nothing overt, mind you. But I always felt your total withdrawal from me. Maybe to protect yourself. Or maybe I just wasn't what you wanted."

She glanced down at his eyes and saw surprise. "Not that I've ever expected any commitment from you," she was quick to continue. "You never made any promises, so I'm not trying to say you did anything wrong. I'm just saying that I figured you'd send someone else to get me yesterday morning or something, because of our kiss. Because you wouldn't really want to see me. I figured I wouldn't really talk to you again until sometime next year. If the pattern held."

Derek was completely still in the chair across from her hospital bed, staring at her. Molly began to get uncomfortable. What if he didn't even know what she was talking about? He had never once brought up the things that had happened between them in the past. What if he really didn't remember?

She looked away toward the door, hoping some doctor or nurse or even one of Belisario's men would come bursting through. Oh, to go back to the good old days where she couldn't get a complete sentence out around Derek. Stuttering and stammering was much better than the hole she was digging for herself.

She glanced back at him to find him still in that frozen position. "You know what? Forget I even said anything. I must still have more of the drug in my system than they thought."

Then Molly did what any adult scientist with a PhD and two advanced master's degrees would do under the same situation: pulled the blanket up over her head.

Chapter Fourteen

Derek was pretty sure this sort of situation had never come up in his Omega tactical team training. It probably would've been in the *How to Diffuse a Bomb Using Acupuncture and Other Impossible Situations You'll Never Get Out of Unscathed* class. Derek had obviously missed that one.

The damnedest thing was, Molly was right. He did withdraw. But he thought he had been all slick about it. That she hadn't really noticed.

Evidently, not only had she noticed, but she'd recognized a *pattern*, he did it so often. But even worse, she thought it was for his own good that he tried to stay away from her. That he didn't want her.

The exact opposite from the truth.

And now she was hiding under a blanket, which Derek found adorable but also proved his point. Molly was soft, gentle, kind.

Entrenching himself in her life would be the most selfish move he could make. Derek could almost live with himself despite some of the choices he'd made in the past, lives he'd taken, darkness he'd embraced. But choosing to surround someone like Molly with his darkness?

Unforgivable.

Still, the thought that she wasn't what he wanted? That

she somehow wasn't good enough for him? It burned like acid in his gut.

He stood and reached for Molly where she hid under the covers, but then stopped. Maybe it was better this way. Derek honestly didn't know.

His phone buzzed. It was Jon.

Derek turned and walked to the other side of the room, answering it. "What's up?"

"Derek, you've got to get Molly out of there immediately."

"Why? What's wrong?"

"Evidently some new 'evidence' has come to light that makes it seem like Molly was the one who purposely caused the explosion in the lab."

"What?"

"There's a warrant out for her arrest."

Derek muttered a curse.

"What?" Molly had pulled her head out from under the covers. "What's going on?"

"Jon, I'm putting you on Speaker so Molly can hear."

He put the phone on the bedside tray and went to get Molly's clothes out of the drawer of the small dresser in the hospital room. No matter what Jon explained, they were still going to need to get Molly out of there.

"Evidently someone went over Drackett's head with the warrant. Steve is pretty furious."

"What evidence, Jon?" Molly asked. "I know I didn't do it, so I'd like to know what evidence it is someone could have against me."

"No one seems to actually know, Molls, that's the thing. All I'm sure of is that they were waiting for us when we got back here," Jon told her.

"Like someone knew we had gotten her out and was making sure they could catch her on this side?" Derek asked, bringing Molly's clothes over and setting them on the bed.

"Exactly like that, I'd say. If she'd been with us, she'd already be in custody."

Derek shook his head. "But *whose* custody, is what I want to know. Not local law enforcement's, I bet."

"Is Molly checked in to the hospital under her real name?"

"Yeah." A misstep on Derek's part, thinking that they were too far for Belisario to reach. But they weren't too far for his partner to reach.

"If this goes as high as we think it might, it won't be long before they've got men at the hospital," Jon said. "Liam is running interference as much as he can, but that will only stall for so long."

Molly had already sat completely up. Derek winced as she pulled the IV out of her arm and pressed down on the bleeding spot with a tissue. She reached for her clothes and Derek turned his back to give her privacy. He picked up the phone.

"I'm getting her out right now. We're going to ground. I will call you in exactly twenty-four hours at a pay phone." Derek gave Jon an address of a gas station not far from Omega HQ that he knew had a pay phone. He'd used it before. "We need to get burner phones. I'll be dumping this one."

"On it. Be safe."

"You, too, brother. And thanks for the warning."

Molly was reaching down to tie her shoes as Derek disconnected the call. He reached down to help her.

"I'm sorry that you don't get to rest yet," he told her as he tied first one shoe, then the other.

"I'll be okay. At least we're not running through the jungle."

She stood and Derek took his phone and jammed it down into the cushion of the chair he'd been sitting in.

"They may be trying to track us through that. Might as well make it as difficult as possible for them to find it," he explained. "Are you ready?"

She nodded. He offered her his hand and she took it. "I'm going to go out to the nurses' station to distract them so you can get out without them realizing you're gone. I'll meet you down at the end of the hall."

"Okay."

"As soon as they're looking the other way, you go."

He waited for her nod, then walked out of her room and down to the nurses. Distracting them wasn't that hard, Derek did know how to use his smile when he wanted to. And he only needed them to look away for a few seconds.

He met back up with Molly at the hallway right where she was supposed to be.

"Any problems?"

"Nope. Just had to be friendly."

"I'm sure." Her look was decidedly sour. Derek chuckled.

"Nobody else around here should know you or question why we're leaving. But your bruised face makes you pretty memorable, so I'm going to keep you tucked next to me as much as possible."

He wrapped his arm around her and pulled her body close to his. Molly kept her head down and let him guide her every time they passed any people. Most would just think she was grieving.

They were coming out the front doors when Derek saw them pull up. Two nondescript sedans, each carrying two men in suits. Derek wrapped Molly more tightly to his side and swung them in a sharp left.

"Head down," he whispered. He hunched his own shoulders so they both would just look like exhausted family members. He forced himself not to speed up the pace to draw any attention to themselves. But he did reach for the Glock in the side holster he wore. When Jon had slipped it to him before they left for the hospital, neither of them had thought it might need to be pointed at federal agents.

Derek hoped there wouldn't be a showdown with people who were just doing their jobs. They probably had no idea they were being used for nefarious purposes.

If Derek and Molly had been fifteen seconds later they would've been caught. But since the agents obviously thought they were arresting people sitting up in a hospital room, they weren't carefully watching the people who were leaving.

As soon as possible, Derek cut them into the shadows. It was a careful balance between not doing anything that would draw attention and getting them out of there as soon as possible. He felt Molly slip her arm around his waist and huddle closer.

"Did they see us?" Her voice was barely more than a whisper.

"I don't think so. They continued on their path inside the building. They probably saw us, but it didn't register who we were."

They stayed in the shadows just a few more moments. Once the agents made it to Molly's hospital room and discovered them missing, the first place they would start looking would be the exits and the parking lot.

They kept a tight hold of each other as they went into the parking lot. Derek ushered her into the car as soon as they found it.

"Stay as low as you can."

He didn't speed out of the parking lot or draw any attention to their vehicle—a black SUV. But as soon as they were clear of the main red light, Derek sped up, keeping his speed just over the limit. When he glanced in the rearview mirror he saw the blue of flashing police lights.

That was fast. Someone had made sure there was backup pretty close by in case those agents needed help. Derek smiled wryly to himself.

"I think you're safe to sit up," he told her.

"Is anybody following us?"

Derek shook his head and glanced at the police lights in the rearview mirror again, now getting farther away. "No, but it was much closer than I would've liked."

"None of this really makes sense. Why would anyone think I started the fire in the lab? And I find it very hard to believe that they had enough evidence to arrest me."

"Trust me, this has nothing to do with the lab fire and everything to do with getting you isolated. Away from the people in Omega who can protect you. Once you were alone, you'd be in trouble."

"But police officers wouldn't hurt me, would they?"

He shook his head, glancing at her for a moment before looking back at the road. "I'm sure it wouldn't be long until whatever real officers arrested you were given paperwork to 'transfer' you somewhere. And that would be it, you'd never be seen again."

"Why would Belisario send someone to kill me here? I already told him that I didn't know anything."

"Not Belisario, whoever his partner is stateside. A partner who is high enough in the US Government to get things done. As evidenced by us almost getting caught in the hospital."

"Someone in *our* government is responsible for all this? Had a part in the Chicago bombing?" Dismay colored her tone.

Derek explained about the Secret Service vehicle that had been spotted at the house in West Philadelphia.

"International terrorists attacking us is bad enough. But the thought that some high-ranking official in the government, someone people trust, having a hand in it? That just makes me sick to my stomach. Why would someone do that?" She turned and looked out the window.

Derek reached over and took her hand gently before he could help himself. "Why? Because some people are just terrible human beings who do terrible things. If you're racking your brain trying to understand it, it just means you're not one of those terrible people."

"It's still pretty inconceivable."

For her he was sure it was.

"Don't you think it's horrible?" she asked.

"Yes, absolutely. I'm just not surprised by anything anybody does anymore. Betrayal, dishonesty, greed, killing, happens everywhere."

Derek was sure she'd be just as horrified by things he'd done, choices he'd made, if she knew. He let go of her hand and put it back on the steering wheel. Right now he needed to focus on getting them to the safe house.

"We need to purchase a temporary cell phone that can't be traced. I'll use that to contact Jon tomorrow."

"Where are we going?"

"To a cabin an old friend of mine owned that he's given to me, near a lake about an hour and a half from here. Nothing about it is in my name and I haven't ever told anyone, at Omega or otherwise, about it." It was from one of the ranch hands who had worked for his uncle. Gary had been more of a father figure to Derek than his uncle had ever been.

Molly nodded and gave a tired sigh.

She needed rest. She needed nourishment. She needed

a chance for her body to heal, or at least stop running off pure adrenaline. Hell, twenty minutes ago she'd still been on an IV. The fact that she was even halfway functional was amazing.

"At the very least the cabin will be somewhere that you can rest and be safe for however long you need. To catch your breath."

"And for us to come up with a plan," she responded, resting her head back against the seat.

"Yes, come up with a plan." He smiled at her, glad for the cover of darkness, so she couldn't see that the smile wasn't anywhere near real.

Because damned if Derek, the tactical team specialist, had any earthly idea what their next move would be.

Chapter Fifteen

After stopping at a local supercenter to get food, the burner phone and some other supplies they needed, including clothes for both of them, they'd made it to Derek's cabin. He mostly came out here when he wanted to be alone, needed to get away from people, or the city, or both. The next nearest building was over five miles away. He'd never even considered bringing someone else here, especially a woman.

The cabin was sparse: two bedrooms, one bath, a living room and a kitchen. No real decorations, everything was built for function. Derek hadn't ever given the lack of coziness any thought, but it occurred to him now that Molly was here.

He didn't know what he expected from her as they'd walked through the door, both of them holding bags from the store. Not complaints about the house, Molly wasn't a complainer. Maybe just a nose turned up or a forehead creased in distaste.

But she'd only just looked around and said, "It's perfect."

They'd made a quick meal of pasta and salad. Molly was still drinking as much fluid as she could, to continue to offset the drugs and dehydration. Then, when he noticed she was falling asleep at the kitchen table, he'd shown her to the bathroom so she could take a quick shower, then had tucked her into the bed.

She had looked at him as if she had something to say, but then whatever was going on in that mind of hers had to take a backseat to what her body needed. And what her body needed was rest.

Derek watched her fall asleep as she was trying to start a sentence.

She didn't wake up for another fourteen hours.

He knew rest was the best thing for her, even more than eating or drinking, so Derek let her sleep. He did check on her, even took her pulse a couple of times to make sure it was steady, but she slept peacefully and deeply so he left her to it.

"Hi."

He looked up from yesterday's newspaper that he'd been reading through. "Feeling better?"

"Much. So much better."

She looked so much better. The swelling in her face had gone down considerably, and the bruises looked less angry. Her skin had a more healthy hue to it, not chalky as it had been.

"I'm just going to take a shower. Brush my teeth. I feel like Sleeping Beauty."

Derek nodded. "Sure." He couldn't stop looking at her.

She looked like Sleeping Beauty, or any other princess, with her rich brown hair falling loosely around her face. She normally kept it pulled back in a braid at work, almost certainly to keep it out of her way at the lab. But down like this she looked infinitely more touchable.

Derek realized he was staring at her and she was staring back.

"I think everything you need is in the shower."

Molly nodded slowly and turned away. "Not everything," he heard her mutter. But chose to ignore it.

Derek made more food, sandwiches this time, while Molly was in the bathroom. The cabin had seemed the perfect place to bring her, but now he realized that he hadn't thought things through completely. What it would be like to be enclosed with Molly in this small space. No reprieve.

Derek turned to the window that was in front of the sink. Yeah, she was safe from whatever might do her harm out there.

What about what might do her harm in here? Him.

He wanted to go for a walk. Take a drive. Hell, go for a swim out in the lake. Anything to create some distance between them. Physical distance. He needed to refortify. But he couldn't risk Molly's safety.

It had been okay while she'd been asleep. He'd even gotten a few hours' sleep out on the couch. But having her awake, right in front of him? What was he going to do?

Derek turned from the window to find Molly standing there, awake, right in front of him. Her hair was damp and hanging loose around her shoulders and back. She had on a T-shirt and sweatpants, both incorrectly sized and cheaply made, and blue socks.

Derek had never seen anyone so beautiful in his entire life.

He knew he was walking on dangerous ground here. One wrong step, one wrong word—hell, one *right* word— and he was going to start kissing her and never stop.

"I was wondering if you'd still even be here when I got out."

"I couldn't leave you."

"I'll bet you wanted to, though. Considered it. Withdraw because we had a moment."

Derek didn't want to address exactly how correct she was.

"Here, I made you a sandwich." He pushed the plate toward her. She looked for just a moment as if she might refuse it so they could continue the conversation, but then her stomach growled loudly enough for him to hear it across the room. He raised an eyebrow at her.

Molly huffed just the slightest bit at being betrayed by her own body, then sat down and promptly demolished her sandwich as well as some fruit and leftover salad. Derek ate with her.

"I finally don't feel like I got hit by a truck," she told him. "I'm sore, but I can tell that the last of the Ketamine is finally out of my system."

Derek stood and began clearing the dishes, but she stopped him. "I'll do it. You fixed lunch. But do you mind fixing some coffee? I feel like I will finally truly think the situation with Belisario is behind me if I can just have some coffee."

Molly was well-known for her love of all things coffee. "Sure," he told her. "But you're going to have to live with Folgers because I don't have any of that froufrou stuff you make at work."

"That froufrou stuff keeps the lab running, so do not knock it."

Derek made their coffee—he knew she also liked hers black—and they walked into the living room. For the first time he wished the cabin had a television or a radio or something. Anything to distract him from the fact that Molly Humphries was sitting in the oversize chair next to the couch with her legs tucked underneath her, sipping coffee. Wearing mismatched clothes under which Derek happened to know she could not be wearing anything because they'd forgotten to buy her underwear last night.

Derek swallowed hard.

"So, can I ask you something?"

Oh, yes, please dear heavens, ask him something. Ask him anything to get his thoughts away from her lack of undergarments.

"Shoot."

She paused for just the slightest moment. "Do you actually remember the night we spent together having sex three years ago?"

Derek had to give himself credit, he at least didn't spew his coffee. But it was close.

"Molly—"

"No. Do not *Molly* me." Her tone brooked no refusal. Where was the woman who had barely been able to get a sentence out around him a few days before? She'd certainly found her voice now. She set her coffee cup down. "I have spent the last three years acting like a total nincompoop around you. *Mousy Molly.* Do you think I don't know everyone calls me that?"

"Molly—"

She shook her head. "No, I deserved it. They were right. I have been mousy. Ridiculous." She took a breath, seemed to be mentally regrouping. "I thought I was going to die yesterday, Derek. In an ugly, horrible way."

Derek breathed deeply through his nose. He had thought the exact same thing.

"I was afraid." Her voice got softer.

"Anybody would be afraid under those circumstances."

"I tried to keep it together." Her shoulders straightened a little. "I *did* keep it together."

"I have no doubt about that." Just the way she'd handled

herself in the jungle, under the roughest possible physical circumstances had proved that. Although Derek had already known Molly was strong.

"Somewhere in the midst of all this, I decided I wasn't going to waste time with you anymore, Derek, wasn't going to be timid and wait. Life is too short. You either want me or you don't. I know that's a hard decision for you to make for some reason. So I'm going to help us get to the bottom of it. Do you remember us having sex three years ago or not?"

He wanted her. He wanted to yell it at her. But instead he sat back in his chair a little farther. Tried to feign a relaxed stance he very definitely didn't feel.

"Molly—"

She shot out of her chair as if it was on fire. "No. Just answer the question."

Derek couldn't sit either, but as he stood he was careful to stay far away from Molly. If he touched her now all would be lost. He walked over to look out the window. Look anywhere but at her.

"Yes. Yes, I remember." He remembered it all. Every touch. Lick. Moan.

"Was it just a one-night stand for you? You got what you wanted and that was it?"

The hesitation in her voice pulled at him. He turned back to look at her. "No. Never that."

"Then why have you been distant since then? Was it because I wasn't a better friend? You were upset that night and just wanted a friend and I forced it into something more…"

This was worse than her thinking he only wanted a one-night stand. He stuck his hands deep in his pockets. He cut her off. "Get something straight. I came to your house that night with every intention of taking you to bed.

Short of you slamming the door in my face, that was an inevitable conclusion."

That got her attention. Evidently she had never considered the possibility that he'd come there to deliberately seduce her.

He very definitely had. Yeah, he'd had a few drinks, but not nearly enough to stop him from his plans.

"Sometimes I've seen you looking at me," she said. "*Caught* you looking at me is a better phrase, and I would think I saw something in your eyes. A heat. But then all the other times you were always so distant. I never knew what to expect."

Derek had been so busy just trying to keep himself away from her, he hadn't really taken into consideration what his actions might be saying to her. She was more astute than he'd realized.

Which...he should've realized she would be.

"Molly." He took a step toward her, then stopped. "I'm sorry."

"Why?"

"For hurting your feelings in any way. For making you doubt yourself."

"Did I misread what I saw? Was it all in my imagination?"

Lie to her. That was all he needed to do. One tiny lie, let her down easy, and this crisis was averted. Moments passed. It was his tactical advantage and he knew he should take it.

But looking into her precious brown eyes, her sweet face, he couldn't do it. "No. You didn't imagine it."

She took a step closer. He took a step back.

"Why, Derek?" Her question was barely more than a whisper. "Why have you stayed away from me all this time? You've had to know I wanted to be with you."

"Molly, our worlds don't mix. I'm not the right person for you."

"Don't you think I should get to be the judge of that?" She took another step closer. She was studying him as if he was something in her lab, a piece of evidence she was trying to figure out.

He tried to take another step back, but found his back was already against the window, so there was nowhere he could go.

"Molly, you don't know the things I've done. Decisions I've had to make in the past. Some really questionable decisions."

She stared at him for a long moment. "We've all made questionable decisions."

"Not like mine."

"I know we all have a past. And I know enough about you to know that you're not still making questionable decisions, at least not lightly. You have to make the hard call sometimes, Derek. I understand that. It's part of being a leader in something as important as Omega Sector."

She took another step toward him.

"I've killed people, Molly. Not just people chasing me through the jungle like yesterday. Too many people when I was in Special Forces."

"Hard, I know. But part of your job," she said softly.

"I was always told by my commanding officers to bring the mark in alive if I could, dead if I had to. I always chose *dead*, Molly. These were bad guys, terrorists, yeah. But I set myself up as judge, jury and executioner. Every time."

"You want to lump yourself in with those terrible people, you think I don't understand, but you're not one of them, Derek." She moved closer to him.

"I once shot a man at point-blank range right in front of

his family." He was desperate to get the words out before she touched him. "In front of his children."

That stopped her movement toward him. He knew it would.

"I had orders and there were reasons he needed to die. But there were other ways I could've done it. Ways that wouldn't have traumatized children."

He turned and looked back out the window. He didn't want to see her eyes now, see disappointment or disgust or whatever he would find in them.

"Our worlds are different. Someone like you doesn't belong in mine."

He didn't expect to feel her arms slip around his waist, or her head laid against his back. "You're right. You made a bad decision. A wrong decision. And you've tortured yourself for it ever since."

She put her hands on the sides of his waist and urged him to turn around. "Answer me one question honestly, and if it's true, then I'll agree with you and promise I'll leave you alone."

He nodded.

"Would you do the same thing if you could do the whole situation over again now?"

Derek closed his eyes. No. Every day for the past ten years he'd wished he could go back. Do it differently.

"No. I'd find another way."

"Exactly," she whispered.

"But you still don't get it. No matter what, I would still kill him. His blood would still be on my hands."

"Derek, that's part of your job. What kind of person would I be if I judged you for taking lives if it means protecting the innocent?"

"But I saw your face when I killed those men in the jungle. The horror, disgust."

"Yes, but not directed at you. Directed at them. The one that almost fell on top of me had already described what he planned to do with me once Belisario was finished."

Derek was running out of arguments for why they should be apart. Both for her and for himself.

"I don't want to hurt you. I couldn't live with myself if I hurt you."

She reached up and wrapped her arms around his neck. "I'm stronger than I look. You're not going to hurt me." She pulled him down to her and pressed her lips against his. He felt her grin. "At least, if memory serves you won't."

He was done fighting this. Couldn't believe he had fought it for so long.

He took her lips with his. There was nothing soft or gentle about it. It was consumption. He kissed her in ways he'd only dreamed about doing in the darkest of nights when he'd been alone, thinking about her.

And she met him kiss for kiss. She may have stuttered and stammered around him for years, but there was nothing shy about her now. He felt her tongue dueling against his and need exploded inside him.

He slid his hands from where they framed her face down her back until they reached her hips and bottom. Squeezing, he lifted her up. Her legs hooked around his waist.

She peeled off her sweatshirt as he walked them both to the bedroom. He'd been right, no undergarments underneath. He kissed her again as he laid her down on the bed. She was the most beautiful thing he'd ever seen.

He knew he'd never be able to stay away from her again.

Chapter Sixteen

For someone who tended to be such a loner and so distant, Derek Waterman sure didn't sleep like it. Molly was still wrapped in his arms, as she'd been for the past few hours. The same way it had happened three years ago. He wanted her next to him while he was sleeping.

Not that she was complaining.

There was nothing that had happened in the past few hours that would cause any complaints from her. From him either if she had to guess.

They had wasted so much time over the past three years. Derek was stupid. She was stupid. Together the whole of their stupidity was greater than the sum of their stupid parts.

Because to think she could've been lying in his arms like this for the past three years if she had just nudged him along, but hadn't? Stupid.

"We're going to have to call Jon soon." Derek's arms tightened around her, squeezing, before letting go.

"What are we going to do, Derek? I can't hide here forever. Sooner or later I'm going to have to face these charges against me."

"I just want to keep you out of sight until we get more of a handle on who we're dealing with here. This mystery government official. I'm sure Jon is already running all of Belisario's known associates to see if he can get any names."

"I just want to do something." She got up as he did and started to get dressed. "I know Director Drackett needs someone assisting with the setup of a temporary lab after the explosion. All the cases that are stalled because of it." It was distressing to think about.

Derek crossed the room and put his arms around her. "I know. And Steve knows you didn't cause the explosion and I'm sure he wishes you were there, too. But not if it means putting your life at risk."

"I still don't like it." She knew she sounded like a grumpy child, but didn't care.

Derek walked into the bathroom to brush his teeth. "I promise I'll find you something to do while you can't be at the lab."

She looked at him standing there in just jeans with no shirt on. She'd kissed every inch of that chest in the past few hours, but definitely didn't mind just sitting here looking at it. If *he* was what she could do while she wasn't at the lab, maybe it wouldn't be so bad.

"Not me, you perverted little scientist." He stuck the toothbrush in his mouth. "Well, not just me." He wagged his eyebrows at her.

It was good to see Derek so much more at ease. Molly wasn't sure how long it would last, but she would enjoy it while she could.

"Can you get my laptop from home?"

Derek put on a shirt. Sadly. "Yeah, Jon could probably get it. Why?"

"There's stuff I can do for the lab to help get it back up and running sooner. Nobody knows those files better than I. I could access it on a neutral server and at least be able to organize some of the lost files."

"You can't do anything that can be tracked back to you."

"I understand, and I won't. This would be completely anonymous. Basically the equivalent of color-coding files, but with electronic documents. It will save me a bunch of time when I get back to work." She thought about that for a minute. "If I ever get back to work. I guess right now I don't really have a job."

"You will still have a job. Nobody at Omega would think you blew up that lab. You work too hard in it, put in way too many hours a day, to ever be the one who destroyed it. Drackett will have your back, believe me."

Molly wasn't so sure, but she hoped so. "Either way, I'd like to get started cataloging. It won't help with your case or any of the other open cases when the lab blew, but I can definitely make progress organizing past cases."

They made sandwiches again to eat, then called Jon. He was right on time and Derek put the phone on Speaker so Molly could hear, too.

"It's an absolute mess here," Jon explained. "Steering clear is the best thing you can do."

"What's going on?" Derek asked.

"Whoever the government official is behind all this is a freaking genius, that's what's going on. The whole division is crawling with Internal Affairs types." Frustration was clear in Jon's tone.

Derek muttered a curse.

"Yeah, no kidding," Jon continued. "You can't do anything around here without someone asking what it's for and which case it involves. We're in red tape up to our ears. Nobody can get into Steve's office. He's in conference with someone 24/7."

"Can you track whose office the bureaucrats are from? That would give us a good clue as to who's behind this."

"It was my very first thought. Joint task force, my

friend. Omega is a joint task force. Four different government offices involved. And we conveniently have people from all of those offices, so no hints there."

Jon sighed. "Oh yeah, Molly is considered a fugitive and a number of people are asking about you, Derek."

Derek's lips tightened into a straight line. "And damn it, we've got absolutely nothing. No clue who the government person is, no evidence left from our lead and no easy way to prove Molly's innocence."

"Thus far it seems like Drackett has been able to side-step any knowledge about us going down to Colombia. Of course, our government bad guy wants to keep his ties to Belisario as close to the chest as possible, so evidently Belisario having Molly has not been made common knowledge, nor has our rescue mission."

That sounded like good news, but honestly Molly wasn't even sure.

"It's overkill again, Derek. Just like with everything else. All these suits in here asking questions and causing delays? It's all a part of our guy's plan to keep us from getting close to him."

"Yeah, well, if he wanted us scattered and discombobulated, he's succeeded," Derek muttered. "And now we're back to ground zero."

"You should probably make an appearance at some point, Derek. Talk to the suits. Lead them away from the Molly trail. I don't think anyone has considered that the two of you are hiding out together. Molly's still the one they're after with an arrest warrant."

Derek slipped an arm around her waist. "I don't want to leave Molly alone. Not for any reason."

"I agree, someone needs to be with her. Maybe Liam or I can take turns."

"Jon, do you think it would be possible for you to get

my laptop from my condo?" Molly asked him. "If I'm going to be stuck out of the action, I'd like to at least get as much done as I can. But nothing that will link me to Omega or be traceable."

"Without a doubt someone will be watching your house in case you come back there. But I can probably find an excuse to get inside. Although if someone really did have a legit warrant out for your arrest they probably already confiscated the laptop," Jon said.

"I appreciate you trying. And bring me some clothes, if you can, okay? I look like I'm wearing a clown suit these clothes are so ill-fitting." She glanced up at Derek. "And bring some underwear, too."

"Something sexy," Derek said low into her ear. Molly shivered.

"Hey, I heard that," Jon chuckled. "Although I will pretend I didn't. Okay—computer, clothes, underwear, anything else? Too bad your lab coat burned, Molly. I'm sure you'd love to have that. I can hardly picture you without it."

Molly smiled. "Thanks, Jon. And actually my lab coat didn't burn, although it smelled like a chimney. It's sitting in my dirty clothes hamper and—"

Oh my gosh, *her lab coat.*

She wrapped her fist in Derek's shirt.

"What?" Derek said, looking into her face. "Molly, what? Are you okay? Does something hurt?"

"What's going on?" Jon asked from the phone.

"My lab coat." How could she have forgotten? "I wore it home after the explosion and took it off when I got in the shower."

"What about it, hon?"

"That evidence you gave me, when you came into the

lab two days ago, or whenever it was… *It's still in the pocket of the coat."*

She watched Derek's blue eyes narrow. "It wasn't destroyed?"

"No. I don't think so, I didn't even check. You put the stuff in my pocket, remember? So I would know which pieces to concentrate on. I didn't have a chance to get to them that night. They should still be in my lab coat sitting in my dirty clothes hamper."

"Jon—" Derek started.

"I'll check what's going on and get over there as soon as I can."

"I know where it is," Molly said. "I can get it."

"No," both men responded at the same time.

"Jon will get into your condo and get any evidence still there," Derek told her.

"They're looking for you, Molly," Jon chimed in. "You can't go to your house."

"Well, you're going to at least need to find another lab or somewhere for me to work once he gets it."

Derek was giving her a look that said he was determined to keep her as far from any danger as possible. "We'll see."

She took a deep breath so she wouldn't punch him. "Fine." She would deal with that later once Jon had the evidence pieces and they knew what exactly they were dealing with.

"Keep us posted as soon as you can get there," Derek told Jon. They exchanged burner phone numbers, and Derek made her memorize the numbers, too. "Jon, be sure to watch your back. There are eyes everywhere."

Chapter Seventeen

Waiting for Jon to be able to get into Molly's condo was pretty agonizing. Derek had a lot more practice waiting, again thanks to his Special Forces background, than her. She was practically wearing a hole in the floor waiting for Jon to call.

He'd already distracted her—hell, distracted them both—right here on this couch, for an hour or so, then distracted her again while they took a shower. But now she was determined to focus on the evidence Jon would be getting from her condo.

She wanted to go, but there was no way he was taking her anywhere near there. Not when her place was undoubtedly under surveillance by multiple groups of people: federal agents, maybe Belisario's men, the unknown government official's men. Everyone was looking for her. And Derek wasn't going without her—leaving her alone was not an option he was even willing to consider. After the scares he'd had with her over the past couple of days, he wasn't sure he'd ever be able to let her out of his sights again.

Derek's phone buzzed and Molly immediately sat down so they could read the text. Jon was finally able to make his way out of Omega HQ and was heading toward her condo.

"Okay, so we should go, right? It will take us at least an

hour and a half to make it back into the city. Jon will have gotten into my place much sooner than that."

They had agreed, Molly using one of their *distraction* times to sway him, to go back into Colorado Springs so she could process the evidence once Jon got it. Or at least look at it and see what needed to be done. They'd use a lab at a law enforcement training facility that Liam had access to.

"If he's just now leaving Omega, he won't be taking a straight route there. He'll have to get rid of any tails he'll undoubtedly pick up."

"How do you know?"

"It's what I would do." Hatton worked for the Crisis Management Unit putting out fires, but the man still had sharpened skills when it came to subterfuge and surveillance.

They got in the car not long afterward and drove toward Colorado Springs. Jon would be contacting them to let them know what he could find. Derek prayed Molly's lab coat was still there and the evidence undamaged.

It was a huge break. The evidence in Molly's lab coat was key to everything. Those pieces were the reason why Omega's lab lay in ruins and Molly had bruises all over her face. And Derek was going to make sure he took down the bastard whose door it led to.

They rode in comfortable silence except for the tension Derek could feel humming through Molly. He wished she would sleep; her body needed rest since it was recuperating from a trauma. But he knew there was no way of that happening, not the way she was wired.

"What's taking him so long?" Molly asked once they were just a few miles outside of the city. "Shouldn't he have already checked in? Do you think something went wrong?"

"No. Don't borrow trouble." He reached over to hold her hand. "Getting rid of someone tailing you can take a long time, especially when you're trying not to be obvious about it."

"I know. This is why I work in the lab and don't do cloak-and-dagger stuff! Just give me a microscope or a petri dish and I'm fine, but I can't stand this."

"Give Jon some more time, baby. He'll be all right."

The phone rang just a few minutes later. Derek put it on Speaker. "How's it going?"

"Not good, man. I have multiple people tailing me. One was definitely government, I lost him. The other two? I don't know who they are, but I can't shake them, not by myself. They're working together."

Derek muttered a curse under his breath.

"Is Liam available?"

"No," Jon told them. "He's running as much interference as he can at Omega. Believe me, he's more help there than he would be here."

There was a moment of silence before Jon continued. "I think the best plan may be for me to lead them away and for you guys to get to her house, Derek."

Derek didn't like that plan, but he had to agree. If they wanted to get the evidence out tonight, he and Molly were going to have to do it.

"Roger that, Jon. Just keep trying to lose them. We'll take care of retrieving the evidence."

"Sorry, buddy." Jon clicked off the call.

"Looks like it's up to us." Derek changed the direction of the car so they were heading toward her house. "But I can almost guarantee you there are other people watching your house. Waiting to see if you come back."

Their best bet was to use the fact that they were together. The people watching her home would be looking for Molly by herself, but not a couple.

But he knew it wouldn't be enough to actually fool anybody watching. No matter if it was her going in alone or her going in with another person, the teams watching her house were going to pounce as soon as Molly showed up.

Derek knew there was more than one group watching. Maybe they would take each other out, trying to get to them.

As far as plans went, that was the worst ever.

The second best plan was him going in by himself. But that would leave Molly outside, unprotected. He needed to stash her somewhere safe.

"Okay, I have a question," Molly said. "Will the bad guys or whoever is watching my condo be watching my neighbor's unit, too?"

"Peripherally, maybe. But not primarily. Why?"

"Mrs. Pope, three doors down, has access to the roof through a hatch door. So does my unit. Something about fire code."

Molly's home was a condo, but the building itself was set up more like town houses. The five units were stacked side by side to each other, rather than on top of each other. Each home was tall and narrow, but it gave them all their own little piece of backyard.

"Two of us together going to your Mrs. Pope's house? That might work. We'll just keep you bundled up so you can't be identified."

He liked it better than leaving her unprotected.

"It's nine o'clock in the evening. We'd better hurry up because she goes to bed by ten, I'm sure," she told him. "She's not going to like this as it is."

If the evidence at Molly's house wasn't so important, Derek wouldn't even try something this risky. But he didn't have a choice. So they were about to go disturb old Mrs. Pope.

They drove for a few minutes before Derek found the

place where he wanted to park, three blocks from her house at the corner of a four-way stop. This would give them multiple directions to leave if one route was cut off. There were also at least five different alleys and side streets if they needed to abandon the SUV and leave on foot.

May in Colorado wasn't hot, especially at night, which was good for how he and Molly would be huddling together down the street to Mrs. Pope's unit.

"Okay, it's just like at the hospital. Stay close to me, head down, so no one can see your face. I'm going to be doing the same, because anybody watching the house may know who I am, too. Just pretend like we're lovers and want to be really close to each other."

She cocked her head to the side and raised an eyebrow. "Pretend?"

Derek chuckled. "Just stay close."

He could feel the tension in Molly as they walked down the block. Her arm was wrapped around his waist and his was down her back and resting at her hip. She was on his left side so he would have free range of motion if he needed to get to his weapon.

"Did I ever tell you I grew up on a horse ranch in Wyoming?" he said to her in a conversational tone. She had to relax or they were going to stick out to anyone looking. "I was raised by my uncle and the other ranch hands."

"Really? I didn't know that. Did you like it?"

"I don't know that I would say that I *liked* it. It was hard, demanding work every single day. Good weather or bad." He remembered many a morning in the winter when he'd had no desire to go outside whatsoever. "But the land there? The mountains? They're carved into my soul."

She nodded. "Wyoming. That's a pretty amazing place."

"And if you're good, maybe I'll let you see me with my cowboy hat on later."

She laughed and leaned closer into him. Which was exactly what he wanted. The more realistic they were in looking like lovers going somewhere, the less likely they were to draw the surveillance teams' attention for the wrong reason.

"I know what you're doing," she said as they continued walking.

"Doesn't matter. You can still see me in it if you're good." He winked at her.

They turned the corner to the street her row of condos was on.

"Okay, Mrs. Pope's house is right here." She gestured to the door three down from her own.

Molly rang the doorbell. Derek stood directly behind her, trying to block her from the line of sight of anyone else. He also tried to keep an eye out to either side of them without making it obvious he was doing so.

They were at their most vulnerable right now. The seconds dragged on. Evidently Mrs. Pope wasn't home.

"Let's go," he murmured. "She's not here."

"No, give her a minute. She's slow and she's probably irritated that it's so late."

Sure enough a few seconds later a woman old enough to be his grandmother opened the door, just slightly, chain obviously still on.

"Hi, Mrs. Pope. It's me, Molly from a couple doors down?"

"Molly, dear, what are you doing here so late?"

"Well, it's a really long, funny story…"

Derek nudged Molly gently in the back. There was no time for a long story—funny or not.

"But—" Molly switched gears "—I won't waste your time with that right now because I know you're probably getting ready for bed. But do you mind if we get to the roof from your access? I locked myself out."

"I keep telling you to make an extra set of keys, dear." Derek prayed the older woman wouldn't make this an object lesson.

"I know, Mrs. Pope, you're so right. And I will, I promise."

"Okay, come on in. I guess your friend can come, too, if he is trustworthy."

Did the woman think he was going to pounce on her?

"Thank you so much, Mrs. Pope. We're sorry to disturb you."

The woman closed the door, and after a long moment opened it again, this time without the chain. Derek could almost feel eyes boring into his back. He needed to get them inside. Now.

He put his hand at Molly's waist and ushered her inside. Mrs. Pope gave an audible sigh at the way Derek moved them all from the porch. He felt better as he closed the door behind them.

Once they were inside, Mrs. Pope got a good look at Molly's face.

"Oh my goodness, Molly. What happened to you?"

Assuming Derek was the cause of Molly's bruises, the older woman literally pulled Molly away from him and put herself in the middle. As if to make herself a barrier between them.

It was actually endearing, the way she was so protective of Molly. Until she turned a glaring eye at Derek. He had to fight the urge not to take a step backward.

"I'm okay, Mrs. Pope." Molly touched the other woman's arm. "I was in an accident. There was a fire at my work."

"Oh, yes, I saw that on the news, dear."

"Derek is one of my…colleagues at Omega. He's very trustworthy."

Mrs. Pope turned an eye back at him again. She didn't looked convinced.

"Well, as long as you're okay, hon."

Molly kissed Mrs. Pope on the cheek. "I am okay, I promise. Thank you for letting us use your roof access."

"No problem, but you get an extra key made soon."

Giving Derek one more glare, she stepped out of the way. The layout of Mrs. Pope's house was the same as Molly's, so he followed her up one flight of stairs, then to a second stairway leading from a side hall to the attic. From the attic was the door outside.

"It's a weird configuration. Obviously since the door is in the attic, it's not really meant to be used a lot. But I always liked that my unit had the access. Mrs. Pope's unit and mine are the only ones that do."

They walked around the multiple years' worth of junk Mrs. Pope had in her attic.

"Mrs. Pope seems pretty protective of you." Derek was glad she hadn't had a knife when she saw Molly's bruises.

"Yeah, she kind of gets in my business sometimes, but that's okay. I try to have a meal with her once every couple weeks or so. I know she's lonely since her husband died about eighteen months ago."

That was more than Derek knew about any of his neighbors and he had lived at his house for over five years. He had definitely never eaten with any of them. He'd never even considered it.

He stopped her as she was opening the door leading to the roof.

"I'm not sure what line of sight anyone may have with this room. Stay low and near me, away from the edge."

Molly nodded.

Derek opened the door and peeked out. He doubted anyone had done enough homework on Molly's building to know about this roof access, but he wasn't taking any chances. He took his weapon out of his holster.

Bending low at the waist, he made his way outside. Molly was right behind him. They moved quickly and directly to the identical door that was attached to her unit. It was locked so Derek had to put a hard shoulder into it a couple times, grimacing at the noise. It couldn't be helped.

The door gave way after the third good hit and they went inside. He kept his weapon in hand as they made their way downstairs. According to Jon, Molly's house was empty, but that was only based on law enforcement reports. Others would not make their presence so known.

He could feel Molly's hand on his back as he first looked around her guest bedroom, then her bedroom. Both seemed to be empty. After the noise they'd made to get inside, Derek was willing to bet no one was in the rest of the house, either.

"It's clear. Let's see if the evidence is still here."

Molly rushed to her hamper and began digging through it. After a minute she looked up at him.

"It's gone, Derek." There were tears in her eyes when she looked over her shoulder at him. "My lab coat isn't here at all. Someone must have taken it."

Disappointment was a bitter taste in Derek's mouth. They had been *so* close. "Okay, let's grab you some clothes and get out of here. We'll have to think of something else."

He watched as she grabbed a pair of jeans and some undergarments. "Can I get my favorite shampoo, too? I still feel like I can smell smoke in my hai…"

Her eyes widened as her sentence trailed off.

"What?"

"It smelled like smoke. My lab coat and other stuff I

was wearing that day. So I didn't want to put them in the hamper. So I—" She broke off and ran into the bathroom.

Derek followed and found her bending into her bathtub.

"So I threw it all in the bathtub." She stood and turned, a huge grin on her face. She held an undisturbed evidence bag in each of her hands.

Chapter Eighteen

Molly looked around the lab where Derek had brought her to do the initial examination of the evidence. *Lab.* She rolled her eyes. This could hardly be called a lab. She glanced over her shoulder at him, scowling.

"What?" he asked.

"This is not a lab. This is a…" Molly searched for the right word. "A *preschool*."

They were at a police training facility outside of Denver. This was where future crime scene and lab technicians came to be trained.

Heaven help us all.

It was a step down from Molly's lab at Omega. She scoffed. It was *twenty* steps down from her lab at Omega. She was amazed anyone could leave this place and know how to do anything except dust for prints and tie their shoes.

Molly had the items recovered from her house on the table in front of her. Knowing they couldn't leave through her condo's front door after finding the items, she and Derek had gone back up to the roof and down through Mrs. Pope's house, explaining they couldn't get in and would need to call a locksmith. Mrs. Pope had just continued to look suspiciously at Derek and escorted them to the front door.

She felt Derek's hands encircle her waist behind her. He kissed the top of her head. "It's all we've got right now. Omega is not an option and it's not like we can get you into any police or federal labs, either. Not right now."

"I'll do my best. Let me see what they have. But I'm not making any promises."

He kissed the top of her head again. "If anyone can do it, you can."

Molly appreciated his faith in her, but she could only go so far as the electron microscope, DNA sequencer, gas chromatography and AFIS would take her. None of which seemed to be available here.

She looked at the items on the table. "You know none of this will be admissible in court. Not after the fire in the lab and me as the suspect."

"I know. But if it gets us a name, it will be worth it. Hell, if it gets us anywhere out of this dead end we've found ourselves in since the lab blew, then it's worth it." He was still standing behind her and put his hands on her upper arms, squeezing them gently. "But whatever we've got there, someone was willing to kill and die for. So it has to be something."

Molly nodded. In one bag was a set of prints. Derek had told her that the prints belonged to a man who had killed himself at the scene a few days ago. She pushed that to the side. She couldn't run them now, although she would check to see if she could access the federal fingerprint database AFIS from here. The other piece of evidence looked like some sort of communication device, although much of it had been destroyed by the house fire. But still it had the potential to tell them a lot, if she could get whatever working pieces were still left out of the melted outer shell.

She didn't want to take the evidence out of the bags

until she was ready to actually begin working on it. That meant she needed to take stock of what was available in this teaching facility.

Molly was hoping for iodine and silver nitrate to lift latent prints, but she wasn't holding her breath.

If they didn't have magnesium powder and ultraviolet light, then she might as well hang it up right now. Not to mention this place should close its doors as a teaching facility. There was no way to observe and record any latent fingerprints without those items.

She took her hair and quickly braided it so it would be out of her way. She rolled up her sleeves and donned latex gloves. It was time to get to work.

As soon as Molly began braiding her hair he knew to get out of her way. This Molly was the one he had known for four years. And she was every bit as sexy as the woman he'd been in bed with a few hours ago.

He knew not to get in her way. She was focused, albeit frustrated at not being in her own lab, and she would work the evidence until she'd gotten as much information from it as she could.

Jon and Liam would be showing up here as soon as they could. Jon had gone to his house, hoping to finally lose whoever had been tailing him. Liam would be coming straight from Omega HQ.

What Molly said about not being able to use whatever evidence she found in court was definitely true. But Derek really didn't care. He wanted to be able to move forward, not just to figure out who was behind the Chicago bombing. He also wanted to be able to know that Molly was safe. Until they knew who was behind this, she would have a target on her back. So would Derek, but he was more used to it, and more capable of taking care of himself.

Not that Molly wasn't capable. These past few days she had proven herself more than capable and much stronger than he'd given her credit for. Okay yeah, she had pulled the covers up over her head at the hospital, but when it had counted she had shown strength and fortitude.

Including when he had told her about his past.

He hadn't expected her to run screaming from the room, but he had thought it would give her pause. Pretty damn considerable pause. Not that she had been flippant about it.

Instead, as was exactly her way, she had looked at it from an angle he'd failed to consider. Derek generally did that—tried to look at situations from multiple angles to get the best possible understanding—but it was a lot harder to do when you were talking about yourself.

Derek's burner phone buzzed in his pocket. Liam was here. Derek crossed to let him in the door. Molly was so engrossed in what she was doing that she didn't even notice.

"Hey." Derek let Liam in, then quickly closed the door that led to the back parking lot of the building. "This was a good idea. Nobody will be looking for us here."

"It's the best forensic lab I could think of that might not have any law enforcement looking for Molly," Liam responded, slapping Derek on the back in greeting.

"Well, she called it a *preschool*, so I don't think she's overly impressed with the facilities."

Liam laughed. "I'm just glad we actually have some evidence to try and process."

Derek nodded. "Me, too. Were you able to update Drackett about what's going on?"

"Yes, since it's nearly midnight most of the Internal Affairs, or whatever they are, are gone. Steve looks like he's been hit by a train."

"When was the last time he went home?" Both men

knew their boss didn't have a family, but everyone needed to go home sometime.

"Honestly, I'm not sure he's been home since the lab explosion. Probably just caught a few hours of sleep on the couch in his office here and there." Liam shrugged, his respect obvious. "Where's Jon?"

"On his way. He couldn't shake his tail earlier so Molly and I got into her house to get the lab coat. Good thing, too. It wasn't where she'd remembered it being. If Jon had been looking for it, he might not have found it." Derek's phone buzzed again. "There he is now."

Derek let Jon in. "Finally shake them off?"

Jon rolled his eyes. "I must be losing my touch when I can't manage to shake five different people following me. I'm pretty sure they think I'm inside my house watching TV. I snuck out a side window and walked a couple of miles, then took a cab and walked another couple of miles. How's it going?"

"Molly's in her element. She's already been at it a couple hours. I tried to help a while ago, but she gave me such a glare that I decided I'd better leave it alone."

Both men grinned at that.

"So what is our plan?" Jon asked.

"Dependent on what Molly finds, we'll have to move from there. It's not going to be legally binding, but it is at least going to point us in the right direction."

"You're going to need to check in at Omega, Derek," Liam told him. "I have made up every story about you that I could about why you haven't been there. Hell, I even had a pretend conversation with you, with the Internal Affairs guys just a few yards away, about how you were sick and would be in tomorrow. I was supposed to bring you soup, by the way, so if you don't show up, I'm pretty sure someone will be coming to your house."

Although Liam had a great gift for storytelling, Derek was sure what he said was true. He needed to show his face at Omega tomorrow.

"And, bad news," Jon said.

"What?" That's all they needed was more bad news.

"Molly's status has been officially upgraded to dangerous fugitive. So that means even uniformed cops are going to be looking for her. I wouldn't be surprised if she showed up on the news."

Damn it. Someone was definitely trying to put the squeeze on Molly. He needed to get her out of here as soon as possible. Out of the city, back to his cabin. Jon or Liam could stay with her while he went into Omega.

Derek didn't like the thought of Molly being with anyone except him. He trusted these two men like brothers, knew they had his back, but the thought of either of them with Molly in that cozy cabin, near the bed where they'd made love all afternoon?

No, he definitely didn't like it. He'd allow it for her safety, of course, but he didn't like it one damn bit.

"Okay," he told the guys, trying not to grimace. "We'll take turns out at the cabin. We'll have to make sure we're not followed, which will be tough, but it's pretty secure. Remote. No reason anyone would be coming out there unless it's to purposely get to the cabin."

"Okay," Jon said. "It won't work for long, but the most important thing is getting Molly out of Dodge right now. Even getting pulled over for a routine traffic stop with her in the car could be disastrous. We've got to get her as far away from any type of law enforcement as possible."

Molly walked over with the evidence bag in her hand. "Hey, you guys are going to have to get me into Omega Headquarters."

Chapter Nineteen

Derek met Jon's and Liam's eyes and they all turned to her.

"No." It was in unison.

Molly blinked and looked at the other two men. "When did you guys get here?"

Jon rolled his eyes. "A while ago, Molls. I'm hurt."

"You can't go to Omega, Molly. Everyone is looking for you," Liam explained. "Things have escalated. Cops down to the last crossing guard have been told to bring you in. That you're a dangerous fugitive."

She held up the evidence bag. "There's a set of prints on here. Those I was able to get off with no problem, even with the substandard equipment." Her disdain was evident. "And I matched them to your dead guy's. I don't know who he is, but I know he touched this. I'm running him through AFIS, to see if we get a hit, but the computers are about the same speed as snails, so we should get it by the time we're all fifty."

Derek shook his head at her melodramatics. He was glad she was able to manually get the print, but Molly was right, a print didn't help them without a name.

"But this." She held up the bag and pointed at something on the communication device. "I'm pretty sure there's a drive on here that has active data. Pictures, documents or something else, I'm not sure. But I can't access it here.

There's too much damage from the fire and I don't have the equipment I need. If I try, I'll probably lose the data."

He saw how she stretched her shoulders and neck, so he moved behind her to rub her shoulders and help work out the kinks. The past couple of days had definitely taken a toll on her body.

"Fine, give it to us and we'll get the data off of it," Derek said to her.

Molly looked over her shoulder at him, and gave him a smirk. "No offense, but you can't do it."

"You can tell me how, and I'll do it. You can walk me through it. Or we can bring in one of your technicians. One that you trust."

Derek looked over at the guys to get them to back him up. But they were both staring at him and Molly with their mouths all but gaping. Derek realized it was because he was rubbing her shoulders.

"What?" he snapped.

That got their attention. "Um, Derek is right, Molly." Jon spoke first. "You'll need to let someone else do it. We can't get you into Omega. As soon as we carded you in you'd get arrested."

Molly's sigh was tired. "I'm not being conceited. I just don't think anybody from Omega can get the information off this drive except me. It's a specialization. The process is too delicate and is going to involve the use of both lasers and acid. It needs to be done in a sterile room. There will only be one chance to get the data drive separated from the casing in any sort of operational fashion."

"Even if we could get you in, Molly, there is no lab at Omega right now." Derek kept rubbing her shoulders, and pulled her back closer to him.

"Yes, there is." She glanced at him before relaxing into his chest. "The old lab, down in the basement."

Derek could remember it, vaguely. It hadn't been used in years.

"She's right." Liam nodded. "They kept it for overflow cases."

"Not that we ever have enough personnel in the lab to get to overflow cases." Molly sighed again. "But yeah, everything I need should be there."

Derek looked over at Jon and Liam. They were both nodding.

Using the old lab changed the factors quite a bit. It was in the older part of the building, less security clearance was needed there. She'd still need a swipe card, but she wouldn't have to go through a live guard to get to the lab.

"It's definitely possible," Jon said.

"Although bringing her into a law enforcement building housing a multiagency task force filled with top-trained agents may not be the wisest thing we've ever done," Liam said. "But then again, not the most stupid thing, either."

Molly turned around to face Derek and smiled. "I'm going to pack everything I need. I'm assuming that since I'm already a fugitive, taking a couple items from here won't really be a problem."

She stood up on tiptoes to kiss him, but that didn't even get her lips all the way up to his. Derek bent the rest of the way to meet her.

"Take your time," he murmured against her lips. "It'll take us a few minutes to figure out the details."

"Okay." She nipped at his bottom lip, then was gone, back to gather whatever she needed. Derek turned to watch her go for just a second.

When he turned back around the guys were staring at him again.

Liam turned to Jon and grabbed the front of his shirt.

"What just happened, Jon? Can you explain to me what just happened?"

"No, Liam. Some mysteries of the universe cannot be explained. Like how Derek finally figured out what a wonderful woman Molly is."

Derek considered punching both of them. "Yeah, you two are a regular comedy team. Like the Black Plague and Europe."

"I don't like the thought of bringing Molly to Omega," Derek said. Jon and Liam instantly got serious.

Liam shrugged. "You have to admit, it's probably the last place they'd expect her to be. I wouldn't head to Omega if I was on the run."

A thought occurred to Derek. "Is the old lab being used for cases since the explosion? If so, there will be too many people around to bring Molly in."

"No," Liam replied. "All lab work has been officially shifted to other agencies. Especially pending the charges against Molly."

"Got any ideas about how to get her in?" Derek asked. She wouldn't have to go past a live guard, but she'd still need to have a swipe card.

"Let me call Andrea Gordon," Jon said.

"The profiler?" Derek asked. He knew her, but not well. She tended to keep to herself. But then again, so did Derek.

"Yeah." Jon nodded. "I'll see if she'll let me use her swipe card to get Molly in. We've worked quite a few cases together over the past couple of years. I trust her. She already knows something suspicious is going on. I'll explain as much as I can. I think she'll be game."

"We'll have to do something to Molly to make her look a little more like Andrea. A blond wig, cover her bruises," Liam said. "She'll still need to look up at the camera when she scans the card."

"I'll see if Andrea can help us out with that, too." Jon nodded and began heading toward the door.

"You're going to need to feel that out carefully, Jon," Derek told him. "Don't tell her anything about Molly if you don't think Andrea will support this. If she decides to call it in, this will all go downhill fast."

"I will, don't worry," Jon said. "I'll let you know if she's in or not."

"Andrea was still at HQ when I left," Liam called out after him. Jon waved his arm in acknowledgment on his way out the door. "I'm going there, too, make sure there're no surprises. Give me a few minutes to get ahead of you."

"Okay. Be careful. Fill Drackett in if you can," Derek said.

"Yeah, that's a good idea. I'll text you when it's clear and Jon has Andrea's key card. Be thinking of a Plan B in case we need it."

"See you in a few," Derek replied. Liam saluted and jogged out the door.

Derek walked over to where Molly was carefully re-bagging the evidence. Concentration furrowed her brows and her long braid fell over her shoulder.

Watching her work should not make him this hot, but it most definitely did. He wished she had her white lab coat on.

"Done," she said, looking up at him. "I'm ready whenever you are. I'll be so glad to get into a real lab."

"Promise me one thing," he said to her, taking a step closer.

"I'll be careful, I promise," she told her.

Derek took another step. "I do want you to be careful, yes. But that's not what I was going to say."

"Oh, yeah? What were you going to, ohhh—" Her words stopped as he grabbed her by the hips and hoisted her up onto the lab table. It put them eye to eye. He slid his hands to cup her backside and pulled her all the way to the edge of the table, her legs falling on either side of his hips.

"I've always wanted to kiss you on a lab table," he murmured, wrapping her long braid around his hand and tugging so she looked up. Her neck was completely available to him. He trailed kisses all along her throat, delighting at her shivers.

"Actually, there's quite a lot more I'd like to do to you on a lab table and I plan to do so soon when all this is settled." He nipped lightly at her neck and she moaned.

"I never knew you had a thing for laboratory furniture," she said, wrapping her arms around him.

"Not lab furniture. I have a thing for *you* on lab furniture." He slid her even closer, still trailing his lips up and down her throat.

She laughed softly, then sighed as he nipped at her throat once more. "And you have to promise me that at least one time you'll be wearing your lab coat."

"You're pretty naughty, Agent Waterman."

"You have no idea, Dr. Humphries, but when this is all over, I plan to show you." He let go of her braid so he could frame her face with both hands and kissed her.

What was it about this tiny woman that allowed her to get to him like no one else ever had? Touched him to the point where it was difficult to think of going back to his life without her as a regular part of it?

When he finally brought his lips back from hers they were both breathing deeply. There was nothing Derek wanted to do more than lay her back on this table and show her just how much he wanted her.

But more than that, he wanted to rid them of the guillotine that was hanging over their heads. He wanted to clear her name and make sure she was safe. He wanted to make sure no one ever put another bruise on her again.

"But right now we need to get over to Omega and let you do your work."

Chapter Twenty

Molly felt like a clown with all the makeup she had on. She knew it was just to cover up any traces of the bruises, but it was so unnatural for her. Especially considering on any given day Molly didn't remember to even brush her hair—thank goodness it could be easily braided and put out of the way—much less put on eyeliner and all the other things currently being applied to her face by Andrea Gordon.

Molly knew looking like Andrea was important because of the security cameras at all Omega doors, including the older section of the building they'd be entering. She appreciated the other woman's willingness to let her use her ID card. Of course, Andrea had only done so after making a call to Steve Drackett to be certain everything about this situation was on the up-and-up.

"I look ridiculous," Molly said for at least the fifth time.

"You don't look ridiculous," Derek called out from the other room.

"He's right, you know. You don't look ridiculous, you just look a little different from what you're used to yourself normally looking like." Andrea continued putting on the makeup. "This is only so you'll look like me for whatever security guard is watching the monitors."

How was Molly supposed to ever look like Andrea? There wasn't enough makeup in the world to give Molly

Andrea's classic cheekbones and full lips, a perky nose
that was just a bit crooked, like maybe it had been broken
at one time. She always had immaculate makeup and hair:
chic, shoulder-length blond bob.

And she always wore heels.

Molly sighed. Next to Andrea, Molly looked like what
she was: a scientist who always chose sensible shoes.

But right now Molly had on a gray pencil skirt and
dark blouse, both borrowed from Andrea. She'd wanted
pants, but she was too short to wear any of Andrea's. So
skirt it was.

Molly looked different.

"You've got a pretty pained expression there," Andrea
said. "I'm nearly done. Torture is almost over."

"And it's not what you're doing. It's just that the makeup
is pretty much a representation of everything I'm not."

"Good," Andrea told her. "Makeup should never be a
representation of what you are."

Although the statement was true, it struck Molly as a
little odd coming from the other woman, especially since
she was applying the makeup with such skill. Molly realized that even though they'd both worked at Omega for
years, she didn't really know Andrea. Molly didn't know
if anyone really did. The woman tended to keep to herself.

"Do you have sisters?" she asked.

The question obviously caught the other woman off
guard. "Um, no. Why?"

"You're just really good at doing other people's makeup.
I thought maybe you practiced on sisters growing up."

"No. I had a...job when I was younger that involved
makeup."

A job when she was younger? Andrea couldn't be more
than twenty-three or twenty-four. It didn't seem likely that
she'd had a career before the one she had at Omega as a

profiler. She must be referring to something part-time in high school or college.

"Oh, okay, like at the cosmetics counter at the mall?"

Andrea smiled, but it didn't reach her eyes. "Something like that. But it was a long time ago." She continued applying the makeup in silence.

Molly hadn't meant to bring up a painful past. Time to change the subject. "Thank you for your help."

Andrea shrugged. "I'm willing to do anything I can to bring down those bastards who bombed Chicago. But to be honest, I'm doing this because Steve Drackett asked me to. I owe him, more than one."

"Well, either way, I appreciate it."

The other woman smiled and this time the smile did reach her eyes. "Okay, makeup's done. No more bruises in sight. Let's get the wig on you."

Andrea had brought a wig similar to her own blond bob. Actually the woman had a number of different wigs in the trunk she'd opened with the makeup, but Molly didn't want to ask her why after how the last questions had gone. Maybe she'd been involved with community theater.

Andrea tucked Molly's braid under a cap, then slipped the blond wig on her. She took Molly to stand in front of the full-length mirror in her room.

Molly couldn't control the little gasp that escaped her. Not only were all her bruises covered, but Andrea had done something with her eyes that made them smoky... sexy. While standing there in the other woman's clothes, with the other woman's hair, and makeup that made her face look exotic and sexy, all Molly could wonder was what would Derek think?

Even after the great night of lovemaking, Molly couldn't help but consider, if she looked like this, dressed like this, would Derek have been able to keep his distance over the past three years?

Maybe this was more of what he really wanted? It certainly would be a better fit aesthetically. Someone like the person looking at her in the mirror—poised, well-dressed, put-together—someone like Andrea should be with Derek. Not Mousy Molly.

"Whoa. Holy cow."

It was Jon. He and Derek were standing in the doorway. Jon's mouth was gaping almost embarrassingly wide.

"You look totally amazing, Molls," he said.

Molly couldn't even look over at Derek. What if he was like Jon and really liked what he saw? Molly couldn't look like this every day. Even without the wig, Molly still wouldn't look like this.

Could never look like this.

Not to mention how impractical it would be in the lab. Heels?

Plus her hair was brown.

Did Derek wish she looked like this?

Finally Molly glanced over at him. Although he was looking at her, his face was completely shuttered.

"I think it's enough to get her through a security check," Andrea said. "It wouldn't fool someone who knows us, but it will get you through the door."

Molly nodded. Yeah, she may not look exactly like Andrea, but she definitely didn't look like herself.

Derek still hadn't said anything. And Molly couldn't read anything—pleasure or displeasure—in his expression.

"All right, let's get this show on the road," Jon said. "Andrea, you've been a lifesaver. Thanks so much." He walked out of the room with the other woman.

Molly couldn't take it anymore. "So what do you think?" She gestured at herself with her hand.

He studied her a moment longer, from her sophisticated blond coif down to her heeled shoes. The shoes weren't as high as Andrea normally wore, but were still unusual for Molly.

"I think you'll pass without any problem. Anyone looking at a scanned ID picture who didn't have reason to think otherwise, would probably mistake you for Andrea."

He turned to walk out of the room, but Molly touched his arm.

"That's not what I meant, Derek." She immediately wished she had just let him go. Was she *trying* to get him to admit he wished she was gorgeous like Andrea?

She heard Derek take a breath through his nose as he turned around.

"What did you mean?" His blue eyes were cold.

"I guess I—I meant what do you think of this new look?" Damn it, now she was stuttering again.

His eyes softened at her slight stammer. He took a step closer. "You really want to know?"

"Yes." No. Why was she asking him this? She was setting him up to hurt her, and she was a fool.

He looked her over again one more time.

"I wish I could tear these clothes off your body." His voice was even more deep and gravelly than usual.

Molly looked down at her feet and closed her eyes. She knew that he would be more attracted to her like this, with all her physical flaws hidden by makeup and great clothes and high heels. Why had she forced him to tell her?

She felt his fingers under her chin. "Molly."

She didn't open her eyes, because if she did she was afraid the tears she could feel gathering might make their way out. Then she would really be mortified.

"Molly. Look at me." His tone brooked no refusal, but she still kept her eyes shut.

She felt his lips on hers. He kissed the side of her mouth, running his tongue over her lower lip, then drew back just the slightest bit. "Look at me, Molly. Right now."

This time she opened her eyes.

"Yes, I want to rip all these clothes off you. The wig and makeup, too. Because all this stuff is not you. Could never be you. And I wouldn't want it to be."

"Really?"

He kissed her again on the lips, softy. "Yes, very definitely really."

"I was afraid—"

He smiled. "I know what you were afraid of. And Andrea's look is for some men, absolutely. But I find myself drawn to long-haired brunettes wearing little-to-no makeup, generally found with their eye stuck to some microscope. Know any of those?"

"Just so happens I do." Molly could actually feel the happiness welling up inside her.

"Good. Now let's get going so we can put all this sneaking-you-into-buildings stuff behind us."

He grabbed her hand and they started out of the room, but he paused and turned to her. "I have to admit, I do like the heels. Puts you exactly at the right height for kissing." And he proceeded to demonstrate.

DEREK WANTED TO KISS every bit of the lipstick off Molly's face. Then take off all the rest of the makeup she had on, followed by that ridiculous wig and those clothes that she looked not quite comfortable in.

Then he wanted to make love to her. Her. Molly Humphries. Not some blonde, uncomfortable impersonation of someone else.

"Hey, don't smudge that lipstick," Derek heard Andrea say a few moments later.

He stepped back from Molly. "Sorry."

But smiled as Molly walked past him into the kitchen.

"I saw your aversion to how she looks. Good for you," Andrea told him.

"Nothing personal to either you or your handiwork. It's just not who she is."

Andrea nodded. "You know, her crush on you is pretty legendary at Omega." She shrugged. "But seeing you now, I realize you're the one who has fallen."

Derek wasn't sure what to say to that. He shrugged. "I just want to keep her alive and safe."

"And with you," Andrea murmured.

Derek could see why Andrea had the reputation of being the most gifted profiler at Omega. Especially for being so young. At least everything but her eyes were young. Her eyes were much older than whatever number her birth certificate said she was. The woman turned and followed the path Molly had taken to the kitchen.

They grabbed a bite to eat, some soup Andrea had available, but Derck could tell every moment they delayed was making Molly more jumpy. He squeezed her knee under the table and she smiled at him, but her smile was tight.

Finally the text came from Liam that everything was clear.

"You ready?" Derek asked Molly. She nodded. He looked over at Jon who nodded, too.

"Thanks, Andrea. I'll get this stuff back to you as soon as possible," Molly told the other woman before hugging her. Andrea was stiff for just a moment, as if she wasn't used to being hugged, before she put her arms around Molly and patted her back.

Fifteen minutes later they were pulling up at Omega. Jon drove all the way around to the farthest side of the building, far from the main entrance. Derek knew that even at this late hour there would be dozens of armed operatives inside.

This was a terrible idea.

"I'm not so sure about this, you guys." Derek had a bad feeling.

But it was Molly who was the voice of reason. "No, we've come this far. This will work. Let's just do it."

They parked and walked up to the door. Derek scanned his card first, then Jon, then finally Molly using Andrea's card. They pretended to chat while they waited for whoever was watching the security camera to buzz them in.

Now it was Molly's turn to be worried. "This isn't working. It's taking too long," she whispered under her breath, too quiet to be picked up by the audio feed.

Derek and Jon laughed as if she'd made a joke and continued talking nonsense about a football game.

But as a few more moments ticked on, Derek began to agree. He glanced at Jon. Had the security personnel figured out who Molly was? That she wasn't Andrea? Would there be agents here to arrest her at any moment?

To run now would be hugely suspicious. But he didn't want them to stay if it was leading to disaster. He reached down and grabbed Molly's hand, and felt her fingers grip his tightly. Both she and Jon were having the same thoughts as him.

Derek was about to turn and have them run, damned how it looked. He had to get Molly out of there.

Then they all heard the electronic buzz of the door being unlocked and opened. They were in.

Chapter Twenty-One

Finally, a real lab. Molly was aware of the price they'd paid to get her here. Derek and Jon, and even Andrea and Liam, were all risking their careers by getting Molly into this lab. Because they believed what she was doing was vital.

Molly didn't plan to let them down.

Even though it felt strange, she kept Andrea's blond wig on. She'd probably need it to get back out of the building.

The first thing she wanted to do was to start running the prints she'd already gotten through AFIS on the much faster computer than the one at the training lab. It should give them results within the hour.

Much more difficult was the process of accessing the data drive of this comm device. Because of the burn damage she was going to have to chemically remove the top layer of the device in order to access the drive. It was tricky, and like she'd told the guys, she'd only get one chance at it—if she didn't get it the first time, then the opportunity was lost. Molly donned gloves and set the comm device, still in the bag, out on the table.

Her operation would have to be done in the clean room, since any air particles—dust, allergens, dirt—could combine with the gasses and chemicals she'd be using and contaminate the surface area of the device, making the recovery of any data from the drive impossible.

Of course, air particles were better than heat elements. Anything remotely flammable near these chemicals and Omega would be losing its second lab in a week. But Molly wasn't really worried about that.

Unlike the training lab, this one was fully stocked and functional. Gathering the materials took Molly a little while since she wasn't as familiar with the layout, but at least everything she needed was here. She would much rather have been working in her lab. She cringed when she thought about poor David. Things might be bad for Molly, but at least she was alive.

Once she had everything ready, she walked over to where Jon and Derek sat near the door. "Okay, I'm going into the clean room. It will take me a while to get into my dust-particle suit. To be honest, I'm not sure how long the process itself will take me. It depends on how many layers of the comm device are burnt and the status and stability of the data drive itself."

Derek stood and kissed her on the nose. "Let's get this done so we can get your name cleared and you can go back to being a brunette."

"That would be my pleasure. I really hope we find something."

"Somebody has gone to way too much trouble to make sure we don't get this far," he told her. "We'll find something."

As long as Molly didn't screw up getting the data. She took a deep breath.

"I can do this."

His large hands came up and cupped Molly's face. "I have no doubts whatsoever."

She turned to the side and kissed his palm. "You won't be able to come into the clean room. I can't take a phone or anything in there, either."

"Then I'll see you when you're done."

Molly nodded and, grabbing the evidence on a special plastic tray, headed back to the clean room. First she went into the changing area on the outside. She put on her protective clothing: coveralls, boots, gloves, hood and face mask. Opening the airlock door, she set the tray with the comm device inside. She closed the outer airlock door and locked it—it was lockable on both sides—then waited for the air shower. The strong blast of air filtered through ultralow particulate air filters removing any contaminants from her person and the evidence bag.

Only after all that was done could she open the second door and exit the airlock into the clean room itself. The only sound she could hear was her own breathing. She wasn't in a clean room very often. Most evidence didn't call for its use, and when cases did call for it, she generally let someone else do the work. It was a unique experience, the quiet, the overall isolation. Molly imagined it was similar to what astronauts must feel.

The entire room was surrounded by glass except for the floor and ceiling. The table in the middle contained all the items she needed to access the data drive from the device, removing the burnt layers. The outer shell wasn't as important, since they already had the fingerprints from it. Molly used a helium-neon laser to carefully cut away the outer layer. Then using hydrofluoric and hydrochloric acid in very controlled doses she was able to eat away some of the burnt layers attached to the drive.

It was repetitive and exhausting work, eliminating the unwanted, damaged parts bit by bit, without hurting the important data drive underneath. The wig itched, but she ignored it. She ignored every discomfort and focused on the task at hand.

Until finally she had made enough of an opening in the device to carefully remove the drive.

As near as she could tell, it was relatively undamaged by either her workings or the fire. She carefully placed it into a new evidence bag. It was barely bigger than her thumbnail. Now they would get it to a computer and see if it was worth all the pain it had caused.

Molly stepped back into the airlock, closed the clean room door and began stripping off the protective gear. There wasn't as much need for care coming out as going in and she was back into the regular part of the lab in just a couple of minutes.

Jon and Derek were huddled around the computer at the desk.

Derek saw Molly. "How'd it go? You looked pretty intense in there."

Molly held up the bag holding the small data drive. "As near as I can tell it is undamaged."

"We got a hit on AFIS while you were in there. The prints came back from our dead guy."

"He was in the system?"

"Multiple times over." Jon responded, but was still staring at the screen. "And it's not good. Although weird as hell."

Molly put the drive down carefully on the table and walked over to them. "Who is it?"

"Not necessarily who as much as who he's associated with. The White Revolution Party, a white supremacy militant group out of Idaho." Both Derek's and Jon's faces were grim.

"That's not who you thought was responsible for the Chicago bombing?" she asked.

"We were considering them. We pretty much always consider them for everything. They're dangerous and brutal," Jon said.

Derek nodded. "So we were investigating them, but they were still part of a pretty long list, and not even near the top of it. But it always sucks even worse when you find out your terrorists are homegrown. Of course, it could also explain how someone in the government could more easily be in bed with them."

"Let's see if we can find out anything more useful on this thing." She carefully took the drive out and connected it to the computer equipment whose primary function was to read any usable data from a drive or any working portion of one.

Data began to flicker on the screen, plans for the Chicago bombing and then pictures.

"That's Lenny Sydney, leader of the White Revolution Party," Jon announced. "All of these guys are White Revolution."

Picture after picture of people in the terrorist group looking at plans for the bombing.

And with them was Senator Robert Edmundson. Obviously involved in the planning.

Derek's curse was angry. Guttural.

"That son of a bitch personally thanked me last week for all I was doing," Derek said. "Called us and asked what he could do to help us get some traction on whoever was responsible for Chicago."

Jon shook his head. "Offered us his personal contacts overseas if that's what was needed."

"Why would he take all these pictures?" Molly asked. "He has to know that these would be highly incriminating."

"Look at them." Derek pointed to the screen. "The way

no one is looking at the same place at the same time. The weird angle. These were taken without either party knowing."

"Somebody was trying to blackmail Edmundson, or have leverage over him," Jon stated.

Derek's phone began ringing in his hand. He immediately put it on Speaker.

"You've got perfect timing, Drackett. You are never going to believe what we found on the drive we recovered."

"Derek—"

"Senator Robert Edmundson is our player within the government, Steve."

"What?"

"I'm looking at irrefutable proof that he is tied to the White Revolution Party and that they planned the Chicago bombing together."

"Damn it."

Nobody wanted to think of someone with the caliber and charisma of Edmundson being behind an attack that took American lives.

"Exactly how we felt," Jon said.

"Well, we've got even more immediate problems," Drackett continued. "Whatever prints you ran connected to the guy from the White Revolution Party? That triggered some sort of alarm with Internal Affairs—obviously Edmundson was waiting to see if anyone would try to run that data," Steve said.

Molly looked over at Derek. The words *alarm* coupled with *Internal Affairs* did not sound good.

"What exactly are we talking about here, Steve?" Derek asked him.

"Local law enforcement are right outside the building, looking for Molly."

"To hell with that." Derek barely let Steve get the

sentence out before he responded. "No way. This is a witch hunt set up by Edmundson to track Molly down and silence her. Now we've got proof of Edmundson's guilt. It won't take a judge five minutes to give us a warrant once they see this."

"I agree. But unfortunately I'm not in charge of what is happening outside right now. I was called away from the building, probably on purpose, right as the locals were being called in. I'm on my way back now. But they're going to breech the building in the next five minutes."

"To hell with that," Derek repeated again. "What's your ETA, Steve?"

"At least fifteen minutes."

Derek looked at Molly. "I'm sorry, Steve." Derek clicked off the phone before the director had a chance to respond.

He turned to Jon. "I'm not letting them take her. I'll sneak her out or use force if necessary. But I'm not turning her over while Edmundson is still out there."

"Then I'm going with you. You can't go out there blind, alone. If she—"

Seriously, they were going to talk about her as if she wasn't even in the room? "Hey, I'm right here! I'd like to be included in this conversation."

They at least looked at her, although both seemed committed to their current course of action.

She continued, "Look, before we do anything crazy like rush out there guns blazing and just get ourselves killed like Edmundson wants, let's think this through. If you sneak me out or use any sort of force, won't that be considered aiding and abetting a known fugitive?"

"It doesn't matter," Derek said.

"Derek, it *does* matter. You both are going to lose your jobs over this, and you know it. Steve isn't going to be able to help you and even when my name is cleared there's a good chance that it won't be enough to save your careers."

"Molly, I'm not sending you out there," Derek said, tone clearly uninterested in further discussion.

Molly looked at Jon, hoping he could be persuaded to see reason.

Jon just shrugged. "I'm with him, Molls. Your life is not worth it."

Why wouldn't they see reason?

"Look, you said it yourself. A judge will give you a warrant for Edmundson's arrest immediately. Let me give myself to the police, you guys hurry up and get that warrant through, and get me out. I'll be okay. Even Edmundson can't have people everywhere all the time."

She could see just the slightest hesitation in Derek's eyes. He wanted to protect her, and she loved him for it, but he knew there were permanent ramifications for what he was about to do.

But then the hesitation was gone, determination back in its place. He was going to protect her no matter what it cost him. And damned if she didn't love him for that stubbornness, too.

"I can't lose you," he whispered.

She realized Derek couldn't be reasoned with, and Jon was just going to fall on the sword with him in some misguided bro-code pact.

Except Molly wasn't going to let them do that.

"Okay, we'll do it your way," she told them. "But I need you guys to help me get a couple of things out of the clean room. If we're leaving, it's got to go with us."

The both nodded. "Okay, then we need to come up with a plan," Derek said. "Do either of you know anything about this section of the building?"

They followed Molly to the clean room quickly. She

opened the airlock door and immediately opened the second door, without waiting for the air shower. That action completely contaminated the clean room, but it didn't matter, it was about to get much more contaminated. She stood to the side and ushered with her arm for the guys to enter.

"I vaguely remember some of this section, but it's been years since I've been over here, honestly," Jon was responding.

As soon as they were through the second door Molly went back out the first one, closed it and turned the heavy manual metal lock on the door.

Derek and Jon were now trapped inside.

She couldn't hear inside the room, but she saw Derek's face as he stopped talking to Jon and looked over at the closed door. His eyes narrowed as he walked quickly through the airlock to the outer door, and realized it was locked.

His fist came up and slammed against the thick glass of the door. Molly startled even though she could barely hear the sound. Fury was written on every aspect of his features. He spoke to her through the glass—angry words—but she couldn't tell what he was saying. Based on his face, she was glad.

He couldn't get out; the clean room seconded as a bomb disposal area and could withstand a relatively large explosion, so hitting or even shooting at the glass wasn't going to help Derek.

She saw him get himself under control and look her in the eyes. He mouthed the word *open*.

She shook her head no.

He flattened both his hands against the glass.

Molly, please.

She walked closer to him, wanting to let him out, but knowing she couldn't.

"I can't lose you," she repeated his words back to him. But it was the truth.

She didn't know if he could understand her, but couldn't stay to find out. She turned back around and walked out the door of the lab and the building, taking off her blond wig as she went. Colorado Springs Sheriff's officers were everywhere. Lights were blazing in the husky dawn light.

She raised her hands far in the air. "My name is Molly Humphries and I am surrendering. The two agents I took captive are inside, unharmed."

She heard the sound of guns being cocked and knew they were pointed at her. As two officers rushed up to her and forced her onto the ground and put her hands behind her back to cuff them she hoped she wasn't making the worst mistake of her life.

Chapter Twenty-Two

As soon as Molly walked out the door, Derek did what he did best: worked the problem. He immediately called Steve Drackett.

"Molly just surrendered to local PD and whoever else is out there," Derek told his boss with no greeting whatsoever.

"Good. That was the best thing to do. I was afraid you were going to do something completely asinine like try to get her out using force. That would not have been a good idea."

"Yeah, well, that was my plan. But she locked us in the clean room and went out on her own."

"She probably saved you a couple of years in prison, not to mention your career."

"Damn it, Steve, I would've gladly spent a couple years in prison, if it would save her life!"

"Molly, as usual, is thinking more clearly than anybody else in the room, it sounds like. This is not a dichotomy, Derek. We know the danger she's in. We can protect her."

Derek rubbed a hand over his face. God, he hoped what Steve said was true. "Get some agents on her, Steve. Right now."

"I've already got three on her. Nothing is going to happen. And the chief of police in Colorado Springs is a personal friend. I will make sure he's apprised of the situation and knows that Molly is not to be handed over to anyone, short of a presidential order."

Derek didn't like Molly being out of his care, but he knew Drackett was right—she'd probably just saved him, or at least his career. He'd thank her as soon as he throttled her.

As soon as she was back safely in his arms.

"We need to start the warrant on Edmundson."

"I already have someone in the office working on the initial paperwork. I'll be there in five minutes. We'll get you out and get Molly."

Derek gripped his phone tighter. "Hurry."

"You just hang tight," Steve told him. "Oh yeah, I guess Molly didn't leave you much choice." He chuckled.

Derek clicked off the phone. Everybody was a comedian.

"Is he on his way?" Jon asked, leaning against the worktable in the middle of the room.

"Yeah. Five minutes."

"I can't believe she locked us in here," Jon continued. "I didn't even see it coming."

"Drackett thinks she kept the two of us out of jail, but she and I are still going to have words about this."

And by *words* he meant he was going to keep her in bed for a week until she promised never to do anything to potentially threaten her life ever again. But Jon probably didn't need to be privy to that info.

True to his word, Drackett, surrounded by a dozen of Colorado Springs' finest, entered the lab just a few minutes later. The police searched the room while Drackett let Derek and Jon out of Molly's prison.

"She's on her way to the station," Steve told Derek

immediately. "Our agents are providing reports every fifteen minutes."

"I'm going there," Derek said.

Drackett stepped in front of him. "No, you have to stay here, get things going with the Edmundson arrest. It's all I can do to convince them that you're not to be arrested with her, Derek. They're not going to let you anywhere near her at the station."

"He's right, man." Jon popped him on the shoulder with the back of his hand. "You can do more good for her here. Let's go."

Derek was still torn.

"Updates every fifteen minutes," Steve reminded him.

Derek nodded, hoping he wasn't making a mistake he'd regret for the rest of his life.

But as the day went on, Drackett's people reported in at the promised intervals, assuring Derek of Molly's well-being and even sending pictures every once in a while. Although she looked uncomfortable, bored and tired, she at least was safe.

Derek could admit to his petty pleasure that she looked miserable in the pictures. Good.

Drackett called in a favor and woke a federal judge even though it was early in the morning. The information on Edmundson and the White Revolution Party was sent to him electronically and within the hour the warrants had been signed for the arrest of the leaders of the white supremacy group as well as Senator Edmundson.

Derek just wished the son of a bitch was here in Colorado, so he could arrest him himself. But he was in Washington, so the local feds were being called in to make the arrest. The arrest would be quiet, of course.

Because this was a terrorist attack, under the Patriot Act he could still be arrested even though these photos probably couldn't be used in court. Hopefully the photos would be enough to get a confession. Either way, every law enforcement agent in the country would be searching for evidence that would further tie Edmundson to the bombing.

That bastard could expect to spend the rest of his life behind bars. If he was lucky.

Liam and Andrea had come in to help in whatever way they could. Jon and Steve were currently poring over the pictures and data found on the drive. Derek was putting in calls to figure out exactly what evidence was held against Molly that had her being detained across town. Nobody seemed to know. Nor could anyone produce a warrant with an actual signature for her arrest.

That would be because there was no evidence linking her to the lab explosion and probably no real warrant.

A video call came through in the conference room where they were all working. Congressman Donald Hougland. Although Steve answered the call, Derek completely turned his back on the man. He didn't have time for yet another speech about how he wasn't doing his job right and as part of *the best of the best*, he should be doing better.

Steve tried to waylay the congressman completely upon answering. "Congressman Hougland, right now is not a good time. We've had a significant breakthrough in the Chicago—"

The congressman held up his hand. "I just heard about Robert. I've known him for years, and have seen him make some questionable judgments for what he thought were good reasons, but this is beyond unforgivable."

Derek turned back around to look at the man. At least he was being reasonable this time.

"Congressman—" Steve started again.

"No, just let me finish. I know some harsh things have been said about your competency over the past few days.

It ends up someone was deliberately hindering your progress, which is sabotage, not ineptitude. So I apologize for my remarks. I was wrong."

"Thank you, Congressman Hougland. Everyone here appreciates that, I'm sure."

The older man laughed. "But they've got work to do, I know, I know. And while they don't want to be rude—or maybe a few do—" he looked directly at Derek "—they don't really want to talk to me. Understandable. Keep up the good work, everyone." Hougland disconnected.

Derek appreciated Congressman Hougland's statement more than the man probably knew. Someone willing to admit when they were wrong, publicly, was the type of person needed in government office.

But right now, he just wanted to make sure Molly got out of that police station. The work was tedious, proving up the chain at multiple agencies that there was no actual evidence on Molly, nor was anyone in possession of a signed, original warrant for her arrest.

Without the warrant, the police couldn't hold her. "Steve, I've traced the stuff on Molly and nobody has a signed warrant. It looks like all the agencies were just following each other with the APB put out on her. Nobody actually questioned it."

"Good," Drackett said. "I'll call Brandon Han and send him over. He'll have her out in no time."

Brandon was a fellow agent and gifted profiler, who also held a degree and license to practice law. The man could run circles mentally around most people. Derek was sure he wouldn't have any trouble getting Molly released.

For the first time since she'd walked away from him in the lab, Derek could feel the pressure in his chest easing. She was going to be okay. Whatever plans Edmundson had for taking her had been thwarted.

But the plans Derek had for her? Those were definitely not thwarted and she was in so much trouble. Spending at least the next two days with her tied to his bed until she saw the error of putting herself in danger ought to be a good start. Derek grinned and had to shift a little in his chair from the way his whole body tightened.

But that was tonight. Right now there was so much paperwork to be done—the necessary, but boring part of any member of Omega Sector's job—it would take the rest of the day to put even a slight dent in it.

After all, it wasn't every day that you were behind the arrest of a US senator. The evidence they had on the leader of the White Revolution Party was more circumstantial, but Derek was willing to bet Edmundson would roll over on everyone at the White Revolution Party if it kept him off death row.

But something about all this was bugging him. Obviously the White Revolution Party and Edmundson had partnered together on the bombing. These pictures were almost irrefutable evidence of that. Not only of pictures of them together, but of them together looking at plans.

The problem was why these pictures and info even existed in the first place. Their existence was not in Edmundson's nor the White Revolution Party's best interest, so they definitely hadn't taken them, or if they had it had been for blackmail purpose.

But Edmundson had known the data drive with the photos existed because he'd blown up the lab rather than have its contents come to light. Understandably so, now that its contents had been made public.

But how had the drive come into existence in the first place? It didn't matter for the purpose of Edmundson's arrest, but it would need to be answered.

Three hours later Drackett got the news Derek had been waiting for and immediately relayed it to Derek.

Molly was out. Safe. Brandon Han was giving her a ride home since she was exhausted and—Steve had written it down so he could get it right—"knew Derek was going to blow all of this out of proportion and she just didn't want to deal with him yet."

Everyone snickered at that.

Maybe three days tied to his bed…

Derek rolled his eyes. "Thanks for the exactness, boss."

Steve smiled. "Just part of my job."

It was late afternoon by the time they were all ready to call it quits. Things weren't wrapped up, but at least the events set in motion by them today could carry on without their direct supervision. It was time to go home. No one had gotten a full night's sleep since the lab explosion nearly five days ago. At least tomorrow was Sunday.

"Molly and I probably won't be here on Monday." Derek told Steve on their way out. "She still needs some recoup time from what happened to her at Belisario's compound." Not to mention that Derek had plans for her that very definitely did not involve Omega.

Steve nodded. "I understand."

"I sent those pictures and all the info from the data drive to you via email," Jon told him. "Just in case you guys are looking for something to do."

"Yeah. We won't be." Derek slapped Jon on the back. "See you guys Tuesday."

Derek drove to his house, willing to give Molly a little more time before he went over there and "blew everything out of proportion." Oh, she had no idea. He'd take a shower, grab a change of clothes and head over to her place. He didn't plan to come back here until Tuesday.

Derek clicked on his computer while putting on his

clothes after his shower. He would take the laptop with him although he didn't plan to spend much time, if any at all, looking at it. He had better things to do.

He uploaded the email Jon had sent with the pictures, so they'd be readily available. He'd need to study them all in close detail later. He was just shutting the computer down when one picture caught his attention.

The man in the corner with Edmundson. He was obviously part of Edmundson's inner circle. But Derek recognized him.

He'd killed him in the jungle near Belisario's house.

This man worked for Edmundson, but obviously worked for Belisario, too. What did that mean? Some sort of double cross? Was Belisario the one who had taken the pictures? To use for blackmail?

Or maybe they'd underestimated Belisario's involvement all along. They'd taken him at his word when he'd said he was questioning Molly for his "partner."

But maybe Belisario wasn't just doing Edmundson's dirty work. Maybe Belisario had a lot to lose also if Molly had discovered and reported the evidence.

Derek grabbed his phone. Jon and Steve had already left the office, but someone would still be there. Derek would email Steve about his theory, but he wanted to make sure someone was already looking into Belisario right away.

Liam answered the phone in the conference room they'd all been working in. Perfect. Liam knew the most about Belisario from his time in Vice. Derek explained what he'd seen in the picture, confirming his theory about Belisario being a key player in the bombing.

"It would be a perfect cover-up," Liam agreed. "A white supremacy group working with Latinos? No one would've been looking for that pattern."

"Definitely."

"Hang on, a report about Belisario came across my desk a couple hours ago, but I haven't had a chance to look at it."

A moment later Liam let out a curse.

"What?"

"Report says Belisario's not at his house, Derek. That he left this morning around seven o'clock in a plane."

Damn it. That was right after Molly got arrested. "Do we know where he was going?"

Liam's curse was ugly. "Colorado. The DEA's inside informant said Belisario mentioned he was coming to Colorado." Derek picked up his home phone while still on the line with Liam on his cell and called Brandon Han's number since Molly didn't have a phone right now. Han's phone immediately went to voice mail.

"Liam, has Brandon checked back in?" He finished tying his shoes while he waited for Liam to check if Brandon's ID had been swiped anywhere in Omega.

"He's not here, Derek. Nowhere in the Omega facility."

"And I just called his phone. He's not answering."

"Let me ping his phone, check his location."

Derek was already running toward his front door.

"He's at Molly's condo."

"I'm on my way there now. Get Jon and Steve and meet me there. But keep this quiet. No locals," Derek told him as he jumped into his car and pulled out of his driveway, tires squealing. He disconnected and threw his phone down in the passenger seat.

Belisario was here in Colorado because he wanted to tie up loose ends.

That loose end was Molly.

Chapter Twenty-Three

All Molly wanted to do was go home, take a shower, sleep and see Derek. Not necessarily in that order.

After the fourth hour of sitting in that interrogation room, with nobody having come in to see her, Molly had been pretty sure she'd made a mistake by turning herself in. How long could they keep her there? Indefinitely? Molly wasn't sure exactly what the rules were when it came to a case that was tied to a terrorist attack. She was pretty sure they were different from a regular case. Maybe she'd die of starvation or old age or boredom right in the room.

She had thought she would be questioned, but apart from the first officers who had brought her in, no one had asked her anything. Which was a little disappointing since she had been looking forward to rebutting whatever evidence had been found against her. Molly worked with evidence all day every day. If anyone could prove evidence was false, it was she.

But they never brought it.

After what seemed like a million hours, there had been a brief knock on the door before Brandon Han stuck his head in.

"Hi, Molly. Steve Drackett asked me to put on my lawyer suit and come get you out. Are you doing okay?"

Molly could've kissed his beautiful Asian face, but he

probably wouldn't have appreciated it. He was a pretty straight-laced guy, not to mention one of the most brilliant around Omega.

"Yes, I'm fine. Just tired and bored."

"I understand." His nod was sympathetic. "It shouldn't be too much longer. I'm filing the paperwork for your release and since no one can find an actual arrest warrant, I'm betting they'll be pretty quick to let you go."

"Great. I'm ready."

"Well, nothing is ever quick when it comes to paperwork at a police station, but I'll be back as soon as I can."

That ended up being another two hours.

But now Molly was out. And Brandon told her that Senator Edmundson had been arrested. So it sounded as if everything had worked out the way it should.

She wondered if Derek was still mad at her. Hopefully she could make him understand why she'd had to do it.

Brandon gave her a ride home, stopping by a fast-food place on the way.

"Do you want to go by Omega or just straight home?" he asked her.

"Home, I guess. Derek is going to blow all of this out of proportion. I don't think I want to deal with him yet."

Brandon raised an eyebrow. "Yeah, you know Waterman. Legendary for blowing everything out of proportion."

Nothing could be further from the truth. But Brandon called it in to Steve Drackett as they drove to Molly's condo.

Brandon parked. "I'm just going to come in and check out your place real quick, if that's okay."

Molly was relieved. After the week she'd had, a friendly presence inside her home was welcome.

Molly stood against the inside of the front door while Brandon inspected the rest of the house.

"Looks clear," he told her, smiling, when he returned. "Do you want me to stay with you? Until Derek, or somebody else, if you really don't want to deal with him, can get here?"

Molly didn't want to be a coward. She was going to have to be alone in her home sometime. It might as well be now. "No, with Edmundson already arrested, I think I'm safe. But thanks for the offer."

"No problem." Brandon reached to open the door. "But don't stay here alone if you get scared. Call Derek, or me, or anyone. Post-traumatic stress is a real—"

Brandon's words were cut off as the door burst open. The butt of a gun cracked him in the head before he could do anything and Brandon fell to the floor unconscious.

Pablo Belisario strode into the room, followed by two of his goons. One shut the door while the other grabbed Molly.

Molly was so flooded by terror, remembering what had happened the last time she'd been in Belisario's presence, she couldn't even fight. Not that she could do much damage to the much bigger man holding her.

They backed her away from the door toward her kitchen. Brandon was lying on the floor unmoving.

"What do you want me to do with him, boss?" the man asked Belisario. "Kill him?"

"Not just yet, but tie him up," Belisario told him, then turned to Molly. "It might end up that the agent can be of some use to us alive. We can always kill him later."

Belisario walked over to Molly and grabbed her chin. She tried to pull away, but his fingers sank painfully into her jaw. The man holding her arm gripped her tighter, also.

"Of course, keeping someone alive can occasionally come back to haunt you," Belisario continued, giving her face a brutal shake. "For example, I was supposed to kill you, but I didn't. And here you are causing all sorts of trouble."

It was clear that Belisario did not plan to make the mistake of keeping her alive twice. Through the haze of fear, Molly tried to figure out why he hadn't already done it. Why he'd come here himself. But as long as she was still alive, she was going to at least try to make the man see reason.

"Mr. Belisario." Molly's words came out funny because of how he held her face. "We found evidence, but nothing had anything to do with you. It was all concerning Senator Edmundson. Evidently, he was working with the White Revolution Party in the Chicago bombing a couple weeks ago."

Belisario released her chin and tilted his head at the man holding her arm. He threw Molly down into one of the chairs at her kitchen table.

"White Revolution Party, the white supremacy group? What a shame the senator got caught up with people like them." He tsked and shook his head. "But sometimes you have to do business with people you find distasteful."

There was obviously something Molly didn't understand here, a vital piece of information she was missing. And it all came down to what could be important enough that Pablo Belisario would be here, in Colorado, himself. That would happen only under the most dire of circumstances, she was sure.

And then the obvious truth hit her. "You're part of the Chicago bombing, too."

"So clever." He touched her on the cheek and Molly cringed away. "I guess I should expect that from a scientist."

"There's something on the data drive that incriminates you also."

"The Chicago bombing was *my* plan. Edmundson already had ties to the White Revolution Party long before that happened. But he was key to me being able to do business with them. They are white supremacists after all, and I am Latino. Ignorance of that magnitude is so difficult to swallow."

"But why would you want to perpetrate a terrorist attack on Chicago? On anywhere in the United States? What would you stand to gain?"

"Interestingly, the White Revolution Party, Edmundson and I were all united on that one point—we all wanted the US Government focused on terrorists and international threats. Something like this happens and everyone in the government gets thrown into a tizzy. Money is flung everywhere."

Belisario's smile made Molly's skin crawl. "Edmundson wanted the government to propel money toward whatever he was trying to get funded. I don't know exactly what it was, and I don't care. He called himself a 'patriot who was willing to slaughter a few to protect the many.'"

He leaned down close to her. "The White Revolution Party and I realized that every time the national focus is on solving some big attack, or finding some elusive Middle Eastern terrorist group, less focus is on us and our activities. I've been able to move billions in product since the bombing, easier than ever before.

"The three of us working together made a perfect triangle. The White Revolution Party planned and created the bombs, since they had the means and knowledge, but they couldn't actually plant them because of how they are watched by federal agents all the time. I had no knowledge of how to make bombs or where to put them, but was not being watched for this sort of activity, so my men could plant the explosives."

His face, only inches from hers, was almost giddy with his own self-importance.

"And Edmundson handled misdirecting the investigation away from you or the WRP," Molly finished for him.

"Exactly." He stood straight again.

"It was a good plan." Molly had to admit it. She also had to admit to herself that there was no way she was leaving this house alive. Not with all the knowledge she now had about Belisario.

Molly had no idea how to get herself out of this. As long as Belisario kept monologuing, she was relatively safe, but that couldn't go on forever.

"But something went wrong, didn't it?"

Belisario's lips tightened into a thin line. "No honor among thieves. That's the saying, is it not? I knew I could not trust either party I found myself partnered with, but especially Edmundson. It would be just like him to try to make himself the hero by proving the White Revolution Party and I worked together on the bombing. Thus the drive with all the pictures of the WRP leadership and Edmundson together."

Out of the corner of her eye Molly saw Brandon shift slightly on the floor, then still himself. Maybe he was awake.

"Ends up my instincts were correct. Edmundson was already giving signs of double-crossing me, threatening to lead law enforcement my way. So I decided I best show Edmundson the damning evidence I had on him, although I didn't necessarily plan to use it."

"The pictures," Molly whispered. She tried to shift farther away on her chair, but a hand instantly clamped down on her shoulder.

"Yes. But then the WRP found out we were meeting and got nervous and sent their own representatives. And that's when your Omega agents caught the trail. The drive wasn't destroyed in the fire and the WRP man was killed.

"Edmundson hired someone to blow up the lab when we learned the drive wasn't destroyed. And asked me to question you to make sure all the data had been eliminated."

Belisario shook his head as if in disbelief. "Despite all our attempts otherwise, that drive is still in the hands of law enforcement. Unfortunately, with Edmundson out of the picture I no longer have a foothold in law enforcement. But I don't need it, because I have you."

"M-me?" Molly stuttered. Although it sounded like a good thing, it was bad. Really bad.

"There are, unfortunately, a couple of photos on the drive that are incriminating for me. One of my men that I had placed within the WRP was in one of the photos. You, and the men who rescued you from my estate, are the only ones who can make the link between him and me."

He smiled almost sweetly at her.

"I need you to call your friends and tell them to come here. Right now."

"But…" Molly did not want to call Derek and invite him to his death. "There were, like, twenty people who rescued me."

The blow from Belisario knocked her off her chair. The world spun as the guy behind her picked her up and plopped her back in the chair.

"That was for the lies, the made-up names you gave me before," Belisario said. He turned and pointed at Brandon Han. "Bring him over here."

They dragged the agent over to the table. Blood was oozing from the wound on his head just behind his ear.

Belisario pulled out a gun elongated by its silencer and pointed it at Brandon's head.

"We know there were two men who broke in to the

estate that night. You will contact them right now, or I will kill this man."

Brandon's brown eyes looked at her, but he didn't say a word.

"One."

Could she trade Brandon's life for Derek's?

"Two."

"Okay, stop!" Molly yelled. "I will call him. But I don't have a phone."

"See, he did come to some use, didn't he?" As if they were having a genteel conversation about dinner plans, Belisario handed her his phone. "By all means, use mine."

She dialed Derek's burner phone number—thank God he had forced her to memorize the new number—and listened as it rang. She thought he wasn't going to pick it up, which would at least take this impossible situation out of her hands.

"Waterman."

"Derek, it's Molly."

"Molly, are you okay? Where—"

Belisario snatched the phone out of Molly's hand. "Derek Waterman is it?"

"Belisario." Molly could hear Derek's voice even though she didn't have a phone up to her ear.

"Oh, good, you know who I am. I will make this very easy for you, Mr. Waterman. I have the lovely Ms. Humphries right here with me at her house. Hold just one moment, please." He put the phone on her table and extended his hand out to Molly. She reluctantly placed her hand in his. When he brought it up to his lips, she barely restrained her cringe.

But then he turned her hand around in his and calmly yanked sideways while twisting on her pinky.

Molly felt the bone break.

White dots flashed in front of her eyes and she let out a scream at the unexpected searing pain. Only the thug behind her with his grasp on her shirt kept her upright in the chair at all.

She saw Brandon stand up and lunge across the table, even with his hands tied, before he was roughly thrown back down by the other man and slugged in the face for his efforts.

Molly tried to get her breathing under control, but could only seem to sob as she cradled her wounded hand to her chest. Belisario brought the phone back up to his ear.

"Now, now," he laughed. "Is that the language becoming of a federal agent? Hold just a moment and let me put you on Speaker so you and Ms. Humphries can hear each other more easily."

Molly knew Belisario wanted her in hysterics to motivate Derek to do what he asked. But even knowing it, she couldn't seem to stop sobbing.

"Molly? Molly, baby, hang in there," Derek said. "I'm coming, okay?"

"That was her pinky, Mr. Waterman," Belisario told him. "I will break another of her bones every ten minutes until you and the other man who was with you at my estate arrive. Alone."

"I've got to find Liam, and I'm across town, you bastard. There's no way I can get there in less than thirty minutes."

"Unfortunately, then, it seems like Ms. Humphries will have three more broken bones by that time."

Belisario smiled at Molly and disconnected the call.

Chapter Twenty-Four

Derek was going to kill that son of a bitch.

He hit the side button on his watch so he had an exact countdown for the time. Because he was sure Belisario would be true to his word about every ten minutes.

Molly's scream as that bastard broke her finger would haunt Derek for a long time. He was still sweating even though the weather was mild. Adrenaline coursed through him.

He was ready to fight.

Liam was on his way, as were Jon and Steve. He estimated Liam's arrival would be in another ten minutes. Jon and Steve's sometime after that, depending on where they were when Liam was able to contact them.

Derek had told Belisario it would take him thirty minutes to get there. He'd lied.

He was already on the roof of Molly's house. And he'd be damned if he was going to let another of Molly's bones be broken.

Eight minutes.

Mrs. Pope had been very surprised to see him when he'd knocked on her door a few minutes ago. He'd shown her his badge. "Molly's in trouble, Mrs. Pope. I need to use the roof access to get her away from the bad people who have her."

He'd expected hysterics, expected her threatening to call the police, expected to have to traumatize the old woman by locking her in a closet.

Instead she'd let him in saying, "Is it like that remake of the *Hawaii Five-O* show? I love that program. I watch it every week."

"Yes, ma'am. Something just like that." He smiled and quickly made his way up the stairs.

"Book 'em, Danno," she'd called after him, giggling like a schoolgirl.

Booking had been the plan before Belisario had decided to start torturing Molly. Now all bets were off.

Seven minutes.

Derek dialed Liam's number. "Bastard called me. Said he would break one of Molly's bones for every ten minutes it takes you and me to get to him."

"Do you believe him?"

"I heard him break one already."

Liam let out a blue streak, which matched Derek's feelings exactly. "I'm five minutes out."

Five minutes was cutting it close to the next deadline.

"There's roof access to her condo. I'm already on it. They won't be expecting me coming from this way or this early."

"Is Han in play?"

Brandon Han was not only the smartest guy they all knew, he was wicked good in hand-to-hand fighting. Black belt in all sorts of martial arts. But if he was dead or injured, he wouldn't be any help to them.

"Unknown. We can't count on him."

Six minutes.

"I'll get in position," Derek told him. "You ring the doorbell. They won't be expecting it to be us this soon. You take out whoever is at the door, I'll try to take out the rest."

"We don't know how many are in there, Derek. We may be way outnumbered."

"I know. But I also know that Belisario has no intentions of letting any of us leave alive anyway. We may as well go down fighting if we have to go down."

Derek grimaced. Molly would be right in the middle of the firefight.

"Jon and Steve are about ten minutes behind me. I'll tell them to just come in hot. Might as well add more partygoers to this throwdown. See you soon, brother. Be careful."

Derek heard the car speed up as Liam disconnected.

Five minutes.

The roof door was still broken from where they'd gotten in yesterday, so Derek inched it open as quietly as possible. The element of surprise was his only tactical advantage.

Weapon drawn, he eased down the steps, opened the door that led into Molly's hallway. No one seemed to be upstairs, but Derek checked again, just in case. Although taking someone out without notifying everyone downstairs of his presence would be just about impossible.

Four minutes.

As he neared the main stairs, Molly's quiet crying tore at his heart. He just wanted to get her to a place where she never had to cry again. To get Belisario out of their lives for good.

Liam would be ringing the doorbell soon and Derek wanted to be in place to do the most damage while they had the element of surprise. The two men talking allowed him to slip down the stairs without anyone hearing him.

He eased himself around the corner and kept to the wall, taking small steps toward the kitchen.

Three minutes.

"So Ms. Humphries, Mr. Waterman didn't think he'd

be here for thirty minutes. And it looks like we're coming up on the ten minute mark. What do you think, your other pinky this time?"

Derek expected Molly to cry more at that, but after a moment of quiet she spoke.

"You know what, Belisario, go—"

Derek couldn't clearly hear the rest of Molly's statement, but he was pretty sure that what she wanted Belisario to do to himself was anatomically impossible. Derek smiled at her spunk. That was his girl.

"We'll see if you're so spirited in two minutes," Belisario replied.

Derek felt the silent vibration in his pocket. A text from Liam.

At least three minutes out. Not going to make it in time.

Damn it. Molly didn't have three minutes.

Forget the doorbell. Derek texted him back. Get here as soon as you can and come in loud and hot.

K. Stay away from the front door.

Derek put his phone back in his pocket and eased to the corner, dropping low so he could peek around without being spotted. He only needed one second to ascertain the situation.

Belisario stood across from Molly; one of his men stood directly behind her. Brandon Han, alive but restrained, was on the other side of the table, injured.

If he had to do this alone, he would round the corner, take out the guard closest to Molly, then Belisario. He damn well wasn't going to sit here while another finger was broken.

Derek was about to make his move when he felt the muzzle of a gun against the back of his head.

Damn it.

"Stand up. Keep your hands up, too." The man took

Derek's weapon out of his hand and nudged him forward with his gun. They rounded the corner.

"Boss."

"Ah, Mr. Waterman," Belisario said. "It seems like you were able to join us just a little sooner than you thought."

"I like to be early for my parties." Derek made eye contact with Molly, giving her a half smile, hoping it would be encouraging. She was pale and visibly sweating.

"And where is the other person who was supposed to be with you? Niam, is it?"

"Liam. He'll be here soon."

"Not soon enough to save Ms. Humphries from another broken bone, I'm afraid."

Derek watched as Molly blanched, the last of the color draining from her face.

"How about if you break one of mine instead, if you've got some weird fetish with the bone-breaking thing." It wouldn't be the first bone he'd ever had broken. Growing up on a ranch in Wyoming had made sure of that.

And it would be much less painful than watching Molly suffer more.

Which evidently Belisario had figured out. "Oh, no," he said. "I'll keep my word. One of Ms. Humphries bones every ten minutes."

Derek dove for the other man, he didn't care if it got him shot. But Belisario's two goons grabbed him before he could pound the man's face in like he wanted to. One on each arm, they dragged him back.

Brandon leapt across the table at Belisario when he came near Molly again, but Belisario clocked him in the head with the butt of his gun. Han fell unconscious to the floor.

Molly backed away from Belisario as he came closer to her, fear obvious on her face.

"Stop, or I shoot your boyfriend in the kneecaps, then still break your finger."

Molly stopped. Belisario took a step forward.

Then the whole front of the building seemed to cave in with a huge crashing noise.

Liam had arrived.

Derek took advantage of the men's confusion and yanked himself from their grips. He hit the first one with an uppercut that no doubt broke the man's nose and sent him straight to the floor. Derek leapt behind Molly's couch, landing hard on the floor, knowing Belisario's other man would be shooting at him. Bullets flew past him, as he grabbed his backup weapon from his ankle holster. He felt a searing pain in his arm as a bullet grazed him.

Scrambling to the side, Derek jumped up from the side of the couch the man wasn't expecting. Derek was able to get off a shot before the man could turn his gun back toward him. He fell dead from Derek's chest shot.

Derek rushed over to Molly, putting her directly behind him as Liam wrestled with Belisario. Derek had his weapon raised and Belisario in his sights. He could take the shot and finish Belisario right here. Rid the world of a scumbag.

He had done it many other times with much less reason than he had right now. Judge, jury, executioner.

But he thought of Molly, could feel her hand tucked inside the waistband of his jeans again like she had in the jungle. She trusted him to do the right thing.

"Belisario, put your hands up right now, or so help me God, I will shoot you."

Belisario stopped fighting Liam. He turned and looked at Derek with such a look of malevolence that Derek was sure he was making a mistake by letting the man live. He would have to spend the rest of his life protecting Molly from this possible threat. It would never go away.

But Derek realized he was okay with that. If it meant proving to her—hell, proving to *himself*—that he wasn't the man he used to be, then it was worth it.

Derek lowered his weapon and brought Molly around to his side, careful not to jar her broken finger, as Liam began reading Belisario his rights. Liam was getting his handcuffs out when the henchman Derek had knocked unconscious began waking up and moaned on the ground. Liam's attention was divided for just a moment as he looked over at the man.

Belisario took advantage of it.

He shoved Liam away and grabbed for the gun on the table next to him. He swung it up straight toward Molly.

Derek didn't hesitate. He put three bullets through Belisario's chest. The man died with the same look of evil intent that he'd had when he'd lived.

Derek didn't regret the kill. Not for a split second. The man he had been, the man he was now and the man he would be in the future would always be willing to do whatever he had to do to keep Molly safe.

No matter what.

Chapter Twenty-Five

"You're a moron, you know." Molly rolled her eyes at Derek.

Derek just sat in the chair across from her hospital bed, holding the gauze against his arm where the bullet had grazed him. After their arrival at the emergency room, Molly had insisted that Derek be treated first. She wasn't a medical doctor, but she knew that his bleeding wound needed more immediate care than her broken pinky. Her finger wouldn't get any worse, unlike what his loss of blood could become.

But he'd refused to let any doctors see him until her finger was taken care of.

So now they were waiting for the numbing to take place in Molly's finger so the doctor could reset it. He said it was a clean break, would just need a splint. No permanent damage. Derek's wound, after a quick glance, had also been deemed of the impermanent kind, although it would still need bandaging.

"I'm glad you killed him."

Derek shrugged. "Once he pointed that gun at you he was a dead man."

Molly reached her uninjured hand out to him and he took it. "I'm sorry you had to do it, though. I don't want the taking of another life weighing on you."

"You know, before he pointed the gun at you, when

he and Liam were fighting, I could've taken the shot. It would've been a clean shot, Liam was far enough out of the way. And I thought about it. After everything that had happened, nobody at Omega would've questioned it."

She ran her fingers over his. "Why didn't you?"

Derek stood up and came to stand in front of her where she sat on the hospital bed. He linked their fingers together so that their palms were against each other. "I realized that what you said yesterday was true. The man I was—the decisions I made in the past—they don't define who I am now. I lived in a dark world. But I don't have to stay there anymore."

Molly brought their joined hands to her lips and kissed his fingers. "Well, I'm glad that I never have to worry about him or any of his goons being inside my apartment ever again. So thank you."

The doctor came in and reset Molly's finger, a painless process due to the anesthesia. Not long after, Derek's wound was cleaned and properly bandaged. After the paperwork, they were deemed clear to leave.

"I don't have a house to go home to now," Molly said as they walked out of the hospital in a much less clandestine fashion as when they had snuck out just forty-eight hours ago.

"Yeah, I told Liam to come in loud and hot, but I was envisioning him breaking through the door himself with some uniformed cops, not tearing down your entire dining room with his car."

"I guess I need to check into a hotel or something." Molly hadn't really gotten that far in her thinking. Now that the danger had passed and she wasn't in pain, Molly was bone-weary exhausted.

"How about you let me do something I should've done

after our night together three years ago? Hell, before our night together three years ago."

"What's that?"

"Move you in with me. Court you. Win your heart. Not necessarily in that order."

Molly smiled up at him as he turned her around and leaned her against the car. "You've already done one of those things. A long time ago. The other two, I think, can be arranged."

Derek looked down at her in the way she had always dreamed of having him look at her. "You're the strongest person I know, Molly. I love you."

He kissed her.

"But you're still in trouble for locking me in the clean room."

Molly wrapped her arms around his neck. "I love you, too. And maybe I can find a way to make it up to you."

"Yes. But after you rest. You need some sleep." He trailed a finger down her cheek.

"Okay, but it involves me wearing a lab coat and heels." She got in the car as he opened the door for her. "And nothing else."

She saw his eyes bug out and his whole body jerk. She smiled wickedly back up at him. He made her feel wicked and sexy and smart and strong.

He leaned down and kissed her, taking her breath away. "Okay, maybe sleep can wait."

* * * * *

Bang!

Amber awoke with a start at the loud noise and was suddenly struggling to breathe as Dex threw himself on top of her, his gaze darting around the room.

"What's going on?" she whispered, as she tried to extricate herself from beneath him, very aware that her nightshirt had ridden up to her belly and that Dex had apparently shed all of his clothes during the night except for his boxers.

He glanced down at her as if only just now seeing her, then rolled off her. "Are you okay?"

"I think so. What was that noise?"

"Gunshot."

She stared at him in shock. "Are you sure it wasn't thunder?" As if in response to her question, thunder boomed overhead and another incredible wave of rain began pouring in earnest.

"That sound came from inside the house."

ARRESTING
DEVELOPMENTS

BY
LENA DIAZ

MILLS
BOON

First Published in Great Britain 2016
By Mills & Boon, an imprint of HarperCollins*Publishers*
1 London Bridge Street, London, SE1 9GF

© 2016 Lena Diaz

ISBN: 978-0-263-91892-2

46-0116

Our policy is to use papers that are natural, renewable and recyclable products and made from wood grown in sustainable forests. The logging and manufacturing processes conform to the legal environmental regulations of the country of origin.

Printed and bound in Spain
by CPI, Barcelona

Lena Diaz was born in Kentucky and has also lived in California, Louisiana and Florida, where she now resides with her husband and two children. Before becoming a romantic suspense author, she was a computer programmer. A former Romance Writers of America Golden Heart Award finalist, she has won a prestigious Daphne du Maurier Award for excellence in mystery and suspense. To get the latest news about Lena, please visit her website, www.lenadiaz.com.

Thank you, Allison Lyons and Nalini Akolekar.

Chapter One

Dex looked out the cockpit window of his Cessna Corvalis at the vast wasteland of the Everglades racing below him at 190 knots. The monotony of sand-colored saw grass went on for miles, broken only by occasional muddy canals and vast islands of mangled cypress, their roots sticking out of the brackish water like giant knobby knees. If the Glades were anything like the marshes back home in Saint Augustine, he didn't know how anyone could stand the rotten-egg stink of rotting vegetation enough to want to visit for very long, let alone live there.

"I don't get it, Jake." He held his cell phone to his ear while he looked out the windows. "You worked your butt off to convince me to front the money to create Lassiter and Young Private Investigations. But just a few months after leaving everyone you know—including me—and setting up shop in Naples, you're ready to close the doors. For what—this swamp full of smelly plants and more alligators per capita than people? Can't you get *Faye* to move instead of *you* moving to Mystic Glades?"

He maneuvered the stick and dipped the wing, veering from his flight plan for a bird's-eye view of the town that had been at the center of their recent investigation but was now going to be his friend's new home. *Unless Dex could talk him out of it.*

"Hold it," Jake said. "What do you mean 'this' swamp? Aren't you still in north Florida?"

"I was. But then you called last week to tell me that you and the former target of our first and only case were an item and that you were quitting. I left my billion-dollar enterprise on the brink of ruin with people I barely trust so I could talk you out of this foolishness."

Jake snorted. "Don't give me that. Lassiter Enterprises runs so smoothly no one will even notice that you're gone. More than likely, you're using me as an excuse to hide from the latest girlfriend you dumped. Who is it this time? That intellectual property rights attorney you introduced me to last Christmas? Didn't you date her for several months? I thought you two were getting serious. Veronica something-or-other?"

"You wound me deeply to imply that I would use our friendship as an excuse to avoid my commitment issues."

"Uh-huh. What's the name of the woman you're running from this time?"

"Mallory. I think she wants to kill me."

"They usually do. Dex? *Exactly* where are you?"

He tapped the touch screen of the GPS navigation system. "Good question. My state-of-the-art airplane isn't acting so state-of-the-art right now. It's blinking like a caution light on steroids." The screen went dark. "What the…?" He rapped the glass with his fist.

"Tell me you aren't flying over Mystic Glades," Jake said.

Dex looked out the side window. "As a matter of

fact, I think I am. And it doesn't look any better from up here than I thought it would. I count fifteen, maybe twenty ramshackle wooden buildings down one long dirt road. Looks like something out of the Old West, or a ghost town, or both. Where are the houses? Where are the cars? Heck, where's the *town*? Is that all there is?"

"It's bigger than it looks. There are side roads hidden under the tree canopies. It's fairly spread out. And most of the townspeople use canoes or ATVs to get around more than they use cars. But I'm pretty sure I've told you most of that already. Do you even remember our last call? The one where I said I was *getting married*?"

"I remember *that* part. It was right before you said 'I quit.'" He pressed the stick, nosing the plane lower while pulling up on the throttle to reduce air speed for another circle. "This place is in the middle of *no*where—as in *no* bars, *no* nightclubs, probably *no* satellite service. How are you going to keep up with football season out here? I-75 or Alligator Alley or whatever the locals call it is the closest thing resembling civilization, but that's miles away. Tell me what it is about this place that you find so appealing, 'cause I'm sure not seeing it."

"I didn't catch everything you said. The cell service near Mystic Glades is unpredictable at best. But I *can* tell you the town has a way of growing on you. About me getting married—I may have…"

The phone went silent. Dex pulled it back to look at it. The call still showed active. He put the phone back to his ear. "Jake?"

"Still here. Can you hear me?"

"I can now. Hang on a sec." He thumped the instrument panel again, but it remained dark, useless. Thankfully, it was a clear summer day with good visibility.

But he was going to raise hell with the manufacturer when he got home. The plane was just a few months out of its shiny new wrapping and still had that new-plane smell. It shouldn't have had *any* issues, let alone a full instrumentation meltdown. He shook his head in disgust. Maybe he should get into the airplane manufacturing business instead of high finance and investing in other people's ventures. He could teach those yahoos a thing or two about quality standards.

"Dex?"

"Yeah. You said something about getting engaged?"

"Uh, about that. We decided on a very short engagement. We're already married."

Dex noisily tapped the side of the phone. "This thing must be messing up again because it sounded like you said you already got hitched. Without inviting me to the ceremony. Which means you can kiss the shamelessly extravagant gift I would have gotten you goodbye. Wait…*when* did you get married?"

"That's what I'm trying to tell you. We did the deed yesterday. We're in the Bahamas for the next two weeks. Freddie—Faye's friend, the one who owns Callahan's Watering Hole—gave us the trip as a wedding present."

Dex shook his head and sent the plane into a turn, heading in what he believed was a southwesterly direction toward Naples Municipal Airport. He'd rather head straight home to Saint Augustine, but he couldn't risk flying that far with a dead instrument panel. "Looks like this was a wasted trip."

"Sorry, man. I had no idea you'd fly out there without telling me first."

"Honestly, I didn't, either. But when I complained about you quitting our little business experiment, my assistant encouraged me to surprise you. He insisted it would be good for me to get away. And I figured I might be able to talk you out of a big mistake. Guess I should have come sooner."

"Marrying Faye *wasn't* a mistake," Jake bit out, sounding aggravated.

"Okay, okay. Sorry. I will graciously admit defeat. I guess I have to welcome Faye into the family now. Maybe I'll even buy you two a present after all."

"Gee, thanks."

"Hey, what can I say? I'm a softie."

"When we get back, I'll call you and we'll decide what to do about the company. You could always try to make a go of it without me. Just drop 'Young' from the name."

"Without my former-police-detective partner there'd be no point. Who'd want to hire an ex-navy pilot turned financier to hunt down a cheating husband or find a missing person?"

"I couldn't have solved Faye's case without your help. You're not too shabby as an amateur sleuth."

"Yeah. I can search the internet and make phone calls with the best of them."

"Actually, most of the time that's exactly what detectives do—research and interview witnesses." A woman's voice sounded in the background. Jake murmured something to her, then cleared his throat. "I've, ah, got to go."

"Wait. Jake?"

"Yeah?"

"All kidding aside. Are you sure about this? About Faye? You haven't known her very long, and half that time you were taking turns pointing guns at each other. I just… I want to know that you're going to be okay."

"Are you getting sentimental on me, Dex?"

"I don't even know what that word means."

Jake laughed. "Well, you don't have to worry. I may not have planned this, but Faye's the best thing that ever happened to me. I love her. She's my whole world."

The certainty in his friend's voice went a long way toward reassuring Dex. Maybe Faye was what Jake needed to heal him from the mistakes of his past. God knows he'd had his share of tragedy and was long over-due for some happiness.

"Then I look forward to meeting her. Enjoy your honeymoon." The call cut out as Jake was saying good-bye. Dex shook his head again and put the phone away as he tried to judge his altitude. Lower than he was comfortable with. He was about to edge the nose up to climb higher when he noticed a young woman in a canoe.

Her dark brown hair hung in waves to the middle of her back. Even from the cockpit he could see the long, shapely tanned legs that paired nicely with a curvy body wearing only a skimpy yellow tank top and khaki shorts. He whistled low in admiration. She looked bet-ter than anything he'd seen in months. He just wished he could make out the details of her face to see if it matched the rest of the sexy package.

On impulse, he waved at her, but she didn't wave back. She might not have seen him waving, but more likely she probably thought he was an idiot. He couldn't blame her for that. He was about to increase air speed when a thick mist seemed to come from out of nowhere and wrapped around the plane like a shroud. He tapped the instrument panel again, hoping he could at least get an altimeter reading. Nothing. He was flying blind.

A scraping noise sounded against the bottom of the

plane. He cursed and put it into a climb. The mist suddenly cleared. An enormous cypress tree stood dead ahead, its moss-covered branches reaching out like giant claws.

He banked hard left while throttling up. The branches made a sickening scraping noise against the underbelly of his Cessna, but she did her job, clearing the deadly tree. He laughed with relief and wiped a bead of sweat from his brow. That was close—too close.

A dull thump sounded from the engine. An alarming shudder ran through the fuselage, making the springs in his seat rattle. Instead of the familiar, reassuring dull roar of the twin turbocharged power plant, all he heard now was the sound of air rushing past the windows. He watched in stunned disbelief as the single propeller began to slow.

The engine had just died.

He immediately tried a restart with no luck. At such a low altitude there wasn't much room to recover. The controls were sluggish. He fought to keep the plane on an even keel and catch some lift beneath the wings while continuing the restart attempt. But it was a losing battle with the engine refusing to catch. He flipped the button on his headset to make the one call he'd hoped never to have to make, and never *had* made in all his years of flying fighter jets in the navy.

"Mayday, Mayday, Mayday. Naples Municipal, this is Bravo Two Seven One Charlie Baker, a Cessna TTX with total engine failure attempting a forced landing in the Everglades. Last known location approximately two nautical miles southeast of Mystic Glades. Mayday, Mayday, Mayday."

No answer. Not even static.

AMBER FOUGHT DOWN her panic and paddled her canoe toward shore. The pilot in that fancy little green-and-white plane had waved at her. But that didn't necessarily mean that he'd recognized her. Maybe he was the friendly type. It wasn't like there was an airport in Mystic Glades, so he was probably just a stranger passing overhead. She'd hidden out here for over two years without anyone finding her. There was no reason to fear the worst now.

Tell that to her shaking hands.

She reached the shore and realized she could no longer hear the plane's engine. The noise had stopped suddenly instead of fading away. A sickening feeling shot through her stomach. She hopped out of the canoe and ran around a clump of trees to look up at the sky in the direction where the plane had gone. It was a small spec now, probably more than a mile away. As she watched, the wings dipped back and forth and the plane dropped alarmingly low. Then it lifted, as if it were gliding and had caught a rush of air, before tilting crazily and disappearing behind a line of trees.

She clenched her hands together, waiting for the plane to rise above the trees again. *Come on, come on.* A full minute passed. Nothing. No plane. No sounds but the usual insects and frogs that created a constant low buzz that rarely ever stopped. He couldn't have crashed. There would have been smoke, wouldn't there? But if he hadn't crashed, she'd have seen the plane again.

Maybe he was one of the drug runners who used the Everglades as their own private highway to ferry their poison from city to city. But usually they used boats to get through the canals. And the plane she'd seen couldn't land on the water. It was sleek and expensive looking, like a minijet with a propeller—without a pontoon in sight.

She started forward, then stopped. *No. Don't try to help him.* People who can afford planes like that don't just disappear. Someone will notice that he's missing. They'll send a search party. At the most, he'll be out here a couple of hours while they figure out how to reach the crash site.

If he'd even survived the crash.

Outsiders would need guides through the swamp. Guides meant hiring locals, most likely from Mystic Glades, which meant soon the place would be crawling with people who *would* recognize her.

She ran to the canoe. Grasping the sides, she put one foot on the bottom, ready to shove off with the other.

What if he survived the crash? What if he's hurt? What if he's hurt so badly that he needs immediate care?

She *couldn't* help him. That wasn't something she did anymore. She'd learned that lesson the most painful way possible. A familiar stab of grief and guilt threatened to overwhelm her. But she ruthlessly locked those useless emotions away.

Okay, assume he's not hurt. He can find his own way to Mystic Glades. But he could just as easily wander into the swamp and get lost. He could stumble into a nest of alligators or step on a snake. The Glades might be beautiful but they were dangerous, teeming with wildlife, emphasis on *wild*. Only those who understood its dangers—and respected them—could avoid them and thrive out here.

He's not your responsibility.
But he's still a human being.

Her shoulders slumped. She couldn't pretend she didn't know he was there. She had to at least check on him.

She stepped out of the canoe and tugged it up onto a muddy rise beneath some trees. Too bad he'd gone down in one of the areas unreachable by boat. She had a good, long hike ahead of her. She grabbed her walking stick, double-checked that her hunting knife was sheathed at her waist and then headed out. She hoped she wasn't making a horrible mistake. But, then again, no mistake could be worse than the one she'd already made.

Chapter Two

Dex drew a shaky breath. He was still breathing—definitely a plus. His heart was still beating, adrenaline making it pound so hard it seemed to be slamming against his rib cage. And the plane wasn't on fire—yet. Two more pluses. But the big minus was that he was hanging upside down, strapped to what was left of his seat, with jet fuel dripping down the ruined fuselage onto his shirt. And he was pretty sure he'd cut his right leg, since sharp pain shot up his calf every time he tried to maneuver his foot out of the tangled mass of metal above him.

His main concern was the jet fuel. The noxious smell made it difficult to breathe. But more worrisome was that if any of the fuel made contact with the hot engine, he was going to go up like a human torch. He had to get out of the plane and out of his fuel-soaked shirt.

Without taking off his seat belt, he couldn't reach his trapped leg to free it. But he didn't want to unclip the belt and fall to the ground. No telling what damage that might do to his leg or what he might land on. He tilted his head up—or down, depending on how he looked at it—to see what was beneath him.

The plane had gone sideways and then turned over

as it went down. A massive tree had peeled the top back like a can of tuna before dumping him and the Cessna onto the ground below. He supposed he should be grateful to that tree, since it had slowed his descent and saved him from diving nose first into the mud. The thick, now-broken branches had cushioned the fall and were now suspending the cockpit a few feet above the mud. All in all it was a miracle that he'd survived.

The muddy grass a few feet beneath his head appeared to be clear of debris. If he could work his leg free he could drop down without doing too much more damage. He used his free leg to kick at the metal trapping his right foot. Once, twice, three times. Another sharp pain in his calf was the price of freedom as the metal snapped and broke away. He pulled his knees up to his chest, put his left hand over his head to protect himself, then released his seat belt. He dropped and rolled, coming to rest on his backside.

He hurriedly shed his shirt and tossed it toward the plane as he shoved himself to his feet. After a quick look around to assess his surroundings, which basically consisted of cypress trees and saw grass, he clopped through the semi-firm ground to the one body of water he could see—a large puddle. Whenever it rained he imagined this whole area would probably be underwater. Right now it was a mixture of soft dirt and soggy bog. He dropped to his knees and sniffed the water to make sure it wasn't jet fuel. The putrid smell wasn't pleasant but at least it was biological, not man-made.

Hating the necessity of it, he cupped the water and used it to scrub his arms and chest and as much of his back as he could reach, ridding himself of the dangerous jet fuel that had coated his torso. Then he sat and yanked his pant leg up to see what, if anything, he could do about his injuries. Blood smeared his skin, but after washing it away he wasn't all that worried. The bleeding had mostly stopped and the cuts didn't look too deep. Except for one small puncture wound, mostly his leg had just been scraped, no worse than skinning a knee.

He dropped his pant leg into place. Now that he was out of danger of being roasted alive, time for his second priority. Getting the heck out of Dodge. He pulled his cell phone out of the clip on his waistband and sent up a silent prayer that the phone wasn't broken as he typed his pass code to unlock it. But a few minutes later, after turning in every direction, holding the phone up above his head, then down toward the ground, the screen still showed the same thing.

Zero bars. No service. *Useless.*

He shoved it in the holder. Might as well face what he'd so far been avoiding. He drew his gaze up to his plane and groaned. Even though he'd known it was beyond being salvaged from what he'd glimpsed while hanging from the pilot's seat, seeing the whole thing now was devastating.

The fixed landing gear pointed up at the sky. One wing was completely sheared off. He didn't see it anywhere. The other, still attached, was snared in a pile of broken branches. The tail had snapped off and had landed in the mud behind the fuselage. He shook his head in disgust. Not because of the money this would cost him. He could easily absorb the loss. But to see a piece of beautiful machinery destroyed like that was akin to a Monet being wadded up and tossed in the trash. It was a damn shame, a waste.

He shaded his eyes and looked up at the sky, a beau-

tiful, bright blue unmarred by clouds, with no sign of
the mysterious mist that had engulfed the plane right
before the engine died. Even if his Mayday call hadn't
gone through, that sky would still soon be dotted with
other planes, or helicopters, searching the marsh for
him. Because even though he was often lazy about filing flight plans, his assistant religiously checked behind
him and would have insured the plan was submitted.

Yes, instead of heading straight to the Naples airport
and then driving from there to Mystic Glades, he'd made
a slight detour to get an aerial view of Mystic Glades
first. But that had only taken him a few miles out of
his planned flight path. As long as the transponder in
his plane was working, a rescue crew would be able to
zero in on his location.

Transponder. *Was* it working? It was part of the instrument panel that had gone on the fritz. But the system had built-in redundancies to insure it could survive
most crashes and send out a signal if it received a ping
from a transmitter, like the kind a rescue plane would
send. He studied the wreckage, looking for any tell-
tale signs of smoke. There were none. After waiting a
few more minutes, he decided to chance a closer look.
It should be safe, as long as he kept an eye out for any
warning signs of an impending fire—and stayed away
from the jet fuel.

He worked his way to the cockpit, approaching from
the far side this time since it seemed fuel-free there. The
instrument panel was a disaster. No way to tell if the
transponder was working or not. If it wasn't, that was
more of an inconvenience than a concern. It wasn't like
he was in an uninhabited area. Mystic Glades couldn't
be more than two, three miles away.

Of course, the trick was making sure he headed in the right direction. But he could use the sun to figure out which way to go. Navigating by sun or stars was a rusty skill, but one that had been ingrained in him during his pilot training in the navy. Still, there was no point in risking getting lost if a rescue effort was under way. Which, based on the anticipated arrival time in his flight plan, should be soon.

Knowing the National Transportation Safety Board would immediately take possession of the plane and site for their investigation into the cause of the crash, he figured he might as well take advantage of his time alone to do some of his own investigating.

Getting to the engine compartment wasn't as difficult as he'd anticipated, since the access panels had been peeled back like the top of the plane. Since the plane was upside down, he ducked down and looked for anything obvious. Most of the engine was intact. Only a few parts had been ripped away or crushed on impact. Everything looked normal.

Except for the electrical tape.

What the…? There were two long pieces of tape, or rather, one long piece that had been burned in two. He pulled out his cell phone and took some pictures, then zoomed the screen. Wait, no, that couldn't be. He shoved the phone in its holder.

Bracing himself on a twisted piece of metal, he followed the piece of tape. One end was attached to the edge of the engine compartment. The other was wrapped around a bundle of wires—a crucial bundle that provided power to instrument panels, including the transponder and the engine. Someone had pulled those wires free of their normal harness and used the tape to hold them in place. Which pretty much guaranteed that during flight, with the heat and vibration from the engine, the tape would fail. The wires would have dropped down onto the hot manifold. If the heat seared through their protective coating, that would have caused a catastrophic failure. Judging by the burn spots on the wires, that's exactly what had happened.

Since electrical tape wasn't standard equipment in any engine compartment, especially a brand-new plane, he could only reach one logical conclusion.

Someone had tried to kill him.

AMBER CROUCHED BEHIND a large fern that protected her from the sharp ends of a massive saw palmetto, totally mesmerized by the way the sun slanted off the golden skin of the impressive male specimen thirty feet away. She didn't know why he'd taken off his shirt, but she certainly wasn't complaining. The way his muscles rippled beneath his skin as he walked was fascinating, and an amusing contrast to his dark blue dress pants and expensive-looking but thoroughly ruined dress shoes. Since his footprints were the only ones she'd found after she'd reached the plane crash site, he must be the pilot. And the lack of bodies in and around the plane reassured her that no one else had been onboard. No one had died.

But based on how he was limping, she wasn't sure that would hold true for long.

His right leg seemed to be the one that he was favoring. From the rips in his pants, she assumed he'd been hurt during the crash and wasn't just suffering from some kind of disability. Unfortunately, the smears of mud on his back and chest meant that he may have washed himself in one of the brackish pools of water near the plane. If he'd done the same to his injuries, he might have introduced some nasty bacteria into his system. People who got lost in the Glades tended to succumb to exposure or infection just as often as other causes. If he didn't get medical attention soon, he might become one of those statistics.

So far he was heading in the right direction, toward Mystic Glades. As long as he continued that way, he'd reach town before nightfall. Her former townspeople might not exactly welcome strangers, but they would never turn away someone in need. Whoever was running The Moon these days would have some kind of medicine or potion to treat him. Or maybe Freddie would drive him to the nearest hospital in her ancient Cadillac, assuming the thing was still running. Either way, the pilot would get the help he needed. There was no reason for Amber to let him see her. All she had to do was keep following him, and somehow steer him if he went off course.

SOMEONE WAS FOLLOWING HIM.

Normally, Dex would have called out to whoever was hiding in the bushes, padding after him in the mud, keeping a good thirty or forty feet back, from what he could figure. But that was before he'd realized someone was trying to kill him. Knowing *that* had changed his perspective a hundred-eighty degrees.

He couldn't imagine his nemesis—whoever that might be—calculating the exact location where he might be when the wires in his Cessna burned through. There were too many variables for that. But it hadn't exactly been a secret at the office that he was flying to

Naples, and that he was going to then drive up to Mystic Glades. Maybe whoever wanted him six feet under had planted someone near Mystic Glades to finish him off if their plan failed and he didn't crash. Or, in this case, if he *did* crash and the impact didn't kill him.

A faint crackling noise sounded behind him, like a twig breaking in half. He pretended not to notice and kept going. He needed to wait until he was near a larger clump of trees instead of just the small groupings he was passing now as he slogged through the marshy grasses. Then he'd catch his pursuer.

Just thinking about someone hiding out here like a coward to attack him was pissing him off. That and this awful heat. He wiped sweat from his brow, surprised to find his hand wet enough to shake off droplets. When had it gotten this hot? Yeah, it was probably around noon, but still, the cooling marsh breezes had been comfortable an hour ago when he'd started on this trek. Now it was as if someone had turned the sun up twenty degrees and was trying to cook him.

His shirt. That had to be it. Without his shirt to protect him from the sun, he was baking out here. Maybe he should sit in the shade for a few minutes and cool off. No, not with someone following him. He had to take care of that problem first. Then he'd sit and cool off.

A group of trees about thirty feet ahead looked like the perfect place to catch his follower unaware. The trees suddenly wavered and shifted. What the…? He stopped, wiped more sweat from his brow and shook his head. He blinked a few times until the trees stopped dancing around. The heat. It had to be the heat. He idly leaned down and rubbed the growing ache in his right leg, then wobbled forward.

He reached the trees and ducked behind the largest one and then crouched down to wait. He pulled out his cell phone, ready to snap a picture when his pursuer came into view, figuring that if he lost this upcoming battle at least there'd be a picture of his attacker for police to find later. It would be a small victory to hold on to as he breathed his last breath. For some reason, that seemed funny—in addition to being pathetic—and he almost laughed out loud, just barely keeping it together, reminding himself he couldn't risk alerting his prey.

His prey? Right. When had he ever been a hunter? This time he couldn't contain his laughter. He clamped his hand over his mouth but changed his mind when he started to lose his balance. He grabbed a low-hanging branch on the tree beside him and kept his phone in his right hand, poised to snap his all-important picture.

Good grief, it was hotter than Hades. His friend Jake was a fool to want to live here.

Half-dried mud crunched like sand beneath someone's feet. Dex leaped out from behind the tree, snapping pictures.

No one was there.

He shifted and heard the crunching sound again. He looked down, wiggled his toes in his shoes. Crunch. Wiggle. Crunch. Wait. Was that him making that noise?

A shadow shifted beside him. He whirled around, snapping pictures as he fell to the ground. The shadow became a beautiful woman standing over him, her face mirroring concern. As she reached out a delicate-looking hand, he snapped another picture, then let his hands fall to his sides. All his strength had strangely drained away.

Her blessedly cool hand touched his brow. It felt so good he pushed his head against her palm.

"You're burning up," she said.

He blinked until he could focus on her face. His breath caught. "Canoe Girl! I waved at you." He frowned and waggled his finger. "You didn't wave back."

"I…must not have seen you. Sorry."

"No worries. I'm Dex. But you can just call me Dex."

"O…kay. Dex. Let's take a look at that leg of yours."

He grinned up at her. "Honey, you can look at anything you want."

She rolled her eyes and moved to his right leg. He lifted his head to watch, but it felt so heavy he dropped it back down.

"Ouch." He rubbed his head, wondering why it suddenly hurt.

Cool air rushed against his heated skin as she pulled his pant leg up.

"Hey, Canoe Girl. What's your name?"

"Canoe Girl works." She drew in a sharp breath. "I'm guessing you didn't have these red lines going up and down your calf before the crash."

"Nope." He dropped his phone and used both hands to lift his heavy head to look at her. "I'm guessing that's a bad thing?"

She nodded. "Could be. If not treated right away." She looked past him. "No one in Mystic Glades knows how to treat something like this, unless things have changed."

"Unless things have changed? You don't live there, Canoe Girl?"

"Um, no." She pushed his pant leg down.

"But you're familiar with it. You *used* to live there?"

She shot him a look. He should have known what that look meant, but her face went out of focus and he closed his eyes.

"Do you have any medicine in your plane?" she asked.

"Nope. Fresh out. Where do you live, beautiful?"

"That must be one bad fever." She brushed her hands on her shorts and stood. "We've got to get you to Mystic Glades. Someone there will take you to the hospital. Come on." She held her hand out to him.

He frowned, not at all pleased. "Do I have to get up? It's kind of comfy down here. It would be even more comfy if you lay down with me."

"No, thanks. We need to get moving. Come on." She grasped his hand.

He sighed heavily and tugged his hand out of hers. "I'll do it by myself. You're a tiny little thing. I wouldn't want to hurt you." He rolled over and forced himself up on his knees. A pair of surprisingly strong arms grabbed him around his waist and helped him stand. He staggered and she pulled his right arm around her shoulders, keeping her other arm around his waist.

Impressed, he smiled down at her and patted the top of her head. "You're stronger than you look, little one."

"And you don't smell anywhere near as good as *you* look. So let's get this over with."

He let out a crack of laughter. "Now that's one I've never heard before. My apologies. I think it's eau de jet fuel mixed with eau de swamp water."

She didn't respond. All in all, his little rescuer didn't seem to have much of a sense of humor. Too bad. Making a woman smile, seeing joy light up her eyes, was one of his greatest pleasures. Especially when they were making love.

The infernal heat seemed worse now. And the growing stiffness in his leg was making walking more and more of a chore. Even with Canoe Girl's help, his steps were growing slower and slower. He stumbled and grabbed a tree for support.

"You can do it," she urged, pulling him back from the tree.

"Actually, I'm not sure that I can. How much farther do we have to go?"

"A hundred yards, give or take."

He squinted at the wavering shapes in front of him then gave her an admonishing look. "You're teasing me. I don't see any buildings. It must be farther than that to Mystic Glades."

"It's a hundred yards to my *canoe*. Make it there and I can take you the rest of the way to town."

A wave of dizziness had him grabbing another tree. "I don't…think I can…make it that far."

"Sure you can. What are you, six-two? You're a big, strong guy. Just put one foot in front of the other. Close your eyes if it makes it easier."

He took a shaky step. "I don't suppose you have a four-wheeler hidden behind a tree somewhere closer than the canoe?"

"I'm fresh out of four-wheelers today."

"Bummer. I would have liked to ride a four-wheeler, especially with a pretty girl. Everything's better with a pretty girl." He winked and tried to grin, but the effort required more energy than he had left. "So…tired." He fell to his knees and surrendered to the darkness.

Chapter Three

Amber groaned and sank to her knees beside the handsome stranger with the corny yet kind of endearing sense of humor. Eau de jet fuel? If she hadn't been so worried about his fever she might have laughed at that. And she couldn't remember the last time she'd laughed.

Now that he was unconscious, how was she supposed to help him? Even though her canoe was a short jog away, it might as well have been miles. There was no way she could drag him that far. And even though he certainly wasn't packing any extra pounds, all those scrumptious-looking muscles had to amount to a lot of weight.

She pressed her hand to his forehead again and grimaced. He was like a furnace. If she didn't get his fever down soon he might have a seizure. And those red lines on his leg meant he had blood poisoning. That was probably what was causing the fever. That kind of infection could easily kill him no matter how big and strong he was.

She pulled his phone out of her pocket. When he'd dropped it earlier, she'd picked it up, planning on erasing the pictures he'd taken of her before returning the phone to him. But right now she just wanted to see if she could call for help, even though odds were high there wasn't any reception out here. When she'd made the swamp her home, she'd had a cell phone but had quickly learned that it was useless in about 99 percent of the Glades. She did know a few spots that got reliable reception, but they were much deeper into the swamp, too far away to be of use right now.

She pressed the main button and it asked her for her password. Shoot. She should have asked him for the code while he was delirious with fever and still conscious. He might have told her without a second thought. The service bars showed No Service anyway, so there was really no point. Making a call had been a long shot.

She shoved it into her pocket.

So, what now? Getting him to the canoe would take hours, assuming she could roll him there, which was the only way she could think of moving him. But she didn't think he had hours, not with that kind of fever. She had to bring it down. But how? Medicine, even if she could bring herself to try to doctor someone again, would take too long to make—and that was only if she could find the right plants. What she really needed was a bag of ice, something not exactly around every corner out here.

Wait. She might not have ice, but she had access to the next best thing. A spring. There were a handful of them scattered throughout the Glades, feeding ice-cold fresh water into the marsh from deep underground aquifers. And there were a few close by, one of them much closer than her canoe. It was worth a try. But how to get him there?

Her gaze dropped to his belt. Yes. That might work. She unbuckled it and worked it free, rolling him to pull it from underneath him. Then she strapped it around his chest below his arms and fastened it on the last hole. His chest was wide and muscular. It didn't give her much play in the belt, but it gave her enough to be able to slip her hands beneath his back and grasp the belt. She was just short enough that this might work.

Bracing her legs wide apart, she heaved backward. He slid easier than she'd expected on the soft mud and she almost fell on her rear end. Through a series of trial and error she finally found the best angle and managed to get him moving at a decent clip. She pulled him around the group of trees toward the spring, which was only thirty feet behind her, hidden in another group of trees. The muscles in her arms burned and her back was aching by the time she'd gotten him just ten feet from their original location.

She had to stop and take deep breaths, letting her shaking muscles rest before she started up again. Any hope that she might be able to use this method to get him to the canoe died a quick death. It would be a miracle if she could just get him to the freshwater. Someone had died once because of her actions. She was determined not to let her inaction be the cause of this man's death. Giving up wasn't an option. She had to keep going.

Fifteen minutes later she finally had him beside the spring, next to a shallow spot where she could sit and hold him without him slipping in too far and drowning. She emptied his pockets of his wallet and keys, leaving them up on the bank. After shucking his shoes and her boots, along with her knife, she took a bracing breath, then slid into the spring.

She gasped and pressed her hands against her

breasts, her teeth already chattering even though she was barely covered by the water as she sat down. Shivering violently, she grabbed the belt around Dex and tugged, hard.

He slipped easily over the soft side and she had to grab his head to keep it above water as his body rolled over. She caught his face against her chest, mortified when his hands came up around her and he pressed his face harder into the valley between her breasts. His eyes, however, were still closed, which was the only reason she didn't slap him.

"He doesn't know what he's doing," she reminded herself as she grabbed his shoulders and pushed up with her knees to flip him onto his back.

His body settled against hers in the V of her legs and she wrapped her hands under his armpits and around his chest, holding him tightly so he didn't slide beneath the water. She lay back against the edge of the bank, her teeth chattering so hard they clicked against each other. But it didn't take long for the incredible heat of his body to begin transferring to her.

He was still so alarmingly hot that she was actually sweating where his head rested against her breasts, in spite of the chill bumps on the rest of her skin. She cupped the cold water and dribbled it on his hair and his face, getting as much of him wet as possible. She continued putting cold water on his hair, his forehead, his neck, all while trying to monitor both of their temperatures. If she ended up with hypothermia, they'd both be in trouble.

She clung to him, freely plastering her body against his to warm herself while keeping him covered in the cold water. All the while she continued to rub the water into his scalp and on his skin.

When her hands and feet started going numb and she started feeling drowsy, she knew she had to get out of the spring. But he was still warm. Not as burning hot as before, thank goodness, but far too warm to be out of danger. She edged out of the water, pulling on the belt to tug him with her. She sat cross-legged on the bank, her skin covered with goose bumps. She managed to pull him half out of the water, keeping her hands locked under the belt to keep him from sliding back in. His rear end and legs were still in the water. Hopefully, that would be enough to continue bringing his fever down while she warmed up for a few minutes in the sun.

When the feeling had returned to her extremities and she was no longer shaking, she slid into the water with him, submerging all of him except his head and going through the same routine all over again.

She repeated the process for what had to be over an hour before he finally began to show real signs of improvement. Instead of the ruddy, red complexion that showed he was in the grips of the fever, the color drained away and he became more pale. When his skin pebbled with goose bumps, he moaned and tried to twist away from her.

She ruthlessly held on to him, determined to make sure his fever was gone before she'd let him out of the water. Unable to let him go for fear he'd drown, she pressed her cheek against the side of his face to see how hot he was. Still warmer than he should be, but so much better than before that it barely counted.

He suddenly jerked away from her and rolled over,

pressing her down into the water. She just managed to grab a lungful of air before she went under. He followed her down, his body on top of hers, his eyes—a startling green—were open and staring at her in confusion as he held his breath and held her down.

His hands grabbed her waist and he pulled back, suddenly lifting her out of the water against his chest as he smoothly stepped up on the bank. She clung to his shoulders, amazed he was so strong after seeming so weak earlier. Water cascaded off both of them as he dropped to the ground with her still in his arms. Whether by design or accident—she wasn't sure—he'd managed to position her so that she was straddling him. And from the widening of his eyes and the sudden movement of him beneath her, he wasn't unaffected by the intimacy of their position.

"Let me go." She smacked at his hands and shoved his chest.

He blinked, then a slow grin spread across his face. "Canoe Girl. I thought you were a dream."

"More like a nightmare," she grumbled. "Let me go."

"I like you right where you are."

So did she. And that was the problem. The spring had done a good job of washing away the stench of the bog he'd bathed in earlier. And up close like this, just inches from his face, she couldn't deny just how devastatingly handsome he was. Add to that how long it had been since she'd even seen a good-looking man, much less done anything else, and it was almost impossible to resist the urge to wiggle against his growing erection beneath her.

Good grief. Maybe she was the one with the fever now.

He was a stranger. An incredibly *hot* one, even when he wasn't running a temperature, but still a stranger.

He frowned. "Why are you all wet?"

She choked at his unintended double entendre and coughed to cover her embarrassment.

"We're, ah, both wet. From the spring." She waved her hand toward the water behind them. "You had a fever and I put you in the cold water to bring it down. Now, if you'll please—"

"If you insist." He yanked her against his chest and brought his mouth down on hers.

She was so startled she didn't immediately pull back. And by the time she thought to do so, he was kissing her senseless and her brain shut down. She slid her hands up his bare chest and around his neck, pressing herself against him as she opened her mouth for his searching tongue. He groaned and fell back against the bank, pulling her with him, deepening the kiss.

A sinfully long time later they broke apart, each of them gasping for breath.

He framed her face in his hands. "You're so beautiful."

"So are you."

He laughed and they reached for each other again.

Kissing him was insane. Crazy. Stupid. And *wonderful*. She'd never, ever been kissed like this before. Every tug of his lips on hers, every swirl of his tongue inside her mouth sent an answering pull straight to her belly.

Stop. This isn't just crazy, it's wrong. He's probably still delirious. He doesn't know what he's doing.

She whimpered, hating her conscience but knowing it was right. If the roles were reversed, she'd be appalled and feel that he'd taken advantage of her.

Shoving against his chest, she broke the kiss and sat back. "We have to stop. This isn't—"

His eyes closed and he collapsed onto his back.

"—right," she finished, then frowned. "Dex?" She shook him. "Dex?" When he didn't respond, she scrambled off his lap and checked his breathing. He was breathing deeply, evenly. His pulse was strong. But he was definitely unconscious.

Alarmed, she pulled his right pant leg up again and drew a sharp breath. "Oh, no." The red streaks were worse, much worse. And they extended well past his knee now.

She shook him. "Dex, wake up. Come on. Dex."

He moaned, as if in pain, but his eyes stayed shut.

Amber sat back, chewing her bottom lip. There was only one thing she knew that might help him, a potion she could make by mixing mud and two specific plants together into a poultice to draw out the poison. But what if she remembered wrong? What if she did more harm than good?

He moaned again, his handsome face scrunching up in a grimace.

If she didn't help him, he'd die. Of that she was sure. The poultice was his only hope.

Please help me remember how to mix it right.

She shoved to her feet, grabbed her knife from the pile of belongings on the bank and took off running.

Chapter Four

Dex twisted against the sheets, fighting through the darkness.

A delicate face leaned over him, her long, brown hair forming a curtain, her brow furrowed with concern.

"Sleep, Dex. Don't worry. I'll watch over you. You're getting better."

He reached for her. "Don't go, Canoe Girl." But she faded away like a ghost.

He cursed and tried to roll over, but every movement was painful. His entire body ached, as if he was back in college and had been in a drunken fraternity fistfight—and had lost.

A cool cloth stroked his arms, his forehead, driving back the awful heat that seemed to constantly surround him. Voices he didn't recognize whispered close by. Footsteps echoed and a door slammed. A glass was held to his lips. He drank greedily and the cool water soothed his parched throat.

Canoe Girl leaned over him again. No, she was sitting this time, raising her arms, then lowering them, over and over, her muscles bunching with strain. She raised her hands, pulling something up into the air. Water dripped from it onto his pants. An oar? Why was

*she holding an oar? She moved it to the other side and
dipped down again.*

*And then she was on her knees in front of him, her
cool fingers brushing against his brow. That worried
frown a constant twin to the look of concern in her eyes.
Sad eyes. So, so sad.*

*She slid her arms around his neck and hugged him
close. "Don't tell them about me, Dex. Please. Don't
tell."*

"I won't. I swear."

He thrashed against the sheets, seeking relief from
the heat. Hot. He was always so hot. He couldn't remember *not* being hot.

The darkness called to him again and he gratefully
surrendered.

DEX OPENED HIS EYES, blinking at the light.

"Well it's about time you decided to rejoin the living.
I was beginning to think the doc was wrong."

He turned his head on the pillow to see a woman
nearly as brawny as him, probably well over twice his
age, with falsely bright red hair, sitting in a ladder-back
chair beside the bed. He looked around the room but
she was the only one there. "Where am I?"

"Callahan's Watering Hole, in the extra bedroom in
my apartment upstairs. I'm Freddie Callahan."

"From Mystic Glades?"

"Either I'm famous and didn't know it or our buddy
Jake told you about me."

He frowned. "How would you know that I know
Jake?"

"I saw your last name on your ID, in your wallet.
Figured it was too much of a coincidence for you to be

named Lassiter and not be from Lassiter and Young Private Investigations. Called Jake—which was a pain since I had to leave town to get reception—and sure enough, he vouched for you."

He started to scoot up in the bed but stopped when he realized he was naked beneath the sheet. He yanked it higher before sitting up. The room was small, with only the narrow bed, a dresser and a single window. A collection of shot glasses and empty whiskey bottles sat on a shelf along the far wall. And a pair of open doors beneath them revealed a closet and a small bathroom. He tried to remember how he'd gotten there, but his mind was a haze of confusing images and impressions.

"I'm sorry," he said. "But I don't—"

"Remember what happened?" Freddie patted his hand. "No worries. We pretty much pieced everything together with Jake's help after I called him. You crashed your plane into the Glades. The airplane folks done packed up what was left of it onto some fancy barge and took it with them to Naples for some kind of investigation. You got an infection and have been unconscious for a while. I had Doc Holliday come out and check on you to make sure you were coming along okay. You're gonna be just fine."

"Doc Holliday?"

Her mouth cracked open in a gap-toothed grin. "I've called him that for so long that I don't remember his real name anymore. He's a city slicker, comes out to the Glades when we have an emergency. He wanted to take you back to town, but Jake and I told him you were family and I kept you here in Mystic Glades. Jake said he'd call your people in Saint Augustine and tell them where you were. Ain't nobody been by to check on you yet, though, which just proves we made the right decision keeping you here."

She crossed her arms and gave him a crisp nod, as if to let him know she wasn't impressed with his family's lack of concern. Of course, she had no way of knowing that the only reason his family would come was if they thought he was already dead and they stood a chance of getting their hands on his money.

A pounding started in his temple as he tried to think back to what had happened. Electrical tape. He'd found it in the engine compartment. Maybe it was a good thing that no one had shown up looking for him in Mystic Glades. Without knowing who'd tampered with his plane, he wasn't sure whom he could trust.

Images of the crash and its aftermath filtered through his mind: cutting his leg, waking to find himself in a freezing cold spring, a beautiful young woman helping him out of a canoe and onto the bank.

"Don't tell them about me, Dex. Please. Don't tell."

He scrubbed the stubble on his face and searched the corners of the room again, part of him hoping she'd be there even though he knew she wouldn't be.

Freddie's expression turned introspective as she studied him. "You're looking for the woman who helped you, aren't you? The one you call Canoe Girl?"

Canoe Girl. He squeezed his eyes shut. He remembered it all now. She'd put some kind of foul-smelling mud on his leg—to draw out the poison, she'd told him. And when he'd alternated between the fever and bone-rattling chills, she'd built a fire and sat with him all night, leaving only to bring him water and some kind of surprisingly delicious stew.

Every hour, without fail, she'd changed the dressing on his leg. And when he'd needed a moment of privacy and, to his shame, was unable to get up on his own, she'd helped him stand and limp to a clump of bushes. When he was done, she'd escorted him to their little campfire.

She'd entertained him with stories about the Everglades and made him laugh when she spoke about her childhood. He'd told her about flying and about later building his empire, only to become bored and start the PI firm with Jake Young for fun.

When the sun came up he'd awakened to find her curled against him beside the dying campfire. In awe of the beautiful creature, he'd tightened his arms, only to find her blinking at him in surprise and slipping out of his grasp. Far too soon, she'd deemed him strong enough to leave and had helped him limp to her canoe.

After taking him to the woods at the edge of town, she'd helped him sit on a fallen log and crouched down in front of him.

"We're just a few feet from the main road," she whispered. She pulled a whistle out of her pocket. "When I blow this, someone will come help you." She slid her arms around his neck and hugged him close. "Don't tell them about me, Dex. Please. Don't tell. Make up some kind of story to explain how you got here, but never tell anyone that you saw me. It's important."

The fear in her voice had him clutching both of her shoulders and pulling her back so he could look her in the eyes. "What's going on? Who are you afraid of?"

"It's…complicated. Please. Just promise me."

"Okay. Yes, I promise. But tell me why you're afraid. I'm sure that I can help—"

She pressed her fingers against his lips to stop him.

"No one can help me." Her mouth quirked up in a rare smile. "Not even a sexy navy pilot turned billionaire financier private investigator." She stood and backed away, then put the whistle to her lips.

The shrill sound shattered the morning, sending birds shrieking and rising from the trees around them.

"Remember your promise." She turned and disappeared into the woods.

Dex shook his head to clear his thoughts. Freddie sat across from him, still waiting for his answer. A feeling of impending doom settled over him. If he'd kept his promise, then how did this woman know about Canoe Girl?

"My memory is still a bit…foggy," he said evasively. "How long have I been here?"

"Three days. Doc said you wouldn't have made it if Amber hadn't helped you with that concoction she put on your leg. But still, it was touch and go."

"Amber?"

"Amber Callahan. My niece, the one you called Canoe Girl when you were delirious. Pretending you don't know who I'm talking about isn't going to change the fact that you talked quite a bit about her."

He fisted his hands in the sheets, guilt and shame settling on top of him like a heavy weight. Canoe Girl—Amber—had saved his life. And, in return, all she'd asked was that he not tell anyone about her. He'd betrayed her, whether he'd meant to or not.

"They're searching for her. Now that we know she's nearby, Holder and the others won't stop until they find her trail and bring her back."

His stomach twisted into a hard knot. "She doesn't want to be found."

"I'm sure you're right."

He frowned. For an aunt, she didn't seem all that worried about her niece's welfare. "Then why is this Holder person searching for her? It's her right to be left alone if that's what she wants. If he thinks she needs rescuing, believe me, she's quite capable of taking care of herself. She's pretty amazing in that department."

She gave him a peculiar look, as if she thought he'd lost his mind. "Mr. Lassiter, Deputy Holder isn't leading a rescue party. He's leading a posse. Amber is a murderer."

Chapter Five

Amber ducked down behind a trash can against the back of Callahan's Watering Hole and waited for the newest group of men to get out of their cars and go inside. The foot traffic in and out of the bar all morning had been incredible, not to mention several suits in a limo a few minutes ago. Half the town and strangers she'd never seen before must have been inside at one time or another. And she didn't have to guess why. They were looking for her, had been for three days now, carrying rifles and shotguns as if they were afraid she'd attack them. The resentment that shot through her was like a physical pain, making her double over. These people had been her friends, her family. At one time they'd have done anything for her. Now they just wanted to put her away.

She could have been safe and sound at home deep in the Glades by now, but she couldn't stop worrying about Dex. She'd watched from a perch in a tree overhead to insure that her plan had worked—that someone heard her whistle and came to help him. And since the first person on the scene was someone she'd never met, she couldn't just assume he had good intentions as far as Dex was concerned. He could have been a thief or some such. So she'd scampered down the tree and followed him to make sure Dex didn't need her. Then she'd safely made it to her canoe and headed out. But she wasn't comfortable with the things that she'd heard when she spied on the crash site and listened to the men gathering up the plane. So she'd gone back to check on him and had made a habit of checking on him every day. Once he was well and awake and able to fend for himself, she'd quit her vigil. But not before then.

The men she'd been waiting to pass finally went inside, letting the screen door slam shut behind them. Amber waited another couple of minutes, peeking out to see if anyone else was approaching and listening for sounds from inside the bar to tell her if anyone was about to leave. Then she hurried around the trash can and raced up the rickety wooden staircase attached to the back of the building that was supposed to be a fire escape but was so rarely used that it had fallen into disrepair. The way the boards sagged as she stepped on each one had her holding her breath the first day she'd snuck up them, but now she knew they were more solid than they seemed and she no longer held her breath as she hurried up to the landing.

The door was unlocked, as always. That was one thing she could be thankful for, that the residents of Mystic Glades rarely locked their doors. She pulled the door open a fraction to peer down the long upstairs hallway with doors opening off either side. With all the people downstairs in the business part of the building, she hadn't expected her aunt to be up here in her private quarters and wasn't disappointed. The hall was empty.

She headed straight to the guest room where Dex was staying. If he was still suffering from his fever she would sit with him as she had the past few days and use a cool cloth to soothe him. She wished she could speak to the doctor who came every evening and ask him if Dex was going to be okay. But with everyone searching for her, that wasn't in the realm of possibilities.

She carefully eased the door open and hurried inside, shutting it behind her and flipping the lock. Movement to her right had her whirling around. A body slammed into her, tackling her to the floor. She landed hard, her elbows and head thumping against the wooden floor a split second before the person who'd attacked her landed on top of her. She grimaced at the pain that shot through her then blinked in surprise to see the very green, shocked gaze of Dex looking down at her. A very naked Dex, plastered to every inch of her body. And like when she'd ended up in his lap out in the swamp, his body immediately responded to their closeness and began to harden against her belly.

He cursed and rolled off her, grabbing her wrists and yanking her to her feet.

"What are you doing here?" he demanded in a harsh whisper as he pulled her to the bed.

She tried to focus on the unexpected anger in his voice, but she couldn't resist a quick look down. The parts of his body that had been hidden from her when she'd been nursing him to health were now fully revealed. And she wasn't disappointed in the least. The rest of him was just as…impressive…as his naked chest had been.

He grabbed a blanket from the foot of the bed and wrapped it around his hips. If they'd been in the swamp, he'd have made some flirty, corny comment. But the teasing flirtation she'd come to expect from him in their brief time together was replaced by a sullen, angry, serious stranger.

Her shoulders slumped. "You know."

"That you're wanted for murder? Yeah, hard to miss that topic around here. About that—I want you to know that I didn't tell them about you on purpose."

She waved her hand. "No worries. You were delirious. It's not your fault."

"How would you know I was delirious?"

She swallowed and shrugged. "A…ah, guess. I knew you still had the fever when I left you. And, since Deputy Holder headed up that posse after me so fast, they obviously knew about me. And I trust you—I know you meant it when you said you wouldn't tell. Again, no worries. Not your fault." She tugged her arm out of his hold. "It was a mistake. I'll go. I'm sorry to have troubled you."

He blocked her way. "Not so fast. There are things… we need to talk."

"No, I need to get out of here before someone catches me."

"If you're that worried, why'd you come here in the first place?"

She blinked as if remembering something, then reached into her pocket and pulled out a cell phone. "You dropped this earlier. I kept it at first to try to erase the pictures of me. But there's no point in that anymore. So…here you go." She handed it to him and he tossed it onto the bed.

"I don't think you risked everything to come here to return a phone. What's the real reason that you're here?"

She blew out a long breath. "Guilt, I guess. I was worried that I'd left you unprotected. You're obviously able to care for yourself now, so my job is done. Time to go."

"Turn around."

"What? Why?"

"Because I'm the only one naked in this room. Either you take your clothes off and we'll be naked together, or you turn around while I get dressed."

She hesitated, half wondering if he was serious.

"That was a joke, Amber. Turn around."

She sighed and turned around, listening to the sounds of drawers opening and the whisper of fabric against skin.

"Okay, you can turn around."

When she did, she was surprised to see him wearing dark gray dress slacks and a burgundy dress shirt tucked in, with a charcoal-gray-and-maroon-striped silk tie. The only thing missing was a suit jacket and he'd look at home in any boardroom. Pity. She liked him better half-covered in mud and jet fuel. He'd been a lot more fun and a lot less serious.

"Nice clothes. I can't imagine anyone around here having a suit you could borrow, though."

"They're my clothes. My assistant brought them."

"Your assistant. Okay. Well, you're obviously doing fine and you have…an assistant watching after you now, so I'll just be on my way." She scampered around him and ran to the door. But he was surprisingly fast for someone who'd just woken from a near-coma after several days and he braced his hand against the door, keeping her from being able to open it.

"Damn it, Amber. We need to talk."

The sound of voices outside the door and footsteps clomping up the wooden stairs had him breaking off.

Amber's eyes widened in dismay. She turned in a circle, surveying the tiny room for a place to hide. The tiny bathroom or the closet. She chose the closet.

"Wait." Dex grabbed her arm in an unbreakable hold.

A knock sounded on the door.

"Please," she whispered, as she tried to pry his hand off her forearm. "Let me go. I'm just going to hide in the closet."

He shook his head. "No. You're not." He half turned toward the door. "Come in," he called out.

Amber gasped in shock as the door opened. Her aunt gaped at her in surprise, then moved aside to let the group of men behind her into the room. The first two men, wearing suits much like Dex's, were strangers to her. But the last man to enter the room was not. She'd seen him two years ago, the day she'd run into the Glades.

The look of surprise on his face was quickly replaced with a look of reproach as he pulled out his handcuffs.

"Miss Callahan." Collier County Deputy Scott Holder pulled her away from Dex and turned her around. "You're under arrest for the murder of your grandfather, William Callahan."

Amber stiffened her spine while he locked the handcuffs around her wrists. Her face flamed hot as she endured the pat down with the others watching, except for Dex and one of the men in a suit who were currently deep in conversation by the window, completely ignoring her. She noted that he didn't seem surprised by the appearance of a Collier County sheriff's deputy at his door, either.

Holder took her knife and sheath from her belt. Then he escorted Amber to the door with her hands cuffed behind her back, past the admonishing look from her aunt. Dex never once looked her way.

"WELL, THIS SEEMS FAMILIAR." Deputy Holder leaned back in his desk chair in the squad room beside Dex as another officer escorted Amber into an interview room.

"Because of Faye Star?" Dex asked, noting that Amber made a point of not looking at him even though she passed less than a yard away from him.

He nodded. "Your PI partner, Jake Young, had Faye in here accused of murder just a couple of months ago. Déjà vu." He cast him a sideways glance. "Let me guess. You think Miss Callahan is innocent?"

"Honestly, I have no idea. But I certainly wasn't going to harbor a fugitive once I found out there was an outstanding warrant for her arrest. That's why I had Freddie call you to come over, so I could tell you what I knew. It was only dumb luck that she was there when you arrived."

"You're supposedly worried about making sure she doesn't run from the law. And yet you're offering your own lawyer to defend her." He nodded at Garreth Jackson as he passed them and went into the interview room.

"She saved my life. I figure the least I can do is make sure she gets a good attorney. Garreth was a criminal defense lawyer before he turned to business law. He can at least advise her until I can bring in someone else."

Holder snorted. "Sounds to me like you're going to a lot of trouble—and expense—for someone you aren't sure is innocent."

"Like I said. She saved my life. I can't put a price on that. Whatever she needs, I intend to provide it. What about you? Do you think she's guilty?"

The interview room door closed and Holder flipped the file open on top of his desk. "Seems pretty cut-and-dried. Her grandfather was the founder of Mystic Glades. He lived in a mansion, of sorts, several miles outside the town proper, with only one other person— Amber Callahan. She was known more or less as the town healer, for lack of a better term. If someone was sick or broke a bone, they went to Amber instead of taking the long drive to Naples. She was the only one with her grandfather the night he died, admitted as much the next morning when she called the police to report his death."

"Her aunt said the old man had been poisoned?"

"Poisoned? Not exactly, but close. He was sick with the flu or something similar and she gave him one of her potions to supposedly help him sleep better. But the potion was laced with peanut oil, something he was highly allergic to. Coroner said his throat closed up and he died of anaphylactic shock. Amber knew about his allergies. Everyone did. And since she was the one who brought groceries and did all the cooking, it's kind of hard to say anyone else brought the peanut oil into the house."

"Did you actually find a bottle of peanut oil?"

He flipped the few pages in the folder and shook his head. "Nope. She must have disposed of it. But the CSU team tested the glass beside his bedside table and found peanut oil residue."

"What did she have to gain by killing him?"

"Plenty. Since he founded Mystic Glades, he pretty much owned the town and leased most of the property to others. Very few of the residents actually own the land or the buildings on them. He was quite wealthy in his own right—old money that's been in his family for generations."

"And Amber is the only heir?"

"Her and her aunt Fredericka. But Amber got the lion's share."

"Is the estate still in escrow?"

He tapped one of the pages. "No, but it might as well be. As soon as Miss Callahan was charged, the courts put holds on both her accounts and her grandfather's accounts. She can't touch a penny without going to court to release the funds."

"Which of course she wouldn't do if she's worried about being arrested for murder."

"Exactly."

Dex blew out a long breath. "I just can't picture her purposely killing her grandfather even if she did want his money. She seems so—"

"Sweet? Nice?"

"I was thinking intelligent, actually. How old was her grandfather?"

"I see where you're going." He thumbed through the report, then flipped to the beginning and ran his finger down a paragraph. "Let's see. Amber was twenty-two, her grandfather was just shy of eighty at the time. He wasn't in the best of health, either, even without having the flu at the time he died. You're thinking she could have just waited and inherited."

"Seems like the logical thing to do. Does that report say why she might have needed the money? Had she planned on leaving Mystic Glades?"

He closed the file. "The report doesn't really say much more than what I told you. Everything I've said was available through old media reports or word of mouth in Mystic, so I haven't given away any secrets. But the rest of the file *is* confidential and I can only release it to her attorney."

"Fair enough. I'm curious about one thing, as long as it's not one of those secrets you mentioned."

"Doesn't hurt to ask."

"You said the grandfather lived in a mansion. What happened to it?"

"The court apportioned some of the estate for the house's upkeep and appointed a trustee to look after the house. And before you ask, no, I can't share the trustee's name because I don't know if that's common knowledge."

Dex raised a brow. "I imagine it takes a lot of money to maintain a large house, especially in an environment like the Everglades. That trustee probably has access to a very generous bank account."

Holder shrugged. "Your words. Not mine."

"I know what it costs to maintain a large estate. I don't guess I really need your answer to that question. It does, however, make me wonder if the trustee could be culpable in the murder."

"In a normal murder case, I might agree with you. But in this one, there's one fact you can't explain away."

"Which is?"

"Amber herself, in the interview the morning her grandfather was found dead, admitted she was the only other person in the house. She said no one else had been there for weeks. Kind of hard to argue that someone else might have killed the old man when she swore no one else had been there."

Dex was inclined to agree with him, but somehow saying that out loud would have made him feel like a traitor to the woman who had worked so hard to save him. He owed her the benefit of the doubt and was determined to keep an open mind.

The door to the interview room popped open and Garreth stepped outside, closing the door behind him. He stopped in front of the desk. "Miss Callahan has decided to retain my services until I can help her interview and hire a criminal case attorney. I'll need a copy of the original police report."

Holder held the folder up. "I figured you might. Keep it. I'll print myself a new copy."

"Thank you." He turned to Dex. "Assuming you still plan to foot the bill—"

"I do."

"Excellent. Then the calls I made in the interview room weren't a complete waste of time. I started the ball rolling to arrange bail. Now we just have to wait for a judge to call us back."

Holder shook his head. "Not going to happen on a Saturday. Miss Callahan will have to cool her heels in jail until Monday, and even then, I highly doubt a judge will grant her bail. She's a proven flight risk."

Dex exchanged an amused look with his lawyer. "I think you underestimate Garreth's abilities, Detective."

Holder shrugged. "Maybe. I doubt it. I guess we'll see. But I—" The phone on his desk rang. When he saw the number on the display, he shot Garreth a frown and took the call.

Garreth gave him a smug look and turned to Dex again. "When you're done here, Miss Callahan has requested to speak with you."

Dex immediately stood but Holder signaled him to wait.

When he hung up the phone, he shook his head. "I can't believe what I just heard." He filled them in on the details.

Dex laughed and clapped Garreth on the shoulder. "You've still got it, my friend."

"I suppose this means your answer is yes, to both conditions?" Holder asked, not sounding happy at all.

"Are you kidding? This is the coolest thing to happen to me in ages. I'm all in."

"This is ridiculous," Holder muttered as he shoved out of his chair. "But I don't guess I have a choice. Hold up your right hand, and repeat after me."

Chapter Six

Amber clasped her hands beneath the table as Dex stepped into the tiny room and closed the door behind him. Her relief at seeing him, apparently unharmed, had her letting out a relieved breath.

He sat in the chair across from her and leaned his forearms on the table. "I'm surprised that you wanted to see me. I figure you have to blame me—"

"For my arrest?" She shook her head. "I was angry, at first. But I knew this day would come eventually. And I couldn't exactly expect a stranger to want to stick his neck out for me." She grabbed his hands in hers. "That's not the point, and not why I wanted to talk to you. You're in danger."

His brows arched as he looked at their joined hands before meeting her gaze. "You wanted to talk to me to warn me that I'm in danger?"

"Yes. I've only just now really put everything together in my mind and I wanted to tell you my suspicions. After I took you to Mystic Glades, I went to the crash site to erase any signs of me having been near there."

"To wipe out your footprints."

She nodded. "I didn't know what exactly you would

tell everyone about how you got to town, but if you did keep your word, I didn't want any signs to prove otherwise."

"Let me make sure I understand. You came to my room every day of my fever and put cold cloths on my head and made sure that I was comfortable."

"What? That's not what I—"

"Wanted to talk about? No, obviously you didn't want me to know. But I remember someone doing that and your aunt looked at me like I was crazy when I asked her about it. So I know you were the one taking care of me far more than she was." He quirked his mouth up in a wry grin. "Thank you, by the way."

She tugged her hands but he laced his fingers with hers, trapping her. She blew out a breath in frustration. "Look, you need to take this seriously. Like I said, I went to the crash site and—"

"And you erased your footprints, again, to make sure that I didn't look bad if I'd kept my word and said I was alone after the crash and that no one helped me. Do I have that right? You were protecting me? Again?"

"Can we get to what matters please?"

"What matters to me is that everything everyone else is telling me about you makes you out to be a killer. But everything—every single thing that I've personally experienced with you—tells me the opposite. You seem to me like an intelligent, warm, caring person who puts everyone else's welfare above her own. Why aren't you berating me for telling about you helping me after I promised I wouldn't?"

"It wasn't your fault. We already discussed this. You were delirious. And it wasn't a fair promise anyway—

to ask someone who doesn't know me to lie for me. I'm sorry I asked. I shouldn't have."

"You're doing it again."

She tugged her hands and this time he let them go, although seemingly reluctantly. She clasped her hands beneath the table again. "Look, Mr. Lassiter—"

"Dex." He grinned "We've slept together. I think we can use first names after that, don't you?"

She blinked. "I don't know what you think you remember, but we most certainly have not slept together."

"I'm wounded. You don't remember us lying together beside the fire? You stayed with me all night, and we both slept, off and on." He winked.

She leaned across the table and thumped it impatiently. "Will you be serious? Please?"

"Oh, I'm always serious about…sleeping."

She threw her hands up. "I can see this is going nowhere. You might as well leave. I'll talk to that lawyer of yours again and tell him—"

"He's your lawyer now, too."

She swallowed hard. "Yes… I suppose. Ah, thank you for that. I promise that I'll pay you back one day. As soon as I can get out on bail, I'll look into a court-appointed lawyer."

"I wouldn't advise that. Garreth's one of the best around, even if he doesn't practice criminal law anymore. He'll make sure to arrange an equally competent criminal attorney. Murder charges are far too serious to skimp on representation. Florida isn't shy about sticking needles in people's arms. The death penalty is nothing to play around with."

She swallowed hard. "I hadn't even thought of that."

"Well, I have. This is serious, Amber. Your life is at stake."

"Aren't you even going to ask if I did it?"

"No."

"Why not?"

He shrugged. "Because I know that you didn't kill him. You're not built that way. You could have left me to die out in the swamp. But even though you knew it might mean getting caught and going to jail, you helped me. If you did that for a stranger, I have no doubt you would never have done anything to harm your family."

"Thank you," she whispered. "You have no idea how good it feels to have someone actually believe in me."

His smile faded. "Yeah, about that. I'm guessing your aunt Freddie hasn't exactly been supportive. She certainly doesn't strike me as someone in your court."

"Well, you can't really blame her. Grandpa was her daddy."

"And yet he left most everything to you. Not her. That seems rather telling."

She shrugged. "They never had the best relationship."

"And you were the one who took care of him every day. Did your aunt help at all?"

"You have to understand Freddie. She's one of the most supportive people out there. She'll do anything for you as long as—"

"You don't do something she doesn't approve of?"

"Pretty much. But she's a good person. She has a good heart."

"Not from where I'm standing." He looked down at his chair. "Or sitting." He grinned.

Even though she didn't feel the least bit happy right

now, she couldn't help the answering smile that curved her lips. There was just something about Dex that lightened her heart and made her feel good. But of course, she couldn't let him distract her from her primary purpose. She cleared her throat and tried again.

"Listen, please. This is important. I need to tell you about the crash site."

"Let me guess. You heard the investigators talking near the engine and someone mentioned the tape in the engine compartment."

She blinked. "You knew?"

"Yep. I even took pictures. I emailed them to the NTSB after I woke up and already spoke to them. They concur, unofficially at least, that the plane appears to have been tampered with. Of course, their official report will take months, or longer."

She pressed a hand against her chest. "Well, okay, then. I thought you didn't know."

"That's why you came back every day to your aunt's, isn't it? To watch over me? To protect me?"

Her face flamed hot. "You make me sound like a saint. Trust me. I'm not. I came back for purely selfish reasons. I didn't want another death on my conscience."

"Another death? You blame yourself for your grandfather's death?"

She nodded. "How can I not? I knew he had allergies. Obviously, I did something to cause him to die. I must have used something to gather the plants and herbs that used to have peanuts in it. Maybe I didn't wash it out good enough. Whatever, there was only one person who could have harmed him, and that was me."

Dex glanced at the door behind him, then at the glass along one wall before leaning forward. "I don't think anyone is behind that glass listening, but I can't be sure. Let's not sling around admissions of guilt," he whispered.

"But I—"

"Loved your grandfather," he said more loudly, "and would never do anything on purpose to harm him. Isn't that right?"

She frowned. "Yes, of course. But no one else was in the house."

"That you know of. Let's not talk about any of that right now. Let's talk about what matters right this minute."

"Getting you some kind of protection," she said. "You seem to have plenty of money. I recommend hiring some bodyguards."

He chuckled. "You really aren't worried about yourself, are you?"

"Well, of course I am. I don't want to go to prison or…worse. But that will have to play out in the courts. There's nothing I can do about it right now. You, on the other hand, are in very real danger and need to be aware of it and take precautions."

"Understood. And thank you for wanting to make sure that I'm safe."

"Okay. Well. Um…thank you, for everything. I really appreciate your kindness in lending me your attorney." She held her hand out.

He chuckled again and shook her hand, squeezing her fingers before letting go. "I wish you nothing but the best, Amber Callahan."

"Maybe we'll meet again under better circumstances," she said. "Preferably not with me in prison."

He gave her a secretive look and then headed to the

door. He rapped his knuckles on it and waited. The door opened and Officer Holder and the lawyer, Gareth Jackson, stood in the opening.

"Ready?" Holder asked.

"Yep." Dex backed up and let them into the small room, which seemed to become even smaller with the three large men standing on the other side of the table from Amber.

"Is someone going to tell me what's going on?" she asked.

Holder put his hands on his hips. "Looks like you lucked into an impressive lawyer, Miss Callahan. Five minutes on the phone with a judge and he's secured your release. But there are some conditions you have to agree to."

Her pulse sped up as she stared at him, feeling completely stunned. "He's granting bail?"

"He is. And Mr. Lassiter is kindly putting up the deposit."

"I…don't know what to say. Thank you."

Dex nodded. "You might want to wait until you hear the rest before thanking me."

"Yes," Holder continued. "There are two conditions the judge is imposing, and one that Mr. Lassiter is imposing in exchange for the bail deposit." He waved at Dex. "This is your show. Why don't you explain?"

Dex stepped forward and took Amber's hands between his. "My condition is that you consent to the exhumation of your grandfather's body so a new autopsy can be performed."

She jerked back in shock, but he kept her hands in his. "I don't understand. Why would you ask me that? Everyone knows he died because of his allergies, and

I don't know that I have the right to approve that even if I wanted to. Wouldn't his daughter, Freddie, have to consent?"

"She already has," Garreth said from behind him. "Asking you is just a courtesy that Mr. Lassiter felt should be extended. We don't need your permission."

Dex shot him an aggravated glance before looking at her again. "I know you were close to him and I don't want you upset if we do this. But I think it's an important first step in proving your innocence."

"You really think a new autopsy might find something that the first one didn't?"

"It's possible. With your life hanging in the balance, it seems like a good idea. Don't you think?"

"O-okay. I guess."

"Excellent. Garreth will work out the details. As for the other conditions, the ones the judge is imposing, first, you can't leave town—as in Mystic Glades. You have to agree to stay there and not go back into the swamp and hide again until all of this plays out in the courts."

She couldn't believe her good luck. Of course, she would agree to that. She could easily slip away again. She'd hidden out for two years. There was no reason she couldn't go back to that life in the Glades again. She was about to agree, but then she realized there was a potentially huge downside.

"How much money did you have to put down to bail me out, Mr. Lassiter?"

"Dex," he gently corrected again. "Does it matter? As long as you don't run, I don't lose my money."

"That's what I'm worried about," she grumbled, low, so only he could hear.

He grinned again, which seemed strange to her under the circumstances, since she'd basically just admitted she planned on running. "Why are you smiling?"

"Because of the judge's second condition."

"Which is?"

"He thinks you're a flight risk, based on your history. The only way he would grant bail under these circumstances is if you're remanded into the custody of someone who will insure that you don't disappear again."

Visions of her aunt Freddie snarling at her and trading insults while she shoved a tray of food into her room and locked the door had Amber's stomach clenching. "Let me guess. My aunt?"

"Nope. This person also has to be an officer of the court."

"Officer of the court? Like a cop?"

"Exactly like a cop. Or a temporary deputy. That would work too."

The grin on his face had her wary. "O…kay. Whatever that means. So, who's my official babysitter?"

He grinned and held out his hand. "Happy to meet you. I'm temporary deputy and officer of the court, Dex Lassiter, your babysitter."

DEX STEPPED OUT of the back of the limo in front of Buddy Johnson's store—Swamp Buggy Outfitters— and waited for Amber to join him.

The deputy thing, though real, was mainly a gimmick to cover the judge if something happened. And Amber had warned Dex that the residents of Mystic Glades wouldn't roll out a welcome mat, or canoe, or whatever for him if they found out he was law enforcement, even in a temporary capacity. So for now, his newfound role would remain a secret between the two of them.

She slid across the leather seat and stepped out beside him, anxiously glancing around at the small crowds of people standing around the wooden boardwalks up and down Mystic Glades' Main Street, all of them watching Amber with a mixture of open hostility and suspicion.

"I think I may have been safer in jail."

Dex put his arm around her shoulders and pulled her against his side, enjoying the startled look she gave him, especially since she didn't pull away. "Don't worry. I'll take care of you."

Her startled look turned to aggravation and she shoved his arm off her shoulders. "I can take care of myself. Have been for quite a while now." She started to turn away, but he grabbed her hand and refused to let it go.

"Are you forgetting something? The conditions of your release?"

Her shoulders slumped and she quit trying to walk away. "Fine. Why are we here?" She nodded toward the store, where Buddy was now standing in the open front doorway.

A raindrop spattered onto his jacket and he glanced up at the angry clouds gathering overhead. "We're here because we need shelter, a place to stay."

"Last I heard, Buddy doesn't take on boarders. And there isn't an apartment over the store like at my aunt's anyway. I thought we were going to stay at Freddie's."

"You thought wrong." He tugged her toward the store while his driver waited inside the car. He stared at the townspeople on the boardwalk until they looked away.

"I'm not about to make you stay with someone who thinks you're a murderer and makes no secret about it."

They reached the first step that led to the board-walk and the door where Buddy was watching them with open curiosity, several of his gray-haired friends crowding the doorway behind him trying to see what was going on.

"Then where are we going to stay?" she whispered to Dex. "There isn't exactly a Holiday Inn around here."

"True. But we're not staying at a hotel." He tugged her forward with him.

"Afternoon. Mr. Johnson, isn't it? I'm Dex Lassiter." He offered his hand and was pleasantly surprised when the other man shook it. He had a much friendlier look on his face than most of the other Mystic Glades residents had.

"I know who you are. You can call me Buddy. Everyone does." His gaze settled on Amber. "It's good to see you again."

She blinked in surprise. "It is?"

"Yep. I don't believe for a minute that you had anything to do with William's death. So don't be worrying about me standing around judging you." He aimed a withering look at the same group of people that Dex had stared down moments earlier. They turned and hurried away. "I heard you made bail and that you were coming back. Have to say, I was kind of surprised. But I'm glad. I reckon you must be here for one thing—the keys to your granddaddy's place. I stocked it up when I heard you were on your way. But you can look around inside and see if you need anything else. No charge. It's the least I can do for my best friend's granddaughter."

He waved them inside and Dex pulled a stunned Amber behind him into the store.

As Buddy went to his office to retrieve the keys to the Callahan mansion, Amber stood beside Dex in the middle of the store. The older men, friends of Buddy's, sat a short distance away on some folded-up chairs near a display of coolers and fishing poles, making no move to talk to either of them.

"I don't understand. Why does Buddy have the keys to my grandfather's house?" Amber asked. "I would have expected Freddie to have them, or at least a friend of mine, like Faye."

"Faye Star?"

Her brows rose. "You know her?"

"I know *of* her. She married my PI business partner, Jake Young. They're both out of town right now. But back to why Buddy has the keys to your grandfather's mansion. He's the executor of the estate, appointed by the court to take care of the property until things with you are resolved. And before you protest that you don't want to take any supplies he may offer, trust me, they're not exactly free of charge. He's got access to a very healthy bank account to take care of that house. Plus, he receives a monthly stipend from the account for his troubles. He's been well paid."

Buddy headed down the aisle toward them, smiling as he twirled a ring of keys.

"How do you know all of this?" Amber asked.

"My attorney."

Buddy held the keys out to Dex, but Dex motioned for him to give them to Amber. "It's her house now."

Buddy's gaze shot to Dex as he handed the keys to Amber. "The charges have been dropped?"

"It's just a matter of time. You mentioned you stocked the house?"

"Um, yes, yes, I did. The pantry and refrigerator are full, even loaded up the deep freeze. You'll have to put sheets on the beds but all of that is there, too. And everything is clean. I hired a service as part of being the executor. The house has been cleaned once a week ever since…well, it's clean."

"Thank you, Mr. Johnson." Amber clutched the keys in her hand. "For everything."

He cleared his throat, looking embarrassed at her thanks. "It's nothing. And I can't remember you ever calling me by my last name in the past. No sense in starting now."

She gave him a small smile. "Buddy. Thanks."

He nodded and grabbed a backpack from a rack close by. "The only thing I didn't see to before you got here was checking on the old generator up at the house. The propane tank should be full, but I haven't cleaned or tested the generator this season. There's a bad storm moving in. You might want to fire the thing up and make sure it's in good order. I'll just get you a few more things to take, to make sure you have everything that you might need." He headed around the store, loading up the backpack with more items, and sent them on their way.

The limo headed out of Mystic Glades up a long, dirt road. The "few miles" from town turned into six before they reached the house, which was unlike any mansion Dex had ever seen. It was a two-story wooden structure that reminded him more of an old farmhouse than anything else, except that it had a wing on each end that seemed to go on forever back into the trees.

There was nothing remotely fancy about the outside, but he could see the locals might think of it as a mansion simply for its size.

"It's certainly…big," he offered, as he held the car door open for Amber.

A whimsical smile curved her lips. "I think Granddaddy always hoped for a large family of kids and grandkids to fill these walls one day. But it didn't exactly turn out that way."

"Why not?"

She shrugged. "He was a bit…crotchety, I suppose. A lovable heart that didn't always show on the outside unless you took the time to really get to know him."

"Thus him and Freddie not being close?"

"Right. And Freddie never married anyway, so no grandkids there. He had three sons and two daughters, but they all left Mystic Glades as soon as they could. Everyone in his family left, in one way or another."

"Except you."

"Except me." She glanced up at him. "Are we going to stand out here in the rain all day?"

He blinked and realized she was right. The fat raindrops from earlier were starting to plop down more consistently, threatening a deluge soon. He waved to the porch as the limo driver handed him the briefcase that his lawyer had gotten for him before they'd left the police station, along with the small suitcase his assistant had sent along when Dex was at Freddie's.

By the time they'd made it to the porch and the limo was heading down the road back to Naples, the threatening rain was starting to come down in heavy sheets, turning the drive in front of the house into a big puddle.

"Ready?" Dex asked, as he set the backpack just inside the open front door along with the briefcase and suitcase.

She straightened her shoulders, facing down the dark entrance like a soldier about to go into battle. "Ready."

Chapter Seven

Amber stood in the massive, two-story entryway, frozen in place. A warm hand touched her shoulder and she turned to see Dex standing beside her, his usual smile firmly in place.

"Good memories? Or bad?"

"Good. Mostly. Except for, well, that last day."

He hiked the backpack onto his shoulder and managed to tuck the briefcase under the same arm that was holding the suitcase. She tried to at least take the briefcase to help, but he declined.

"They say the only way to get over a bad experience is to face it head-on," he said.

"Do they? Who are they?"

"Hmm. I'm not sure. But it seems like good advice."

"Maybe. I guess I'm not used to doing that exactly. But unless you're going to turn your back and let me take off—"

"I'm not. You're stuck with me, at least until the results of the autopsy come back."

"I can't imagine that will make a difference."

"Then you're not thinking positive thoughts like you should be."

"Well, I never said I was an optimist."

"Pity. We optimists have much more fun. Speaking of fun, are the bedrooms upstairs?" He winked, making her face flush hot as he grabbed her hand in his free hand and pulled her toward the stairs.

She tugged her hand out of his grasp and took the lead. "You really need to stop trying to tow me around all of the time. I can walk perfectly fine without you pulling me along."

His hand settled onto the small of her back, sending all kinds of pleasant sensations skittering up her spine.

"Just looking after my investment," he said. "I'd hate to lose my bail bond deposit if you scamper off somewhere."

She reached the top of the stairs and turned right. "Exactly how much did you have to put down?"

"A hundred thousand dollars."

She jerked to a halt and turned around. He dropped the suitcase and briefcase and grabbed her shoulders to keep from running into her.

"A little warning might be nice next time," he muttered as he dropped his hands.

"A hundred thousand dollars?" she squeaked. "Are you crazy?"

"According to my last girlfriend, probably." He grinned.

"Stop it. Stop with the charming stuff. This is serious."

His smile faded. "Okay. Serious. Would I have survived the night in the swamp if you hadn't put that poultice on my leg to draw out the poison?"

"Um, maybe. Maybe not."

"According to the doctor your aunt brought in to see me, the answer is a definite no. You saved my life,

Amber. Anything I can do to help you is the least that I can do to try to repay you. So stop worrying about me."

"But, a hundred grand. I could never repay that much."

He cocked a brow. "And you won't have to, as long as you don't take off. I won't lose more than the bail bondsman's fees unless you intend to disappear and not show up in court for your hearing whenever the date is set. You aren't, are you? Planning to take off and make me lose all that money?"

Her shoulders slumped and she turned around, leading the way down the hallway again. "Not anymore," she grumbled beneath her breath. He coughed behind her, sounding suspiciously as if he was hiding a laugh.

She stopped at the first door on the right and opened it. "There are a ridiculous number of bedrooms down both of the side wings, but this is my favorite guest—" He set everything down and continued along the hall past her. "Wait, Dex, where are you going?"

She hurried after him, catching up to him five doors down. When she saw the police crime scene tape and seal on the door, she felt the blood rush from her head.

"This is your grandfather's room?" Dex asked.

"It was. Yes."

"It's still sealed." His voice sounded incredulous.

She shrugged. "I guess so. I certainly had no reason to go back inside it. And Buddy must have told the maid service to leave it alone."

He grabbed her shoulders. "Do you realize what this means?"

"Um, that you don't get to stay in the master suite?"

He rolled his eyes. "It's a fresh crime scene, even though it's two years old. We can get some investigators out here and if they find anything to help prove your innocence it will still be admissible in court. Because nothing has been touched. The police seal on the door is proof of that."

She stared at the tape and official notice with renewed interest. "You really think there's a chance they can explain Granddaddy's death some other way?"

"The current theory is that you killed him by putting peanut oil in his tonic. Did you do that?"

"Not on purpose, no."

"Do you even remember having any peanut oil anywhere?"

"Well, no, but the coroner said it would have taken only a small amount. What if I had some peanut butter left on my hands from lunch or something and when I fixed his tonic I accidentally got some in the glass?"

"Did you have a peanut butter sandwich that day?"

"It was a long time ago."

"According to the police report, when you were interviewed the morning your grandfather was found, you said you had a turkey sandwich for lunch. Your memory would have been a lot more fresh back then. So I think it's safe to say you did not have peanut butter on your hands. Plus, you knew he was allergic, so you wouldn't have taken chances if you had. You would have washed your hands."

She pushed his hands off her shoulders and faced him with her hands on her hips. "Look, I appreciate what you're trying to do. But I racked my brain after Granddaddy died. I stepped through everything I'd done that day, over and over, trying to figure out how peanut oil could have ended up in his tonic. I couldn't figure out any way for it to happen. Do I wish I could point the finger at someone else and say they were here and they're the ones to put that in his drink? Of course I do. I wish I could say I saw someone outside, or heard a door slam, or saw someone running away. But I can't. Because I didn't see anything like that. It was raining, much like it is now. No one would have come all the way out here in that kind of weather, even if they did want to hurt Granddaddy."

"Why are you so determined to take the fall for this when you obviously didn't do it?"

"Because it's my fault." She clenched her fists beside her. "He was a sick old man with just a few months to live and all I had to do was take care of him for a little while. He trusted me, relied on me, and I let him down."

"Wait, what do you mean he only had a few months to live?"

"He had bone cancer, and it had spread all over his body. There was nothing else the doctors could do for him."

"Well, that pretty much destroys the police motive that you killed your grandfather for the money. All you had to do was wait two months and it would have all been yours. Amber, the more I hear about this, the more I think the only reason you're facing these charges today is because you ran. Running implies guilt. Why did you run?"

"Your room is this way." She turned around and headed back to the first guest room. "I'll be across the hall." She didn't wait for him to catch up to her. She headed into her old bedroom and shut and locked the door behind her.

DEX STOOD IN the hall, his hands on his hips as he stared at Amber's closed door. Something wasn't right, but damned if he could put his finger on it. Everything he'd learned about Amber Callahan in the past twenty-four hours told him she was a good person, that she cared far more about others than herself—a very rare trait that was incredibly refreshing to him after the users he met and worked with every day. Most of the people he knew wanted him for his money and power. But here he was offering Amber all of that, trying to help her, and she was instead doing everything she could to avoid his help.

Yes, she'd agreed to let him put up the bail money, but only because she hadn't realized how much. Based on her reaction a few minutes ago, he had no doubt that she'd have refused his help and stayed in jail had she realized he'd put up a hundred grand to get her out. But even after she'd grudgingly agreed to let him help her, later in the limo she'd been far more interested in trying to convince him to hire a bodyguard and worried about his safety more than hers. The only thing that had made her drop that line of conversation was when he'd promised that he would indeed get his lawyer to interview and hire a bodyguard service in the next few days.

Which brought him back to her story about the peanut oil. A woman as intelligent and caring about others as Amber obviously was wouldn't risk even having something in the house that might harm her grandfather. In fact, Dex was willing to bet his entire fortune that she'd never brought a jar of peanut butter or so much as a Snickers bar into this house. She just wouldn't risk her grandfather's life that way.

Then why was she so intent on letting people think that she was the one who'd killed her grandfather, even if it was just a mistake? There was only one reason that

Dex could think of that made sense, given what he knew about Amber.

She was protecting someone else.

AMBER STOOD IN front of the bathroom mirror, eyeing her baggy clothes with distaste. She'd obviously lost ten or fifteen pounds since she'd begun her nomad-style life, because none of her old clothes fit. Well, at least they were clean. She'd have much rather gone back to her little hut and grabbed some of her clothes that she'd bartered in exchange for a few odd jobs here and there at the Miccosukee Indian reservation. But she wasn't going anywhere without Dex, not if it could cost him a hundred thousand dollars.

She grimaced at the amount. Even if she worked two full-time jobs at the reservation, she'd never earn enough to pay him back that kind of cash. Assuming she didn't end up in prison in the first place.

She sighed and tightened her belt another notch to make sure the jeans didn't fall to her knees, then headed into the bedroom and out into the hall. The rain had stopped and the sun was going down. She hadn't eaten all day and her growling stomach was reminding her every few minutes. It was time to see what Buddy had stocked, and fix something for Dex, too. He had to be just as hungry as she was, unless he'd gone downstairs and grabbed himself something to eat while she'd been hiding out in her room for the past few hours.

His door was closed, so she knocked. "Dex?" No answer. She knocked again, then decided he must have taken a nap, so she went down the stairs, automatically avoiding the right side of the third stair from the top out of habit. It had always squeaked, and she didn't want to wake Dex with the noise. He'd been through a lot in the past few days and probably still needed extra sleep for his body to fully recover.

Most of the house was filling with shadows as the sun's last rays disappeared from the windows. But she didn't need lights to find her way through the warren of rooms. Granddaddy's eccentricities had guided all the home's rather unique additions, which often meant a wall was right where you'd least expect it, and a door might end up leading nowhere. She'd loved learning all the newest quirks of the maze of rooms and false walls with hidden staircases and hallways every summer when her parents had dropped her off to spend the time between school classes with her grandpa. Sometimes she'd wondered whether he'd designed the house the way he had just to make her laugh.

The thought of her parents squelched any urge to laugh, as it always did. She pushed thoughts of them away and finally—after going through the front entryway and a maze of smaller rooms—she arrived in the kitchen. It was about a third of the way down the west wing and was the only truly modern part of the whole house. She loved to cook, and the summer after her grandpa found that out, she'd arrived to find an ultra-modern kitchen that would have made even a decent-sized restaurant groan with envy. Of course, it had been a waste on just her and her grandfather. But she'd whipped up all kinds of exotic meals to try to justify the expense of the kitchen, and to see the way his eyes closed in bliss when he tried any of her new recipes. Even the meal disasters were appreciated by her grandfather as he pretended to enjoy them.

She made her way around the marble-topped island

in the middle of the expansive room and checked out the Sub-Zero refrigerator. True to his word, Buddy had fully stocked it. And like her grandfather used to do, he'd gone overboard—loading up enough food to keep her eating for months except for perishables like milk that would have to be replenished. The deep freeze on the other side of the kitchen was loaded with all kinds of meats and desserts. And the pantry, which was hidden behind a wall of what appeared to be ordinary cabinets but was actually an enormous door, contained every spice and raw ingredient her chef's heart could possibly desire.

This was one of the few material things she'd truly missed after making her decision to leave two years ago. Cooking in a real kitchen, creating culinary masterpieces, was something that made her happy like nothing else—except for seeing her grandfather's smile, of course.

She sighed and reached down to grab a couple of Delmonico steaks from one of the freezer racks.

"That sigh could fell a tree."

She jumped, bumping her head against the top of the freezer. She turned with the steaks in hand to see Dex standing near the door that led to the backyard and the vegetable garden she used to tend so long ago. The mud streaked on the bottom of the jeans he was now wearing, plus the shoeless socks peeking out from beneath them, told her he'd been outside even if he wasn't standing by the door. At least he'd had the sense to leave his muddy shoes by the door, on the little mat.

"Sorry," he said.

She closed the freezer and arched a brow in question.

"About you bumping your head," he said. "Didn't mean to startle you."

"No harm done." She started across the room, then stopped. "You're not a vegetarian, are you?"

"Definitely a meatatarian. Especially if those are steaks."

"They are."

"Yum." He headed to the sink.

"What are you doing?" She placed the steaks in the microwave to thaw them out.

"Helping. What do you want me to do? Put some potatoes in the oven to bake? Or cut them up to fry?" He washed his hands under the faucet.

"Either, I guess. Whatever you want."

"Baked sounds good." He dried his hands on the kitchen towel. "Point me to the veggies."

She laughed, both surprised and delighted that he was going to cook with her. "Over there, to the right of the freezer. Pull the door on the third cabinet in the middle."

When he did, and the entire wall opened up, he arched his brows. "Cool. Are there other surprises like this around here?"

"Everywhere."

"Tour?" he asked, looking as excited as a little boy.

"After we eat. Absolutely."

"I'll eat fast."

She shook her head at his enthusiasm and set the now defrosted steaks onto a plate to rub seasoning on them. The process of cooking, eating and then cleaning the kitchen, all the while listening to Dex talk about his time as a navy pilot and then later his adventures starting what became a billion-dollar corporation, relaxed her far more than she'd been in ages. He was an engaging speaker and made even the most mundane topics sound interesting. Just watching his eyes light up when he threw around financial investment terms she'd never much paid attention to in the past was pure joy.

She dried her hands on the kitchen towel and tossed it to him to do the same.

"And then you decided to go into business with my friend Faye's husband and become a private investigator?"

He hung the towel over the faucet to dry. "Jake was more the private investigator, because he was a former police detective when he lived in Saint Augustine."

"Where you live."

He nodded. "Faye was the target of our first case actually. She was suspected of murder."

"You're kidding."

"Don't worry. Things worked out. She was innocent— Jake proved it."

"With your help."

"Some. I can't take much credit. He's the one with the investigative skills."

"Somehow I doubt that. Or at least, I can't imagine you trying something without becoming pretty adept at it. You don't know how to fail."

"Trust me. I've been known to fail a time or two." His eyes darkened and it seemed that a shadow passed over his eyes. But then, he smiled again and seemed to shake himself out of whatever memories had bothered him. "I'm pretty sure you mentioned something about a tour earlier."

"I'm pretty sure you're right. Come on. I'll show you the general layout of the house for starters." She glanced at his socks. "Although, you might want to take those off or you'll be sliding all over the hardwood floors. The only place with carpeting is the bedrooms."

He tugged off his socks and shoved them in the pockets of his jeans. "Ready."

She took him through the west wing first, then the east wing, before finally making it upstairs nearly an hour later. He leaned against the banister, then jumped back when it wobbled.

"Whoa. That needs some tightening," he said.

She frowned in surprise. "Granddaddy was meticulous about keeping this place well repaired. I don't know why the banister would be loose like that."

"It has been two years. Maybe Buddy wasn't as worried about home maintenance as your grandfather. Do you have any tools around here? I can hammer a few nails into the base to temporarily stabilize it until we can get someone out here to do it the right way."

"Are you sure?"

He wobbled the banister again. "Positive. This is dangerous. I wouldn't want you to grab it to save yourself from a fall and have the whole thing come loose."

"All right. There's a maintenance shed out back. That's where Grandpa kept everything when I lived here. I assume the tools are still there, though he didn't use them much himself in the last few years that he was alive. He'd really slowed down by then."

"From the cancer or age?"

"Age at first, then cancer."

They went to the kitchen and he pulled his socks and shoes on before holding the door open for her.

A shadow moved by a stand of trees twenty feet away

and hurried around the back of the very building that Amber had been about to take Dex to.

"What the...? Stay here." Dex shoved her back inside and slammed the door. Then he took off running toward the building.

DEX FLATTENED HIMSELF against the side of the building and eased toward the next corner. He'd already searched the inside and made a full circuit around the outside and decided the intruder had gotten away. He was about to head back to the house when he heard a muffled sound and turned back toward the building again.

A few more feet, closer, closer. He turned the corner. Moonlight glinted off a gun. He grabbed for it and tackled the intruder to the ground, twisting the gun away from them then pressing it against their forehead.

Amber's hazel eyes stared back at him in shock.

He cursed and jerked the gun away from her, pointing down at the ground.

"What the hell are you doing out here? With a gun, no less?"

Her brows lowered. "What were you doing out here without a gun? You could have been hurt."

"And I could have shot you just now with your own gun."

She swallowed hard. "Well, yes, there is that."

He swore again and pulled her to her feet, then shoved the pistol into his waistband. He looked around to make sure that whoever he'd seen wasn't sneaking up on them, then put his hand on the small of her back because he remembered how she hated him grabbing her hand and pulling her after him.

"Come on," he urged. "Let's get inside before whoever was out here decides to come back."

Once they were inside the kitchen, he turned the lock on the door and yanked out his cell phone.

"What are you doing?" she asked.

"Calling Deputy Holder. Assuming I can get cell coverage."

She shrank away from him. "If you're worried about the gun, it belonged to my grandfather. It's registered."

"I'm not worried about the gun. I'm worried about whoever we saw skulking around the property. With you and me both outside looking for him, there was no one watching the unlocked kitchen door."

Her eyes widened and she turned around, looking at the dark opening that led into the next room before backing up against the wall beside Dex. "You think he's inside?" she whispered.

"I have no idea. But I'm not about to take any chances." When Holder came on the phone, Dex told him about the shadowy figure he'd seen behind the house. After ending the call, he pulled the gun out of his waistband. "Let's sit at the kitchen table until Holder gets here with some deputies to help search the house."

She sat beside him while he aimed the pistol at the doorway.

"Why didn't you tell Holder about the gun?" she asked.

"Because before he gets here, we're hiding the gun. He doesn't need to know it even exists."

"Why?"

He glanced down at her before looking back at the opening. "Because I'm pretty sure someone out on bond for a murder charge isn't supposed to have any weapons. They could yank your bail and lock you right back up."

She shivered beside him. "I hadn't thought of that. Thank you."

"It's my job to think of things like that."

"Your job?"

"You know…as a deputy and all." He grinned.

She rolled her eyes.

"Where was the gun hidden anyway?" he asked.

She waved vaguely toward the far wall. "In a hidden panel."

"How many of these hidden panels are there?"

"Too many to count."

"Do they all contain guns?"

"Of course not. Just the ones by the front door, the back door here, and in Grandpa's bedroom upstairs."

He shook his head.

"What?" she asked. "Why does that seem to worry you?"

"Well, let me see. The house has been vacant for two years. And someone was skulking around the property like they know it really well and managed to slip past me even though I was out there trying to find them. I have to think they know this place, and if they've been slipping in and out of the house for the past few years, they might know all of the hiding places, too."

"Meaning they could have one of Grandpa's guns."

"Yep. And Holder's a good hour outside Mystic Glades. I'm thinking we might want to hunker down somewhere more defensible than this kitchen while we wait for backup."

"I couldn't agree more."

"Is there a room without any windows close by?"

"The pantry, I guess?"

"That works." They headed toward the wall of cabinets.

A distant squeak sounded from somewhere deep in the house. They both froze.

"Any idea what that was?" Dex asked.

"Yes. It was the stairs," she whispered. "Someone's inside the house."

Dex hurried to the cabinets and yanked the door open. "Get in."

She went inside but stopped and turned around when he didn't join her. "What are you doing? Come in here with me."

He shoved the gun into her hands. "Barricade the door and don't let anyone in but me or Deputy Holder."

"Wait," she whispered harshly. "Dex, you're not going out there without the gun. And I'm not hiding in here while you're risking your life."

He leaned down and tilted her chin up. "Amber, there's no way in hell you're going with me. And I'm not leaving you here defenseless. Take the gun, and barricade the door."

He gently shoved her back and pulled the door closed.

Amber gritted her teeth and yanked the door open.

But Dex was gone, and the lights were off.

Chapter Eight

Dex crouched against the wall, keeping as still as possible as he peered down the second-floor hallway in the east wing. Unless he remembered incorrectly, there were no balconies off this section of the house. Which meant whoever he'd followed up here was trapped. And that made him dangerous.

There. A dull thump, from one of the rooms on the right. He inched his way down the hall and stopped in front of the door that seemed the most likely to be where the intruder was hiding. A second later, another thump.

Dex carefully turned the doorknob, then threw the door open and ran inside. He saw the silhouette of someone by the window, but he knew that silhouette now.

"Damn it, Amber. How did you even get up here?"

The light flicked on overhead. Amber stood a few feet away, the pistol wedged in her waistband. "I wasn't about to cower in the pantry while you went off after an intruder. Especially since you left the gun with me."

"Did it occur to you that I'm trying to protect you?"

"Yes. And I appreciate it. But welcome to the modern age. I can protect myself."

He sighed. "I suppose you can. But that doesn't mean

I'm not going to try to protect you anyway. I'm clinging to my Neanderthal roots."

She laughed.

He grinned. "You should do that more." His grin faded and he turned around. "Since I don't see anyone else up here, I'm guessing the bad guy got away before I made it upstairs. How did you get up here without passing me?"

"I used the back stairs."

"Back stairs? Where?"

She stepped to the wall and pressed a decal of a flower. A panel slid back to reveal a dark hole. Dex peeked into the opening.

"I should have expected something like that in a house like this. You left this off the tour."

"Yeah, well, I hadn't intended to show it to you, to be honest." At his questioning glance, she added, "But that was before I learned about the exorbitant fortune you put down to bail me out. I guess I can show you the rest of the house and all of its secrets now that I'm not going to run away again."

He eyed the opening. "If I came up the main stairs, and you came up these back stairs, where did the intruder go?"

"Like you said, he had to have gotten downstairs before you made it from the kitchen to the second floor."

"I'm not liking this at all. He could be anywhere. This house is way too big to secure. I think we should move back to your aunt's bar until this is over. At least there I knew where the exits were and there weren't any hidden panels or staircases to worry about."

Amber bit her bottom lip and looked away.

Dex blinked at her. "There are hidden panels and staircases at Freddie's?"

She nodded. "A couple. Honestly, they're all over this town. My grandfather was a bit...eccentric. And he founded Mystic Glades. He pretty much left his stamp on everything."

"So, who all knows about these hidden passageways?"

"Everyone, I guess."

"Even in this house?"

She shrugged. "I suppose not. I mean, people are bound to assume that there are hidden passageways. But unless Grandpa or I took them on a tour, they wouldn't know where the openings are or what to look for."

"Can you think of anyone besides you, and his children obviously, who might know?"

Her look turned guarded, and he immediately knew she was hiding something. Again. The only question was why.

"Not really," she said. "Grandpa wasn't big on socializing and I certainly never had anyone over."

He waited, hoping she'd level with him, but when she didn't say anything else, he swallowed his disappointment. "Okay. Then we're back to assuming no one knows about the hidden areas. So as long as Holder helps us search the house to insure no one's still inside hiding somewhere, we should be okay."

"Agreed."

He moved toward the door. "We might as well go downstairs and wait for Holder below. We can set up a defensible position in the main living room in the front, with our backs to the fireplace."

"You're not going to try to make me hide in a closet?"

He rolled his eyes. "I've given up on trying to make you do anything."

Half an hour later, red-and-blue flashing lights lit up the windows on the front room. Per their agreement, Amber hid the gun in a wall panel before Dex answered the door. Holder stood on the porch with three other deputies. The lines at the corners of his eyes were tense and his right hand hovered near the pistol on his belt.

"Bring me up to speed," he said.

A few minutes later, two of the deputies were searching the property in the back where Amber and Dex had seen someone skulking by the maintenance building, while the third deputy stayed with Holder inside the house. They made a circuit of the entire house, one with Amber and one with Dex so they could show them through the maze of rooms. By the time they were done, Dex was convinced no one was in the house, and that no one had probably ever been inside, because the only footprints they saw were those of Dex and Amber.

"The noise we heard on the stairs earlier must have been the house settling," Dex said.

Amber didn't look convinced, but she nodded anyway.

"Well, everything's locked up safe and sound now," Holder said. "We did find footprints in the backyard that don't match either of your shoes. So there was definitely someone out there. Probably just some neighborhood kid curious about someone being at the Callahan mansion since it's been vacant for so long. Whoever they were, they're long gone now." He arched a brow. "If you're worried about staying out here alone, I can take you back to Naples with me. You can set up in a hotel."

Dex looked at Amber. "It's up to you."

She immediately shook her head. "I'd rather stay here, if it's all the same to you."

"We'll stay."

"Suit yourself," Holder said. "Oh, since I'm out here, I might as well update you about the case, Miss Callahan. Your grandfather's body has been exhumed and the private coroner that Mr. Lassiter hired will begin the autopsy in the morning."

"So soon?" she said.

He slanted a glance at Dex. "Money is known for making things happen. I reckon you'll have results later tomorrow, if not sooner."

"Thank you," Amber said, her voice small.

Holder nodded. "Call us if you need us, but remember we're an hour out. So if something happens again you might want to seriously consider getting someone to bring you back to town." He cocked a brow at Dex. "Unless you've decided to give up your glamorous new role as a cop and want to turn Miss Callahan over to me to take back to jail."

"And give up my shiny gold star?" He rubbed his shirt as if he really did have a star on it. "I don't think so."

Holder shook his head and herded his men out of the house. After the police cars were heading down the driveway, Dex closed and locked the door. Amber stood silently staring at the floor.

"Amber, you okay?"

She looked up and shrugged. "It just seems so… wrong…to dig up my grandfather's body. We already know how he died."

He put his hands on her shoulders. "I don't think he'd

mind us disturbing his grave if it means we might find something to help prove your innocence."

Her gaze didn't meet his as she nodded, which only reinforced his earlier suspicion that she was hiding something.

"If there was something about your grandfather's death that you haven't told anyone, you'd tell now, wouldn't you? Knowing it could mean the difference between prison and freedom? And remember that Florida is a capital-punishment state. The prosecutor could go for the death penalty."

She shivered and rubbed her hands up and down her arms. "I know. I'm tired. I think I'll head on up to bed." Without another word, she headed up the stairs and disappeared into her room.

Dex sighed, retrieved the gun from the panel in the family room and then headed up to his room.

AMBER LAY IN bed staring at the ceiling. She couldn't sleep, not with so many worries on her mind. Who was the intruder who'd been in the backyard? What did he want? Was it really just a teenager—or someone more sinister?

And what, if anything, should she do about telling the truth about what happened to her grandfather?

Years ago she'd made a decision that she'd wondered many times about later on. But after coming back to Mystic Glades, she'd seen the reason for her lies and felt the same surge of protectiveness that she had before she'd left. What she was doing made sense because she knew it was what her grandfather would want. And it had never hurt before, until she'd met Dex. Now she was feeling things she hadn't felt since she was in high school: that delicious rush of heat every time she looked at him, the pleasant tightening of her belly when she'd seen him without his shirt, the tingle of anticipation when he held her hand. She had a crush on Dex Lassiter. There was no denying it. Except that this crush was far worse than any she'd ever experienced before. She couldn't stop thinking about him or seeing his face whenever he wasn't around. And it was because of these overwhelming feelings that she was in the trouble she was in right now. If she hadn't been so eager to see him again, and so driven to make sure that he was okay, she'd be home right now, "home" being her place in the Glades instead of this monstrosity that she still thought of as her grandfather's house.

It wasn't her home. Not really. It was her sanctuary and refuge when her parents had left her here each summer, a way to escape the constant bickering and fighting and tension in her house between two people who supposedly had loved each other once, a very long time ago. Her grandfather had been very private and pretty much regarded as the town scrooge, but he'd seen through her pain as a teenager and had rather forcefully insisted that her parents go off on an extended vacation in Europe the summer of her junior year. The fact that he'd dumped a boatload of money on them to sweeten the pot had worked and they'd jetted off for a vacation. And Amber had spent that first, awkward summer with her grandfather, feeling abandoned and unloved. Until she got to know him. And then she saw the marshmallow inside him and knew he loved her deeply and that he'd been trying to save her, in his own way.

From then on out they'd become each other's champions, existing in a usually quiet but comfortable camaraderie with each other. And when her parents ended up staying in Europe after her graduation, she knew her grandfather was behind that, that he must have made it a financial windfall for them to stay away. She'd gone to college and spent all her breaks with her grandfather, and had mostly done the same thing that her parents had done to her—she'd forgotten about them. Until her grandfather's death, when they'd returned just long enough to find out that they weren't mentioned in his will. Then they'd done what they were so good at—they'd disappeared, without hanging around long enough to see what had happened to Amber.

She shoved the covers back and slid out of bed. Enough of this. She was making herself miserable thinking about the past, about the only people in her life she should have been able to count on and rely on who'd never, not once, been there for her.

A board creaked in the hallway outside her bedroom. She froze and looked around for some kind of weapon, but Dex had taken her gun. She grabbed a heavy bookend from a bookshelf by the bed and tiptoed to the door. Then she quietly, carefully, turned the knob and yanked the door open.

Dex swore and grabbed the bookend out of her raised hand. "Good grief, Amber. What are you doing with that?"

"I heard a noise."

He grimaced and stepped to his left, making a board squeak. "Was that what you heard?"

"Yes. What are you doing outside my door?"

"I was pacing the hall. Couldn't sleep. But as soon as I stepped on that board I was worried you might have heard it and might be scared. I was waiting to see if I'd woken you so I could reassure you that the noise was just me."

"Oh." She felt her face flush hot. "I wasn't scared."

He set the bookend on a decorative table against the wall. "Of course not." He winked. "Well, sorry again for waking you. I'll just…go back to my room."

"Okay. Night."

"Night." He hesitated, his gaze dropping to the night-shirt that barely came to the tops of her thighs before he seemed to wrench his gaze away. He cleared his throat. "See you in the morning."

She watched in silence as he went into his room across the hall and shut the door. The heat in his gaze was unmistakable and had sparked an answering tug in her belly. And suddenly she was thinking things she shouldn't be thinking. Because having a crush was one thing. But taking it to the next level, to a level where there was no coming back from, was quite another. She shouldn't be thinking about holding him close, about running her fingers over his rippling muscles. About seeing if he kissed as good when he was conscious as he had when he'd been burning up with fever back by the spring.

No, it was wrong to think about being with him, even if he wanted her as much as she wanted him. Because there was no future, no possibility of one, while she was wanted for murder and had no way to prove she hadn't done it without destroying someone else. Lying, even though she hated it, was accomplishing the only good thing she'd ever done in her life. If protecting her grandfather's best friend from the horrible mistake that he'd made meant sacrificing herself, it was a price she was willing to pay. Because it was the only way she could repay her grandfather for being the only person who'd ever really cared about her. And she never wanted to be the selfish, self-centered type of person that both of her parents had been. Living a life like that was no life and wasn't a future she was willing to contemplate. She'd rather have no future and die knowing that she'd done the right thing.

She started to step back and close the door, but she stopped and stared longingly at the closed door across the hall. She'd had so little love in her life, and only one disastrous intimate relationship in college with a guy who'd ended up more concerned with notches on his bedpost than the lasting relationship she'd hoped to have. So how could she even consider what amounted to a one-night stand with Dex? She barely knew him.

But she already knew he was worlds better than the immature boy from her past.

Dex was all man—tall, strong, incredibly appealing in every way. And he had that sexy smile that made her want to grab him and kiss him every time he aimed it her way. But he was so much more than that, just based on what he'd said when he'd been delirious. She knew that he'd been worried about leaving his company to fly out to Mystic Glades, but he'd done it anyway because he wanted to protect his best friend from what Dex believed might be a very bad decision. And as soon as he'd realized his friend Jake had thought it all through and was determined to continue on the route he'd chosen, Dex had supported him in that decision.

And then when he'd found himself here, even knowing that someone was trying to kill him, he'd continued to put his life on hold to help her, a stranger, simply because he felt an obligation to her for helping him after the crash. He was putting all his resources behind trying to help her. And then he'd risked his life for her twice tonight—first going after the intruder by the shed and then going through the house in the dark, without a weapon, to find the intruder because they'd both believed him to be inside. What did she know about Dex? She knew that he was a good person, kind, and genuinely caring.

She curled her fingers around the doorjamb. If loving him, just this once, was a mistake, why did the thought of being in his arms feel so right? She was tired, so tired, of being on guard and worrying all the time. Just this once, she wanted to push all her worries aside and simply live. Especially if she'd be spending the rest of her life in prison or—worse—facing the death penalty.

With that thought, she pushed herself forward until she was standing at Dex's door. This was what she wanted, one night of joy, one night to treasure and hold close to get her through the darkness that surely lay ahead.

She turned the knob, then slowly pushed the door open. "Dex?" she whispered. If he was asleep, she'd go back to her room and know that this was a mistake.

The covers rustled in the big four-poster bed. "Amber? What's wrong?" He slid out of bed, the moonlight glinting through a slit in the curtains, revealing that he was wearing only boxers.

Her mouth went dry at the sight of all that skin and those sculpted muscles as he strode toward her. He stopped in front of her and moved her to the side as he peered into the hallway. Always the protector. She loved that about him, even though she knew she could protect herself.

"Nothing's wrong," she said.

He stepped back and turned around. "Then why—"

She pushed the door closed and, for emphasis, turned the lock. "I don't want to be alone tonight."

His Adam's apple bobbed in his throat and his hand shook as he swept her hair back from her face. "Canoe Girl, don't tempt me. Because since I met you, I've been thinking about little else but getting you into bed." He dropped his hands to his sides, his fingers curling into fists as if to make him stop from reaching for her.

"Why fight it, then? I want the same thing." She reached for her nightshirt to take it off, but he grabbed her wrists.

"Don't. I'm trying to be noble here. You're just feeling beholden to me because I paid your bail and hired a lawyer. I wouldn't want you to feel obligated. Please, go back to your room." He reached for the doorknob, but she moved in front of him.

"Amber—"

"Dex," she whispered back, as she swiftly pulled her nightshirt over her head and tossed it to the floor.

His eyes widened and his mouth dropped open as he looked his fill. She was completely naked and knew she was being unfair. But just the fact that he was trying to be noble had made her want him even more. He truly was a good guy. She just wished she'd met him years ago, that he could have been her first, and maybe her last, and that she could have been anywhere but here back when her grandfather had gotten sick. Maybe, just maybe, things would have turned out differently.

She ruthlessly stepped forward, sliding her hands up his glorious chest, reveling in the catch in his breath and how his muscles tensed beneath her fingertips. She slid her fingers up, up, up until her body was pressed flush against his and her hands were behind his neck. A shudder racked his entire body, and he groaned. It was a groan of surrender, because suddenly he was pulling her tighter against him, against the hardening erection pulsing against her belly, and molding his lips to hers.

His kiss was like fire, igniting all her nerve endings, tightening her belly almost painfully and melting her insides. She shifted against him, their mouths greedily moving against each other as she tried to get closer, closer. He reached down and lifted her into his arms, one arm beneath her bottom, his hand molded against her thigh as the other wrapped around her back. He turned with her in his arms and pressed her against the door.

His tongue dueled with hers, tasting, teasing, fanning her pleasure higher and higher. He broke the kiss, both of them gasping for air as he moved his mouth to the side of her neck. She leaned her head sideways, shivering in delight at the feel of his lips, his tongue, against the sensitive skin of her collarbone.

Unable to bear the growing pressure inside her, she rubbed her body against his and angled one arm down his back to his hip. He jerked against her, the cloth of his underwear the only barrier keeping him from penetrating her. He shuddered again and moved back to her mouth. But, instead of kissing her, he stared down into her eyes.

"Are you sure about this?" he whispered.

In answer she stroked her hand down his flank.

He growled low in his throat and captured her lips in a searing kiss as he turned and stumbled toward the bed. Holding her with his hand beneath her bottom, he used his other hand to rake the covers back, then gently laid her down on the soft mattress. But, instead of following her down, he pressed a quick, hard kiss against her lips and let her go.

"Dex—"

"I'll be right back."

She turned her head on the pillow and watched him cross the room to the dresser. His suitcase was sitting open on top. He fumbled inside and when he turned around she realized what he was holding. A condom. Or, more accurately, a box of them. He tore the top off, grabbed one and let the box drop to the floor as he hurried back to the bed and sat down on the side of the mattress.

"You always travel with a box of condoms?" she asked.

"My assistant packed them when he sent everything to me." He hesitated, the packet in his hand. "If you want to stop, I'll understand. I'm not exactly a celibate guy or a wait-until-marriage kind of man. Some might even call me a womanizer. Obviously my assistant thinks so, since he made sure I was prepared for any…ah…emergency." He gave her a lopsided grin.

He waited, looking like he fully expected her to tell him to forget it. But just the fact that he was being honest was an added turn-on for her. Honesty was so rare, and to her knowledge Dex had never lied to her, about anything. And even though "womanizer" wasn't in the least bit flattering, he'd readily admitted that the label might fit. But did it really?

She ran a finger down his thigh, delighting in how his muscles tightened beneath her touch. "Are you one of those one-night-stand kinds of guys?"

He slowly shook his head, watching her finger as it moved toward his inner thigh. "No." His voice was raw, tight. "If this…what we're doing…is a one-night stand, then I'd have to admit it's a first for me. But I'm not one for being alone, either. I like being in a relationship." He gave her a wry smile. "I'm just not very good at them."

She stopped with her hand poised just inches from his erection, tenting his boxers. "Are you in one now, a relationship?"

He frowned. "Of course not. I would never cheat on anyone."

She hooked her finger inside the elastic band. "Then what are we waiting for?"

His smile in the dark made him look like a charming rogue. "I have no idea." In no time he'd shucked his underwear and rolled on the condom. Then he was pressing her back against the mattress, the light matting of hair on his chest tickling her sensitive skin.

Any doubts or worries that she'd had disappeared beneath the flood of sensations he was awakening inside her. Like a master, he stroked her body like a fine instrument, stimulating every nerve ending, making her restless and yearning beneath him, never knowing where the next stroke would occur. Although he seemed to touch her everywhere, his movements were unhurried as he fully devoted himself to wringing out every last bit of pleasure that he could in one spot before moving to the next.

It was as if he wanted to leave no part of her untouched, unclaimed, before he finally moved up her body and captured her lips again. For the first time ever, she let go, allowing herself to submerge completely, awash in the flood of emotions and feelings he'd created inside her. She was just as eager as he, touching everywhere, stroking, petting, caressing until she felt she'd die from the pleasure of it.

And then he moved above her, looking deep into her eyes as he poised himself at her entrance and laced his fingers with hers above her head. He leaned down, slowly, oh so slowly, and gave her the sweetest kiss ever as he pressed inside her. It had been so long, too long, and she tensed against the invasion. But he whispered reassuring words in her ear, then made love to her mouth with his lips and tongue in rhythm to the movements of his hips, capturing her gasps of surprise and pleasure. She relaxed beneath his sensual onslaught and was soon just as frenzied as him, straining toward the next peak, riding the sensations higher and higher until an explosion of pleasure shot through her and she cried out his name.

He soon joined her in his own climax and collapsed against the mattress, rolling to his side with her in his arms.

Chapter Nine

Dex put away the last frying pan and plopped the dish towel on the countertop as he eyed Amber washing the kitchen table.

She glanced up at him, then quickly looked away, her face heating to a pretty shade of pink that wasn't actually so pretty since he knew why she was blushing. She'd barely been able to put together two words since they'd woken up in each other's arms this morning. What he didn't know yet was whether she regretted making love with him or whether she was just being shy because she was so inexperienced.

He winced. How many lovers had he had over the years? A dozen? Maybe more? And if he guessed right Amber had probably had only one lover other than him. And the only reason he figured she'd even had one was because she wasn't a virgin. He'd taken her boldness at the beginning of the evening as a sign that she was comfortable with what they were going to do, that she wanted him as much as he wanted her. Now he wasn't so sure. Regrets? Yeah, even if she didn't have any, he sure as hell did. He knew better than to take advantage of someone as innocent as her. In the light of day, knowing her future was so uncertain right now, he felt doubly like a heel, as if he'd really taken advantage of her when he should have been protecting her from the harsh world that her aunt certainly didn't care about protecting her from. Amber had no one in her corner. He should have been her champion, should have been strong enough to say no when she came to his room. He swore beneath his breath.

Amber jumped and turned, her hands clutching the damp paper towels that she'd just used to clean the table. "Something wrong?" she asked, her gaze darting to the back door as if expecting to see another intruder.

He shook his head. "No. Sorry. Just thinking." He glanced at his watch, then at the dark clouds hanging in the sky. "It's closer to lunchtime than breakfast, not that you can tell with the clouds blocking out the sun. I imagine Garreth will call soon to give us an update on the case."

She tossed the paper towels into the trash can beneath the sink and shut the cabinet. "You don't think the medical examiner would really have something to say already about my grandfather do, you? Won't he have to run tests?"

He shrugged. "Can't say for sure. I'm no expert on things like that. But I'm hopeful it won't take long." As much money as he was paying his lawyer to encourage him to speed things along any way possible, he'd be surprised if it took long at all. Garreth could work miracles, and Dex made a point of not asking how he did it. Most of his lawyer's tactics fell into a need-to-know category and Dex figured he didn't need to know. Plus, in this case, his lawyer had already told him that "samples" had been taken and preserved from the original autopsy, so the testing had begun last night courtesy of a private lab in town that had been generously encouraged to work all night. Dex was not a patient man and he had enough money that he didn't usually have to be patient.

He leaned back against the counter with his legs spread in front of him. "The investigation would probably go much faster if you admitted whatever you know about what really happened."

She met his stare, unblinking. "I've said everything that I'm going to say. There's nothing else that I can say."

"Why? Who matters to you so much that you'd lie and risk the death penalty to protect them?"

This time it was her turn to wince. Obviously she didn't relish the idea of facing a death penalty. Maybe that was the weapon that he could use to get her to tell him the truth.

He shoved away from the sink and moved to stand directly in front of her, making her crane her neck back to meet his gaze. He was much taller than her and he wasn't above using that to his advantage, to intimidate. Usually he used his height and his brawn to intimidate men across a boardroom table or in a dinner party that was really more of a mental wrestling match to see who could gain the upper hand with a potential client for a future investment. But if using his physical size and strength to get Amber to back down would save her from prison, or worse, he was all for it.

"Tell me about that night," he said.

"I already did, and it's part of the public record that I'm sure you've already read."

"Tell me again. But this time, don't leave out the part about why you supposedly would want to kill your grandfather."

She shook her head. "I never said that I wanted to hurt my grandfather. I didn't. It was an accident."

He may have found the perfect weapon, even better than the threat of a death penalty. Amber obviously loved her grandfather very much. The idea that she'd hurt him on purpose was repugnant to her. She wouldn't want anyone else to believe that, either.

"Did he ever leave the house?"

"Once or twice a year, maybe. Other than that, he pretty much stayed on the property. He liked to work in the garden out back."

"You were in charge of the groceries, then? Buying everything for the household?"

"Yes."

"If you didn't want to hurt him, why would you buy peanuts, then, when you knew he was highly allergic?"

"I…must have made a mistake. Grabbed them by accident and tossed them in the pantry without thinking."

"Then why didn't the police find anything in the pantry?"

Her gaze dropped from his as she tried to think of something plausible, which only had Dex fisting his hands together. It was so painfully obvious that she was innocent. How could the police not have seen that years ago? He'd have to ask Holder and Garreth to review the original interview. She'd never been taken to the police station, had only been questioned at the house. So maybe that was the problem? They hadn't had the kind of in-depth questioning that might have revealed her subterfuge, and whoever had asked her questions didn't note her body language or hesitation or just plain didn't know how to read someone.

"Amber?" he prodded. "Why didn't the police find

anything to do with peanuts when they searched the house?"

"Maybe I...threw it out?"

"They looked through the trash. If you're going to lie, you need to come up with something better than that."

Her face reddened. "It was a...traumatic event that morning. I wasn't thinking straight. I was more worried with trying to save Grandpa. If there weren't any peanuts or peanut oil here, then maybe one of the jars that I used to mix his tonic had been used for peanuts in the past. And I didn't wash it well enough. I don't know. All I know for sure is that no one else was here, no one else could have done it."

Again, her gaze slid away. And again, Dex knew, with absolute certainty, that she was lying.

He shoved his hands in his pockets and moved past her to look out the back windows. "You know, they say lethal injection is far more painful than people think. You don't just go to sleep and feel nothing."

"Don't you think I know that?" she snapped.

"Then tell me what happened that day."

She joined him at the window and stared out. "He was sick, with the flu or something similar. And he was miserable, achy. I wanted to take him to Naples to see a doctor, or get a doctor to come see him here, but Grandpa was...stubborn. He insisted he'd be okay and refused to see anyone. He wanted me to take care of him. And I had been doing that for a long time—always have been a healer, basically. So when he refused a doctor I went into town to get a few things I'd need in addition to the plants I grew in the garden for mixing potions. When I got back, I mixed his tonic and gave it to him. He was resting comfortably at bedtime so I went to bed with-

out another thought about it. When I woke up, he was…
gone."

"You went to town? Where? For what?"

Her shoulders tensed, and he knew she must have
slipped, in telling him about going to town. Had something happened in town that made her suspect who
might have something to do with her grandfather's
death? And if she loved her grandfather so much, why
would she protect him or her?

"I needed…supplies."

"Okay. So you went where?"

"Here and there." At his exasperated look, she said,
"I'm pretty sure I went to The Moon."

"The Moon? I saw a shop across from Buddy's that
was called The Moon and Star. Faye Star owns it, from
what Jake told me. Is that what you're talking about?"

"Yes. It was just The Moon when I lived here. They
have potions, too, and sometimes I use those as raw ingredients in the things that I mix up."

"So maybe you grabbed something with peanut oil
in it on accident?"

She shook her head. "No. Impossible."

"Why do you say that?"

"Because as soon as we realized that Grandpa had
most likely died of an allergic reaction, I called and
asked about peanuts. The owner of The Moon at the
time was also allergic to peanuts and never has them
in the store, in any form. The tonic couldn't have gotten contaminated that way."

"Because you checked. Which just goes to prove
that you really don't know how the peanuts ended up
in there, do you? But you suspect someone else who
may know, right?"

"Why do you keep saying that?"

"You have an honest face, Amber. Every time something bothers you it shows in your eyes, in the way you tense up. And in your voice. It's like you have a light bulb on top of your head and it blinks every time you try to talk around the truth. And you've done nothing but talk around the truth every time I ask you about your grandfather's death. You're hiding something. You may not know exactly how he died, but you suspect someone. I thought you loved your grandfather?"

"I do. I did. Very much."

"Then why would you protect the one person that you think might have been responsible for his death?"

She closed her eyes as if in pain. "It's not that simple." She shoved the back door open and walked out onto the porch.

Dex followed her out, refusing to let her drop their conversation. They didn't have a lot of time, especially with Garreth pressing for answers. If those answers ended up being nothing to change things, then Amber was in a world of trouble. He had to make her see that.

"You said you loved your grandfather, and yet you're protecting someone who could very well have killed him. Explain that to me."

When she didn't say anything, he gently cupped her face. "Amber, trust me. I want to help you. But I can't, not if you don't tell me the truth." He stared down at her, waiting. "Amber, where else did you go that day? Besides The Moon?"

She stepped back, shaking her head.

A bush near the bottom of the steps rustled. Dex shoved Amber behind him just as a man stepped out from behind the shrub. Buddy Johnson. He wore the same faded jeans and red-and-black-striped shirt he'd worn yesterday at his store, but they looked rumpled, like he'd slept in them. And big bags beneath his eyes told the story of a very restless night.

"Mr. Johnson," Dex said, "What are you doing here?"

His sad eyes lifted from Amber, who had moved back beside Dex, and rose to meet Dex's gaze. "I can tell you where else she went that day, Mr. Lassiter. And I can tell you whom she's trying to protect."

"Buddy. Don't," Amber pleaded.

He gave her a sad smile. "You're a good person, Amber Callahan. And I hate to admit that I was one of the ones who thought you might have had something to do with your granddaddy's death right after it happened. But I know better now. And I know who you're trying to protect."

"Who?" Dex asked. "Who is it?"

Buddy straightened his shoulders. "Me. She's trying to protect me."

"THIS DOESN'T MAKE any sense." Dex rested his forearms on his knees as he sat forward on the couch in the living room across from Amber and Buddy on the opposite couch. "Amber, you thought Buddy was the one who killed your grandfather?"

"Accidentally. Yes."

"How?"

"I went to Buddy's store to buy a new blanket because Granddad loved those thermal ones Buddy sells and Granddad's was threadbare. Buddy is the one who packed the blanket and some other supplies into my backpack, including some new jars that I always order from him for making my tonics. Since I knew I didn't have any peanuts in the house, those jars were the only way there could have been any peanut residue. I realized that later, and I knew Buddy would never intentionally harm my grandfather. They were best friends. I figured he had to have had the jars stored with peanuts or something and didn't think about it."

"But why wouldn't you tell the police?"

She and Buddy both shared a frown, a united front, before she continued. "The police have never shown much love for Mystic Glades residents. I didn't trust them to think it was an accident. I couldn't risk something happening to Buddy."

"But why? Why would you sacrifice yourself to protect him, especially if it was an accident?"

Buddy put his arm around her shoulders as if to protect her from Dex, which was really rather ludicrous, given the situation. "Mr. Lassiter, Amber's a good woman and I'm sure she thought I wouldn't be able to handle prison and she could. We always stand up for each other and she's always respected her elders."

Dex suspected there was more to it than that, but for now, he let it drop. "Okay, so is Amber right? That the jars you gave her were tainted?"

"I think so, yes. But I didn't realize it at the time. I thought— Well, I'm sorry, Amber, but I couldn't figure out any other way, so I assumed you'd done it."

She shrugged. "How could you not? Even my own aunt thought the same thing. Still does."

"Yes, well, it was a few weeks later that I was unpacking the rest of those jars when I realized a shipment of peanuts had come in the same box and were sitting beneath a layer of tissue paper. I figured during the shipment some of the peanuts had shifted and gotten oil on the jars. But by then, Amber was gone and there was nothing I could do to help her."

"You could have helped her yesterday, by going into town and telling the police what had happened."

He nodded. "You're right. But I was scared, and ashamed. It took me a bit of time to come to my senses. I wanted to tell her first, and I came out last night to do that very thing. But then you saw me and came after me and I ran."

"It was you out by the shed?" Dex asked.

"Yes. Like I said, I lost my nerve, so I took off. But I'm here now to tell what I know. You can call the police and I'll confess."

Dex rolled his eyes. Confess? He'd never seen two innocent people more intent on confessing to their crimes before. "Confession is for guilty people, Mr. Johnson. You didn't try to kill Mr. Callahan any more than Amber did. It was one big accident all around. I just have one more question before I call Deputy Holder. Why did you go into the house last night?"

Buddy's brows lowered. "Go into the house? I didn't. Why would you think that I did?"

Dex exchanged a look with Amber. "We heard something and thought someone was inside."

Buddy shook his head. "I didn't try to go inside. I had no reason to."

"Okay," Dex said. "Maybe there's another explanation, like the house settling. I don't know. I'll call Holder. I just wish we had some kind of proof to make the case stronger to help Amber."

"Oh, I have proof. Right here." Buddy took an envelope from the pocket of his shirt and handed it to Amber.

She opened it and pulled out two pictures. Dex got up and squatted down in front of the couch, looking at the pictures with her. They showed a box of bottles with tissue paper beneath them but flipped up at one corner to show a bag of peanuts that had a rip in it, with the peanuts all over the bottom of the box.

"That's your proof?" Dex said. "You could have taken that picture today."

"Nope. Look at the bottom right corner, the label on the box."

Amber raised the picture higher as she and Dex tried to read the date. "It's from the week when Granddaddy died," Amber said.

"It sure is. With my store's name on it. And the peanuts, you can tell, are fresh. The picture is legit."

"Okay, then, what about proof that Amber actually bought some of those bottles at your store that day?" Dex asked.

"I keep records of all of that in my logbooks. I can get them."

"No, don't bother. We'll wait until Holder gets here and then he can get them. That will be better. Speaking of which, I'll call him now."

He left Amber and Buddy holding hands and whispering to each other like long-lost friends as he stepped into one of the rooms without windows in the middle of the mazelike house just far enough away so no one could hear him. He explained to Holder exactly what he'd just been told.

"Interesting," Holder said. "That certainly makes it plausible that there was no intent to harm. And, combined with what the coroner found, I'm sure Miss Callahan is going to be quite pleased."

"What did the coroner find?"

"Mr. Callahan didn't die from an allergic reaction."

Dex's hand tightened around the phone. "You're kidding me."

"Nope. There was peanut oil in that tonic, but only faint traces, probably enough to corroborate the story that the glass was packed in a box with peanuts as opposed to someone trying to add enough oil to kill him. But when the coroner performed some tests, at your lawyer's insistence, she determined the ingredients in the tonic would have rendered any allergic types of reactions irrelevant because the tonic was a natural antihistamine. It would have counteracted anything to do with the peanut allergy even if it were triggered. Mr. Callahan's death is now being labeled as 'natural causes.'"

"Heart attack?"

"Respiratory. The cancer weakened his lungs and the flu was the final straw. He just couldn't take it. As of right this minute, all the charges against Amber Callahan are dropped."

Chapter Ten

Amber stood on the back porch, watching the play of lightning across the dark afternoon sky. Heavy rain clouds warned of another storm that would break across the Glades and probably turn the small water inlets into fast-flowing rivers for the next few days.

Dex stood beside her but, instead of watching the sky, he was watching her. "You should be happy," he said.

"I am. I guess. It's just so…surprising. Sudden."

"Sudden? You lived in exile for two years."

"I know. That's not what I mean. One day I know who I am and what I'm doing and less than a week later a plane drops out of the sky." She turned to face him. "And everything changed. Now I have a life again, a future. And I have you to thank for that." She entwined her arms around his neck and stepped into the cocoon of his arms.

He hugged her tight and rested his cheek on the top of her head. "I still don't understand. Why did you try to cover for Buddy?"

She tightened her arms around him. "You won't understand, even if I explain it."

"Try me."

She closed her eyes and rested her head against his chest. "All my life, the only person who ever cared about me—in my family, at least—was my grandfather. And my friend Faye, of course. But my grandfather was the one who was always there for me no matter what. From the time I was little until the day he died. He did everything for me. He basically saved me by bribing my self-centered parents to move away and leave me with him. He gave me security, love, financial stability, and he only asked one thing in return—that I take care of his friend, Buddy."

"What do you mean? Buddy's a grown man. He doesn't need anyone to take care of him."

She pulled back and looked at him. "Buddy doesn't need money—he's got plenty of his own because of some kind of swamp buggy invention. Grandpa just wanted me to always make sure Buddy was okay even after Grandpa was gone. So when he died, and I realized that Buddy may have been responsible—purely by accident—I couldn't risk him going to jail."

"So you decided to allow the blame to fall on you. That's crazy."

She stiffened and pushed him, but his arms tightened and he didn't let her go.

"I didn't say *you* were crazy, just that the decision you made was crazy. I can't imagine your grandfather wanting you to sacrifice your future just to keep his best friend from going to jail."

"That's because you didn't know my father," a voice said from the yard. "He was cold and mean, even to those he supposedly loved."

Dex and Amber turned to see Freddie Callahan standing at the bottom of the stairs, in pretty much the same place that Buddy had been standing earlier in the day.

"What is it with you people sneaking up on us all the time?" Dex grumbled.

"What do you want?" Amber said, not sounding particularly welcoming, and Dex couldn't blame her for that. Freddie had never been supportive of Amber and had just insulted the man that Amber held up as her hero.

Freddie held out her hands in a plaintive gesture. "I came to apologize. Amber, I know I always assumed you had something to do with my father's death. But you can't exactly blame me since you ran the way you did. Now that Buddy has explained to everyone what really happened, I'm here to, well, like I said— apologize. I'm sorry that I couldn't support you more. Without knowing the truth, I couldn't. Even though I didn't even like him, he was still my father. And I owed him more loyalty than to welcome back the niece who'd played a role in his death." She held her hands out as if to hug Amber. "But I'd like to welcome you back now. If you'll let me."

Amber leaned into Dex's side. "I don't know that I'm ready for hugs, but if you want to visit, to get to know me better, I'd welcome you into the house." She looked up at the ominous sky. "You might want to hurry before the storm opens up, too."

Freddie looked up at the sky. "You've got that right. This is going to be one for the record books. I can feel it in my bones." She hurried up the steps and Amber led her into the kitchen, with Dex following close behind.

No sooner had they gotten inside than the rain began

pouring down so heavily the trees in the backyard were nearly hidden from view.

"Wow," Freddie said. "Good thing I rolled up my windows before parking out front. I rang that doorbell a bunch of times, but you must not have heard it since you were out back."

As if on cue, the doorbell rang. They all hurried through the maze of rooms toward the front of the house. When she opened the door, she was surprised to see Buddy Johnson standing on the porch, along with a young woman of eighteen or nineteen that she didn't recognize.

"Buddy? What can I do for you?"

He motioned to the young brunette beside him. "This is Amy. She works part-time at The Moon and Star and has been covering while Faye and Jake are on their honeymoon. We thought it might be nice to bring you dinner to welcome you back. I hope you don't mind. We thought it would be fun to surprise you."

She stood in the opening, not sure what to do. Yes, she'd taken the blame for her grandfather's death to protect Buddy. But it still stung that no one had questioned her guilt. No one but a stranger named Dex Lassiter.

He chose that moment to put his arm around her shoulder and pull her against his side. "Amber," he whispered, low, "unless you have an ark to put them in to send them back to town I think you might need to step back and let them in."

She sighed and moved aside.

Dex leaned down toward her. "Very nice of you to welcome them," he whispered. "And from the looks of the storm, they might end up being overnight guests."

"Wonderful," she grumbled.

They were about to step back and close the door when a set of headlights appeared from the dark monsoon and inched its way past the other cars to the far end of the porch, where another set of steps angled down from another opening in the railing.

"I don't think I know anyone who arrives in limousines," Amber said. "Must be someone you know."

"Probably Garreth, our attorney."

She smiled at the way he'd said "our" and headed with him down the long porch to where the car had parked. The lights turned off as the driver cut the engine. Then he hopped out in the rain, opened an enormous black umbrella and hurried to the far side to open the door. Three men and a woman scrambled out of the car and hurried up the porch, followed by the driver carrying small bags as if the people planned on staying for a while.

Dex cursed and stopped when he and Amber were still halfway to where the others were. She glanced at him curiously and stopped as well to wait for their newest arrivals to reach them.

"Who are they?" she asked, raising her voice so he could hear her over the rain.

He grabbed her shoulders and turned her to face him. "No matter what, remember what happened between us last night. And what I told you. I care about you, Amber. And I would never cheat on you or anyone else."

She frowned in confusion. What had happened was that they'd made love most of the night. Her face flushed hot at the memory. What did that have to do with these new arrivals? Or anything that he may have told her in the dark? Or…cheating?

He dropped his hands and faced the group as they stopped in front of them.

"Garreth." He shook hands with his attorney. He shook the driver's hand before pulling Amber against his side in a show of affection that had her staring intently at the remaining two men and woman standing there and wondering just what kind of bombshell was about to be dropped on her.

"Mitchell Fielding, Derek Slater." Dex presented the men to Amber. "This is Amber Callahan, owner of this house. And I'm sure that Garreth must have told you she's the one who saved me after the crash."

Amber looked up at Dex expectantly.

"Mitchell is my assistant at Lassiter Enterprises. And Derek is a board member."

"And his wingman." Derek winked at Amber.

"Ah, I see." She really didn't and didn't appreciate the wink, either. But she shook their hands anyway.

"Aren't you going to introduce me, Dex?" The woman beside Mitchell flipped her long, blond hair over her shoulder to hang in a perfect straight sheet cut to razor-sharp precision in the middle of her back. The black dress she wore revealed far more cleavage and leg than Amber had ever dared to bare and had Amber feeling like a worn-out old shoe in comparison. This woman was the epitome of class and chic style, like one of those fancy models on a magazine. She latched on to Dex's arm as if she owned it and rubbed up against him like a well-fed cat, her too-blue-to-be-real eyes narrowing at Amber.

Since Dex seemed to be searching for words, Amber held out her hand. "Hello, I'm Amber Callahan. And you are?"

The woman shook Amber's hand in a noodle-like grip before snatching her hand back and rubbing it on Dex's shirt. "Didn't Dex tell you, darling? I'm Mallory Rothschild. His fiancée."

DEX SIPPED HIS whiskey and Coke and glared out of bleary eyes at Amber on the other side of the massive room that she'd called the great room. The only thing great thing about it was that it was huge and could accommodate the crazy mixture of Mystic Glades residents plus his own associates—nine people in all, including him and Amber. She, Freddie and Amy had spent the past hour getting everyone drinks and snacks. Dex had never seen anyone more intent on being a gracious hostess than Amber was at this minute. And since he already knew she wasn't keen on any of these people being here, he knew she was doing it for one reason and one reason only—to avoid talking to him.

Which was why he was on his third whiskey.

"More, darling?" Mallory purred in her chair beside him. She held up the decanter.

He slapped his hand over his glass, more to be obstinate than anything else. "Don't you have somewhere else you need to go? Like back to Naples to catch a plane?"

She set the decanter down on the silver tray and ran her finger across its discolored surface, her perfect nose wrinkling in distaste. "You know we're all stuck here because of this storm. You might as well stop being so stubborn and just accept that we're here for the duration. Everyone over there—" she waved airily toward the other side of the room where Buddy, Freddie and the other Mystic Glades people were sitting "—said there's no way to make it back into town in a storm this bad. The road is bound to be washed out."

"I'm sure Amber probably has a canoe around here somewhere. You're welcome to use it."

She patted his arm. "Stop trying to be funny. It's not working."

He grabbed his glass and downed the last of his drink. "Garreth, I can understand you bringing Mitchell and Derek to go over business matters if there are decisions I need to make. But why exactly did you feel it was a good idea to bring my ex-fiancée?"

Garreth cleared his throat. "Perhaps you can ask Mitchell about that. He's the one who brought her with him to the airport in Saint Augustine."

"Okay. Mitchell. Spill."

"Oh, for goodness' sakes," Mallory said. "Stop talking about me as if I'm not here. Mitchell hasn't severed ties with me like some people around here. And when he heard about the crash he told me about it. Naturally I was worried and wanted to see for myself that you were okay. Is that really so hard to understand? After all, we meant something to each other once. Didn't we?"

The naked pain in her voice had guilt squeezing Dex's chest and made him feel like a heel. He'd never loved her, and she'd never loved him. That wasn't a secret. They'd just latched on to each other for convenience, because talking was easy and they were both getting older. It wasn't until it was time to set the date and make real wedding plans that he'd realized he just couldn't do it and had broken it off. She'd agreed easily enough, almost seeming relieved. Or so he'd thought. Had he been wrong? It had never occurred to him that she might really care about him beyond being a really good friend. But it should have.

"I'm sorry, Mal. For everything."

Her eyes widened as if in surprise before she nodded and turned away. But not before Dex saw the moisture in her eyes. Wonderful. Now he felt like an even greater jerk than he had a moment earlier. When had everything become so screwed up?

His gaze caught Garreth's, who winced and took a sip of his drink—water. Come to think of it, Dex didn't think he'd ever seen his lawyer drink alcohol, but he'd never really thought about it until now.

"Speaking of being concerned about you," Mitchell said as he leaned forward to be seen from Garreth's left. "Veronica Walker stopped at the office asking about you as we were packing our briefcases for the trip out here. She'd heard about the crash on the news and demanded to know if you were okay."

Dex blinked in surprise. "Ronnie asked about me? I find that hard to believe, unless she wanted to come out here with you to make sure I never came back."

Mallory was suddenly just as interested in Mitchell's response as Dex was.

Mitchell cleared his throat, perhaps realizing that this might have been something better left said in private. "Actually, she seemed genuinely concerned. I told her you'd managed to land the plane, more or less, near Mystic Glades and that we were going to check on you." He cleared his throat again. "I didn't tell her anything else."

Dex glanced around the room, toward the windows, suddenly feeling as if a ghost had just danced on his grave. Of all the people he'd want knowing where he was at this very moment, Ronnie was last on his list.

The few months they'd dated had started out perfectly, but she'd quickly become possessive and almost… stalkerish. He'd considered getting a restraining order by the time he'd managed to disentangle himself from her clutches. But she'd been more of a nuisance than someone he considered to be dangerous so he hadn't pursued any legal action. He'd just had his security guards at the office keep an eye out for her to insure she didn't get into the building. And he'd changed his phone numbers. Now, knowing she was still asking about him had him wondering if she knew anything about planes and how to sabotage them.

"Garreth, when we get out of here and have a chance to talk to the NTSB again—"

"I know. Tell them to add Veronica Walker to the list of potential suspects. Will do."

Dex took another gulp of whiskey, feeling increasingly uneasy as he thought about Ronnie. He tried to pretend that Mallory wasn't staring at him curiously and, above all, tried to ignore the urge to run across the room and drag Amber somewhere private so he could try to explain everything to her. But he didn't want to embarrass her, or himself if she refused to talk to him. His shoulders slumped. This whole evening had been a disaster.

He set his drink on a nearby table. "Mitchell, Derek, if you're so inclined, perhaps we can have an impromptu business meeting and I'll look through the papers you brought down for me to sign. May as well do something today to make it not a total waste."

"I'll accompany you, if you don't mind. Just in case I need to review some of those papers," Garreth said.

"Of course." Dex turned to Mallory and put his hand

on hers, still feeling guilty. "Good night, Mal. And I really am sorry. I shouldn't have doubted your sincerity in coming out here. Thank you for wanting to check on me."

The look of surprise on her face had him feeling even lower. Just how much of a jerk had he been to her in the past? He'd always thought the breakup was mutual. Now he wondered if he'd mowed over her without even realizing she might have felt differently.

"Good night, Dex," she whispered, looking thoughtful. "See you in the morning."

He nodded, looked toward the other side of the room for Amber and saw her laughing and talking to the young woman who helped out at the Moon and Star, Amy. He shot out of his chair. "Follow me, guys." He stalked through the room, aiming a glare in Amber's direction before heading through the side door into one of the many hallways in the back of the mansion on the west wing.

"Where are we going?" Garreth asked.

"I have no idea. But this mausoleum is big enough that I'm sure we'll find somewhere to sit down with relative privacy if we just get moving." He turned to his right, then to his left when a wall blocked him. A few minutes later he found what was probably a library, based on the number of books on the walls. But it had the main requirement he'd been hoping to find. A fully stocked bar. "Bless you, Granddaddy Callahan." He strode across the room and grabbed the first bottle he could find.

AMBER QUICKLY ENDED her conversation with Amy, giving her a lame excuse that she needed to use the bathroom. She smiled and nodded at the others as she made her way to the end of the room where her aunt Freddie was standing.

"Do you mind playing hostess for me? I'm afraid I've a bit of a headache. I think I'm going to call it a night."

Freddie patted her shoulder. "Of course. Don't you worry about a thing. I'll just tell everyone to pick a room and make up their own beds. There are dozens of them in this monstrosity. It's all under control. See you in the morning, dear."

She kissed her aunt's cheek, feeling genuine warmth toward her at that moment. She cast a glance toward Dex's fiancée, who was silently sipping her drink and looking lost in thought. Then Amber slipped through the same doorway Dex had a few moments ago.

She didn't know where he'd gone with his lawyer, assistant and board member, and she told herself she didn't care. Which, of course, was a lie. She headed up the main stairs to her room to escape.

THUNDER BOOMED OVERHEAD, startling Dex from his stupor. He jerked upright in his chair and looked around. Still in the library, but he was alone now. He rubbed his eyes and glanced at his watch. Midnight. The business meeting had ended hours ago. Everyone must have either gone back to the great room or found a bedroom to hunker down overnight. It was time that he did the same.

He started down the main hallway back toward the great room but quickly got lost. It took a good half an hour before he found a staircase and started up it. Hopefully, it would lead him back to his own room. If not he'd just commandeer one of the many rooms in the mansion. He tightened his grip around the bottle of whiskey in his hand as he topped the stairs and started in what he believed to be the right direction.

For once, he was right and ended up at his bedroom door. Finally. He shoved the door open and kicked it closed behind him, stumbling to the bathroom. He set the bottle on the sink and took care of nature's call. By then the bottle no longer seemed quite so appealing. He was beginning to feel as green as he probably looked. Just how many glasses had he had tonight? One too many, that was for sure. And he didn't have to guess why he was in such a foul mood. Mallory showing up tonight had made him face things he hadn't wanted to face. It wasn't a good feeling to realize he'd hurt her and, therefore, possibly others. And now he'd hurt the one person he really truly cared about, Amber.

If only he could have gotten Amber alone so he could explain. But as soon as Mallory had introduced herself, Amber had made herself scarce, using the excuse of seeing to her guests.

He looked around the bedroom, which seemed much lonelier now than it had before. Of course, having shared it with Amber, there was no longer any appeal in being alone. He stared at the bedroom door. Amber was just across the hall. If she'd gone to bed by now. Maybe he could talk to her.

He headed across the room, pulled the door open and was inside Amber's room in no time.

She jerked upright in bed, her eyes widening in the glow from the open closet door. Apparently she liked to sleep with a light on. He vaguely wondered how she'd managed to survive in the wilderness all this time if she was afraid of the dark.

"Get out," she ordered.

"Shh." He put his fingers to his lips, or tried to, but he missed and poked his eye. "Ouch." He cursed and slid to the floor, holding his eye.

"Oh good grief." Amber flipped the covers back and hurried over to him, getting down on her knees beside him. "Let me see." She pulled his hand back, then waved her hand in front of her face and wrinkled her nose. "What did you do, drink an entire bottle of tequila all by yourself?"

He lifted his bottle and shook it. "Whiskey. Good stuff, too. Your grandpa had good taste." He tried to unscrew the cap but couldn't quite manage it. "Will you open it? The damn thing keeps slipping."

She took the bottle from him. "I'll take care of it." She stood and set the bottle on top of a chest of drawers, then reached down for his hand. "Come on. I'll help you find your way back to your room."

He grabbed her hand but, instead of getting up, he yanked her down onto his lap and wrapped his arms around her. "We need to talk."

She shoved against his shoulders and tried to wiggle out of his hold. "I don't talk to drunks, especially when every other word is slurred. I mean it, Dex. Let me go."

Her tone made its way through his stupor and he dropped his arms. "I'm sorry." He scrubbed his face as she hopped up.

"So am I. Now go. It's late."

He tried to push himself up, but his wobbly legs didn't want to work. He collapsed back against the wall. "Can't I just stay here? I won't be much trouble. Promise."

She rolled her eyes and put her hands on her hips. "Won't Mallory miss you?"

He winced. "That's what I wanted to talk about."

"Well, I don't. If you want to stay, stay. But be quiet. I'm tired and I'm going to sleep." She moved back to the bed and flounced down on the mattress, jerking the covers up around her neck and turning to face the window.

Dex let out a deep sigh and pushed himself on all fours over to her bed. "Amber," he whispered.

"Go away."

"I'm tired. Can I please get in bed with you? The floor is hard."

"Then go to your room and get in that bed."

"It's too far. I don't think I can make it. Please?" Thunder boomed overhead and lightning lit the windows. The rain was coming down even harder than before. "Please? Don't make me sleep alone in the rain."

She flipped her covers back and turned to glare at him. "You're drunk, Dex. And a cheater. Neither of those make you particularly appealing or make me want to share a bed with you again. Especially not at—" she glanced at the beside clock "—almost one in the morning. Good grief."

He sighed heavily and propped his head on his hands as he rested his elbows on the mattress. "I may be drunk, but I'm not a cheater. Mallory and I used to be engaged. But we broke up. Two months ago."

She narrowed her eyes. "If that's true, why did she introduce herself as your fiancée?"

"Because she hasn't accepted it yet. I'm hard to forget."

She rolled her eyes again and flounced over on her

side, facing away from him. "I've already forgotten you, so that can't be true."

"Okay, okay. I think she's mad at me."

"Now, that I believe." Her voice was muffled against her pillow.

"Amber?"

"What?"

"It's a big bed."

"Oh, for the love of… Okay, get into bed. Just stay on your side and leave me alone."

He grinned and slid into bed beside her, right where he wanted to be. He scooted as close to her as he dared, not wanting to make her mad. Then he plopped a kiss on her shoulder. "Good night, sweet Amber."

She wiped her shoulder as if to erase the kiss. "Good night, drunken Dex."

AMBER SIGHED AS Dex's heavy, even breathing told her he'd already passed out. She really should have made him leave. But it was hard to argue with him when he was so adorably drunk and kept giving her puppy-dog eyes.

She was fairly certain he was telling the truth about Mallory being his ex. If he was anything like her, then he wasn't good at lying while intoxicated. Liquor was more likely to loosen lips and make the truth come out than to make someone better at concealing something. And she was more relieved than she probably should have been to learn that Mallory had lied and that they weren't engaged.

She brushed his hair back from his forehead, then smiled when he swatted his face as if to swat a fly. And when he reached for her in his sleep, this time she didn't pull away. She snuggled back against him and pulled his arms around her waist.

Chapter Eleven

Bang!

Amber awoke with a start at the loud noise and was suddenly struggling to breathe as Dex threw himself on top of her, his gaze darting around the room.

"What's going on?" she whispered, as she tried to extricate herself from beneath him, very aware that her nightshirt had ridden up to her belly and that Dex had apparently shed all his clothes except for his boxers during the night.

He glanced down at her as if only just now seeing her, then rolled off her. "Are you okay?"

"I think so. What was that noise?"

"Gunshot."

She stared at him in shock. "Are you sure it wasn't thunder?" As if in response to her question, thunder boomed overhead and another incredible wave of rain began pouring in earnest.

"That sound came from inside the house. Definitely not thunder. And your gun is in my room."

She scooted to the edge of the bed and pulled the drawer open in the side table. "Here." She handed him a Colt .45 revolver.

He shook his head. "Really? How many guns do you have around here?"

She shrugged. "Way of life. The Glades can be a dangerous place. And don't worry about it being rusty with age or anything. I cleaned it earlier, before I went to bed."

"Good to know." He threw his pants on, checked the gun's loading, then hurried to the door and peered out. "Wait here." He locked the door, then shut it behind him.

Amber shook her head. When would the man stop telling her what to do and thinking that he needed to protect her?

She grabbed her pile of clothes from the chair beside the bed and quickly dressed. She was just tugging on her sneakers when a knock sounded on the door.

"It was thunder after all, wasn't it?" She unlocked the door and pulled it open.

Her aunt Freddie stood in the hallway, her face lined with worry. "No, it wasn't thunder."

Amber stepped into the hall, surprised to see a small group of people milling around the doorway across from her. The door to Dex's room.

"What's going on?" she asked. She didn't wait for her aunt's reply because she saw Dex coming out of the room with Buddy and two of the men who had arrived in the limo yesterday—Derek and Mitchell.

She hurried to Dex, but he quickly closed the door, blocking her view. He tested the knob, perhaps making sure he'd locked it as he'd closed it.

"Stay back," he said. "Everyone get back. We need to preserve the scene for the police." He motioned the increasingly growing group of people back, as others followed the noise to the upstairs corridor.

"What scene? What happened?" Amber asked.

"It's Mallory," he said, his voice tight. "Someone killed her."

She gasped and motioned toward the door. "In your room?"

He nodded.

Buddy put his hand on Dex's shoulder. "I don't think it was Mr. Lassiter, though. He was just reaching the door when I topped the stairs."

"Maybe he'd just come out of the room," Freddie said. "After all, it was his bedroom."

Mitchell and Derek shared a surprised glance, as if only just now considering that Dex might have been involved.

Amber held up her hands. "You can stop that rumor right now. Dex was with me, in my room, when a gunshot rang out. He's not the one who killed Mallory." She looked to Dex. "I'm assuming she was shot?"

"Yes." His voice was tight, clipped, making Amber wonder if he still harbored some feelings for his ex-fiancée after all. Then again, if they'd been engaged to be married, of course he would still have some kind feelings for her.

She grabbed his hand and held it tightly in hers. When he looked down at her, she silently mouthed the words, *I'm sorry.*

He squeezed her hand in response, then let it go. "Does anyone have a cell phone?"

Buddy handed him his. "Not that you'll get a call out in this storm. Even the areas that get coverage around here, like this house, usually don't work in storms. Don't know why. But you can try."

Sure enough, the call wouldn't go through. He handed

the phone back to Buddy. "If anyone else has a phone, maybe with a different carrier, can you please try calling nine-one-one?"

Aunt Freddie tried, and so did Mitchell and Derek. Both of them shook their heads after trying to get a call out.

"Okay," Dex said. "We all need to assemble in one place so we can verify that everyone is safe and accounted for. Who all are missing?"

Aunt Freddie held up her hands and started counting off her fingers. "There should be eight of us now, minus Miss Rothschild. But I only count seven. Someone's missing. And it's not one of us locals." The tone of her voice said what she hadn't, that it made sense to her that the missing person—allegedly the killer—would *not* be one of the Mystic Glades residents.

Dex looked around. "It's Garreth. Does anyone know what bedroom he was staying in?"

Derek shoved to the front of the group. "He was in the room next to mine, in the east wing. Come on. I'll show you."

He led them down the hall, past the staircase. Bare feet and shoes clomped and shuffled against the hardwood floor as the entire herd followed them. When they arrived at the closed door, Dex motioned for everyone to stay back as he drew the Colt from his waistband and reached for the knob.

A flurry of activity and noise had him looking back over his shoulder. His mouth dropped open when he realized that the locals, except for Amber, were now holding guns and pointing them at the same door he was about to open. Even Amy, who didn't look old enough to be out of high school, was pointing a pistol at the door.

"Good grief," he said. "Where did you all get those?"

Buddy gave him a confused look. "We always carry guns when we go deep into the Glades, and this house is as deep as we go."

"Well, point them somewhere else. I don't want to get shot."

Buddy looked sheepish and lowered his gun, then motioned for the others to do the same. Mitchell and Derek stood away from the others, looking as shocked as Dex felt. And none of them had guns. The theory that the killer wasn't a local looked pretty flimsy to Dex, considering only the Mystic Glades people were armed. And how would someone in his group have brought a gun out here after flying down from Saint Augustine? They couldn't have gotten any guns through security.

Even Garreth, who'd been here a day longer than the others, couldn't have brought a gun. And Dex couldn't imagine him running out and buying one in Naples. There was no way his staid, serious lawyer who saw only right and wrong with no gray areas would ever consider buying a gun. And he certainly had no reason to kill Mallory.

Dex knocked on the door and shoved his own borrowed gun back into his waistband, feeling silly for even having it out in the first place. Garreth wasn't a killer. Period.

"Garreth? It's Dex. Are you in there?" He knocked again. "Garreth?"

"He's probably done run off," Freddie said. "After shooting that lady friend of yours."

"He's a lawyer who has dedicated his life to the pursuit of the law. He's not a murderer," Dex said.

"So you say." As one, all the locals nodded as if to lend their belief to hers. Including Amber this time.

Dex rolled his eyes and knocked on the door again. "Garreth?" When his lawyer didn't answer, Dex turned the knob, then pushed the door open. He stepped inside as Garreth bolted up in the bed, staring at him in alarm.

"What's going on?" He pulled a pair of earplugs out of his ears and looked in shock first at the gun in Dex's waistband and then past him.

Dex didn't have to turn around to know that his band of followers in the hallway were probably all crowded around the doorway peeking inside, if they hadn't already come inside.

"There's been a shooting," he said. "You didn't hear anything?"

Garreth held out the earplugs. "No. Was someone hurt?"

"Mallory. She's…dead."

Garreth's mouth fell open and his face turned pale. "Mallory's dead?" he choked. He cleared his throat. "I don't understand. What happened?" He tossed his earplugs onto the bedside table and grabbed his robe from the foot of the bed, tugging it on and tying the belt.

"Good question. Looks like now that we've found you, everyone is accounted for. Which means either there was an intruder, or—"

"Or one of us is the killer," Garreth said.

Dex nodded. "We need to corral everyone somewhere, take away their guns—"

"Guns?"

"It seems to be standard issue out here. They all have them."

Garreth's gaze dropped to Dex's waistband, his eyes widening. "Including you."

"I borrowed it. After I heard the gunshot."

The color began returning to Garreth's face and he straightened his shoulders, looking all business again. "As your lawyer, I strongly recommend that you return the gun to whomever you borrowed it from. It could likely be the murder weapon and since you'd be the first suspect, given that the victim is—"

"He didn't kill her." Amber stood beside Dex. "And that gun was in my drawer in my room when the gunshot went off. It can't be the murder weapon."

Garreth looked pointedly at how close Amber was standing next to Dex and frowned. "Given that Miss Callahan was only recently suspected of murder herself, I suggest that you keep your distance from her. It doesn't look right."

Dex put his arm around Amber's shoulders. "That little bit of advice isn't going to be followed. My suggestion is that you get dressed. We'll all meet in, um, the…" He glanced down at Amber and arched a brow.

"In the great room where we were last night. It's at the front of the house, to the left of the front door. It's close to the kitchen so we can fix coffee or sodas for everyone."

"Right. The great room. We'll see you there."

Garreth grabbed his cell phone from beside his bed.

"Don't bother," a chorus of people called out from the doorway. "No service."

Dex held Amber's hand and made his way through the throng and headed toward the stairs. "We're going to the great room and we'll figure out what to do," he announced to the others.

"Follow Dex and Amber," Buddy announced. "Dex is Jake's friend, and a private investigator. He'll know what to do and he'll be able to figure out who the bad guy is."

"He's also a sheriff's deputy. He was deputized in town before he came out here," Amber added, as if to give him some legitimacy.

Dex rolled his eyes again but since everyone was following him without complaint, maybe using his temporary deputy status was a good idea. He flipped on lights as the group tromped and clomped through the hallway then down the stairs into the massive two-story foyer.

When they reached the great room, Dex spotted a trunk with a lock on it. "Amber, do you have the key to that trunk?"

She shook her head. "I don't think so."

Buddy hurried to the medieval-sized fireplace at the end of the room and pulled a picture on hinges away from the wall. On the back was a hook with a small ring of keys. "It should be one of these."

"Well, that's a dandy place to hide keys," Dex grumbled. "A burglar would find that in no time."

Buddy handed him the keys and gave him an admonishing look. "We don't have burglars in Mystic Glades. And until tonight, we didn't have murderers, either."

"Too bad you didn't make that clear back when Granddaddy Callahan died and everyone blamed Amber." Dex leaned forward and snatched the keys from Buddy's hand.

Buddy turned red.

Amber stepped between them. "Stop it. There's no point in rehashing the past. And it was just as much my decision to leave after Grandpa died as it was Buddy's to not speak about what he thought happened. We both made mistakes."

Dex didn't understand how she could be so forgiving of her fellow townspeople after being ostracized for two years, but he respected her wishes to drop it and didn't say anything else. He bent down in front of the trunk and tried several keys before one fit. When he opened the trunk, he found it half-full of blankets, with plenty of room for his purposes. He stood and held his hand out to Buddy, who was still looking sullen and standing a few feet away.

"I think we'll all be safer if we lock up the guns. Buddy, you first." He held out his hand.

Buddy looked at him as if he thought he'd lost his mind. "I don't think so."

Amber put her hand on Buddy's shoulder. "Dex is right. Like it or not, someone in this room shot Mallory. We need to lock all the guns away both as evidence and to insure that no one else gets hurt."

"If someone wants to kill one of us, they can do it with or without a gun," he grumbled.

"Buddy," Amber admonished.

"Okay, okay." He pulled his gun out of his waistband and handed it to Dex.

"Thank you." Dex used one of the smaller blankets as a glove of sorts so he didn't touch the gun. He put the gun in the trunk.

Freddie and Amy put their guns in the trunk, as well. And, finally, Dex put his borrowed Colt .45 in with the others. As he locked the trunk, a feeling of relief settled over him. Knowing no one was running around with a loaded gun made him feel much less worried.

"Are there any more guns in the house, Amber?"

He didn't bother mentioning the one that may or may not be in her grandfather's sealed room and knew she wouldn't either.

"I don't think so, at least not that I know of."

Buddy walked to the fireplace at the end of the room. "I'll start a fire. It'll be cozy and good to have in case the lights go out. Although the generators should kick in. But you never know."

"I'll help," Aunt Freddie said.

They both began loading kindling and logs from a wooden box to the right of the hearth. Everyone else split off into groups, sitting on the various chairs and couches around the room.

Dex led Amber to one of the front windows. "If one of us drives into town, do you think we could get phone service there to call the police?"

She shook her head. "Even if we could get service somewhere in town, it wouldn't matter. No one can leave here until this weather clears up."

He gave her an exasperated look. "I'm not afraid of a little rain and lightning."

"You don't understand. Rain like this, for as long as it's been raining, will make the roads impassable. This house and the surrounding property become an island. There's no way to get into town."

"How can you be sure?"

She let out a deep sigh. "Come on. I'll show you." She headed toward the foyer.

"Should we come, too?" Buddy called out.

"No, no. We'll be right back," Dex assured him.

When they reached the front door, Amber opened a drawer in a small decorative table against the wall and pulled out a flashlight.

"Let's hope the batteries still work or that Buddy has kept fresh ones stocked as part of watching after the estate." She pressed the button. The flashlight remained dark. "One more chance." She reached into the back of the drawer and pulled out a pack of batteries. "Voilà." She exchanged the old batteries for new and the flashlight sparked to life.

"Come on, outsider. I'll prove my point."

He shook his head and followed her to the railing.

She aimed the flashlight toward the front yard and slowly moved it from the trees to the left, across the road, to the trees to the right. Except there wasn't a road anymore. There was a river, flowing left to right and forming a moat around the property.

Dex clutched the railing. "That's crazy. We're stranded."

"Totally. Don't worry, the water won't get into the house. The foundation is on concrete pylons driven deep into the ground. The water would have to rise another six feet to come inside. And as far as I know, it's never gotten that high. Grandpa knew what he was doing when he built this place."

"How long before the water recedes?"

"A good twenty-four hours after the rain stops. Like it or not, we're all stuck here together. With a dead body."

"And a murderer."

She set the flashlight on the railing and faced him. "While we've got a moment alone, tell me what you saw in your bedroom."

"Why?"

"Because I want to know the details and you wouldn't let me in the room. It's my house now. I have a right to know what happened."

"I suppose you do. Okay. Mallory was lying in my

bed, under the covers, facing the other way. I didn't know who was in the bed at first. Her hair was covered by a blanket. All I saw was blood." He swallowed hard. "Buddy and I both ran in together and I soon realized it was Mallory. There was no point in performing CPR. She was already dead, and the bullet did... too much damage."

She seemed to think about what he'd said for a moment. "I think you need to consider that whoever killed your fiancée—"

"Ex-fiancée."

"—might have been trying to kill you, instead."

"Because she was in my bedroom?"

"Yes. Everyone knew where you and I were staying because we'd already claimed those rooms and told the others to choose different ones. And someone did sabotage your plane. If Mallory was under the covers, the killer might have thought it was you."

"Makes sense. Makes more sense than someone wanting to kill Mallory. No one here has any reason to want her harmed."

"Are you sure about that? Did they all know her very well?"

He frowned. "Derek knew her, of course, since we double-dated in the beginning. But I don't think he kept in touch with her after we broke up. Mallory did mention last night that she'd heard about the plane crash from Mitchell. That surprised me, since I wouldn't have expected that Mitchell and she would have had anything to do with each other after we ended the engagement."

"And Garreth?"

"He was going to be the best man at the wedding,

so of course he knew Mallory. But he didn't have any reason to want her dead."

"What about you?"

"What about me?"

"Your lawyer seemed concerned that someone might think you had something to do with her murder."

"He's just being protective since I'm his client. But I had no reason to want her dead."

"Are you sure?"

He tightened his hands on the railing. "What exactly about me makes you think I'd kill someone? Especially a woman I was going to marry?"

She met his stare without flinching. "Since you were in my room when she was killed, I obviously know that you didn't harm her. What I'm asking is whether anyone else would have reason to suspect you'd want to kill her."

His anger faded as he considered what she was saying. "You think someone killed her to frame me?"

She shrugged. "Just looking at all of the possibilities."

"Maybe I should change Lassiter and Young Private Investigations to Lassiter and Callahan."

She grinned. "Maybe you should."

Lightning cracked across the sky, briefly illuminating the growing river like a strobe light. "Standing out here doesn't feel too safe right now. I think we might be better off taking our chances inside. Come on."

They'd just stepped inside when the lights went out.

Chapter Twelve

Dex stood on the back porch beside Garreth, Amber and Buddy, eyeing the swirling, brackish water that covered the fifty yards between the house and the maintenance shed. Conveniently, the shed—which housed the generator—was on pylons, which meant it was above the water level, but inconveniently, it was still through the swamp.

"I don't suppose the rain and lightning will keep the snakes away." Dex stared at the dark water.

"Or the alligators," Garreth added.

"Probably not," Amber agreed. "Honestly, there's no reason to go out there. We've got plenty of firewood and candles for light. And it's not exactly cold outside. We'll all just sweat a bit with the air conditioner off."

Dex grimaced. "Speaking of sweating, and no air-conditioning, if we're going to be stuck in this house much longer, there's something else to worry about." He grimaced and looked at Amber. "Mallory. We need to do something to…" He swallowed hard. "Preserve her."

"Oh. I hadn't thought of that. Well, there is a deep freeze in the kitchen. I suppose we could, ah, empty it and…"

"I suppose we could," Dex agreed, bile rising up

in his throat at the idea of putting his former fiancée's body in a freezer. Even though they hadn't loved each other, they had been friends. And the idea that someone had killed her had him clenching his fists and wishing for someone to punch. "All right. That alone means I have to get that generator going. Buddy, you said any tools I might need are in the shed, too. What about fuel for the generator?"

"The fuel is in a tank on the far side, outside the structure. I'm sure it's full. The problem is more likely a fuse. All this lightning must have overloaded a circuit."

Dex stripped out of his jeans down to his boxers, then pulled on his tennis shoes, which he'd grabbed from upstairs. He took the keys out of his pocket. "Amber, we'll need that flashlight. Maybe Buddy can shine it on the water so I can see where I'm going. And will you unlock the trunk and grab the .45? You'll be on snake-and-gator patrol while I swim over."

"This is crazy, Dex. It's too dangerous. You have no way of knowing what's in that water. And as fast as it's moving it could suck you out into the swamp."

"I don't have a choice. I can't let… Mallory… I have to get the generator on. Okay?"

She sighed. "Okay. I get it. Just give me a minute."

She ran inside and returned shortly with the gun. She checked the loading, then held it down by her side. "Ready."

Dex leaned down to press a quick kiss against her lips, but she put her hand around his neck and pulled him in for a deeper kiss full of longing. When she broke the kiss, his traitorous body was straining against the front of his boxers. He shook his head and grinned.

"You're dangerous, Amber."

She stepped closer, shielding him from the others. There was no sign of humor on her face though as she looked up at him. "Be careful, Dex. I mean it. If you get in that water and the current is too strong, get out. No heroics. It's not worth it."

"Are you saying you'd miss me if something happened to me?" he teased.

"Yes."

Her quick, serious answer had his body tightening almost painfully. "There's no way in hell that I won't come back to you." He kissed her again, then headed down the porch steps before she could try to stop him. As soon as Buddy shone the flashlight on the roiling water at the base of the steps, Dex stepped into the abyss.

The water wasn't overly deep, only up to his hips. But Amber was right. The current was incredibly strong as water rushed from the surrounding higher areas and was sucked out toward the Glades. Every step was a struggle to remain upright, and soon he was sweating and breathing heavily as if he'd been in a tremendous battle. But other than dodging some dead branches floating past him, he made it to the maintenance shed without incident.

He pulled himself up on the concrete steps, catching his breath as he looked back toward the house. Amber waved at him and he waved back to let her know all was well. Then he opened the door and went inside. Too late he realized he should have brought a flashlight. The interior was as dark as midnight. He ran his hands along the wall until he located the light switch and flipped it. Nothing.

He felt along the walls for a fuse box, and tripped

over several tools and unknown objects before he found it. Not wanting to stick his wet hands inside the box, he felt around for a while until he found a bucket of rags and wiped his hands dry. Then he returned to the box and carefully patted the interior until he found the main switch. He shoved it up until it clicked, then pulled it back down to reset everything. Since he didn't hear the hum of the generator outside kicking on, he started flipping each breaker individually. Halfway through, the generator suddenly belched to life.

Dex shut the panel, went back to where he remembered the light switch being and flipped it on. A single, dim light popped to life overhead, revealing an incredibly unorganized pile of tools, old paint cans, a riding lawn mower and hundreds of other odds and ends. He grabbed a machete out of one pile and hefted it in his hand. If it came to a fight with an alligator or a snake, that machete would be good to have. But it also wasn't something he wanted in the house for the killer to get a hold of. The idea of someone like Amber coming up against a weapon like that had him leaving it where he'd found it. Too dangerous. He couldn't risk it. He'd just have to brave the waters outside again and hope he was as lucky the second time as he had been the first—that he'd encounter no wildlife of the slithering or biting variety.

When he went outside, he noticed Amber and Buddy still waiting for him, but Garreth was nowhere to be seen. Maybe he'd had to flip fuses inside the house? Lights shone from both the first and second floors, so the generator was definitely doing its job. And he could see the silhouettes of several people in the kitchen behind the porch.

He studied the brackish water for any sinister shadows beneath the surface or the shine of snake scales, then waded back in. If anything, the current was stronger this time. And the water had risen noticeably and was now halfway up his chest. By the time he struggled to the porch steps, he saw the water was cresting just below the second highest step, a foot below where the bottom floor began. Amber's worried gaze confirmed his own fears as he emerged from the water.

"Has it ever gotten this high before?" he asked.

"Not that I know of," Buddy interjected, clicking off the flashlight.

Amber agreed and handed Dex a towel to dry off. "I think we might need to move everyone upstairs, just in case."

"I think you're right." He motioned toward the kitchen door. "What's going on in there?"

Amber gave him a haunted look. "Garreth is directing everyone to empty out the freezer."

He gave her a tight nod and pulled on his jeans before pulling his T-shirt on over his head.

When they went inside, Dex stopped in surprise. Everyone was sitting around the huge kitchen island. Stacks of pints of ice cream formed a mound in the middle and the group was sorting through them, apparently grabbing their favorites.

Mitchell handed a chocolate-mint pint to Amy and she gave him a shy smile in return. Derek shoved a spoonful of Moose Tracks into his mouth, then held out his hands in a helpless gesture.

Garreth looked disgusted with all of them as he leaned against the kitchen wall like a general watching over his unruly troops.

Freddie motioned toward the refrigerator. "We put most of the veggies in the refrigerator freezer, but there wasn't anywhere to store all this ice cream. Might as well enjoy it before it goes to waste, right?"

Dex's stomach clenched with nausea and he headed through the archway without a word.

Amber hurried behind him and caught up to him when he was at the bottom of the stairs.

"What's wrong?" she asked.

He looked down at her. "It just seems…disrespectful, to sit there enjoying ice cream, knowing the reason it was taken out of the freezer." He shrugged and headed up the stairs. "Stupid, I know."

She hurried after him. "Not stupid at all. I totally get it. Where are we going?"

"I'm getting a shower to clean all that swamp muck off me."

"Okay. But what are you going to wear?"

He stopped at the top of the stairs, his gaze shooting to the closed door on his room. "Good point. I need my suitcase." His steps were much slower as he approached the door. "Do you still have that ring of keys?"

She pulled them out of her pocket and held up the skeleton key.

"Thanks. Here, hold this while I go inside." He handed her the gun.

She looked around the dark hallway. "Hurry," she whispered. "It seems creepy up here now, you know."

"Believe me. I know." He unlocked the door and rushed inside, keeping his gaze averted from the bed.

Once he had his suitcase, he was just about to step into the hall when movement off to his left had him whirling around. The room was empty. There was no one there, no one except…Mallory. He glanced quickly to the bed, as if to assure himself she was still there and hadn't become some disembodied ghost haunting the mansion. She still lay in the center of the bed where he'd found her. He swallowed hard and looked away. He stood there for a full minute, trying to figure out what he'd seen.

"Dex?" Amber's voice called to him from the hall-way. "Is something wrong?"

Yes. But what? What had he seen out of the corner of his eye?

"Dex?"

"Coming." He left the room and locked the door behind him.

AMBER STOOD IN the opening between the great room and the kitchen, facing the great room and keeping the others from going into the kitchen. Not that anyone else wanted to, but Dex was being his usual protective self and obviously wanted her where he could see her, but didn't want her to be a part of what he and his fellow outsiders were doing—storing Mallory's body in the freezer.

There hadn't been the need for a discussion about who would take care of the task. The Mystic Glades residents had respectfully kept their distance while the outsiders took care of one of their own, gently wrapping Mallory in the comforter from the bed upstairs and then carefully carrying her downstairs in a solemn procession that had reminded Amber of a funeral.

The top of the freezer clicked into place in the kitchen behind her, and soon she heard the sounds of the men taking turns washing their hands at the sink.

Then, without a word, Garreth, Mitchell and Derek filed past her into the great room, each of them looking deflated and depressed.

Dex stopped beside her, crossing his arms as he surveyed the room.

"Are you okay?" she whispered.

"I will be. I didn't expect it to hurt so much, putting her in there." His voice was too low for the others to hear, but even so she could hear the pain behind his words.

She sidled closer until her hip pressed against the side of his thigh, offering him comfort with that one small touch. "I'm here for you."

He let out a shuddering breath. "I know. Thank you."

Thunder boomed overhead, making her jump. "Good grief. I can't believe this rain." As if remembering the rising flood in the backyard at the same time, they both turned around and headed to the back porch.

"What's up?" Buddy called out, hurrying to catch up to them. He stopped on the porch beside the two of them. "Oh, my God."

The water was lapping against the edges of the porch boards.

"We have to go upstairs. Now," Amber declared.

They all hurried back inside, but Dex hesitated and glanced at the freezer.

Amber put her hand on his arm. "There's nothing we can do now. The lower floor is about to flood."

"I can't just let…" He rushed past her to the great room. "All right, everyone. The water is rising and is about to come into the house." A collective gasp went up around the room. "We'll need to head upstairs. But first, everyone grab what you can from the pantry. Grab things we can eat and drink without having to cook.

Don't forget cups, plates, utensils. Garbage bags would be good too. Hurry."

There was a big rush into the kitchen and everyone started grabbing things from the pantry.

"Amber, we'll need can openers. And is there something we could use to heat beans or anything in cans?"

"I think there's a hot plate." She grabbed Amy as she headed past her. "Amy, help me find it, okay? I think it's over in one of these cabinets." She and Amy rummaged through the cabinets and found two hot plates and a can opener. Amy ran through the great room to the stairs to take them up.

Amber looked around for Dex and froze when she saw what he was doing. He'd gathered his friends and they were wrestling with the heavy freezer, lifting it on top of the marble-topped island. Their muscles bulged and strained as they moved it into place.

Amber noted they'd had to unplug it. The cord dangled over the side. She grabbed an extension cord out of the pantry, sliding past Buddy as he made a second run for more food. She plugged the cord into an outlet above the sink, wrapped most of the extra slack around the freezer handle to keep it from dragging on the floor, then plugged the freezer's cord into it.

The freezer hummed to life. Dex pulled her against him in a fierce hug, then kissed the top of her head. When he pulled back, he framed her face in his hands. "You're a wonderful person, Amber Callahan. Thank you. Again."

She smiled, then let out a little squeak as water began soaking into her shoes. "The water's coming in. Hurry up, everybody. We have to get upstairs."

Everyone made a last dash to the pantry, then ran

through the great room, through the maze, to the stairs. The water was already coming in through the front door, too, and seeping in through the walls.

Dex ushered everyone from the room, waiting until they were all safely out of the kitchen and on their way toward the stairs before joining Amber at the archway. He put his hand on her back, encouraging her forward, but she froze and looked back at the great room.

Dex turned around, shoving her behind him as he looked for the threat.

"Dex, the trunk, the trunk."

He frowned back at her and she pointed to the trunk over by the fireplace. The one with the guns locked inside. Except it wasn't locked anymore, and the lid was standing open.

She and Dex splashed through the water that was already up to their ankles and reached the trunk at the same time.

The guns were gone.

Chapter Thirteen

Amber perched on the edge of a wing chair by the window in the house's second library, the upstairs one, while Dex finished making his rounds on the other side of the room, insuring everyone was okay. Like the great room, the east wing library had plenty of seating, but it was spread out in small groups throughout the stacks of bookshelves so that not everyone was visible at once. That's why Amber had chosen these specific two wing chairs for her and Dex—because at least there was no one behind them, just a floor-to-ceiling bookshelf. Ten feet away, the bookshelf ended and there was an aisle that opened up, like a hallway in the middle of the room. She kept watching that dark opening while trying to keep an eye on Dex.

He finished speaking to Freddie and Buddy, who were seated to the right of the door that led into the hall, nodded at Mitchell, who was curling up to go to sleep on one of the couches, and headed toward Amber.

He glanced toward the bookshelf behind them, perhaps to make sure no one could possibly squeeze behind it to listen to them, and took his seat. They both leaned toward each other, but they continued to watch the others.

"What did you find out?" she said, keeping her voice low.

"I didn't want to announce the guns were missing, because I didn't want to cause a panic. Instead, I was more subtle, or tried to be, asking each person if they were okay, if they'd gotten what they needed from downstairs." He motioned to the stacks of goods everyone had deposited in the common area against one wall, their new pantry, essentially.

"I'm guessing no one admitted to sneaking into the great room and breaking into the trunk."

"Well, I didn't think they would. But based on what everyone said, I was able to pretty much corroborate most of their stories. I'm ruling out Amy, Freddie and Derek. And, of course, you and me. But so far I can't prove the rest of them didn't have an opportunity to get to that trunk. The lock was busted, which implies the thief didn't have a key. But the only person who did have the key was me, so that doesn't help."

"Aren't you ruling out Buddy?"

He shook his head. "No. I can't. No one seems to remember seeing him carrying anything but a case of water upstairs. If he wasn't carrying other things, then where was he while the others were in the pantry?"

She stared across the room at Buddy and Freddie, who were sitting on opposite ends of a couch now, eyes closed, apparently falling asleep sitting up. "I just can't imagine that Buddy would take the guns. Assuming that the person who took the guns is the killer, why would Buddy shoot Mallory? He didn't know her. And if you're the true target, which seems likely, then again, Buddy barely knows you. What motive would he have to want you dead?"

"Okay, with me as the target, who stands to gain something by my death? It would make sense that only Garreth, Derek and Mitchell should be the true suspects. I pay each of them a healthy salary, with excellent benefits. Even Garreth, who takes other clients besides me, earns a generous retainer whether he does work for me each week or not. And our contract pays him escalating amounts above the retainer if he ends up working full-time on any particular issue. With me out of the picture, he'd be at the mercy of my replacement, who might very well hire a different lawyer for future work. I just don't see him gaining anything with me gone."

"All right. Makes sense. As long as the gain is financial. Have you done something to him that might make him want revenge?"

He laughed. "Revenge? Garreth? We're not exactly drinking buddies. It's all business. If anyone had revenge on their mind it would be Derek. We've both dated the same women before, although not at the same time, of course."

She rolled her eyes. "Of course."

He grinned. "There's been some jealousy in the past, on his part. He claims sometimes women see me and leave him because of my money."

"Is that true?"

He shrugged. "Probably. But we usually end up laughing and drinking over the memories later. So far neither of us has been particularly successful in the relationship department, long-term."

"Was Mallory one of the women you both dated?"

He shook his head. "No. She was my mistake alone." He grimaced. "Sorry, that sounds callous now. There've only been a couple of women we've actually both dated.

The last was Ronnie—Veronica Walker. She was a bit… aggressive. It took some convincing before she understood that it was really over. I considered a restraining order until she finally quit coming around. I heard Derek dated her a few times after I broke up with her. But, as far as I know, that was very brief."

Amber tapped the arm of her chair and considered what he'd said. "Okay, so Garreth has no obvious reason to want you dead and seems to benefit more with you healthy. Derek is a friend and you've had some quibbles in the past, but it doesn't seem to have impacted your friendship or his position on your board. You did say he was a board member?"

"Yeah. He's one hell of a smart guy. He sits on several boards, not just mine."

"Does he get to run the company with you out of the picture?"

He smiled. "That's not how it works. For one thing, it's privately owned, not publicly traded. So the company would pass to my benefactor in my will."

"Who's your benefactor?"

"Jake Young."

"Faye's Jake?"

"One and the same. He doesn't know he's the benefactor, though. I'm sure he assumes I've willed my assets to my family."

"Your family?"

"Mother, father, brother. All of them live in California. I haven't seen them in years. And there's no reason to talk about them."

She disagreed, but since they were trying to solve a murder, she was willing to let it drop for now. "Then we've got one more person to consider—Mitchell."

Dex grew quiet and stared out the window. Was he thinking about his family? Or was he maybe thinking that Mitchell was their best suspect? She gave him a minute, but when he didn't respond, she waved her hand in front of his face.

"Dex? We were talking about Mitchell. Do you think he could be our suspect?"

He turned to look at her, his eyes dark, troubled. "As a matter of fact, I do. Mitchell's been my assistant for a couple of years, but I don't know much about his private life. Except for one thing. He was infatuated with Mallory." He waved his hand as if to dispel any bad thoughts she had. "We didn't both date her or anything like that. I brought her to an outside-the-office company event where everyone brought their families or dates."

"Like a company picnic?"

"More or less, a get-to-know-you kind of thing, supposed to make teams work better together according to a consultant who recommended that I do those. We hold them twice a month, usually at a restaurant. But sometimes we'll go to a movie or bowling or something like that. Just the top execs and their families, about twenty-five or thirty people at any particular outing. I remember Mitchell being like a puppy dog following Mallory around that first time. When she mentioned it to me later, I didn't think much of it. But he did it again, at another event, and I had to tell him to leave her alone."

"How did he take that?"

"As you'd expect. He's a grown man. He was embarrassed and resentful but got over it fairly quickly. Or, at least, I'd thought he had. When he found out that I'd broken up with Mallory, I remember hearing from one of the other guys that Mitchell called her to offer his sympathies and a shoulder if she ever needed it. I remember thinking that was a bit odd, to offer your boss's ex-fiancée a shoulder to cry on. Especially when the two of them weren't even close."

"Sounds kind of creepy."

"Yeah, knowing that Mallory's dead now, murdered, it seems way creepy." He glanced around the room. "And I don't have a clue where Mitchell is right now." He suddenly rose from his chair and held out his hand. "Let's get out of here. We're both tired after not getting much sleep last night. And I'd feel a lot safer closing my eyes with a locked door between us and whoever has those guns—whether it's Mitchell or someone else."

THERE WAS NO passion or heat between them this time. They were both far too tired for that. But nothing felt better to Amber than being curled up in Dex's arms on the big, soft feather bed in her room. It had only taken a few minutes for both of them to fall asleep, and she'd slept better than she had in years, feeling safer than she ever had, even knowing that Mallory's killer was still in the house somewhere. The door was locked, her Colt .45 was sitting on the bedside table. She had no reason to worry, as long as they were cocooned in here together.

Or, at least, she shouldn't. But something had jerked her out of a sound sleep, and she had no clue what it was. The sunlight against the window blinds, what little peeked through the cloudy skies outside that were still dumping rain down on them, told her it was probably already afternoon. But the sun wasn't bright enough to have woken her. So what had?

Dex's arms tightened around her and his mouth

moved close to her ear. "You heard it, too?" he whispered. "Close your eyes. Pretend you're asleep."

She squeezed his hand around her waist to let him know that she'd heard him, and she kept her eyes closed, breathing deep and even.

The tiniest creak, like a squeaky door hinge, sounded from across the room.

Suddenly Dex jumped out of the bed. Amber opened her eyes just in time to see him disappearing through an opening in the far wall, his footsteps echoing back to her. She blinked in shock as she realized what she was looking at was a hidden door, much like the small panels her grandpa had for storing things in the walls. But this opening was large enough for people. It looked like a hallway. She turned and reached for the gun on the table, but it was gone. She curled her fingers into her palms. *Please let it be Dex who took the gun.*

She hopped out of bed and ran to the opening. It wasn't completely dark. A wall sconce about ten feet in cast more shadow than light, but it allowed her to see enough to realize what she was looking at. She'd lived in this house off and on for years and had never realized it had secret passageways. Was that how the killer had shot Mallory and disappeared so quickly? Had he discovered one of the openings and used it to get in and out of her room?

"Dex?" she whispered, in case he was still close enough to hear her. No answer. And she couldn't hear footsteps, either.

She couldn't believe he'd chased whoever had opened that panel. It was foolhardy and dangerous. And brave. She couldn't fault him for that. He wanted to catch the killer as much as she did, but he should have waited for her. She knew this house inside and out. Okay, not the secret passageway, or passageways, but she knew the rest of the house. Dex didn't. If he went through another panel he might get lost in a part of the house he'd never been in. And he was following a killer who had at least four guns—the one he'd used to kill Mallory, plus those that Amy, Aunt Freddie and Buddy had given up.

She had to help him.

She ran to her dresser and grabbed some jeans and a T-shirt and quickly tugged them on. Then she took the only weapon that she had, her knife, and attached the sheath at her waist. Bringing a knife to a gunfight wasn't the best possible scenario, but at least it gave her a chance. She drew a deep breath, then stepped into the passageway.

DEX FLATTENED HIMSELF against the wall, the revolver in his hand as he inched toward the next turn. He'd only caught glimpses of the person he was following, but he'd seen enough to know that he was definitely chasing a man—which ruled out Aunt Freddie and Amy, not that he'd really considered them suspects. But he was also chasing a young man, which ruled out Buddy, and he was chasing someone over six feet, close to his own height of six-two, which ruled out Derek, who was an inch shy of the six foot mark. That left only two possibilities—his assistant or his lawyer. Both of those possibilities left a bitter taste in his mouth. He'd trusted them with some of the most intimate and important details of his life, and one of them had betrayed him in the worst way, by killing an innocent woman. And now, whoever was stalking these dark halls had committed another sin—he'd threatened Amber by opening that panel into their room.

Dex hadn't been taking the search for the killer all that seriously, hoping to just wait it out until the storm cleared and the water level went down and they could get the police in here to take over. But now he realized he couldn't risk waiting any longer. He had to step up his game and figure out who was behind everything. Waiting and risking that Amber might get hurt—or worse—was unacceptable.

He tightened his hold on his gun and ducked down to make himself less of a target, then whirled around the corner, pointing the gun out in front of him. There, the silhouette of a man at the far end of the passageway ducked back behind the corner.

"Throw your gun out and give up, Mitchell," Dex called out, making a guess as to the identity.

Laughter echoed back to him, then the sound of running feet.

Damn. What did that mean? That it wasn't Mitchell? Was it Garreth, then? Dex took off running toward the next corner. He stopped and ducked down again, peering around the edge of the wall. The light from a sconce reflected off metal. He swore and lunged back just as a bullet ripped through the corner of the wall, its boom echoing through the tunnel.

Dex raised his gun again and ran past the wall, firing off two quick rounds. The man at the other end dove behind the next corner. Dex took off, running as fast he could. Both his footsteps and the other man's pounded against the hardwood floors. When he reached the next turn, he didn't stop this time. He raced around it, ready to end this.

He turned the corner at full speed. Ah, hell. He raised his arms to protect his face, unable to stop as he slammed against the wall that marked the end of the passage. Stinging pain shot through his shoulder as he busted through a hole in the drywall and slid to the floor. Plaster and dust rained down on him and he waved his hand in front of his face.

Footsteps pounded on the wooden floor again, from the direction where he'd just come from. He raised his gun and aimed it at the corner. He kept his finger on the rail beside the trigger, waiting, waiting.

His nemesis rounded the corner at full tilt. Dex jerked his gun up toward the ceiling just as Amber barreled into his chest. He grunted as he caught the full brunt of her to keep her from crashing into the wall. She let out a little shriek of fear a second before she recognized him.

After quickly stowing the gun, he cradled her against him, his hand shaking as he rubbed it down her back. If he hadn't hesitated long enough to realize she was far too small to be the man he was after, he could have shot her. And, at this close range, he wouldn't have missed.

"Dex, ease up. I can't breathe," she choked.

He forced himself to relax his grip, but he couldn't bring himself to let her go. "Amber, what are you doing in here? I could have killed you," he rasped.

She pushed against his chest and he reluctantly let her go. "I'm sorry. I heard shots. I thought you might be hurt, or need help. I was so scared."

"Scared for me?"

She nodded. "Of course." She ran her hands up and down him as if searching for wounds.

"I'm fine. He didn't hit me. But he got away. I chased

him around this corner, but he was gone. There must be another panel here somewhere."

She sat back on her knees. "You saw him?"

"Only in shadow. But I can rule out everyone but Garreth and Mitchell. I'm leaning more toward Garreth now."

"Why?" she asked, as he stood and helped her to her feet.

"Because I called out Mitchell's name and whoever I was chasing laughed."

She shivered. "Creepy."

"Yeah, tell me about it." He felt along the walls. "The panel has to be here somewhere. He couldn't have gotten back down the passageway past me." He ran his hands along the walls, looking for a seam.

Amber stepped farther back toward the corner. "Dex, there, look. I can see some light under the wall over here."

He bent down and studied where she was pointing. "You're right. But I don't see a seam in the wall. It's all drywall."

She shook her head. "I don't think the panel is in the wall. It's in the floor."

He backed up, and, sure enough, there was a darker square of wood in the center of the floor. Once he bent down and studied it, the opening mechanism was immediately clear. A wood knot had been removed and in the depression was a small, round knob no bigger than a quarter.

"You okay covering me?" he asked, holding up the revolver.

She rolled her eyes. "Is a spatterdock yellow?"

"Well, since I have no clue what a spatterdock is, I really couldn't say."

"Of course I'll cover you." She took the gun.

He hesitated. "Be careful. Stand back." He grabbed the little knob, then flung the wooden panel up on its hinge and stood back, expecting the gunman to be hiding below. But no shots rang out. He eased back to the edge and leaned down to get a look inside.

"It's a short tunnel, more or less about ten feet long. Goes in only one direction. Back toward the way we came. Wait here."

"No way. We're doing this together. No more running off into danger without me. We're a team, Dex."

He didn't like the idea of putting her in danger, but leaving her behind while he continued deeper into the bowels of the house didn't feel safe, either. "All right. But I go first. And before you say it, no, you keep the gun. No arguments on that."

She didn't appear to like his conditions, but she gave him a tight nod.

He braced his hands on both sides of the opening and dropped down into the cramped space, which was only about three feet tall. As soon as he did, the opening above him shut. He glanced up in surprise, noting the ropes and pulleys that had automatically closed the trapdoor and the rubber gasket on this side around the opening, which had stifled any sound.

The door opened again, and Amber looked down at him. "What was that about?"

He motioned toward the pulley system. "Looks like your grandpa designed the door to close on its own so he wouldn't have to close it himself. Assuming he ever ran around in these corridors."

She lowered herself over the opening and Dex grabbed her around the waist. He gently set her down and the trap door again quietly but quickly closed behind them.

"Cool," she said. "I can't believe he built all of this and never told me. I would have had so much fun as a kid in here."

"Maybe that's why he didn't tell you. He didn't want to worry about you running around in the walls and maybe getting lost or hurt. But why would he even build these tunnels?"

"He was always a bit paranoid. Maybe he thought they'd give him a way to escape if an intruder ever got into the house. Who knows? Do you see another way out?"

He nodded. "This is apparently a short crawl space beneath the floor above, but it's not low enough to be on the first floor or we'd be in water right now. There's another panel on the ceiling, at the end. Probably opens into another passageway. Do you have any idea where we are right now?"

"If I had to guess, from the directions I ran above, we're somewhere near the second-floor library."

They moved to the end of the crawl space and Amber reached up for the panel above them, but Dex pushed her back.

"I go first," he said. "If the killer is waiting for us on the other side, I don't want you to get shot."

"Well, hello, the feeling is mutual. And I'm the one with the gun."

"Doesn't matter. Step back, Amber."

"You're being a Neanderthal. I can protect myself, you know."

He cupped her face in his hands and leaned down to give her a soft kiss. When he pulled back, he searched her eyes. "I know you can protect yourself. You protected *me* back in the swamp. In fact, you saved my life. Now it's my turn, okay? I couldn't forgive myself if something happened to you."

Her eyes turned misty. "You say the sweetest things." She pulled him down for another kiss, and this one wasn't soft. By the time they broke apart, both of them were panting.

Dex was left resenting the killer even more, because if it weren't for him, he'd be back in the bed with Amber right now showing her just how sweet he could be.

He forced himself to step away from her and temptation and studied the panel above him to see how to open it. There, on the top corner, another knot had been removed and there was a knob. At least Grandpa was consistent. Dex reached for the knob.

A muffled scream sounded from above them.

Dex shared a surprised look with Amber, then shoved the knob. The panel flew open, the pulley system helping raise it quickly and silently like the other panel. Dex stood up, noting Amber had been right. This was the library, and the opening was back in a corner surrounded by floor-to-ceiling bookcases. He quickly hopped out and braced the panel to keep it from automatically closing, while Amber followed close behind.

The scream sounded again.

Dex and Amber took off running down an aisle between bookshelves and came out into the end of the library, close to where they'd been sitting earlier that morning.

Aunt Freddie was sitting on one of the couches, her

face ghastly pale. Buddy was using a magazine to fan her. Derek stood beside them, and all three stared at Amber and Dex in surprise.

"Where did you two come from?" Derek demanded, his surprise turning to suspicion.

Amber gave Dex a puzzled look as they hurried to the group.

"What's going on?" Dex asked, not bothering with explanations. "Who screamed?"

Aunt Freddie pushed Buddy away and shakily rose to her feet, half leaning on him as he helped her up. "I did." Without another word, she pointed across the room.

Dex and Amber both followed the direction in which she was pointing. There, on top of a side table next to a chair, was a bunched-up white blouse with red splotches on it that looked like blood.

"It's Amy's," Freddie announced. "And she's missing."

Chapter Fourteen

Everyone started talking at once.

Dex held his hands up. "Hold it. Everyone quiet."

The library fell silent. As one, Aunt Freddie, Buddy and Derek looked at Dex. He lowered his hands.

"Okay, I'll start. Amber and I noticed the guns were missing from the trunk earlier, as we were all escaping the floodwaters to go upstairs."

Derek fisted his hands beside him, his jaw tight and angry. "And you didn't think it was a good idea to tell the rest of us?"

"I didn't want to panic anyone. We knew the killer already had a gun somewhere, so it didn't really change things."

"Except to make you the only one with access to a gun." He waved at the Colt that Amber now had tucked into her waistband. "Or the two of you. Hell, maybe you're both the killers."

Buddy stepped forward, using his bulk to force Derek back a few feet. "No one is going to blame Amber again for another murder, so you can just stop that right now. And as far as that other lady goes, like I already said, Dex and I reached the room at the same time. He couldn't have killed her. Plus, I know who took the guns."

"Who?" Dex and Derek asked at the same time.

"Me. I didn't cotton to the idea of the murderer being the only armed one around here, so I hid them in case we needed them. Looks like that was a good idea after all." He eyed Derek with distaste. "Except I'm not sure who to trust around here."

Derek's eyes narrowed. "Are you accusing me of something, old man?"

"Well, you were the one getting cozy with Amy earlier. And now she's missing."

Derek stepped forward, his hands in fists.

"Stop it, you two." Dex shoved Derek, who glared at him in return. To the others, Dex said, "Derek isn't the threat here."

"And how do you know that?" Aunt Freddie chimed in, standing close to Buddy in a united front against an angry-looking Derek.

"Because someone opened a hidden panel in Amber's room a little while ago. And I'm pretty sure I saw another panel open in Mallory's room earlier and just didn't realize it at the time. The killer is using hidden passageways to get around the house. And I saw him. He's definitely not Derek."

"You saw him?" Derek asked. "Who is it, then?"

"One of the only two men not in this room, Mitchell or Garreth. I only saw him in shadows."

"Then how do you know it's not this guy?" Buddy waved at Derek.

"Because the man I saw was—"

"Taller," Derek said, sounding weary. "I'm the short man out. I get it. Fine. So it's Mitchell or Garreth. One of them has Amy. I say we tear this place apart and find them. After we get those guns."

Buddy shook his head. "Nope. Like I said, I don't trust you. I'll give Freddie a gun, and Dex, though."

"You'll give me one, too." Derek drew himself up as if to intimidate Buddy, but the old man just ignored him. "I'll go get them."

"Wait." Dex held up his hand. "Buddy, Derek arrived in that hallway outside Mallory's room at the same time that we did. And he's not the man who shot at me in the passageways. So I think we can all agree he's not the killer. Derek needs to protect himself, too."

"There are only three guns," Buddy grumbled.

"I've got my knife," Amber said. "And I'll give Dex my gun. You three get the rest of the guns. And we all stay together. We'll all be safe that way."

"She's right. As long as we stay together, we should be safe," Aunt Freddie said. "Give him a gun too, Buddy."

"Oh, fine. Come on. They're over here. I hid them in one of the bookshelves when we brought the food up here." He led them to a shelf at the other end of the room and pulled out the guns. "I don't have any extra ammo, so if we get in a shoot-out, we'll have to be careful."

"Good grief," Dex said. "There's not going to be a shoot-out. If those guns are the types with safeties, keep the safeties on."

"Only a sissy needs a safety." Buddy passed the guns around.

Dex had a very bad feeling about everyone around him being armed, but he couldn't exactly justify being the only one with a gun. "Everyone, please, be careful. I don't want anyone getting shot by accident."

"Son," Buddy said, "the only ones around here who might be careless with firearms are the townies like you and this Dexter feller."

"Derek," Derek corrected.

"Whatever."

Derek shook his head and gave Dex a pained look. For whatever reason, Buddy had taken a dislike to him and wasn't going to drop it.

Dex figured it had to do with the way Derek had been cozying up to Amy earlier. He remembered how the town had been against Jake as an outsider when he'd first come here. But they now considered Jake to be one of their own. They had their hearts in the right places, being protective of one other. But he could well understand Derek's frustration. If it weren't for his own ties to Jake, they'd probably be treating him the same way.

"Okay, when Amber and I got here, we'd just heard you scream, Freddie. So what happened?"

"Something woke me up. I'm not sure what. And I got up and looked over there and saw Amy's blouse, all cut up." She shivered. "Then I went looking for her on the couch on that other side of the room where she and Dexter had been earlier—"

Derek rolled his eyes.

"—and he was lying there asleep but Amy was gone. That's when I screamed."

"So no one saw Amy leave? Or anyone else in here?"

They all shook their heads.

"Maybe she went back to her room," Amber said. "And the killer put that blouse there to scare us?"

"What about the blood?" Derek asked.

She shook her head. "I don't know."

"Let's go to Amy's room and see if she's there before we go down that line of thought," Dex said.

As one they headed toward the door. Dex made them wait while he looked out in the hallway. Clear. Lightning lit up the windows behind them, casting eerie shadows down the hall. But so far the generator was keeping up and the sconces down the hall showed enough that he felt it was safe to step outside.

"Which way?" he whispered to Amber.

"She was in the west wing, a few doors down from… Mallory's room."

He nodded and headed out, with Amber keeping pace with him. The others followed close behind. Dex tried not to think about the fact that they had guns in their hands. His back itched, expecting someone to stumble any minute and shoot him.

"Keep an eye on the doors, and listen for anyone else," he whispered back to them.

Buddy gave him a salute as if Dex was a general, and he whispered to Freddie. She nodded and the two of them aimed their guns at either side as they made their way down the hall behind him. Dex noted that Derek kept his gun shoved into his waistband and stayed well back from Freddie and Buddy, apparently as nervous as Dex was with the two Mystic Glades residents walking around with their guns out.

They passed the open railing that looked down on the foyer below and, as one, they paused. Amber gasped and clutched Dex's arm.

He could well understand her surprise and dismay. Water covered the bottom two steps of the staircase and lapped at the third. "I'm sorry," he said. "I know this is your family home."

She nodded, looking miserable. "I never thought I'd see the day when the water would rise like this. We've had floods in the past, but they never got this high."

"I think the rain's letting up," he said, trying to make her feel better.

She looked out the windows above the front door. "You're right. That's something to be grateful for, at least."

"Come on." He urged her forward, not liking that they were essentially targets out in the open two-story foyer. If Mitchell or Garreth was bold enough to shoot at him, then he wasn't going to assume the man would be worried about getting wet down on the first floor. The attacker could be behind an archway even now, waiting for a good shot.

They passed the open railing and Dex breathed a sigh of relief with walls on both sides again, blocking any shots from below. When they reached Amy's door, Dex didn't bother knocking. If the killer was inside with her, he wanted to use the element of surprise to put the odds more in his favor. He drew his gun, carefully turned the knob, then shoved the door open and ran inside.

Another scream met him as Amy backed up against the wall, clutching a towel against her naked body, her hair dripping water onto the floor.

Dex lowered the gun and shoved it into his waistband. "Are you okay?"

She blinked at him and looked at Amber. "Why does he have a gun? What are all of you doing here?"

Amber hurried to her and gave her a fierce hug before pulling back and answering. "We thought the killer had you."

She frowned. "Why would you think that? I was just taking a shower."

Freddie and Buddy stepped up beside Dex. "One of your shirts was in the library, with blood on it."

Her face turned a light pink. "Oh. Sorry. I scratched my arm against an old nail on one of the bookshelves earlier this morning when I woke up before everyone else. I had a tank top underneath, so I took off my shirt to stop the bleeding. I forgot and didn't take it with me when I left later to take a shower." She frowned. "Where's everyone else?"

Dex shoved his gun into his waistband. "I'm not sure where Garreth and Mitchell are. We think one of them must be the killer. Now that we know that you're okay, our next stop will be to look in Garreth's and Mitchell's rooms to see if either of them is there."

"Okay, but where's Derek?"

Her words seemed to sink into everyone at the same time. They all whirled around.

Derek was gone.

DEX STEPPED OUT of Garreth's closet and crossed the bedroom to where Amber was rifling through Garreth's suitcase.

She looked up and shook her head. "I don't know what he brought with him, of course, but everything seems to be in order. No obvious gaps like anything's missing. What about that briefcase he had with him?"

"It's in the closet. I couldn't open it since it's locked. But it's present and accounted for. Unlike Garreth."

"And Mitchell and Derek," she added.

"Told you I shouldn't have given him a gun," Buddy

grumbled from his position on the other side of the room next to Amy and Freddie.

"He's not the killer," Dex said. "It has to be Mitchell or Garreth."

"How tall am I?" Buddy asked.

"Excuse me?"

"You heard me, son. How tall am I?"

Dex considered him for a moment. "Five-eight?"

Buddy drew himself up, and Dex immediately realized his mistake. Buddy had been slouching.

"Closer to six foot," Dex admitted.

"Five-eleven," Buddy confirmed. "You willing to bet your life, and ours, that you were right that the man you saw in those hidden passageways wasn't that Dexter fellow?"

"You're right. I shouldn't have made any assumptions. The hallway was dark. And he was far away. I have to allow for the possibility that the killer could be anyone, including *Derek*."

"You mean the killer could be anyone except us." Amber waved her hand to encompass everyone in the bedroom.

"I'm not assuming anything at this point," he said.

Buddy gave him an irritated look. "We're going back to the library."

"Wait." Dex hurried to the door. "The library isn't a safe place to stay. It has one of the passageway entrances. Amber, is there some other room we can all easily fit in, somewhere more defensible?"

She shook her head. "Other than the bedrooms, there are no other big enough rooms upstairs where we could gather."

"Then we need to search the upstairs library to make

sure we know where all of the passageway entrances are and block them off. If we have to, we'll scoot furniture on top of any trapdoors or throw a pile of books on them. Before we go back, does anyone need a bathroom break or anything from their rooms? I don't want anyone wandering around on their own."

Amy shook her head no.

Buddy and Freddie both raised their hands like children in a schoolroom.

"Bathroom," Freddie said.

"Me, too," Buddy chimed in.

Dex sighed. "Amber? Where's the nearest bathroom?"

"Just down the hall."

They went through the same routine, Dex looking down the hall and then everyone keeping behind him as they headed out the door. But this time, both Amber and Dex kept looking back to make sure they didn't lose anyone.

Once they were finally in the library and Dex was satisfied that they'd located the only passageway entrance—the one he and Amber had used earlier—and it was covered by a very heavy couch that had been difficult for all of them together to scoot over to the trapdoor, Dex pulled Amber to the side away from the others.

"I need you to stay here and keep an eye on the others, make sure they don't try to go anywhere. Lock the door behind me."

"Hold it." She put her hand on his arm to stop him. "Where do you think you're going? The rain has stopped, yes, but the water won't recede for a while. We need to wait here until we can get back to town and call the police. Even then, we'll likely have to pile into a canoe to get there since the cars are probably all flooded out."

"A canoe? You have one around here?"

She shook her head. "No. I was being facetious. I wish I had a canoe. I could get us out right now, since the lightning has stopped. But I don't."

His excitement at hearing her mention a canoe took a nosedive and cemented his earlier decision. "Okay, let's take a hard look at what we're up against, then. There are three men out there somewhere—two of whom are either already dead or could be soon if I don't find them, and the third is armed and has already killed once for sure and tried to kill me in the passageway. Amber, I can't sit here and wait an entire day for the water to go down while two people are somewhere at the mercy of a killer. I have to search for them."

"Fine. Then I'm going with you."

He grabbed her arm this time. "No. You're not."

"You listen to me, Dex Lassiter. I survived in a dangerous swamp for over two years. Trust me, it's not just the reptiles and wild animals that I had to watch out for. Drug dealers and other unsavory people use those swamps as their personal hiding place and sometimes as a route to ship their illegal cargo. I've had more than a few run-ins with them and I'm still standing here to talk about it. Don't assume that I'm not good in a fight just because I'm a woman. You need someone to watch your back, or you can watch mine. But, regardless, I am going with you."

He gritted his teeth. "How am I supposed to focus when I'm worrying about you out there with me?"

Her face softened and she pressed her hand against the side of his face. "The same way that I will. I care about you, Dex. And I don't want you hurt any more than I think you want me hurt. But I, too, am not going to sit around while your friends need help."

He cupped the back of her neck and pulled her in for a quick kiss. "Damn it, Amber. I don't like you being in danger."

"Neither do I. I'll be careful. We'll both be careful. And we'll get through this together."

He nodded. "All right." He quickly told the others what they were going to do. "Don't let anyone else in this library, no matter what."

"What if Derek comes back?" Amy's concern for him was obvious in the worry lines on her young forehead.

"I suppose you'll have to use your own judgment," Dex said. "But I'd feel a lot better if you kept that door closed until either Amber or I return. We'll search the house in a grid pattern and check in once an hour, which means that our first check-in will be—" he looked at his watch "—three o'clock."

Buddy rose from the couch where he'd been sitting with Freddie. "What are we supposed to do if you aren't back by three?"

Dex took Amber's hand in his and exchanged a long look with her before answering. "Pray."

Chapter Fifteen

Amber held up her thumb, silently letting Dex know that the bathroom connected to the bedroom he was searching was clear. He nodded and headed into the walk-in closet while she waited against the wall by the door, her hand poised on the top of her knife sheathed at her waist. This was the last bedroom to search in the east wing, and they were bumping up against the one-hour mark so they'd have to hurry back to the library for their check-in if they weren't going to worry the others.

She wished they hadn't agreed to the one-hour check-in since it would disrupt their search. But she tried to imagine herself sitting in the locked library, waiting, and realized she'd probably go nuts if hours passed without any word if someone else was out searching. Dex knew what he was doing when he'd told them he'd come back. It was as much for the others' peace of mind as it was for her and Dex's safety. Because she had no doubt that if she and Dex didn't check in, Aunt Freddie would be pushing Buddy to go search the house for them.

Dex emerged from the closet, shaking his head. He met her beside the door and pointed to his watch. She nodded, and they looked out into the hall, then hurried back toward the library, watching every table, every alcove, every door as they passed. She and Dex had made a point of closing and locking each door after they searched a room. So if any of them were open, they'd know that's where someone else had gone.

Their quick trek down the hall was uneventful. Aunt Freddie must have been waiting at the door, because as soon as Amber announced that it was her and Dex, the door swung open.

While Dex spoke to Freddie and Buddy, Amber hurried to Amy, who was staring out the front window at the water below. Amber was just about to speak when she saw Amy's reflection in the glass and hesitated. Instead of the pale, scared-looking young girl that Amber was used to seeing when she looked at Amy, the reflection against the dark windowpane seemed much older, harsh, angry. Her brows were drawn down and her lips were compressed into a tight line.

Amy raised her hand and pressed it against the glass.

Amber's eyes widened and she leaned forward to see what Amy might be looking at.

Amy suddenly turned around, her eyes wide, her face looking frightened like usual as she pressed a hand against her chest. "Amber, my gosh, you scared me."

"I'm sorry. I didn't mean to." She forced a tight smile. Had she only imagined the angry expression on Amy's face reflected in the window? Was it just a trick of the light?

Amy's brows drew down in confusion. "Amber? Is something wrong?" She raised her hand to her throat. "My God. Please tell me you didn't find Derek, and that he's…he's…" She bit her lip and made a small sound in her throat as if she was trying not to cry.

Guilt rose inside Amber and she pulled the other

woman into a hug. "I'm so, so sorry. I'm tired and on edge. I should have been more careful and shouldn't have worried you. No, we haven't found Derek." She pulled back and took Amy's hands in hers. "We have to believe that he's okay." *If he isn't the killer.*

"Everything all right over here?" Dex asked from behind her.

Amy's shy gaze darted away. "I'm fine. I over-reacted, thought maybe something had happened to Derek."

Dex smiled. "You really like him, don't you?"

Her face flushed. "He's okay."

"We're doing everything we can to find him. Don't worry."

She bit her bottom lip and wrapped her arms around her waist. "Thank you."

He nodded. "Amber? Ready to search the east wing?"

"The east wing?"

"Yes. The one we haven't searched yet. Ready?"

Something in his gaze told her to go along with what he was saying, even though she knew they'd already searched that wing. "Yes, yes, of course. Let's go."

Dex led her to the door, then stopped and spoke in low tones to Buddy, before pulling Amber out into the hall.

When they were in one of the bedrooms in the west wing a few minutes later, Dex closed the door.

Amber swung around to face him. "Okay, spill. What did you say to Buddy? And why did you lie about where we were going?"

"I told Buddy the truth about us searching the west wing next. But I didn't want Amy to know. I warned Buddy to keep an eye on her, that I didn't trust her.

And that if he got a chance to get her gun away from her without openly confronting her, he should take it."

"What? Why?"

"Because if Amy is our enemy, instead of an ally, and she sneaks out of the library to come after us, I don't want her to know where to search. There was some-thing…creepy…about the way she looked at you when you talked to her. For a moment, it almost looked like she…hated you. I hurried over as soon as she turned around."

Amber's eyes widened. "I thought the same thing. Only I noticed her reflection in the window, that she seemed…different, harder, angry. But that doesn't make sense. And why would she hate me? I only just met her."

"I don't know, but since we both got the same vibes, I say we be careful not to turn our backs on her."

"Good grief, is everyone after us now? Do we have to be afraid of all of them?"

"I'd rather be alert and stay alive than take any chances. Come on. Let's get through this wing as fast as we can. I have a feeling we won't be any more suc-cessful than we were on the other side."

Sure enough, their search yielded nothing new. No clues. No more passageway doors that they could find or trap doors in the floors. And no sign of Garreth, Mitchell or Derek.

"After the next check-in," Amber said, "I think we should search the only two rooms we haven't been in yet. They're both locked, but the killer may have been able to get inside through the passageways and panels."

"You're talking about your grandfather's bedroom, which has been sealed for years, and my old bedroom—where Mallory was…killed."

She nodded. "I don't like the idea of going in either room. And I know we wanted to keep the crime scene pristine for the police. But we're running out of places to search."

He glanced down the dimly lit hallway toward the closed and locked door where Mallory's body had been found, not looking any more excited about the prospect of going inside than she was.

"How much time do we have?" Amber asked. "We searched faster this time, now that we're in a routine."

He checked his watch. "You're right. We have fifteen more minutes."

"Do you still have the keys?"

He patted his pants pocket. "Okay. Let's do this."

She followed him to his old bedroom door and they both pressed their ears against the wood, listening for any sounds from within.

Dex very carefully and quietly put the key into the lock and slowly turned it. As soon as the lock clicked, he shoved the door open and ran inside, sweeping his gun out in front of him.

Amber ran in after him, holding her knife out. When she saw what was on the bed, she pressed her hand to her throat. "Oh, no."

Dex was already shoving his gun into his waistband and hurrying to the bed. He bent over Garreth and pressed his fingers against the side of his neck, checking for a pulse.

Amber stopped beside him. "Is he…" She couldn't bring herself to say it. There was blood all over his shirt and his face was incredibly pale.

"No, he's not dead," Dex said. "But his pulse is very

weak." He leaned closer. "Garreth, can you hear me? It's Dex."

Garreth moaned, his eyelids fluttering then opening. "Dex?" His voice came out a bare whisper of sound.

"Where are you hurt?" Dex asked, as he opened Garreth's suit jacket. "Oh, no."

"He's been stabbed," Amber said. "Twice, that I can see. We've got to stop the bleeding." She ran into the adjoining bathroom and came back with some towels. Dex was pressing his hands against both wounds. Garreth writhed beneath him, alternately cursing and begging him to stop hurting him.

"I'm sorry," Dex gritted out. "I have to keep the pressure, Garreth."

"I don't think he can hear you." Amber felt his forehead. "He's hot, but I don't know if it's from the blood loss or if he's already got an infection."

"You can help him, though. You helped me."

She gently pushed his hands away and laid the towels on top of Garreth's abdomen, then stepped back for Dex to press down again. Garreth wasn't struggling anymore. He'd passed out from the pain.

"Amber?" Dex's tortured voice called to her. "Please. You have to help him. I don't know what to do, but you do."

She bit her bottom lip. "You don't understand. I don't…do that anymore."

"Amber, you're not responsible for your grandfather's death, if that's what this is about. I know you tried to save him with your tonic, but you couldn't save him. It was the cancer that took his life. You did everything you could. It wasn't your fault."

She clenched her hands at her sides. "I know. Logically, I know that. But in my heart, I can't help wonder if there was something else that I could have done."

He bent down, capturing her gaze. "You can do this. I know you can. What do you need? Tell me. How do we stop the bleeding? How do we bring his fever down? There have to be medicines around here for that, right? A needle? Thread?"

She could do this. She could do this. "Yes, yes, there should be headache powders in my grandfather's bathroom." She swallowed hard at the idea of going in there without Dex. Not because she was scared, but because facing the ghosts of her past would be so much easier with him there to support her. "And I've got needle and thread in my bedroom."

"Take the gun with you. And the keys, so you can get into your grandfather's room." He put his hand on hers. "Be careful. If the crime scene seal from two years ago is broken, don't go in. And even if it isn't, be extremely vigilant." He frowned. "It could be dangerous. I should go. You should stay here."

"No. Stay with your friend. I've got this."

She grabbed his gun and ran before he could stop her.

DEX SWORE, REGRETTING that he'd let her go. But he couldn't do anything about that right now. He'd just have to hope she was okay, as much as it killed him not to chase after her.

He lifted the towel, cursing again when he saw how much blood had saturated it. He tossed it to the floor and grabbed the second towel that Amber had left with him. One of the wounds seemed to be clotting, but the deeper wound wouldn't quit seeping. And Garreth couldn't afford to lose much more blood.

He looked up at the door. Amber had locked it on her way out. He hadn't meant for her to do that, but he understood why she had—to protect him and Garreth if the killer came back. Everything she did seemed to center around others—keeping them safe, nursing them back to health, protecting them in every way possible. She never put herself first, no matter what. It was the main quality, that and her never-ending courage, that astounded him. He was used to working with people who always put themselves first, who put making a dollar above everything else, including relationships and families. And since almost dying in the plane crash, and then realizing that one of the people he'd trusted every day at his company was also trying to kill him, he'd had to reevaluate his own life and how he treated others.

And he didn't like what he saw.

He'd known Garreth, Derek and Mitchell for years. And yet, faced with the knowledge that one of them was a killer, he had no real gut feeling for which one it might be. How could he work with them, even double-date with them in the case of Derek, go to football games and supposed team-building events, and never really, truly know them? The longer this debacle went on the more he despised himself and the more he realized that Amber was a better person than he could ever be. She deserved so much more than she had, and he vowed if they survived he would do everything he could to make sure that she never wanted for anything ever again.

Garreth groaned, drawing Dex's attention.

"Dex?" he whispered, sounding groggy. For the first time since they'd gotten there, Garreth's eyes were clear and focused. "What happened?"

Dex laughed with relief. "Hey, man. You tell me. You've got a pair of nasty cuts on your belly."

Garreth winced. "Hurts like hell. Did I get shot?"

"Stabbed. You don't remember?"

He shook his head. "Last I remember we were putting that freezer on top of the island in the kitchen."

Dex frowned. "You must have gotten conked on the head." He chanced lifting one hand off the towel and felt along the back of his friend's head. "Yeah, you've got a huge goose egg back there, but it's not bleeding. Not anymore at least." He put both hands on the towel and kept up the pressure even though his arms were starting to ache.

Garreth looked around. "Where are we?"

"My bedroom. Or what was my bedroom, until Mallory went in there and…" He shook his head. "This was where we found her earlier. Amber and I searched this wing for you and the others and decided to look in here. Glad we did."

"The others?"

He winced. "Derek and Mitchell are missing. I have to assume one of them killed Mallory. I just don't know which one."

Garreth closed his eyes. "You thought I might be the killer, didn't you?"

"Sadly, yes. I have to admit I don't really know you or Derek or Mitchell like I thought I did. Hell, I don't even know if you have a girlfriend."

A small smile played on Garreth's lips. "Yeah. Her name is Veronica Walker. One of the many women you've dumped on your way to someone else. We're madly in love and plotting our revenge against you for how you treated her."

"Don't make me press harder," Dex joked. "I'm not proud of my past and am only now beginning to realize what a jerk I've been."

Garreth laughed, then groaned. "Damn, that hurts. And I was kidding. No girlfriend. No time. My boss is a real pain in the ass, and the belly, apparently."

"Your pain-in-the-ass boss is going to give you a month off with pay if you promise not to die on him."

"Careful what you promise. I might take you up on that."

"I'm counting on it." He looked toward the door. "Where the hell is Amber?"

"Right here, right here." Her voice sounded from behind him. "You were so busy talking to Garreth that you didn't notice when I came into the room."

"Well, that's a scary thought."

She shrugged. "No harm." She smiled down at the bed. "Nice to see you awake, Mr. Jackson. Let's see about stitching you up and getting that fever down, okay?"

"If it will make this jerk stop pressing on my stomach, I'm up for anything."

Garreth held still like a trouper for Amber to stitch him up, in spite of not having anything more powerful than the headache powder to dull the pain. It was when she and Dex tried to roll him over to check for other injuries that he passed out again.

"What's wrong with him?" Dex asked, worried that they'd hurt him by rolling him over.

Amber finished feeling along his back and motioned for Dex to lay him down before replying. "His belly isn't distended and I don't see any more injuries. I think he's just exhausted and passed out from that and the pain of being moved. I'm certainly no doctor but I don't think he has any internal bleeding. I think your friend's going to be fine."

"You should have let him bleed to death," a familiar masculine voice called out from the doorway.

Dex clawed for his gun.

"Draw on me and I'll shoot both of you."

Dex forced his hand to relax and stared in disbelief at the man he'd trusted and worked with for years. "What's going on, Mitchell?" He positioned himself in front of Amber, hoping to shield her.

"Oh, how sweet. You *are* a couple, aren't you? That was pretty obvious from the get-go. Well, now it's my turn to answer the question you asked our dear friend Garreth there. I do have a girlfriend. Or I *did*, until you *stole* her from me and then cast her aside like garbage, like you do *all* your women." His hand tightened on the pistol he was pointing at Dex. "And her name really was Veronica Walker."

Dex blinked in surprise. "I knew Derek dated Ronnie a while back. But I never knew that you—"

"Shut up. I don't want to hear it."

"But this doesn't make sense. Why are you doing this?"

Mitchell raised the gun higher, squarely pointing it at Dex's chest. "I don't want to hear anything else come out of your mouth except 'yes, sir.' Understood?"

Dex flexed his fingers, dearly wishing he could draw his gun. "Yes, sir," he gritted out.

"Toss the gun on the bed. Oh, and Miss Callahan, toss your knife on the bed, too. Quickly. We don't have much time."

Not seeing a way out without risking getting Amber

shot, Dex laid his gun on the bed while Amber discarded her knife.

"Why don't we have much time?" Dex asked.

"Well, because of the floodwaters, of course. The rain may have stopped, but the water's still rising as the runoff from higher ground drains down onto this property. I should know. I've spent a lot of time outside since we got here. In fact, I'd say I know this property just about as well as Miss Callahan now. Maybe better."

"And why do we care about the rising floodwaters?" Dex pressed.

"Oh, I didn't tell you yet? Because if you don't get to Derek soon, he'll drown, of course. The water will be going over his head. He's tied to the maintenance shed. If you hurry, you just might be able to save him. Of course, the question is, will I shoot you *before* you do, or *after*?" He shrugged. "Who knows?" He stepped away from the door and motioned with his gun. "Get moving."

Derek. How could Dex have ever doubted his friend? And now both Derek and Amber were in danger because of his clouded judgment.

He pulled Amber with him toward the door, keeping himself between her and Mitchell's gun.

Chapter Sixteen

Amber hesitated halfway down the staircase with Dex at her side and Mitchell a few steps behind him. Her toes curled inside her sneakers. Mitchell had been right. The water was still rising even though the rain had stopped and there was no more lightning or thunder. She didn't know how many stairs were underneath the water, but the brackish mess was halfway up the front door. What worried her more than the water was what was under that water. Could a gator have worked its way through one of the windows or the back door?

"Move," Mitchell ordered, from behind her and Dex. "Head to the kitchen and the back porch."

She exchanged a glance with Dex. His brow was furrowed with concern and he gave her a barely perceptible nod, as if to reassure her. She nodded to let him know she was okay. But she really wished she had her knife right now. Or the Colt .45 that they'd been forced to leave back with Garreth. Thank God, she'd finished sewing up his wounds before Mitchell got to them. At least Garreth would have a chance now.

But what about Derek? Was he even still alive? And why was Mitchell doing this? She couldn't imagine that Dex would have treated Veronica so poorly that

Mitchell felt bound by some kind of old-fashioned honor code to defend her this way. And even if he did, why had he killed Mallory? She desperately wished she could talk to Dex, that they could try to figure this out together. But she was afraid to do more than breathe after the way Mitchell had pointed his gun at Dex back in the bedroom and ordered him not to say anything.

She held the banister and plopped her foot down to the next stair, splashing into the water. Dex stepped into the water with her, matching her step for step. He was obviously doing everything he could to stay glued to her side, to protect her if he could. But nothing could protect either of them if Mitchell decided to pull the trigger or they stepped on a water moccasin.

Another step, the carpet runner squishing beneath her feet. Another, another. Soon the water was up to her chest, but thankfully her feet were on the floor now. It wouldn't get any deeper. The water was only up to Dex's hips. He reached for her hand and held it tightly as they waded forward.

"Watch out for snakes," she whispered, hoping Mitchell wouldn't hear her and retaliate for her talking. "And gators."

He cursed and watched the water around them with renewed interest.

Mitchell splashed down into the water behind them, not close enough for her or Dex to try to overpower him but not far enough away that he couldn't still shoot them or give them the opportunity to dodge around a corner and hide.

Amber plowed forward through the maze of rooms, through the great room and into the kitchen. She was amazed that the electricity was still on in this part of the house. She'd have expected the water to short-circuit the lights. The kitchen was as bright as ever but looked utterly bizarre with the deep freeze up on the island, water lapping at its base. The familiar hum had her skin crawling at the knowledge that a body was inside that freezer.

Dex squeezed her hand, as if to lend her strength and keep her calm. She glanced up at him as they continued toward the back door where Mitchell had told them to go.

"If there's any way for me to jump him, I will," he whispered. "And you need to run back in and get to Buddy, get the guns and hide somewhere."

"I'm not leaving you," she muttered.

His jaw tightened but he didn't say anything else because Mitchell splashed up behind them.

"Onto the porch," he ordered.

Dex wrestled the door open against the current and stepped out onto the porch. Or what was left of it. Amber couldn't believe the destruction she was seeing as she joined him. They both held on to the posts where the railings were attached, or had been. She moved her foot forward and encountered nothing where she knew a railing should be. Behind the house, trees were down, their branches rising out of the water like ghostly fingers ready to snare an unsuspecting person in their grasp.

"Dex," a voice called out. "Dex!"

Amber followed Dex's gaze. As Mitchell had said, Derek was tied to the post that supported the overhang of the maintenance building fifty yards away. His hands were above his head, roped to the post. And he was struggling to keep his chin above the waves the current made as it lapped against the building.

"Go ahead," Mitchell said. "Go help your friend. Unless you want to save your own hide, like always. That's what I'd expect you to do, of course—stay here and watch out for your own safety rather than brave that murky water. Because that's what you do, put yourself before others."

Dex took a step toward Mitchell.

Mitchell raised the gun toward his head. "Give me a reason, boss. I've been wanting to do this for a long time."

"Really? How long? Before or after you sabotaged my plane?"

Mitchell laughed, the same eerie laugh Dex had heard in the passageway outside Amber's bedroom earlier tonight. Maybe if he'd paid more attention to his employees, to the people in his life, he'd have recognized that laugh. And he'd have known earlier who the killer was. Of course, Mitchell had already disappeared by then, so it wouldn't have mattered. But what did matter right now was saving Amber and Derek and the others inside. He just wished he knew how he was going to manage all that.

"Mitchell, you're not a bad person. I know something must have happened to make you snap. A jury would understand that, too. Stop this, before it goes too far."

Mitchell sneered at him. "Too far? I've already killed Mallory. I'd say I've already gone too far. I didn't mean to kill her, you know. She caught me sneaking into your room with a gun. It was you that I wanted to kill. I shot her without thinking about it."

Dex edged closer to Mitchell. Amber looked toward the maintenance building. Derek's cries were getting weaker. She didn't know how much longer he could keep his chin above the water.

"You panicked then," Dex said, his voice soothing as he spoke to his assistant. "People will understand that. Like you said, you didn't mean to kill—"

"Stop it," Mitchell shouted. He wrapped both hands around his pistol and shook it at Dex. "Just stop it. You and your smooth talking. Do you think I'm stupid?"

Dex held his hands up placatingly. "Of course not. I think you're very smart. You've been practically running my company for years. You do a far better job than I ever could."

"Damn straight, I do." Mitchell lowered the gun ever so slightly. "And what do I get for it? I get to watch you, year after year, treat people like they're nothing."

"Mitchell—"

"Let me finish! You do, you know. You act all nice and polite on the surface, but do you really care about anyone? No. We're all replaceable, interchangeable. Me. Ronnie. Mallory. I liked Mallory, you know, even though she didn't like me back. Ronnie does, though. She loves me. Because after you threw her away, after you broke her, she came back to me again. You didn't know that, did you? I was there to help her pick up the pieces, to make her realize she had worth. To let her know she mattered and shouldn't have been thrown away like that. You don't give a damn about anyone, Dex. I thought killing you with the plane crash would be quick and painless and would end it all without anyone else getting hurt. I was being merciful. But, of course, you had to survive—the golden boy. Well, now I'm teaching you a lesson before you die. Because for the first time ever, I've figured out what you really care about."

"Mitchell, look, I'm—"

"Don't you even want to know what it is?" he shouted.

"Of course, of course. What do I care about?"

Mitchell swore. "Even now, you don't know. Because you're shallow, empty. Move, get over there."

"No."

Amber stiffened behind Dex. She wanted to see Mitchell's reaction, but Dex kept adjusting his position every time she tried to look around him. He was keeping himself firmly between the two of them.

"Dex?" Derek cried weakly across the darkness.

"Give me the gun, Mitchell," Dex said. "No one else has to get hurt. Let me help Derek and then we'll sit down and talk about what I've done to wrong you. I'll make it right. I promise."

A guttural, pained sound like that from a wounded animal came from Mitchell. Water swished. Amber looked back at the wall of windows in the kitchen. She could see his reflection now. He'd waded through the water and was standing directly in front of Dex, with his pistol jammed against Dex's forehead.

"Don't tell me what to do ever again," Mitchell spit out. "Now, go save Derek like a good boy. And the one thing you care about, the one *person* you care about, will stay here. With me." He suddenly reached around Dex for Amber.

Dex grabbed Mitchell's arm and shoved the gun up toward the ceiling. "Run, Amber! Run!"

The two men struggled for the gun. It went off, firing into the porch ceiling. They fell backward, a tangle of arms, with Mitchell snarling and cursing at Dex as they both struggled for control of the pistol. They fell into the water and disappeared below the surface.

Amber took a deep breath and crouched down under the water, but when she opened her eyes she couldn't see anything and the burn and sting of the dirty water had her squeezing her eyes shut again. She felt the water move violently around her and she hurriedly stood up above the surface again, wiping at her eyes as she tried to see what was happening.

Dex and Mitchell were standing up again, pressed against the back of the house, still fighting for the gun. Dex managed to free one arm and swung his fist toward Mitchell's jaw. Mitchell jerked to the side before it could connect.

"Amber, get the hell out of here," Dex yelled at her, meeting her gaze in the reflection in the windows.

She realized several things at once. There was nothing she could do to help Dex in his deadly struggle with Mitchell without getting in the way. She was distracting him by staying here. But there was one thing she could do to help. She could save Derek.

She moved toward the edge of the porch.

"Amber, no, it's too dangerous!" Dex cried, confirming her fear that she was distracting him.

"Don't worry about me," she yelled back. "I've got this." She jumped into the water.

DEX LET OUT a guttural roar and crashed his fist into the side of Mitchell's face. Mitchell grunted in pain but didn't let go of the pistol. Dex twisted violently, renewing his struggles in a frenzy, but it took all his strength to keep from getting swept away in the current and still keep Mitchell from lowering the gun and aiming it toward Amber.

Dear God, Amber. He couldn't believe she'd jumped into the water. He had to help her.

"I'm sorry for whatever you think I did to you," he yelled. "Killing Amber or anyone else isn't going to make up for it, though."

Mitchell snarled and kicked toward him, but the force of the water slowed his movements and Dex was able to turn his thigh to block him. Still, the blow knocked him back enough so that Mitchell was able to tug his non-gun hand loose from Dex's hold and put both hands on the pistol. Slowly and surely he began to turn the pistol down toward Dex's head.

Dex swore and shoved Mitchell harder against the house. The mad light in Mitchell's eyes told him there was no reasoning with him. And, damn, the man was stronger than he looked. Dex grabbed the pistol with both hands and lifted his feet. He crashed back against the water's surface, pulling Mitchell down with him under the water.

Chapter Seventeen

Amber struggled to untie the ropes that held Derek to the post. Her hands kept slipping in the brackish water. "Hold on, Derek. Just hold on."

His mouth went under water and again Amber grabbed him and yanked him higher. He coughed out some brackish water and drew a shaky breath. His arms were shaking from the effort of trying to keep his elbows bent to hold himself above the water, but it was a losing battle. He was exhausted.

"If I can just get this knot free." She pulled and plucked at the knot. Derek didn't respond and she didn't expect him to. His eyes were closed. He was using every ounce of strength he had just trying not to drown. He must have been struggling out here for hours and there was nothing left. He seemed ready to pass out from exhaustion. And from the bruises already beginning to form near his temple, she suspected that Mitchell might have hit him. A head injury and exhaustion could be a lethal combination right now. She looked past him to the porch and froze. Where were Mitchell and Dex?

Derek went under again.

Amber grabbed his chin and pulled him up. "Come on, cough it out."

Derek's head lolled back toward the water.

"Derek, Derek, wake up. Cough out the water." She let go of the post and cupped his face with both hands. The current tried to drag her away from the building. She was forced to grab the post again and wrapped her legs around it before reaching for Derek, who'd dropped his face back beneath the water.

"Come on," she yelled. She slapped his cheeks, again and again.

He flinched and opened his eyes. Then he started violently coughing. Water and vomit rolled out of his mouth.

Amber tilted his head so he wouldn't choke. "There you go, that's it. We'll get you out of here. You just have to hang on a little longer."

Water splashed beside her. She gasped and whirled around. A dark shadow rose from below the surface. Gator! No! She grabbed Derek and kicked out with her feet, hitting the reptile under the water.

It broke the surface, coughing and spitting water. Amber's jaw dropped open. This was no gator.

"Dex? Dex! How did you get here? Are you okay?"

He grabbed the post beside her and rubbed his chest. "You have a mean kick. I'm not sure you needed my help, after all." Impossibly, he grinned. And winked.

She sputtered. "I can't believe you're smiling at a time like this."

His smile faded. "Me, either." He looked back to the house. "I don't know where Mitchell went. I knocked the gun loose but he disappeared beneath the water. He could be anywhere." He looked at Derek and the ropes holding him to the post. "Hold on. I'll be right back."

"Dex, don't leave me, don't…"

He disappeared beneath the surface again. Where had he gone? What was he doing? She focused on keeping Derek's chin above the water, cradling his head against her chest as she kept an eye on their surroundings. She didn't know if she was more worried about gators or Mitchell. Both were deadly.

Metal creaked behind her somewhere. She jerked around. "Dex?" Nothing.

Derek coughed up more brackish water.

"It's okay," she soothed, keeping his chin up. "It's okay. Dex wouldn't really leave us. He'll come back."

"Damn straight."

She whirled around. "Dex!"

He smiled again and pulled a machete up from beneath the water. "I remembered this from before, from inside the building." He pulled himself to the backside of the post and held the machete with both hands as he hacked down against the wood. The ropes split and fell away.

Derek slipped from Amber's hands into the water. "No, no!"

Dex dove under and came up seconds later with his friend, holding his head up. "Come on, Amber. Let's get him back to the house and get out of this swamp."

"You don't have to tell me twice."

They swam on both sides of Derek, wrestling against the current and to keep him from going under. He'd completely lost consciousness now and was deadweight, threatening to drag them away or under. Something splashed not far from them.

"Keep swimming," Dex yelled. "Hurry."

His urgency had her putting everything she had into her strokes as she kicked her legs behind her. They reached the porch and she grabbed the post to pull herself up. Dex gave her and Derek a mighty shove forward, which propelled them all the way to the kitchen doorway. She wrestled Derek inside and propped his arms up on a countertop to keep his head above the water.

She turned back to see where Dex was and saw him raise the machete above his head at the edge of the porch and bring it slashing down. An enormous gator snapped its jaws inches from his face, then disappeared beneath the water.

"Dex!" Amber screamed.

He dropped the machete and dove toward the doorway. He pulled himself inside and shoved the door closed. A loud thump shook the door but it held. The gator must have given up because it didn't try again. Dex turned around, his face pale and his eyes wide. "Tell me that did not just happen."

Amber's hands shook as Dex rose to stand in the hip-deep water and helped her hold on to Derek.

"I can't believe you just fought an alligator," she said, her voice hoarse. "And that was a big gator."

He grinned. "Something to brag about later." His smile faded and he glanced around. "If we survive this, that is. I'm not going to assume that Mitchell drowned. We need to get out of here. We're too exposed." He pressed his hand against Derek's chest, then felt the side of his neck. "He's breathing, and his pulse is good. Let's get him upstairs with the others."

"How will we—"

In answer, he lifted Derek and draped him over his shoulder in a fireman's hold. "Let's go. Hurry."

They waded through the kitchen to the great room.

Some of the furniture was floating and they had to maneuver around it.

A guttural roar and a splash sounded behind them. They whirled around. Mitchell pointed his gun toward Dex. He dove out of the way. Shots boomed. The front windows exploded in a hail of glass.

Amber grabbed Derek, who was floating facedown, and turned him faceup in the water. Mitchell whirled around, not seeming to notice her. He was too busy looking for Dex. She took advantage of his preoccupation and floated Derek to one of the chairs that was bobbing in the water. She wrestled Derek's arms and upper body into the chair and made sure his face was well above the waterline before she let go.

Mitchell turned toward her, as if just realizing she might be a threat. She dove down below the water. A concussion of movement burst just past her head in the water as a bullet shot at her. She couldn't see, but she swam toward where she remembered the nearest wall to be. When she reached the wall, she used her arms and legs to kick the water to stay below the surface until her lungs were burning. Unable to stay there any longer, she stood up and drew a deep breath as she looked around for Dex or Mitchell.

Mitchell stood ten feet away, his back to her. But he must have heard her as she'd broken the surface. He whirled toward her, gun in hand. Water splashed on his other side as Dex rose above the water with something in his hand. The poker from the fireplace! He brought it crashing down as Mitchell brought his gun around. The gun went off as the poker slammed into the side of Mitchell's head. He cried out and fell back into the water. He raised the gun again, but Dex brought the poker down and knocked it out of his hands. Mitchell sank below the surface.

Dex held the poker at the ready, watching the water all around him. When Mitchell didn't reappear, Dex swore and dropped the poker. He disappeared beneath the water.

Amber pushed off the wall to help him. She'd just reached where she'd last seen Dex when he stood up, pulling Mitchell with him. Mitchell's head lolled against his chest, blood running from the nasty gash in his scalp where the poker had hit him. His eyes were closed.

"Is he…is he dead?"

Dex pressed his hand against Mitchell's neck. "No." He swallowed hard, his Adam's apple bobbing in his throat. "But I hit him hard, too damn hard."

Amber was shocked at the anguish in Dex's voice. "Dex, you did what you had to do. You saved us."

He nodded, but she didn't think he was necessarily agreeing with her. "Derek?"

She pointed to the chair. "He's okay."

He nodded again and started pulling Mitchell toward another chair floating beside that one. He'd just propped Mitchell up when bright lights shone through the hole where the front windows had been shattered.

"Get behind me," Dex ordered. He reached for her just as the front door burst open. Then he grinned and let out a relieved laugh as a man whom Amber had never seen before led a rescue crew of a half dozen Collier County firemen into the house.

"If you're here to save us," Dex said, "you're a little late."

The man in front of the others splashed toward them.

His brow was lined with worry as he took in the scene, looking from Derek to Mitchell, then to Amber and Dex.

"I thought we were rescuing you from what I'm told is the worst flood this place has seen in decades. But you managed to up the ante to a whole new level. What the hell happened?"

"It's a long story. I'll explain it all, but first we need medical help for these two."

As the firemen tended Mitchell and Derek, Dex led Amber through the water to the stairs with the man he'd just spoken to following behind.

"There are more people upstairs." Dex helped Amber out of the water and onto the first dry step.

"Aren't you going to introduce us?" Amber nodded to the man beside Dex.

"Oh, sorry. Amber Callahan, this is—or was, until he quit—the other half of Lassiter and Young Private Investigations. Meet Jake Young."

AMBER PAUSED IN the doorway to Derek's room in Naples Community Hospital, with two paper coffee cups in her hand. Derek was asleep, resting comfortably in spite of the IV he'd vehemently opposed when he'd first gotten there. Apparently he was afraid of needles, but Amy had shamed him into "taking it like a man," and had added the extra insult that Garreth was being much less of a baby in his room down the hall, even though Garreth's injuries had been more severe.

Chagrined, Derek had allowed the nurse to put the IV in his arm. They were giving him antibiotics through that IV to counteract any bacteria he may have swallowed when he'd nearly drowned in the swamp. And they were monitoring him because of the concussion he'd suffered. But he'd probably be released in a few days as long as he didn't show signs of a fever.

Amy was asleep, too, sitting in a chair pulled up beside the bed, her upper body and arms draped across Derek's chest. Their hands, even in sleep, were laced together. Amber had a feeling this wasn't a mild infatuation that was going to blow over. The two of them seemed completely enamored with each other. The anger that Amber had thought she'd seen in Amy's reflection in the library window? She realized now it was probably a mixture of anger and pain because she was worried— and mad—that someone might have hurt Derek.

Amber backed out of the room, allowing the door to quietly close behind her as she turned and balanced the coffee cups.

"Is one of those for me?"

She looked up sharply, expecting to see Dex. But instead, it was his friend, Jake.

"You don't have to look so disappointed." He shoved away from the wall.

"Oh, sorry. I wasn't… I thought…" She held out one of the coffee cups. "If you like cream and sugar, it's yours. I was bringing it to Amy, but she's asleep."

He grimaced but took the cup anyway. "I prefer black, but right now I'll take anything warm after being submerged in that nasty swamp. Thanks." He took a deep sip and grimaced again. "Or not." He tossed the cup in a nearby trash can.

Amber eyed her own cup. "That bad, huh?"

"I wouldn't try it if I were you."

She tossed it in the trash. "Thanks for saving me. Again."

He shook his head. "I didn't save you. Dex gets

all the credit for that. Speaking of which, he's asking about you."

She cleared her throat. "He is?"

"Uh-huh. He wanted me to come get you. He's sitting with Mitchell. I couldn't get him to leave the guy's side."

"Mitchell? Why would Dex sit with him after everything that happened?"

"You can ask him that yourself. Come on. I'll take you to him." He offered his arm like an old-fashioned gentleman. Amber smiled and took it and walked with him down the long hall to another wing of the hospital. He stopped at room 222.

"I'll be in the waiting room, just around the corner when you come out," he said. "Faye just got to the parking lot. She's coming up. She'd love to see you."

"And I'd love to see her."

He nodded and headed to the waiting room.

Amber could see why Dex liked Jake. He was a nice guy. And he and Faye had cut their Bahamas honeymoon short to check on Dex, after hearing about the terrible storm and that the plane crash had been deliberate. They'd been keeping tabs on him through Freddie until Freddie told them they were heading to the old mansion to celebrate Amber's charges being dropped.

After that, when the impending storm was on the news, Faye had had a premonition that it was going to get worse than the weathermen thought. She'd convinced Jake they should fly back from the Bahamas before the weather prevented them from doing so, and check on Dex and the others.

But the storm had come in even faster than Faye's premonition had told her. And it had taken a long time to work their way to Mystic Glades. By that time, they knew anyone in the mansion might be in trouble, so Jake had rounded up some firemen and some canoes and they'd made their way through the flood.

"You coming in or planning on standing in the hall-way all day?"

She whirled around at the sound of Dex's voice. He was standing in front of her, outside Mitchell's door. Amber raised a shaky hand to her chest. "You and Jake are both good at that."

"Good at what?"

"Surprising people." She waved her hand. "Never mind. Jake said you wanted to speak with me."

He pushed open the door behind him. "Do you mind talking inside?"

She hesitated. "In Mitchell's room?"

"He's in a medically induced coma, to keep the brain swelling down. He won't hear anything we say."

She rubbed her hands up and down her arms, not at all anxious to go near Mitchell again. "I've heard of studies that say that people in comas *do* hear what is said around them."

"Amber. Please."

His quiet, resolved tone had all kinds of alarm bells going off in her head, but she pushed back her res-ervations and followed him into Mitchell's room. She stopped just inside, surprised to feel a tug of empathy when she saw the machines and tubes hooked up to the man who'd tried to kill her and Dex a handful of hours earlier.

"He can't hurt you now." Dex waved toward one of two plastic-and-metal chairs beside the window.

She crossed the room and sat beside him. "Why are you here? With him? After everything he did?"

"That's what I wanted to talk to you about."

He scrubbed the stubble on his face. His exhaustion was broadcast by the tiny lines around the corners of his eyes and the dark circles beneath them.

He took her hands in his. "The doctors performed a CT scan. But it wasn't where I hit Mitchell with the poker that they're worried about. What they're concerned with is the mass they found, something called anaplastic astrocytoma. I'm sure I'm pronouncing it wrong, but basically he has a malignant brain tumor."

She blinked in surprise. "A brain tumor?"

"They'll do surgery, radiation, maybe chemo, too. His prognosis doesn't look good. But they'll do everything they can to control the pain and alleviate his symptoms." He tugged his hands out of hers. "He must have been having terrible headaches the past few months. I never even noticed. I was oblivious. How many times did I say good morning without really talking to him, to see how he was really doing?"

"Wait. Dex, is this why you're sitting here with him? You feel guilty?"

He shrugged. "I am guilty—guilty of not paying enough attention. Guilty of being so self-absorbed that I didn't notice that an employee, a friend who's worked for me for years, was acting differently, that he was in pain. I'm guilty of everything he accused me of when we were fighting on that porch." His bleary gaze captured hers. "I'm sorry, Amber. That's what I wanted to tell you. I'm so sorry if I ever treated you that way. And I'm sorry that I took advantage of you. I made an unforgiveable mistake. I shouldn't have—"

"Stop it. Stop it right now. You did not take advantage of me. And I refuse to sit here while you characterize our sleeping together as a mistake. Dex, I wanted to make love with you. I still want to make love with you. Nothing Mitchell said has changed that, or how I feel about you. I want to be with you. Don't you want to be with me?"

His brow furrowed and he looked away. "Of course I want to be with you. But I can't. It's not right."

"How is it not right?" When he didn't answer, she followed the direction of his gaze. He was watching the readouts on the machines by Mitchell's bed. "The tumor affected Mitchell's judgment, didn't it? I'm sure the doctors must have said something like that. Mitchell skewed everything in his mind because he couldn't help it, he couldn't control what the tumor was doing to his brain, to his thoughts."

She waited, but when he didn't say anything, she tried another approach. "Okay, Mitchell has an out, then. There's an explanation for why he did what he did. It will be hard to forgive him, but I'll try because I understand it wasn't entirely his fault. But I can't forgive you."

He jerked his head toward her, his eyes wide. "What?"

"You heard me. If you choose to go down this path of self-loathing and give up the one good thing sitting in front of you, don't expect me to participate in your pity party. I deserve better. *You* taught me that."

"Wait, I taught you that? What do you mean?"

She sighed. "Dex, I gave up two years of my life because of guilt. Oh, I was pretty sure that I hadn't killed my grandfather with that tonic. I figured there had to be another explanation, and even after I heard about the peanut oil, I wasn't totally convinced that was the cause of his death. But I chose to run, not just to draw suspicion away from Buddy, to protect him if he'd made a horrible mistake. I ran because I knew that living in that swamp would be incredibly difficult, maybe even impossible, but I didn't believe that I deserved any better. I thought I deserved to struggle every day because of the horrible mistake that I'd made."

He frowned. "What mistake? Your grandfather died of cancer. Even if you didn't know it back then, you said you didn't think your tonic killed him."

"No, I didn't. But it didn't save him, either. I was… arrogant. I healed people even when Aunt Freddie's Doc Holliday couldn't heal them. My herbs and potions had never failed me before, and I believed I could do better for Grandpa than real doctors." She shook her head. "My arrogance is what killed my grandfather. I should have insisted that he go to the hospital instead of just assuming that I could take care of him. Would it have made a difference? Probably. But not for long. All it would have done is buy him a few more weeks, weeks filled with pain because of the cancer. I know that now. And because of your faith in me, in getting me to help Garreth and making me fight for others, I realized I was guilty of what you're doing now—of feeling sorry for myself while life passed me by."

She clasped her hands in her lap. "Dex, I wasted two years of my life over guilt when I should have been making up for my wrongs by helping others. The guilt that ate me up is something I have to move beyond if I'm going to make up for my past mistakes. And that's what you have to do. You have to let the guilt go, move on."

She waved at Mitchell, lying in the bed. "You're not responsible for Mitchell killing Mallory. But if you believe he was right when he talked about you using others, about not paying attention to those around you and being self-absorbed, then do something about it. You can start by admitting the truth—that you care about me."

He stared at her as if in shock. "You heard what he said, about Ronnie, about how I treated her. She and Mallory were only a couple of the women I've treated badly over the years. How could you even want me after knowing that?"

She thumped his chest. "It's precisely because you're sitting here acknowledging your past mistakes that I want you. You're a good man." She flattened her hand over his heart. "You're a good man, here. Where it counts. That's the man I'm falling in love with. Because he cares about his impact on other people, and he wants to make it right."

He suddenly scooped her onto his lap. He hugged her so tightly she could barely breathe, but she didn't push him away. Instead, she wrapped her arms around his neck and held on tight, pressing her head against his chest, listening to the solid beat of his wonderful, caring, loving heart.

He kissed the top of her head and loosened his hold, pulling back to meet her gaze. "I don't deserve your faith and trust, or your…love… Amber Callahan. But I'll spend the rest of my life trying to earn it. That is, if that's what you want."

She blinked back the moisture suddenly blurring her vision. "The rest of your life? That's quite a commitment from a commitment-phobe when you barely know me."

He framed her face in his hands. "I know you. I know the kindness inside you, the way you put others first. I know that you're one of the few people who's ever stood up to me, told me I'm not perfect, that I'm wrong. I've surrounded myself by yes-men and yes-women, afraid to tell me the truth. I need you to keep me honest, to tell me when I'm being an ass, to remind me to stop, and listen, and pay attention—to make me a better person. You're everything I need and want in my life. If you'll have me."

Her lips trembled and she drew a shaky breath. "If that's a proposal, you'd better be sure about it. Because I just might take you up on it."

"Is that a yes?"

"It's a qualified yes."

He frowned. "Qualified?"

"I'll only say yes if you agree to take me away from Mystic Glades. I don't ever want to go back there again." She shivered with genuine abhorrence at the thought of returning to the swamp she used to love but that had become the symbol of all her failings.

He cocked his head, looking deep in thought. "I don't know. It might be hard giving up being a cop. Especially if I can convince Deputy Holder to give me a gold star to wear on my chest."

She arched a brow. "So you like the swamp, the alligators, the water moccasins?"

A sexy grin curved his mouth, taking her breath away. "I like *you*, Amber Callahan. And if I have you, with me, forever, I can give all of that up."

"Even the gold star?" she teased.

His grin faded and his gaze searched hers. "I would give up anything, everything, for you. I love you, Amber. Marry me?"

She smiled through the tears freely coursing down

her cheeks now. Had she thought she was falling in love with this man? She'd been wrong. She'd already fallen. She was madly, deeply, in love with him. And she couldn't imagine her life without this amazing, caring man in it.

"I love you, too, Dex Lassiter. And the answer is yes."

He kissed her, and for the first time in years, she felt protected, cherished, loved. From the beginning, when she'd spent those summers with her grandfather as an escape from her parents, and later when she'd fled to the Glades, she realized she'd been running *to* something as much as away *from* something. She'd been searching for that one thing her whole life—a home. And she'd finally found it, the place where she belonged. She'd found her home at last, in Dex's arms.

* * * * *

Look for more books in Lena Diaz's
MARSHLAND JUSTICE
series later this year!